JIMMY'S GAME

The 'Ruthless' Series
Book One

KAREN CLOW

Copyright © 2013 Karen Clow

This work is registered with the UK Copyright Service
Registration number: 281544

All rights reserved. No part of this book may be
reproduced or transmitted in any form or by
any means electronic or mechanical including
photocopying, recording or any information storage
and retrieval system without permission in
writing from the author or publisher.

Karen Clow has asserted her right under the
Copyright, Designs and Patents Act 1988
to be identified as the author of this work.

www.karenclow.com

Find the author on Facebook:
www.facebook.com/karenclowbooks

This novel is a work of fiction. Names and characters
are the product of the author's imagination and
any resemblance to actual persons living or
dead is entirely coincidental.

> ISBN: 1489531157
> ISBN-13: 978-1489531155

IN MEMORY

Mum and Dad with love xx

Roger Hopper with love xx

This book is dedicated with love to Ronnie and Kate, who in the early stages sat through listening to me reading this book every Wednesday. Special thanks to Kate for reading the dirty bits when I was too embarrassed!

For all the women who cry in silence and live in fear of violent, jealous, controlling men.

FOREWORD

'Jimmy's Game' was my first eBook, which went onto the Amazon Kindle platform in April 2013. I would be the first to admit how naïve I was back then. I knew my books needed editing, but financially this wasn't something I could afford, so I took a chance and hoped for the best. I was shocked at how popular this book became in just a few weeks. Thankfully, most people were kind with their reviews and loved the book, although a few did comment constructively on the grammar, spelling and the need for editing. Despite this and much to my surprise, the book rallied a lot of support with people stating, despite the errors and a little overkill on some storylines, they loved it!

Due to the success of the series, I now have two wonderful ladies who help me edit and proof read. I'm thrilled to say my more recent books in the 'Ruthless Series' have received wonderful reviews on all counts. I am now having the earlier books edited; suffice to say this is the new copy of 'Jimmy's Game.' Hopefully the other two early books will be ready soon as, due to popular demand, I am currently writing Series 3.

Maybe the time and effort put in will bring me a step closer to securing an agent? I hope so as so many people asked if they could buy the book in paperback, or if it's going to become a TV drama. I've actually had this book converted to script initially; which we affectionately refer to as England's answer to the Sopranos and now, using the wonders of Createspace, into its first ever printed version. I hope you enjoy it.

KAREN CLOW

ACKNOWLEDGMENTS

To my many friends who encouraged me not to give up, my heartfelt thanks to them, they know who they are. My lovely friends on Facebook who have read, commented and shared my book snippets, you inspire me!

I also want to thank some very special people who, without their help and belief in me, my lifelong dream would never have come true.

My wonderful family, **Pete, Michelle, Melissa and Ruth** for their love, patience and understanding.

Ian Paton, my very own earth angel, wonderful friend, critic and inspiration. I would be lost without his support.
Sue Fairman, who for over thirty years has been my confidante, loyal, reliable, honest friend, a lady I hold very close to my heart.
Helen Deeprose, not only my sister-in-law, but my dear friend. Her addiction to my books encouraged me to write more in the series.
Jan Norse, my lifelong friend, whose knowledge and friendship started me on this amazing journey; she also has a special place in my heart.
Shelly Grant, my nutty friend who has put up with my constant moaning whilst preparing my books for publishing and whose encouragement and laughter has meant so much.
Pamela O'Keefe, my dear friend who came to my rescue in the eleventh hour and did a fantastic job.
Sallyann Cole, (www.facebook.com/sallyssneakypeeks) my dear friend, who inspires me and does so much for me.
Last but not least my dog;
Fat Freddy, my loyal, faithful boy who keeps me company through all those long, lonely night hours when I'm writing.

KAREN CLOW

CHAPTER 1

Like a caged animal, Jimmy Dixon paced up and down his lounge floor. He glanced at his watch every few minutes; patience wasn't his strong point and what little he had was beginning to run out. From the window of his luxury apartment he looked out over the river Thames and scanned the streets below. His hope was to see Shaun Flanagan's car but it was Saturday and as always the streets outside were a hive of activity. For a few minutes he watched the people go about their business, instantly picking out the day trippers at a glance. Whilst looking along the endless stream of traffic for Shaun's car, the reality of what he'd done the previous night at the poker game began to sink in. Nick Orphanides wasn't someone to mess with, Jimmy knew that from past experience, but it was too late to take back what had happened, what was done was done. His thoughts were simple, he hoped Nick would accept that he'd lost the bet and keep to his end of the deal. Had the bet been for money, things would be different but the prize had been the girl and Jimmy knew better than anyone that Nick would be reluctant to give her up, especially to him. The arrangement had been Nick's bodyguard, Shaun Flanagan, would deliver her to Jimmy's apartment later that morning. Nervously he tried not to think negatively as he watched and waited, but he'd already decided that if she wasn't there by eleven he would go and get her, regardless of the consequences.

It was just past ten thirty when the intercom buzzed. Although he had anticipated this moment all night, now it was here he could feel his stomach churning and his palms sweating. In his mind he tried to convince himself he'd only made the bet to free her from Nick and she could simply leave if she wanted to, but in truth he wanted her. Every Friday night at the poker game he'd thought about having her. When she leaned over to fill his glass, he had wanted to reach out and touch her as the smell of her perfume aroused him. Since the first time he laid eyes on her, he wanted her. On rare occasions, his dark side would surface when he lay in bed after the game thinking of her. If he had her would he want to keep her prisoner as Nick did, knowing only him, never allowing anyone to get close to her? Then he'd remember his mother and the prisoner she became through fear and violence. There were times alone in the darkness when he thought he heard his mother's voice say, 'Don't be like your dad Jimmy, be better than that.'

Answering the intercom, he immediately noticed the Irishman sounded less calm than usual.

"Quick Jimmy let me in!"

Hearing panic in his voice, Jimmy pressed the entry button and waited at the door for the lift to arrive. Moments later he was looking across the hall at them, but he had not expected the sight which now confronted him. Of course he knew there would be consequences over the previous night, but not like this. Shaun stood in front of him cradling the girl in his arms; she was barely conscious and covered in blood.

"Oh my God!" exclaimed Jimmy, "What the fuck happened?"

"Nick that's what happened," replied Shaun as he carried her into the apartment and gently laid her on the sofa. Shaun said he'd been careful when Jimmy asked if anyone had seen him.

"Should I phone an ambulance or a doctor Shaun?"

"Nah best not, just get me a bowl of warm water and a towel."

Returning a few minutes later, Jimmy passed him the items he'd requested. Standing over her, he watched as the big bruiser gently bathed her cuts and swollen face. Shaun glanced at him and asked if he had any ice. When Jimmy nodded, Shaun instructed him to bring him some in a cloth.

Returning quickly with the ice, Jimmy continued to watch as Shaun tended her. In all the years he'd known Shaun, he never realised he had such a compassionate side. He was well known for being a hard man, always ready to beat someone to a pulp if Nick ordered him to.

Shaun told him to leave her to sleep and pour him a drink. Passing him a scotch, Jimmy asked why Nick had done that to her. Shaun's reply was simple; he had her and Nick wanted her back. If he hadn't turned up when he had, Nick would have killed her for certain. With rage in his eyes, Jimmy stated he was going to fucking kill Nick; he wasn't going to let him get away with it, that hadn't been the deal.

"Just leave it Jimmy, there's been enough blood spilt for one day. Just let things calm down and take my advice, keep out of his way, he's dangerous."

Jimmy had a look of curiosity and mistrust as he asked Shaun why he was helping him; everyone knew his loyalty was to Nick.

"Aye you're right Jimmy, but not this time, you see I love the wee lass."

Shaun noticed he looked shocked by his remark and quickly stated his love was pure; he loved her like a father.

"Really?" said Jimmy with a tone of disbelief.

"Aye really. It's like this Jimmy, every Sunday for the past two years she has attended church with me and the family. It was the only time she was allowed out; even then I had to ensure she spoke to no one. It was hard convincing Nick to let her come with us; I had to call in a couple of favours. Aye, she was such a young wee scrap of a girl back then. I knew what was going on but there was nothing I could do. Believe me if I didn't have my family to think of it would have been different, but Nick's an evil bastard. I couldn't take the chance; we both know what he's capable of."

Looking a little humbled, Jimmy never knew that, but quickly said Nick was a fucking psycho!

Shaun agreed that was why he'd always looked out for her. He'd asked her once if she wanted him to take her to a train station. He'd offered her money and said he'd tell Nick she'd run away, but she'd refused. Since then he'd asked her several times over the years, but she'd always refused. She knew if Nick found out he would kill both of them.

Jimmy nodded and stated she had probably been right before asking if Shaun would be ok returning to Nick's.

"Aye for sure, with any luck he'll have calmed down by the time I get back and believe me he will listen to reason once I make him see sense. You know as well as I do the last thing he'll want is a war, especially with you Jimmy."

Despite what he'd just said, Shaun knew there would be repercussions over what had happened. He'd worked for Nick long enough to be certain this wouldn't be an end to the matter. Looking at Jimmy he could see the burning hatred in his eyes, he had that look about him which told Shaun he wouldn't back down, not even from Nick. Jimmy had grown up tough on the streets of London, into organised crime at seventeen. Now nearer forty than thirty, a real hard man, his whole demeanour shouted; 'don't mess with me or you'll be sorry.' Standing five foot eleven, with short cropped fair hair, well built with a muscular physique. A faded scar above his left eyebrow, which was not as a result of fighting, but a souvenir of a merciless beating he had taken from his abusive father when he was just seven. Tattoos across his arms and chest all but hid other reminders of his violent past.

Finishing his drink, Shaun stood up and after reminding Jimmy to stay out of Nick's way, said he'd see himself out.

The two men shook hands as Jimmy thanked him. He wasn't surprised when Shaun said no thanks were needed, but just for him to take care of Maria.

For the next four hours, Jimmy sat watching over her. Feeling anger raging through his body as he thought about the vicious beating she'd taken because of him. His mind questioned why he'd thought for one minute his actions from the previous night would end well. Why had he imagined for an instant that Nick would be ok about it. How could he have been so stupid? Clenching his fist he pounded the arm of the sofa, only controlling his temper because the noise made her stir although she didn't wake. Again his mind questioned his logic, like everyone else involved in organised crime, he knew that within your own crew there was a line which you didn't cross and he had been stupid enough to do just that.

Sweeping her hair back from her face, he felt the stickiness of her blood on his fingers. Gently he wiped her hair with a towel, only stopping momentarily when she opened her eyes, but before he could say anything to her she began sinking back into unconsciousness. Sitting there quietly he looked at the young woman who was lying, bleeding on his sofa, her beautiful face unrecognisable; every inch covered in cuts and bruises. He went over in his head what had happened just a few hours earlier, the series of events which had led to her almost being beaten to death.

Taking his thoughts back to when he and his best friend, Mickey Mann, had arrived at Nick's penthouse for the weekly poker game. The other players were already there. Jimmy pictured the faces of the men; especially Nick who as always was smirking, ever confident that he was going to be a big winner that night. Jimmy could feel his adrenalin pumping as he thought about Nick and what he'd done to her.

That Friday night hadn't started any differently to any other poker night, same faces same chit chats. Like most of the players, Jimmy was there because it was expected. Everyone at the game knew Nick saw himself as the boss who revelled in the fact that at the ripe old age of forty two he had done so well. Always boasting, he loved to show off. Nick knew he was a handsome man, with well-kept black wavy hair and dark brown soulless eyes, standing over six feet tall with a great body from working out daily. Carrying an air of arrogance about him and looking more like a Hollywood leading man than a crime boss, nobody loved Nick as much as he loved himself. A confident, arrogant, self-made man who bragged about liking kinky sex and recreational drugs, although he rarely indulged in anything stronger than coke because he liked to be in control. It was no secret he had a hard on for young girls, a real control freak and sadist. His real name, Nikodemus Orphanides, a descendant from Greek Cypriots, his family had moved to London from Cyprus when he was seven. They shared a house with his uncle who, like his father, was heavily involved in organised crime. Nick learnt quickly that being tougher than the next kid would guarantee him respect. At just thirty two he became the head of his family when his uncle died from cancer, and less than a year later his father was killed in a pub brawl with a rival crew. His mother and two sisters returned to Cyprus, never again to return to Britain. One thing every criminal in London knew was never to cross him; he's a hard ruthless bastard who would have no trouble putting you down, although rarely getting his own hands dirty; that would be left to Shaun Flanagan, the big Irishman who had kept his word and brought the girl to

Jimmy's apartment earlier that morning. Shaun never says much and no one really knows what brought about the union between him and Nick. Apart from money and the fact they're both hard men, they have little in common. Before becoming Nick's bodyguard, Shaun worked the doors in his clubs for a few years, yet despite the closeness he shares with the other crew members Shaun carries an air of mystery about him. He's the type of man you could know for twenty years and still never really know him. A giant of a man, standing no less than six feet five inches tall, with fiery red hair now flecked with grey and held back in a ponytail. In his fifties and slightly overweight, he still poses an awesome figure and despite his undisputed reputation as a hard man, he's a devout Catholic who goes to church regularly. Always carries rosary beads and looks after his family of seven children and six grandchildren, all of whom he adores. Probably the only man who knows most, if not all, of Nicks dirty little secrets. Always with him, yet despite his loyalty Shaun keeps his own counsel. Unlike his boss, Shaun is content with his lot and well aware that Nick is dangerous because he's power hungry. Nick's into everything, prostitution, drugs, gambling. If there's money to be made, he's into it, allowing nothing to stand in his way. He doesn't care about who he has to hurt or kill to stay on top. Having little compassion or respect for anyone or anything, in Nick's world everything has a price.

There were eight players including Jimmy at the game, all of whom were heavily involved in organised crime. With the exception of the one black man, Maurice Lamar, everyone there had grown up tough on the streets of London. Unlike them, Maurice moved to Britain from the Caribbean in his late teens and was quickly spotted by the then crime boss. Despite Jimmy doing business with Maurice he doesn't care for him, due to the fact that he's a sadistic bisexual with an unhealthy liking for young boys. In truth, he represents everything Jimmy hates.

The player sat next to Jimmy was his closet friend and business partner, corrupt solicitor and entrepreneur, Mickey Mann. They had been best friends since early schooldays. It was Mickey's father, Den, who introduced them into organised crime when they were seventeen. Their dissimilarities in looks are about the only thing to separate them, both approaching forty and single. Despite a totally different upbringing, in many ways they're closer than brothers. Jimmy had seen more than his fair share of trouble and violence, especially when it came to fighting, which was usually brought about because of the short fuse he had regarding his temper. Never one to walk away from a fight regardless of the odds, he knew Mickey was always there watching his back. Had they not been able to coerce influential people into providing airtight alibis on certain occasions over the years, no doubt Jimmy would have done hard time.

Mickey was the slightly taller of the two, dark hair, naturally slim; normally wore suits, hair and nails were always immaculate. Certainly looked the part as a professional, although he could handle himself should the need arise. Both men had married in their early twenties and both were divorced by the time they were thirty. Mickey has a fifteen year old daughter, Charlotte, from his marriage. She works in his legitimate law office during school holidays; mainly helping his secretary with run of the mill stuff like filing and making coffee. Mickey makes sure she never knows exactly what he does outside of his office and despite the fact she is an intelligent girl, he also forbids her to date any boys whose families are connected to the criminal world. Charlie, as she prefers to be called, lives with her mother and stepfather, but spends weekends and school holidays with Mickey. Privileged to attend one of the best schools in London, paid for by Mickey. It's no secret she adores Jimmy, often joining him for dinner at one of their restaurants when her dad is out on business. Everyone knows Jimmy loves her like a daughter; nothing is too good for her. If she asked him for anything he would endeavour to get it. Fact is he loves Mickey's family as though they were his own after they'd taken him in many times during his troubled childhood.

Mickey's parents, Den and Mary, made Jimmy feel as though he belonged with their family. Den was not only a great father figure, but a great accountant. Well respected locally as a good family man and husband. They appeared to be the perfect family; apart from Den keeping books for the mob, they were. It was a total contrast to the life that Jimmy had, with an abusive alcoholic father and a downtrodden mother who was terrified of her husband. Finally, when Jimmy was fifteen his mother committed suicide. She left him a note telling him how sorry she was for not being able to protect him from his father, but she couldn't stand another day living with this dreadful man who she hated but was too afraid of to leave. She told Jimmy to ask Mickey's parents if he could live with them until he was old enough to get a place of his own. The note ended with her telling him how much she loved him and how sorry she was that she'd let him down. The final line read, 'always respect women Jimmy, don't be like your father.' There was two hundred and eighty pounds wrapped inside the note. It was all his mother had after eighteen years of marriage; she was thirty eight years old when she died.

Everyone knows the bond between Jimmy and Mickey is airtight, not just because of their childhoods; it goes much deeper than that. Even when Mickey went away to university to study law, Jimmy stayed with his family. It was Den who then introduced him to the boss. By the time he was twenty one, Jimmy had his own crew working a protection racket. For his twenty first birthday his crew gave him his best present ever, they murdered his father. Rumour has it two heavies lured him to a train depot where they beat him to death before laying him on the track. Jimmy kept the newspaper clipping, it read, 'Local man James David Dixon killed by train, a widower who leaves a son James. There were no suspicious circumstances. The police believe he was drunk and fell onto the track knocking him unconscious.

By the time Mickey returned from university, Jimmy was already turning over big money. They bought their first club, Dixie's, at age twenty six, around the same time Mickey became a partner in a law firm. By the time they were thirty they were high up in organised crime. Everyone at the poker game was a self-made man. Despite having had a little help from older family members they had all made it on their own and very successfully. Ironically, none of them really answered to Nick, but in one way or another they needed him. He was the man with all the contacts and it was definitely healthier to work with him than against him.

Yes, life in organised crime was sweet and very profitable, however no one, especially Jimmy, had foreseen that something would happen that night which would change everything. That particular poker game would bring about the fall of an empire and result in a brutal murder.

CHAPTER 2

Aside from the eight poker players, there was Maria, the young girl Jimmy was now looking at lying on his sofa. Known to the crew as Nick's trophy virgin, he never spoke about how they had met or where she came from, only that she had been raised by the nuns at St Augustus. Regularly on poker nights Nick would humiliate and tease her about being a good Catholic girl, the previous night being no exception. It was obvious to everyone she was terrified of him. Rarely speaking; she simply did what he told her to. If someone had an empty glass he would snap his fingers at her and she would fill it. Hour after hour she would sit motionless, just waiting for her next order. Stunningly beautiful, looked to be about nineteen, long dark hair to her waist with smouldering green eyes and a figure to die for. She had lived with Nick for the past three years. Although rarely seen during the first twelve months, for the last two years she had attended the poker night. Often seen sporting black eyes and bruises to her face and body. Jimmy would sometimes say to her, 'what you done to your face, how'd you get that black eye?' Nick would always answer for her, usually blaming a fall or a cupboard door. There were the odd times when he would try and look macho by saying something like, 'that's what happens when you don't do as you're told, isn't it Maria.' Black Maurice would be the only one who would laugh; the others would simply look at Nick and think 'arsehole.' If any of the men tried to make conversation with her, she would immediately look to Nick and he would speak for her.

Sitting in his lounge looking at her bruised and battered body, Jimmy remembered clearly the reasons why he had made the bet on her. As the poker game went on into the early hours of the morning, Nick had been drinking heavily and everyone knew he was getting a kick out of embarrassing her. Jimmy could still picture the look of fear on her face as Nick mauled her when she filled his glass, openly pushing his hand up her top and fondling her breasts. It was obvious to the other players that he enjoyed watching her squirm. Yet despite begging him to stop, she never raised her voice against him, even when he'd continued to humiliate her and said, 'when the games over and we're alone you're going to suck my cock before I fuck you and you'd better be good!' She just stood there and quietly pleaded with him to stop, her beautiful eyes welling with tears. It was when he slapped her and ordered her to stop crying, Jimmy had wanted to punch him. Everyone just sat and watched as he humiliated her; it would be more than anybody dare do to try to stop him, they all knew what he was capable of. Maurice seemed to enjoy the show, everyone else just tried to ignore it, everyone except Jimmy. Watching her became too much for him, so he tried to help her by trying to talk Nick into getting on with the game. He saw in her the same dread he had seen in his mother. He hated men like Nick who treated women like dogs. Several times in the past, Nick had questioned why he was always the one to say something over Maria, almost goading him into admitting that he fancied her but Jimmy was no fool, he knew exactly how to handle him. Just like that night when Nick had made reference again to Jimmy fancying her.

"Although she's very beautiful Nick" he'd replied "I thought we were here to play poker and I'd never let a woman distract me from the game. You know me; I'd hate to lose money because of a woman."

He remembered the look of relief and gratitude on Maria's face when Nick replied he would never let a woman come between him and winning and if he was fucking her on the table he could still beat Jimmy.

"Precisely Nick, we all know you're the better player and it would be unfair to distract me. Surely with your reputation you wouldn't want people to think you had to win by using a woman."

"You're right Jimmy I am the better player, so let's play the fucking game!"

No one paid any attention to what had been said, simply because on many occasions they'd heard the same type of conversation. Very often Nick would send her out of the room, but last night he didn't, he just ordered her to go away.

Mickey knew Jimmy really liked her and despite the fact she rarely spoke, he knew by the way she looked at Jimmy when she thought no one could see her, she felt the same way about him. Often on their way home after the game they would talk about her. There was one such occasion a few months earlier when Jimmy hit the dashboard so hard with his fist that he cracked it, making it quite clear to Mickey he hated the way Nick treated her. Mickey would tell him to just let it go. It was just the way things were, she was Nick's property and there was nothing they could do to change that, making an issue of it would just be asking for trouble. He knew that although Jimmy always agreed with him, one night Nick would go too far and Jimmy would show his true colours. Little had he known when he picked Jimmy up for the game that Friday, it would be that night and everything would change.

The pot was around twenty grand as the time approached three that morning, the atmosphere was intense. Most of them had just about broken even, although Nick had won several big hands and Jimmy had lost the previous two to him. As the game continued the ante rose, which saw several players folding until finally it was just Jimmy and Nick left in the game. After ordering Maria to pour him a drink, Nick gathered his thoughts. With over thirty grand now on the table, Nick tried to rattle Jimmy by reminding him that he'd lost the previous two games to him.

When Jimmy arrogantly stated he didn't need reminding, Nick looked smug; he had simply been stating a fact. It could cost Jimmy several thousand to stay in the game, only to lose to him again.

A deathly silence had fallen over the table when Jimmy stated in a clear firm voice, he was staying in the game. Nick laughed, he thought he was bluffing. With an air of arrogance, Jimmy told him to name the stakes, anything he liked. Nick had sat back in his chair, calmly took a slug of scotch before stating he still thought he was bluffing, so he would raise him two hundred big ones against Jimmy's club, Dixie's.

Mickey had shaken his head and urged Jimmy to fold. They loved that club, especially Jimmy because it had been their first. You could almost cut through the atmosphere with a knife; tension was at an all-time high. The smell of stale tobacco and alcohol hung in the air like a thick cloud as Jimmy looked Nick in the eye and said it wasn't enough, the club was worth three times that. Undaunted, Nick cockily told him to name his pleasure because he was going to lose so Nick need not worry.

Everyone watched silently as Jimmy wrapped his hand around his chin and hesitated for the briefest of moments before telling Nick, he would take the bet against Maria.

In an outburst of anger, Nick sprang to his feet and shouted, "Fuck you Jimmy, who the fuck do you think you are!"

Before he'd had time to say anything else, Jimmy started laughing, he was just testing him and maybe Nick wasn't so sure about winning? Nick was ready to explode.

"Fuck you Jimmy; I'll see you for what's on the table and her!"

Flipping over his cards, they all watched in horror as Nick produced a straight flush; two of hearts through to the six of hearts.

"Jesus Christ," said Mickey looking at his friend, "what the hell have you done Jimmy?"

Nick, with a smirk, said it looked like he'd be changing the club name from Dixie's to Nicky's.

Slowly Jimmy looked up and laying his hand on the table, calmly stated. "Not this time Nick."

The tension was electric, everyone sat holding their breath. You could have heard a pin drop as Jimmy slowly turned his hand over and produced a royal flush; ten of spades through to the ace. Mickey had thrown his arm around his shoulder and shouted that Jimmy certainly knew how to scare him.

Nick looked evil and implied that he must have cheated. Instantly he ordered Shaun to search him. The other players stuck up for Jimmy, arguing he was no cheat.

After frisking him, Shaun confirmed he had won fair and square. Knowing he was beaten but needing to save face with his crew, Nick would have her delivered to Jimmy's in the morning, but it wasn't over, he wanted her back!

"It is over Nick, you have no respect for her," said Jimmy looking menacing "if you had, why did you gamble her? I'll take her now!"

Having no intentions of letting him take her that night, Nick needed to convince him that his reasons for keeping her were sincere. Holding back his true feeling of anger, he acted calmly and in an effort to convince him said, she'd need to sort some things out. He would get Shaun to bring her to him in the morning.

Knowing that the situation could have quickly spiralled out of control, Mickey intervened and advised Jimmy to agree.

"I'll expect her by eleven," snapped Jimmy "don't make me come over and get her!"

After their heated exchange of words, Nick ordered Shaun to get everyone out.

Believing everyone had left and now alone with Maria; Nick grabbed her by the hair and dragged her into another room. From outside the apartment, Jimmy could hear her screaming and begging him to stop, but his attempt to re-enter the apartment was blocked by Shaun. From the doorway Jimmy shouted for Nick to leave her alone, she was no longer his property. From inside, Nick shouted back she was his till the morning that was the deal!

At that moment, Shaun bundled Jimmy out into the lobby in the hope of defusing the situation. Had it not been for his assurance that he would honour what Nick had said and bring her to him later that morning, Jimmy would never have left. Shaun only managed to calm him down by telling him it was just Nick's way because he didn't like to lose, but he would make sure he kept his word.

Jimmy could feel his adrenalin pumping as he thought about Nick; it was only when Maria stirred he came back to the present. Reassuringly and gently he touched her face.

"Sshh babe, everything's ok."

Instantly she settled back into a deep sleep. Jimmy continued to sit with her as he tried to imagine exactly what Nick had done to her when he'd left. The one thought going through his head was, 'Why did I leave her there? Why didn't I insist on taking her last night?'

After leaving her at Jimmy's, Shaun had thought about her, if anything he felt worse, because he knew something would happen once everyone had left despite his reassurances to Jimmy. Thinking back to the previous night, he could remember feeling reluctant to leave after the others had gone, even though Nick had told him to. In an effort to stay he'd said he wasn't in any hurry and he should stay in case Jimmy came back. Nick was having none of it. He knew as well as Shaun the likelihood of that happening was remote, especially as Mickey had taken Jimmy home; he knew he would talk him round to leaving things till the morning. He also knew, despite Shaun's loyalty to him, he would defend Maria. In the hope of lulling Shaun into a false sense of security he'd calmly replied.

"In that case, I'll pour us a drink Shaun, but I don't think Jimmy will be back, he agreed to the deal. I'll make sure she's ready to go by half ten, there'll be things she'll need to pack."

Shaun hadn't believed one word of what he'd said, he could remember replying "Aye there will and like you said Nick, a deal is a deal. I wouldn't want to see anything happen to her, she's just a kid."

The look on Shaun's face told Nick he feared leaving her with him. Keeping his anger hidden he'd tried to act rationally.

"I won't hurt her Shaun; it wouldn't be good for business. I was just angry with myself for letting that bastard win. Anyway I'll work something out with Jimmy, she won't be gone long. Now finish your drink and get off home, I'll see you in the morning."

Although unhappy about leaving, Shaun did as Nick ordered and put his glass down on the coffee table before heading towards the door. Had he known how bad it would be for her, he would have refused to leave. Unbeknown to him, Maria had overheard the conversation from the bedroom. On hearing Shaun leave she felt panic. Sitting on the bed she shook violently as she waited for Nick to enter.

Back in the lounge, Nick poured another scotch and waited until he was certain that Shaun had left. Knocking his drink back in one, he walked towards the bedroom. The moment he opened the door, she scurried up the bed like a frightened animal crying and shaking. As he approached her, she begged him not to hurt her. Ignoring her plea, he looked evil as he stood over her. Knowing what was coming, she curled herself into a ball in the hope of protecting herself. Then it began. Nick grabbed her by the hair and punched her in the face before dragging her off the bed and throwing her onto the floor. Terrified she'd begged him to leave her alone. During her time there he had always beaten her, but never with such ferocity and rage. Kicking and punching her he shouted "This is your fault! Don't think I didn't see you encouraging Jimmy to bet for you! You're just a fucking whore!"

Begging him to stop, she pleaded for him to believe that she hadn't done anything, but in his drink fuelled rage he was void of any feelings for her. Dragging her up from the floor by her hair, he'd thrown her across the bed.

"Do you think for one fucking minute I'd let you go? You're my property you fucking whore! I'll see you fucking dead first!"

Grabbing her by the throat he pinned her down, tightening his grip before raping her with such force that she passed out. Simply raping and beating her wasn't enough, he needed to make sure she would never forget that night. Being a sadistic bastard, he kept an assortment of implements for inflicting pain.

As she laid there in an unconscious state, he branded her. As the hot iron burnt into her flesh she came round and, trying to endure the brutality of what he was doing, begged him to stop before she passed out again. When he finished, he punched her face so hard it loosened her teeth. It was as he continued to punch her, she regained consciousness, be it all for only a few minutes. Despite the vicious beating she was taking, all she could think about were the many times she had contemplated taking her own life, yet every time she had convinced herself that God would help her. The countless nights she would pray and ask God to give her the strength to go on. That night God listened and she found an inner strength. Believing God had sent Jimmy to save her, for the first time she'd tried to fight back, but her efforts were futile. Nick was strong and powerful, she was no match for him. Finally, when he stopped she was lying on the floor motionless. He kicked her several more times as she lay there, but she didn't move. He never checked to see if she was alive or dead, when without any conscience, he just walked away and returned to the lounge. After drinking several large scotches, he collapsed onto the sofa.

It was five hours later, just after nine that morning when he was woken from his drunken stupor by Shaun ringing the intercom. In a dazed state he'd answered it, momentarily forgetting she was lying, as he thought, dead in the next room. The moment Shaun entered; he knew something had happened when he noticed the dried blood on Nick's hands. He'd listened to Nick's pathetic excuses as to what had occurred.

"Where is she Nick?"

"I'm not sure Shaun," replied Nick with a smirk "I think she's gone. Make me a coffee then we'll talk about it."

Shaun noticed he'd looked towards the bedroom door. Without any thought for himself, he headed towards the bedroom. Nick immediately raised his voice in an attempt to stop him.

"I told you to make the fucking coffee Shaun!"

Ignoring him, Shaun opened the door. Nick shouted again that Shaun worked for him and he'd told him to make coffee.

Seething with anger, Shaun was just about to reply when he saw her lying on the floor. Rushing over, he knelt down next to her. Pressing his fingers onto her neck, he felt a weak pulse. Picking her up, he walked out into the lounge. Nick was sitting down as he looked at Shaun.

"She's dead Shaun, get rid of her!"

"She's alive" replied Shaun aggressively "I'm taking her to Jimmy's!"

"Put her down, she's not going anywhere! I told the bitch I would see her dead before I'd let her leave. Now fucking put her down!"

"I work for you Nick, but you don't own me!" said Shaun defiantly, "now like I said, she's going with me. It's up to you. We can do this easy or hard, but I'm not leaving her here! If I were you I'd pray she doesn't die. We're leaving now, so you'd best get out of my way. I'll be back later!"

Aware that Shaun wasn't about to back down and needing to save face, Nick told him to take the fucking whore. With any luck she'd be dead by the time he got there and Shaun needed to remember who paid him.

CHAPTER 3

Jimmy knew nothing of what had happened between the two men, other than what Shaun had said about Nick killing her if he hadn't have turned up when he did.

Gently stroking her hair and holding her hand, he felt a surge of guilt for leaving her at Nick's. Leaning over, he gently kissed her forehead. Slowly she opened her eyes and tried to focus on his face, but even in her semi-conscious state she immediately put her arms up to defend herself before pulling her knees up under her chest to protect her body. Realising she was absolutely terrified; Jimmy scooped her trembling body up into his arms and in a gentle voice told her nobody was going to hurt her.

Laying her head against his chest, she drifted in and out of consciousness. It was several hours before she woke again. Slowly opening her eyes she could see him looking at her. He smiled and said he'd made some tea as he proceeded to gently help her sit up to drink. Her lips were so badly cut and swollen she could barely sip from the cup. Laying her back down, he sat down opposite her. She watched as he clasped his face in his hands and asked her to forgive him.

Barely able to speak, but forcing the words out, she asked forgive him for what

"For doing this to you," he replied with sadness in his voice.

Instantly she told him he hadn't done it, Nick had.

"No, not technically babe, but if I hadn't been so fucking stupid in the first place, none of this would have happened!"

Before he could say anything else, she drifted back off. The hours passed until she gradually woke again.

Looking at him, she slowly nodded her head when he asked if she felt better, but despite his earlier reassurance, he could tell from her eyes she was afraid of him.

Without taking her eyes from him, she shook her head when he asked if she needed anything. Just lying there she remained silent for the next three hours. He noticed that every time he moved or stood up she flinched and looked afraid.

The day had passed and the evening drew in. When she woke he asked if there was anything she needed. To his relief along with surprise, she nodded her head. He waited for her to say what it was, but it was as though she was too afraid to ask.

"Ok babe what happens now," he asked with a grin "do I have to guess, or are you going to tell me?"

"Am I allowed to use the bathroom?"

He was surprised at the way in which she asked and wondered why she didn't just say, 'I need to use the bathroom.' Disturbingly, he knew she would simply have sat there unless he gave her his permission.

"Of course babe, would you like me to run you a warm bath?"

Instantly a look of absolute dread appeared on her face as she quickly shook her head. Jimmy had seen that look before on his mother's face; having a vague memory from his childhood that he had witnessed his father holding his mother's head under the bathwater. Scanning his memory, he tried to recall exactly what had happened to his mother, but it was futile. Perhaps as a child he had tried to erase such a dreadful memory, or perhaps it was never a real memory at all; maybe he had seen something on television as a child and confused it with reality. Whichever it was, one thing was certain, Maria was terrified, she was still trembling several minutes later.

Reassuringly, Jimmy had only said about the bath because he thought it might help her feel better. He suggested running it and then she could decide if she wanted to use it, he added she could lock the door.

Tearfully she nodded her head in acceptance.

"I'm not sure what you can wear babe; only Shaun didn't actually bring anything of yours. I'm pretty sure I have some pyjamas somewhere and a dressing gown. They'll probably swim on you, but at least you'll be comfortable."

Leaving the bath water running, he went to find her the robe and pyjamas. Several minutes later he returned to the bathroom, the huge Jacuzzi bath was ready. After placing the clothes over a beautiful peacock chair in the corner of the room, he returned to the lounge and told her it was ready.

Slowly she tried to get to her feet, but the full effect of Nick's beating was now taking its toll. Every bone in her body was hurting, large dark bruises had developed on her face and her left eye was swollen shut. Wanting to help he walked towards her, but she immediately backed away.

Having no choice but to trust him when he said he wasn't going to hurt her, she took his arm and walked slowly towards the bathroom.

Although he was concerned about leaving her, he didn't want to push the issue. Hearing her lock the bathroom door, he returned to the lounge and loaded a classical CD into the player. Jimmy wasn't someone you'd expect to like classical music, but as a child he had often listened to it with his mother and he had grown to like it. Turning the volume down low, he pressed a button so the music piped through to the bathroom. The entire apartment was wired with state of the art technology.

With the music playing, he listened outside the bathroom door, he could hear her in the bath and believing she was ok, his first thought was to phone Mickey and bring him up to speed over the day's events. The phone seemed to ring forever before his friend answered.

"Alright Jimmy," said Mickey breathlessly "I'm glad you've phoned, I was going to bell you earlier but I thought you'd be preoccupied."

Jimmy knew he was referring to Maria being at the apartment with him.

"Oh mate," sighed Jimmy, "you've no fucking idea!"

Something in his voice told Mickey not everything had gone to plan; although he had warned him the previous night that he didn't think Nick would take it lying down. He asked Jimmy what had happened.

Jimmy was just about to reply when he heard someone else in the background, it sounded like a woman. Jimmy asked if he was alone and wasn't surprised when his friend said no, Monica was with him. It was unusual for her to stay over at weekends because Charlie normally stayed then.

Mickey was quick to tell him Charlie wasn't staying that weekend; she'd gone to a show with his parents and was staying over with them.

Mickey heard panic in his voice when Jimmy said they could speak the next day and was sorry for interrupting him. It was the type of panic he remembered hearing when they were kids, when Jimmy would run to his house after his father had attacked him and his mother. Mickey knew his friend needed to talk, so without hesitation told him he'd be there in five minutes.

Thanking him, Jimmy asked if he could stop at one of their restaurants and pick them up something to eat along with some chicken soup. Mickey didn't question his request for the soup.

Forty minutes later, the two of them were sitting in Jimmy's lounge. Mickey asked where Maria was and what was going on. Jimmy explained she was taking a bath and had been in there since he'd called him. Mickey looked concerned and asked if she was ok.

"Yeah I heard her moving about a minute ago. Wait till you see her, Nick's beaten her to a pulp. Shaun reckoned he'd have killed her if he hadn't turned up when he did. She's fucking terrified Mick; he's not getting away with it. I'll fucking kill him! I'm going to make him pay for what he's done!"

Mickey felt concerned at the display of anger Jimmy was exhibiting. Trying to calm him down and succeeding when he said if she was as afraid as Jimmy thought, she'd be too scared to come out if he kept shouting and swearing.

The moment Mickey stopped talking they heard the bathroom door unlock. Moments later she was standing in the lounge doorway.

"Jesus Christ!" said Mickey as he looked at her, "fuck me babe you look bad. Nick really did a number on you."

Maria just stood there visibly shaking. Jimmy stood up and helped her to the sofa. Asking if she felt better for a soak, he joked that he'd wondered if she'd drowned.

"Fuck me Jimmy, she needs to see a doctor; she may have internal damage for all we know, Shaun was right; he's tried to kill her!"

The two friends debated whether to take her to hospital or to call a doctor; their thinking was hospitals would ask too many questions, which could be costly. Their debate was interrupted by Maria telling them she was ok, she just felt a bit sick. Jimmy asked if she was hungry. Without replying she simply nodded her head.

After telling her she was in for a treat as Mickey had stopped at one of our restaurants on his way over there and they make the best chicken soup in London, he left her with Mickey while he sorted out the food.

When he returned and placed the food on the table, Mickey smiled at her and asked if she would prefer hers on a tray on her lap.

Shaking her head at his offer, he helped her to her feet and led her to the table. What Jimmy had told him was right, he'd noticed how frightened she looked when he'd approached her. Mickey could feel her trembling as he held her arm and pulled the chair out for her to sit down.

While the two men tucked into grilled chicken and fries, she slowly sipped her soup. Every mouthful was painful, but she was hungry. She hadn't eaten anything since before the poker game, a full twenty four hours earlier. Both men were aware that she kept watching them as she sipped each spoonful. Sitting in the oversized clothes Jimmy had given her, she struggled to keep the shoulders up, stopping every few minutes to adjust them. Mickey watched her; it made him think back to when his sister Fay used to play dress up in their mum's clothes when she was about ten. She would always be pulling them up because they were far too big for her. They had been close; he missed Fay since she married a doctor and moved to America, although they kept in touch regularly and Fay and her family would try and visit every couple of years. Watching Maria struggling with the over-sized clothes, he noticed that she had a large bite mark on her shoulder. With a sincere look he said she should get that looked at as human bites can be dangerous.

"Let me see," said Jimmy reaching over to pull the robe down.

Instantly leaning away from him, she looked terrified as she quickly pulled it up tight to her neck. Jimmy gently touched her hand and assured her he wouldn't hurt her, he just needed to look. Slowly she pulled the robe down just enough to expose the bite. Both men could see her neck and shoulder was covered in bites and bruises. Telling her

Mickey was right and she should see a doctor, Jimmy would give Doc Daniels a call.

An hour later the doctor arrived. He was the doctor that the criminal underworld used if anyone got hurt and didn't want it on record. Jimmy had first met him when he was fourteen after he'd run to Mickey's house one evening after taking a bad beating from his father. Den had sent for Doc Daniels to check him over. Obviously at the time, Jimmy had no idea who he was, but since that first meeting he had seen him several times over the years; usually for stitches after a knife attack or similar. Back then the Doc had been a relatively young man, now in his sixties, balding and wearing glasses, a mere shadow of his former self. Years of heavy drinking had taken its toll; nevertheless, he was still a good doctor.

Jimmy thanked him for coming so quickly. When Doc asked who the patient was, Jimmy pointed over at Maria who was sitting at the table. Doc smiled and said, "Hello Maria."

Jimmy asked if they knew one another. Doc enlightened him, they'd met several times and he presumed this was Nick's handiwork. She simply nodded. The Doc helped her to her feet; they should go somewhere private so he could examine her.

Jimmy walked over and opened his bedroom door. He would sleep in the guest room until she was well. Mickey poured them a drink while they waited for the Doc to return. He tried to talk about Nick, but it was futile, Jimmy was too preoccupied with what was happening in the next room. He looked agitated when he asked Mickey what was taking so long. Mickey's theory was the Doc was just being thorough.

Thirty minutes later they heard the bedroom door close. Walking into the lounge, Doc looked at the two friends and shook his head, "Nick's gone too far this time Jimmy. I've warned him so many times that one day he'll end up killing her."

Jimmy asked if she was going to be ok.

"I think so, but it's going to take a long time. She's got numerous burns and bites and a blood vessel in her eye has burst, it should heal, but it will be bloodshot for a few days. Multiple cuts, bruises and she's sustained some vaginal tearing, hopefully that will heal within a few days too, but it must have been a very sadistic rape. I've given her a shot of antibiotics to stop any infection from the bites and a sedative to help her sleep; it's the best healer of all. I would have preferred her to go to hospital for some x-rays, but she's too scared to leave here. I'll call in on her in a couple of days. In the meantime, when she wakes up give her two of these every four hours, they'll help with the pain."

Doc handed Jimmy a small bottle of tablets as Jimmy asked how often he saw her.

"About every two months, it depends on Nick; if things go well for him it's better for her. I've been her doctor for the past three years and every year the beatings get worse. I've tried to talk to her about leaving, but he's always there, even when I give her the birth control injection, not that I think she would say anything if he wasn't, she's terrified of him. It's none of my business Jimmy, but if she goes back he will end up killing her."

"Don't worry Doc," said Jimmy with a look of pure hatred on his face as he handed the Doc an envelope, "she won't be going back."

He thanked the Doc when he told him there would be no charge; seeing Maria was on the house.

The two men shook the Doc's hand and thanked him as he left.

The moment he closed the door, Jimmy started shouting that he was going to make Nick pay for what he'd done. Mickey saw a rage in his eyes, a deadly rage he'd come to recognise over the years. He knew his friend meant it and there would be little he could do to stop him.

"You'll have to be patient and bide your time Jimmy, these things take a lot of planning, so let's take a breather here."

The two friends talked about Nick. They both knew he would be okay for a while because he wanted her back without a war; especially a war within his own crew. It wasn't good for business and regardless of how he felt about her, nothing was more important to Nick than business. Having built his empire, he wouldn't jeopardise it for a woman. This would be Jimmy's ace card, especially if Nick thought that she wasn't sleeping with him, it would give them more time to work out a plan.

Mickey suggested he could speak to Nick and make it known she was in a bad way. They knew Nick well enough to know he'd be less likely to push the point if he believed there was definitely nothing happening between her and Jimmy. If Mickey was clever, he could even imply Jimmy was having second thoughts about her staying.

"Sounds good Mickey," laughed Jimmy "I must congratulate you on being such a devious bastard."

"Well I learnt from the best!"

Jimmy thanked him, he really appreciated his help. There was never any doubt Mickey would back him, but as his friend he felt compelled to say he knew Jimmy felt sorry for her, so did he and he agreed that Nick was a first class bastard, but he wouldn't feel right if he didn't advise him to think carefully about this. Nick was a very dangerous bastard and did Jimmy think she was worth the devastation that may follow? He would stand by Jimmy whatever happened, but he was worried how all this would turn out; people could get hurt. He knew Jimmy fancied her, but was she worth dying for?

"I appreciate your concern Mick and I can't say whether she'll be worth it or not; but sure as hell I'm not backing down now. Nick's a bastard; I won that game fair and square. She needs my help, I got her into this mess and I'm not fucking sending her back so that fucker can beat her senseless! This is one fight Nick's going to lose, I'll take the fucker out myself if need be!"

"Fair enough Jim, I just needed to know how far you're prepared to go. You know you can count on me and, unless I'm mistaken a few others too. Let's face it; Nick's not exactly Mr Popular is he?"

Mickey left two hours later. After watching the TV for a while Jimmy took a shower then checked in on Maria before retiring to the guest room. Whatever the doc had given her was working; she was fast asleep, not even stirring as he pulled the duvet up over her shoulders.

In the next room he lay awake; he could not erase the image of Shaun carrying her out of the lift, her limp bloodied body draped over the big Irishman's arms. Trying to imagine what Nick had done to her because she'd looked so terrified. The anger surged though his body the more he thought about it, but he knew Mickey was right, there could be no mistakes.

When Shaun returned to Nick's apartment, he expected trouble, especially as he'd defied his boss and taken her to Jimmy's. Knowing he'd done the right thing, he'd made up his mind, if Nick gave him a hard time he would be looking for a new bodyguard. Unexpectedly, Nick could not have been nicer even telling him that he had been right about taking her. Totally shocked by Nick's sudden change of attitude, he knew something was wrong and unable to simply accept this, he questioned Nick's change of heart.

"I've been thinking about her Shaun," he said smugly "she knows I'll get her back. It's just a matter of time. Even Jimmy's not stupid enough to take me on. I'll just make him an offer he can't refuse."

Shaun didn't believe for one minute that Jimmy would give her up that easily, but his only concern was for Maria, at least she was safe for the time being.

Nick told him he wanted him to accompany him to a meeting that night. He was meeting some Russian associates. Shaun didn't ask any details, he simply nodded.

An hour later they were parking the car. It was the first time Shaun had actually come face to face with Nick's Russian associates. He'd heard Nick talking with them on the phone on several occasions, but for reasons best known to Nick, he had preferred to keep his relationship with them quiet. Shaun's theory on the matter was simple; it involved sex trafficking which Nick knew was something the others, with the exception of Maurice, would be reluctant to get involved in. Shaun was well aware that Maria had come to live with his boss under very strange circumstances, even he hardly saw her for the first year. He would have asked her outright if he thought for one minute she would tell him, but her fear of Nick was enough to guarantee her silence, even to him.

The meeting was held in a restaurant's back room. Uri Karpov the Russian boss, along with two big Russian bodyguards were waiting for them when they arrived. Uri ordered his two heavies to sit at another table with Shaun while he discussed business with Nick. Shaun couldn't hear all that was being said, but he did catch the name Jimmy a few times, and it was obvious from the way the Russian spoke, he was unhappy about Nick gambling Maria at the poker game. Several times the conversation became quite heated between the two men. When they finished talking about Maria, Shaun heard the Russian say he had business to attend to in the Ukraine and he wanted Nick or Nikolai as he referred to him, to go with him.

When Nick said that may not be possible as he had things to sort out here, Uri insisted stating there was nothing that couldn't wait. He would deal with Jimmy himself if need be, but their business in the Ukraine was more important. Nick was quick to say he would deal with Jimmy and there was no hurry as Maria would keep her mouth shut.

"If she doesn't," said Uri threateningly "I will hold you responsible and I will expect you to deal with her and this Jimmy!"

Nick said he would and then asked him when the trip was and who would be there.

"That is not important Nikolai; all you need to know is they are looking at England to sell girls. We are looking for someone to run things from here, I suggested you. We could make a lot of money, and if you're lucky I'll get you a new girl to fuck! We leave tomorrow night, probably be gone a week maybe ten days. I will send a car for you at eight tomorrow evening."

The Russians were still drinking when Nick and Shaun left around four that morning.

"You probably heard I'll be going away for a few days," said Nick as Shaun drove, "keep your eye on things here Shaun. If you run into any of the others don't tell them where I've gone, understood? I'll deal with Jimmy when I get back. If she's let him touch her, I'll kill her myself!"

Shaun didn't reply, but his thoughts were, he may work for Nick, but he wouldn't be party to taking out Jimmy and he definitely wouldn't hurt Maria, whether his boss ordered it or not. Shaun hardly spoke on the drive back; he just listened to Nick bragging about how much money he was going to make from his business arrangement with the Russians.

CHAPTER 4

Jimmy woke the following morning to the sound of someone moving about in the apartment. Throwing on a robe he went to investigate.

Entering the kitchen, he could see Maria getting a glass of water. Aware that she was still very nervous he smiled and said good morning. Taking the glass from her, he told her to go and sit down and he would get her water. Frozen to the spot she just stood there looking terrified. Noticing her fear, he asked if she was ok.

"I'm sorry I woke you;" she said looking terrified "please don't be angry that I took the water. I promise I won't do it again, but I was thirsty."

Immediately realising her dread, he reassured her he wasn't angry. He was glad to see her up and about and she could help herself to anything. When he asked how she was feeling, again she hesitated before replying "Better thank you, I'm a quick healer."

He commented that her face didn't look quite so swollen and she was definitely talking better. With a grin he talked about breakfast and stated he did a mean scrambled egg. Despite her talking, she still looked terrified, so he attempted to lighten the mood and humorously asked her not to look so excited, it was only scrambled eggs.

For the first time since she arrived, she actually replied without hesitating.

"It's not that I'm not grateful, it's just I can't remember the last time anyone offered to cook anything for me."

Then suddenly without warning she burst into tears.

Reassuringly he told her not to get upset as he placed his arm around her shoulder. Instantly he could feel her trembling as she pulled away.

"I'm sorry, I'm sorry," her voice was panicky.

Shocked, he asked what she was sorry for. He listened with disbelief as she told him everything was her fault. With conviction, he stated none of it was down to her and she must stop worrying about it. She needed to concentrate on getting well, so she must stop crying and leave the worrying to him.

Reaching out to her, he pulled her close to his chest; he could sense she was apprehensive about him touching her. With a smile he told her to go and make herself comfortable while he got on with the breakfast. Nervously she nodded and moved away.

Just as he placed the breakfast on the table, the intercom buzzed. Jimmy moaned and questioned who the fucking hell was ringing the bell that early on a Sunday morning. Immediately she sprang to her feet as a look of sheer terror came over her face, "Oh God Jimmy, its Nick!"

Telling her to calm down as it was probably someone who'd hit the wrong button, it happened all the time. Jimmy spoke into the intercom and asked who it was. To their surprise it was Shaun.

Moments later the big Irishman was standing in front of them holding a small suitcase. Smiling, he said he'd brought her a few things and how was she feeling.

Jimmy noticed she seemed to trust him when she said she was ok and thanked him for helping her.

"You're most welcome darling, I'm only sorry I didn't get there sooner. You'll be alright here though, Jimmy's a good sort. Now you get on and eat your breakfast."

When Jimmy asked if he'd seen Nick, he shook his head, not since the previous night. He never mentioned he'd gone to the meeting with the Russians. Jimmy asked if Nick was gunning for him. He was angry when Shaun said not at the moment because he was confident he'd get her back.

"No fucking chance," snapped Jimmy "after what he did, I'll see the bastard in hell first!"

"Don't underestimate him Jimmy; he's a very dangerous man. Best to let sleeping dogs lie at the moment, let's just wait and see, don't be too hasty. Anyway you won't have to worry about him for the next week; he's going away on business."

When Jimmy asked if he knew where, Shaun shook his head and said he thought Europe, but Nick was keeping things close to his chest, no doubt they'd find out soon enough.

Jimmy knew that none of their crew had any drug deliveries connected with Europe that week. Tony Ramon handled most of the overseas deals and he hadn't mentioned any coming up. Obviously Nick was working on his own which straight away made him think it wasn't something the others would be keen on, but he decided not to ask Shaun. He'd already helped them enough and it would be unfair to expect any more from him.

Jimmy asked what was in the case and joked he hoped it wasn't a bomb.

"If Nick had his way it would be," laughed Shaun "I hoped to bring Maria some of her clothes, but I didn't feel it was a good time to ask him. So I asked my daughter Bernadette to let me have a few things, she's about the same size."

Looking humble, Jimmy thanked him, he owed him one.

"You don't owe me nowt Jimmy, I did it for Maria and anyway, Nick would grill me by the bollocks if he knew I was here!"

Standing up she walked over and hugged him. Shaun reached into his pocket and pulled out a set of rosary beads. Handing them to her he smiled, "There you are darling; I thought you might get some comfort from these."

On the brink of tears she thanked him.

After telling Jimmy to look after her, Shaun left. As they sat back down, Jimmy said it was a nice surprise to see Shaun.

Nodding her head she smiled. Neither of them had touched their breakfast. So he suggested they eat.

Jimmy watched her as they sat quietly eating. He noticed she put the tiniest amount of food on her fork and, just like before she never took her eyes off him. Breaking the silence he asked her age.

She swallowed the food she had in her mouth before telling him she was nearly nineteen.

Doing the math, he asked if she was sixteen when she moved in with Nick. He looked horrified when she shook her head and looking tearful said fifteen. Wondering how she came to live there at such a young age and thinking it probably wasn't legal, his curiosity got the better of him. He asked if she had been a runaway or something. Unable to give him eye contact, she looked down at the table as she shook her head. Realising she was getting upset, he leaned over, gently touched her hand and apologised for upsetting her.

"It's not that, it's just," she hesitated for a moment, "Oh nothing Jimmy, it doesn't matter."

Caringly he said it did matter and he wanted to know what she was going to say.

"Please Jimmy," she blurted out as she burst into tears "tell me why you're doing this for me. If you intend using me then I would rather you just did it and stopped being so nice. I know this a set up for Nick to test me."

"Fuck me Maria" stunned by her reaction "is that what you've been thinking?"

Barely able to answer him because she was shaking quite violently, she muttered something as she nodded. He gently took her hand and told her she couldn't be more wrong. He hated the way Nick treated her and he would never treat her like that. Tearfully she apologised and stated she should have known better, especially after what Shaun said.

Jimmy said Shaun seemed to look out for her. With a nod she said he did, he was her guardian angel; he'd helped her many times. She thought it was because of their faith.

"Maybe you're right babe; I've certainly seen another side to him since you've been here. I've always seen him as a hired thug who wouldn't think twice about breaking someone's arm or worse. Still as the saying goes, it's always the quiet ones that surprise you. I've got some business to take care of with Mickey later today; will you be okay by yourself? I can get someone to come round and keep you company if you like?"

Maria assured him she would be fine, she was used to being on her own. Before he left, he showed her where he kept his DVD collection and how to operate all the different remote controls for the TV and DVD player. He'd only be a couple of hours and she could help herself to anything.

Despite being unhappy about her staying on her own, he knew she'd be safe for the time being because of Nick's business trip.

A short time later she watched from the window as he got into Mickey's car; it was unmistakable, a red Ferrari Spider.

"No news on Mr Janders then?" asked Jimmy as he shut the car door.

"No," snapped Mickey, "and if that fat bastard thinks he's getting away with it a third time, he's making a fucking big mistake! I thought we could use Jacky Boy and Kevin for this, what do you reckon?"

Jimmy nodded and stated he thought they'd be up for it. Mickey grinned; he'd already asked them to meet them at the club.

The club didn't open on a Sunday so it was always a good place to talk business. Ten minutes later Mickey pulled in to his parking space outside the club. They could see the two lads waiting.

The two friends got out of the car and walked towards the club door where the two lads were standing.

Kevin and Jacky Boy had worked for them for several years; they were what Jimmy would refer to as 'good boys'. Both looked the part as doormen, hard men. Jacky Boy was around thirty, six feet tall of muscular build, but not huge like a lot of doormen; his shoulder length hair was well kept in a ponytail. He was well liked amongst the club staff and punters, especially the females. Kevin was a couple of years older and slightly larger, with receding short fair hair. A real player with women, most weekends he would leave the club with a girl on each arm.

As they entered the club, Mickey told Kev to grab a bottle. Moments later the four men where drinking scotch and ready to talk business. Kevin asked why they'd wanted to meet up.

"Well it's like this Kev;" said Mickey "that fat bastard, Patrick Janders down at the Clifton Arms seems to think he can fuck us about! For some unknown reason he thinks he doesn't need to pay us anymore. So we think you and Jacky Boy ought to pay him a visit and convince him that he does. Nothing too heavy, we don't want to put him out of work, just scare him a bit."

When the lads said they would call on Patrick Janders that night, Mickey said they could drop the money into the club as either Jimmy or he would be about. While the men talked, Mickey asked if Jacky Boy was still dating the little blonde party who worked in the office at AJ's.

"Oh fuck me," interrupted Kev "is he still seeing her, he's fucking loved up Mick; they're like a fucking old married couple. All he ever fucking talks about is me and Lisa did this, me and Lisa did that; gets right on my fucking nerves!"

The four men laughed.

Mickey suggested the two lads taking Lisa and a friend for a meal on the house at one of their restaurants after they'd sorted fat Patrick out. Both lads liked the idea and readily thanked them.

Leaving the two bosses talking business, the lads left.

Once alone, Mickey told Jimmy that Nick was definitely pissed off with him, but arrogantly confident about getting her back.

"Over my fucking dead body Mick, I've tried talking to her, but most of the time she just cries. She thinks this is all a set up between me and Nick to test her loyalty. One thing's for certain, he's really screwed her up; she won't ask for anything, all she keeps saying is sorry. Fuck only knows what she's gone through. Oh and another thing; she was only fifteen when she moved in with him."

"Fuck me, I know he likes them young, but fifteen, what is he a fucking paedophile?"

Jimmy nodded; he thought there was more to her situation. Something, somewhere just didn't seem right.

Mickey's first thought was maybe the rumours about Nick being involved in sex trafficking were kosher. That was probably why he was so desperate to get her back, he was afraid she'd tell them some of his sordid little secrets. He advised Jimmy to find out as much as he could about the circumstances of how she came to be at Nick's. Although Jimmy agreed, he knew it was easier said than done because she was fucking terrified. Telling him to give her time and she'd come round, Mickey asked if he thought Shaun knew anything. Jimmy nodded and said how Shaun had surprised him when he'd turned up that morning. One thing was certain, he cared about her. Mickey said perhaps at a later date they could have a little chat with Shaun, but in the meantime, Jimmy should simply stay out of Nick's way. He felt relieved to hear Nick had gone on a business trip to Europe and he'd be gone about a week. However, like Jimmy he was curious. He knew they had nothing coming in from Europe. Tony's delivery was coming from Asia. Mickey would try and find out, but from the sound of things Nick was working alone. Referring to Nick as a slimy bastard, Mickey was convinced he was up to something. On a positive note, it did give Jimmy another week with her.

Not wanting to leave her on her own for too long, the two men left. Mickey dropped Jimmy off fifteen minutes later, but declined his offer of a drink because he had court business to go over.

Entering his apartment, Jimmy called out to her. Moments later she appeared in the hall. With a smile, he said she looked better and the clothes Shaun brought round looked good on her. Smiling she nodded. After checking everything had been ok while he was out, he asked if she needed anything. When she asked if she could shower, he grinned and questioned why she hadn't simply taken one while he was out. He noticed she began to tremble as she said she hadn't asked his permission. Assuring her she didn't need it and could do whatever she liked, he asked what she fancied to eat. He would send out for whatever she liked, Indian, Chinese, Thai, English, the choice was hers. With a blank expression on her face she started crying and asked him to choose. When he repeated it was her choice, she looked nervous and burst into tears again.

"Hey it's no big deal," he said reassuringly "it's only a takeaway, don't get so upset. What about an Indian, a nice curry or something?"

Nodding her head, she regained her composure, stopped crying and told him she was sorry, but it was because he was being so nice. Nick never asked her what she'd like. It was the first time in years she'd been given a choice.

"Fuck me are you serious, what is he some sort of fucking control freak?"

She nodded.

Forty five minutes later they were sitting down looking at their meal. Being unsure exactly what she'd like and not wanting to risk upsetting her again by asking, he'd ordered just about everything possible; the table was full of takeaway dishes. After telling her to tuck in, he began taking food from the dishes. Unsurprisingly, she just sat there and looked at him. Grinning he told her again to eat as the food would get cold. Despite being shocked when she asked what she could have, he smiled, she could have whatever she liked.

Hesitantly, she picked up a spoon and began placing a tiny amount on her plate from each dish. With every spoonful he was aware she was looking to him for approval, so throughout the meal he kept smiling at her. Still hurting from Nick's beating she chewed her food slowly. Despite the swelling having gone down slightly, there was still the split lip and two loose teeth to contend with.

Staring at her, he couldn't help wondering what makes people like Nick do such things; did he think it made him look tough? Why had his own father given his mother such ferocious beatings? What makes men like them tick? Could it have been they were abused as children? Even if that was so, Jimmy could not accept it as a reason to hurt someone else. He wouldn't have a problem hitting another bloke, but not a defenceless woman or kid.

With a sigh, he said he was stuffed and asked how she was doing. Swallowing her food, she nodded and said he'd ordered too much. When he asked if she fancied watching

TV or listening to music, again she just nodded her head and said it was up to him.

"Oh no not all that again," he joked "just decide babe."

Trembling she just sat there looking at him, tears were welling in her eyes. Realising it was all too much for her, he held out his hand. Nervously she took it; moments later he led her into the lounge.

Once they were both sitting down he smiled and asked if she wanted TV or music. Several seconds passed before she plucked up the courage to tell him she'd really liked what he'd played when she was in the bath. Jimmy used the remote control and played classical favourites.

Despite sitting on the sofa at opposite ends; he could sense she was beginning to feel slightly more relaxed with him. Wondering if then might be a good time to try to coax some more information from her; he smiled then casually made conversation by stating that Nick treated her badly. Even though she simply nodded, there were no tears, so he continued and asked if she'd never thought about getting away with Shaun's help. He could see she was uneasy answering his questions, but she wasn't crying, so he leaned over and patted her arm to reassure her. He hadn't expected to hear what she was about to say.

"I can't talk to you Jimmy, he will kill me. I know this is a test, please tell him I never told you anything when he comes for me."

Lifting his hand up, he gently touched her face; she flinched and quickly sat back against the sofa. Determined not to stop, he reached over and gently cupped her face in his hand and gave his word it wasn't a test and nobody was going to hurt her. Tears ran down her cheek onto his hand. Gently moving his thumb he wiped them from under her eyes. When he asked why she thought it was a test, she was too afraid to answer, she just stared at him. Swearing to her that he'd won the game fair and square, so why did she think it was planned. Patiently he waited several minutes for her reply.

"He always warned me that if I ever told anyone anything about him, he would kill me. I told him I would never do that, but he would laugh and say; 'Well maybe one day I'll test your loyalty, but you'll never know when or who with.'"

Jimmy gently squeezed her hand and swore on his mother's grave it wasn't a test and he fucking detested Nick. Something inside was telling her to trust him, but she knew just how cunning and calculating Nick was. If it was a setup he would kill her for sure, but as she looked at Jimmy she felt a strange sense of calm. Hesitating for a moment, she took the rosary beads from her pocket and clasped them.

Maria said he was right about Shaun helping her, but she could never have escaped. Nick always said if she ever tried, not only would he kill her, but also her best friend Melanie. She knew he meant it; he used to tell her all the time. He would have killed her yesterday if Shaun hadn't turned up. She talked about the night of the poker game and how Nick had told her he was going to kill her, despite her begging him. He would rather see her dead than with Jimmy.

"The fucker actually said that?" said Jimmy feeling his temper surfacing.

Nodding her head, Nick thought it was her fault because she'd led him on at the game.

Unable to suppress his temper a moment longer, Jimmy raised his voice and shouted that Nick was a fucking psycho; and they'd barely said more than five words to each other!

"I know," she replied nervously "but it wasn't the first time he'd said it."

While waiting for her to reply after asking what she'd meant, he noticed she was rubbing the beads and trembling. Recognising his display of anger had probably scared her, squeezing her hand he said he was sorry.

Mustering all her courage, she took a breath and told him that many times when he had humbled Nick over her during poker nights, he would take it out on her afterwards.

Calling him a fucking bastard, Jimmy was by then inwardly raging with aggression. Maria watched him clenching his fists. Sensing she was scared, he apologised again.

"It's ok Jimmy, it doesn't matter now anyway; Nick was right, I did really like you. I knew you were trying to protect me."

"Oh yeah I was protecting you alright, getting seven buckets of shit knocked out of you!"

Tearfully she looked at him, her beautiful eyes all bruised and swollen as she asked him not to say that because until the previous night, she used to pray every day that Nick would kill her and put an end to it all. Then when Jimmy won her, she wanted to live; that was why she fought back. Gently he touched her hand and stated she wasn't his property and he wouldn't force her to stay at the apartment. Tears were rolling down her cheeks. The fear and torture she had endured was etched on her face, she wanted to stay there. For the first time in years, she felt like a person and not a possession.

"What the hell did he do to you Maria to make you so afraid that you wanted to die?"

Unable to contain her emotions, she burst into tears. Moving closer to her, he placed his arm around her shoulder and said they didn't have to talk about Nick and he shouldn't have expected her to.

Suddenly she felt an overwhelming desire to get closer to him. For years she had been denied all tender human contact, yet she found herself wanting to hold him. Slowly she rested her head on his chest and placed her arm across him. Gently he stroked her hair, they could talk another time, but for now they could just enjoy listening to music.

She wanted to talk; her fear was that Nick would come for her and by telling Jimmy it might stop Nick from doing what he'd done to her to another girl. Placing his hand under her chin, he gently raised her head and swore no one was coming for her and if anyone did, he would deal with them. Again he promised he wouldn't let anyone hurt her.

She knew in her heart that Jimmy was a good man, but she also knew Nick would get to her. She needed to tell him everything before that happened. Trusting her instinct that he wouldn't hurt her, she remained calm as she began telling him that he was right. Nick was an animal who used to beat her, chain her up and do terrible things to her. Sometimes the beatings and torture went on for days.

Curiosity was getting the better of him; he had to ask what the terrible things were that Nick did.

With her hands trembling and her eyes filling with tears; it was clear she couldn't talk about the torture. She rested her head back on his chest and wiping her eyes said she needed to show him something. Rising slowly and standing up, she turned round to face away from him. Jimmy wondered exactly what she was going to show him as he sat looking at the back of her. Slowly she undid her trousers and pulled them down just past her buttocks. Silently he watched. He had no idea what to expect, but the sheer horror of what he saw turned his stomach. Both of her buttocks had been branded by a crucifix; at least two of the burns were fresh. As she dressed, he stood up and held her in his arms.

"I promise you he will pay for this Maria, as God is my witness, he's not going to get away with it. I'll see him dead before I let him touch you again!"

Hearing his words, she wrapped her arms around him, "May God forgive me for saying this Jimmy, but killing him would be too good, he needs to know what it feels like to be terrified every day like I was."

"That's not impossible" he replied with a grin "I know certain people."

At that moment for the first time ever, he saw a spark in her, a spark which Nick had failed to extinguish. It was then she shocked him again when she stated she didn't want Nick killed, she really wanted him to suffer day after day like she had. With a grin he said that could be a bit trickier.

"Not necessarily Jimmy, you cannot live with someone for all those years without seeing and hearing things, even when they think they have total control over you. I'm talking about sending him to prison for a very long time."

"Whoa, slow down there girl. A hit is one thing, prison's another. Nick's far too clever; he'd never leave anything that incriminated him."

Instantly she stated he was wrong, she knew things which involved not only her, but several other girls. She would tell him about them, but she felt exhausted and asked if they could leave it until the morning. She needed to sleep.

Before she left the room for bed, he asked if she would mind if he invited Mickey to join them the following morning. He grinned when she said she was going to ask him to, a good solicitor may be just what she needed.

As she walked towards the bedroom, she turned and with sincerity thanked him for saving her. That night she would ask God and the Blessed Mother to keep him safe.

Without replying to what she said, he simply smiled and told her to get some sleep.

Jimmy tossed and turned the entire night. What exactly did she know? Lying in his bed gazing at the ceiling, he kept telling himself he should have encouraged her to tell him before she went to bed. Now his mind was going into overdrive, there would be no rest for him that night.

CHAPTER 5

Jimmy was woken the following morning by the sound of his mobile ringing. Fumbling to answer it, he rallied to gather his senses. Through blurred eyes, he looked at the number and seeing it was Mickey asked what he wanted. Mickey stated he'd had a call from Nick and he was adamant he would get Maria back; he wanted them to meet him to discuss it. Jimmy's instant reply was there was nothing to discuss, she was staying with him. Mickey agreed, but after telling him to calm down said they needed to play for time and meeting him was their best option. Jimmy's feelings on the matter were they should find Nick and beat him senseless, but he knew his friend was right; they had to pick their moment. He wasn't surprised when Mickey said he'd already arranged the meeting. It would take place at their club, Dixie's, when Nick returned from his trip. Mickey asked if there had been any developments with Maria. His curiosity was buzzing when Jimmy spoke about the previous night and that Maria wanted him present when she told them details about her time at Nick's.

Before the call ended, they arranged for Mickey to come round that afternoon. Jimmy also said he needed to pop into Sweet Cheeks at some point. His choice would be that afternoon as his cleaning lady, Gladys, was due round then. Mickey would pick him up and go with him.

It wasn't until Jimmy closed his phone, he realised he could smell something cooking. Throwing on a robe he went to investigate. Maria was cooking breakfast. As he entered the kitchen, nervously she said good morning and asked if he was hungry. A smile replaced her worried look when he replied, "Starving babe!"

"That's good because I've cooked you some eggs and bacon, is that alright? Only you never said what time you wanted to eat. I can do you something else if you prefer."

It was great, he hadn't expected anything. Placing his breakfast on the table, she asked if he wanted tea or coffee. Moments later, he was tucking into his meal as she placed a mug of tea down. When he asked if she would be joining him, she shook her head. Looking around he noticed that the kitchen was clean and tidy; gone were the remnants of the previous night's Indian. When he said she didn't have to clean as he had a cleaner, Gladys, who came in a couple of times a week and today was one of her days, Maria said she had wanted to clear up for him. At Nick's she had to do it, only then if she didn't do it good enough, he would beat her.

He just looked at her. Despite the bruises and the swelling she was still beautiful. Had things have been different for her; she could have been a model. His curiosity over her comments got the better of him and he asked what she'd meant by 'he'd beat her.'

"Every day he would check that everything was perfect, nothing out of place. If it wasn't perfect he would hit me. It was the same when I cooked, if it wasn't right, he would hit me. Sometimes he would just stop my food for a couple of days, it just depended what mood he was in."

With disbelief he questioned that Nick wouldn't let her eat. Tears welled in her eyes as she nodded. He asked her why she didn't eat when Nick went out. With disbelief, he listened as she told him she was only allowed to eat when Nick ate. On the occasions when he was out all day and night, he would leave her some crackers.

Jimmy could feel his temper rising, he wanted to ask her more, but for the first time she seemed relaxed talking so he decided he would change the subject rather than push the issue and upset her. They talked about his cleaning lady Gladys. She had been a friend of his mother's and she had always been kind to him, especially when he was a child.

Nervously, Maria asked if Gladys would mind her being there. Jimmy laughed, she'd love it. It was likely all she would want to do would be to sit, drink tea and talk. Noticing she looked uneasy with this information, he asked if she was ok about it. Although she nodded, she asked what she could talk about as she'd never been anywhere worth talking about. With a grin he told her not to worry as Gladys could talk for England, getting her to stop was the problem! Maria would be lucky to get a word in edgeways. Immediately her expression changed from one of happiness to dread when Jimmy said he wouldn't be there when Gladys arrived, he had to go out. As they continued to chat, he mentioned that Mickey had arranged a meeting with Nick when he returned.

Almost begging him, she asked him not to meet him; she knew Nick wouldn't let her stay and something bad would happen. It was best if she just went back.

Reaching over, he touched her hand as she fought back her tears, reassuring her she wasn't going back and she should stop worrying. If she wanted to stay then Nick would just have to accept it one way or another.

With a sad expression, she just looked at him, she so wanted to believe him, but she knew Nick wasn't going to let her go. Jimmy continued to try and reassure her by saying; even Mickey thought avoiding Nick would only make things worse. Jimmy couldn't avoid him indefinitely; his hope was he'd be able to keep his fucking hands off the bastard! Pleading, she asked him not to meet Nick; she knew just how dangerous he was and the things he'd done. Jimmy assured her he wouldn't give him any reason to kill him and he was confident Nick wouldn't do anything at the club as it was Jimmy's turf. Looking at his watch, he exclaimed that Mickey would soon be there so he had to get ready, but he was dying to find out what she knew.

Thirty minutes later he was ready to go and thanked her when she said how nice he looked. Wearing a pair of black trousers and a white designer shirt, he looked very smart. All finished off nicely with a black leather jacket, Rolex watch, gold ring and a solid gold neck chain which was just visible through his open top button.

She asked him what she should say when Gladys arrived. Seeing the concern on her face, he would call Gladys and say he had a friend staying who was having trouble with an ex-boyfriend.

They heard Mickey's car horn outside. She called for him to take care as the lift doors slowly closed behind him.

Locking the door, she stood in the hall thinking about him. Although she barely knew him, she felt she could trust him. Despite what Nick had done to her, she found herself wanting to be with Jimmy. For the past three years she had only known cruelty and violence, but she never gave up hope that God would help her. Her prayers had finally been answered, Jimmy was her saviour. Momentarily she slipped into the most wonderful daydream, imagining that in time they could be like any regular couple. Jimmy would be kind and loving and maybe one day she would become his wife. Then the harsh reality that Nick would see them both dead before he would allow that to happen pounded through her head.

Outside the apartment block, Jimmy got into Mickey's car and after saying hello called Gladys to tell her about Maria. Mickey joked and asked if he'd told Maria she'd need earplugs, because Gladys loved to talk.

The club was only fifteen minutes away. During the drive, Jimmy told him what Maria had said the previous evening. Both men wished she'd told him more and were interested to find out what she knew.

"Let's just hope it's something we can use," said Mickey, "but for now let's just concentrate on what to do about Nick. We both know he's not going to let her stay and he's far too arrogant to let it drop. Whether you won the bet or not, this is one game he doesn't intend losing. I think things could get messy Jim."

"Well like I said before, I'm not backing down. You should see what the bastard did to her Mick; he's branded the cheeks of her arse with a crucifix! It turned my fucking guts when she showed me!"

Mickey referred to Nick as a sick twisted bastard who would get his comeuppance. As they pulled up outside the club, two of their lads, Shane and Billy, were unloading beer crates. Jimmy asked them if anyone was in the club. Billy said just bar staff and a couple of dancers practicing their moves.

The two friends made their way inside followed ten minutes later by the two lads.

Billy asked Jimmy what he was going to do about Nick's bird, only rumours were flying round the place.

"Well let's just say, Nick's not too happy about losing and no doubt the fucker will make an issue of it. Thankfully he's away on business at the moment Billy, but I dare say the shit will hit the fan when he comes back!"

Billy had a look on his face, a look which said he wanted to say something. He was probably the closest to them and without a doubt the man they relied on to keep things running smoothly at the club. He'd worked for them for years since joining their crew when he was just nineteen. Now in his late twenties; he was big, bald and brawny. Known to be a tough cookie, but with a kind heart, totally loyal and reliable and never one to shirk his responsibilities.

"Tell you the truth Jimmy, I'm curious as to why you ever made that fucking bet in the first place, we all know Nick's a fucking psycho! Why didn't you just say one of his clubs or brothels? I've seen that bird once or twice and yeah, she's definitely got something, but is she worth having your bollocks cut off for? After all, you do have to work with the fucker!"

Everyone laughed; they all knew Billy wasn't one to mince his words. They waited for Jimmy to reply. Moments passed when he looked at Billy and said it just seemed to be the right thing to do at the time. Everyone knew Nick treated her like shit and someone had to help her.

"Oh, so it didn't have anything to do with the fact that you wanted to shag the fucking arse of her then Jimmy?"

"Well there was that as well Billy, but it was worth every minute that night just to see his fucking face. Mind you, what he did to her afterwards made me wonder if I did the right thing. One thing's for sure though, she ain't going back. It's a fucking miracle he didn't kill her, the sadistic bastard!"

Billy heard on the grapevine that Nick had messed her up pretty bad. The two doormen listened as Jimmy told them what had happened to her and that she was only fifteen when she moved in with Nick, their theory was he had bought her.

Looking shocked, Shane said that was disgusting, nobody loved pussy more than him, but a fifteen year old that was fucking sick! However, Billy had been right about having to work with Nick.

"I don't have to work with him," snapped Jimmy arrogantly "he just thinks he's fucking indispensable, well he's not! Truth is I think maybe it's time to reconsider our business relationship with Nick. I think the real reason he's making such a fucking big deal over her is because she knows too much; probably about dodgy fucking deals that we know fuck all about!"

The lads agreed and Billy said they'd thought for a long time Nick was doing some dodgy stuff. Personally he wouldn't trust Nick the slimy bastard any further than he could throw him. They knew he was genuine, if things got tough with Nick they could count on him and Shane. They fucking hated him, he was a cocky bastard, especially when he came into the clubs and ordered Billy about like some fucking errand boy! Billy didn't even work for him; Jimmy and Mickey were his bosses!

"When the Nick fan club closes." said Mickey with a grin "I'd like to say with any luck we'll be able to sort this out peacefully. Who knows, Nick may just decide to leave it. Although what you both said is appreciated. We'll know who to call if we need someone to send him for a midnight dip!"

"Be my fucking pleasure," said Billy "I'll even supply the fucking concrete boots!"

They all laughed. There was definitely no love lost between Nick and the doormen, especially Shane. There had been several times over the years when Nick had ruffled his feathers, but like everyone else, Shane knew most of the time Nick did it to get at Tony Ramon. Shane was tight with Tony, usually working his clubs. It was only when Tony could spare him he worked for Mickey and Jimmy. They were just about to continue talking when Simone, one of the dancers walked over to them and asked if they minded her practising her new pole routine.

The four friends looked at her, standing in just a pair of skimpy hot pants, a good looking girl in her twenties with a great body. Billy was the first one to grin and reply, "Oh I think we could stand it, what do you lot reckon?"

They all laughed and joked saying things like, "Well of course you've got to practice babe, we understand. If you like we'll watch you and give you a few tips!"

With a giggle she called them a dirty load of bastards!

It was as she walked away, Jimmy noticed a large bruise on her thigh. Pointing at it, he asked what she'd done. No one was surprised when she told them it was a gift from her ex, Alfie Stubbs.

Jimmy referred to Alfie as a wanker, but said he thought they'd separated. Simone said they had but when he'd been drinking he was punchy and seemed to forget they weren't together. When he asked if Alfie still worked the doors at the Paradise club, she nodded. Then he asked if she was going to shake her tits for them. Laughing she began walking away before she called over to Shane to put her music on.

They watched her gyrate up and down the pole and made several lewd comments as she danced. When Billy said he wouldn't mind giving her one, it was obvious the feeling was mutual amongst the men and especially Shane, as he'd slept with most of the dancers. He was very good looking and built like an ox, there was never any shortage of girls.

They waited until she finished dancing before leaving the club. The time was just after four.

CHAPTER 6

Nick had arrived in the Ukraine with the Russians. Uri had booked him into a high class hotel before taking him to meet with another man at a club. Uri introduced the man as Sven; he was the man who wanted a partner in England. Sven and Nick shook hands.

"So Nicolai" said Sven, "Uri tells me you are interested in doing business with us?"

Nick nodded, but said it would depend on the business. Sven repeated what Uri had told him about them wanting to send girls to England. Sven knew there were many people there who would pay good money for the right girl. He could supply girls, but he needed someone who could deliver them to the buyers. Nick asked him what sort of money they were talking about should he agree to work with them. He listened as Sven said for every girl; Nick would be paid three thousand pounds in English money. He could send maybe three to three hundred and fifty a year. Nick liked what he was hearing and asked exactly what he'd have to do.

"Just keep them somewhere for a few days Nicholai, until their buyers are ready. I send about fifteen at a time. Over a year you make a million, a good deal yes?"

The Russian could see that Nick was keen to know more. Thinking about the offer, Nick knew that keeping the girls would not be a problem. He had several properties and warehouses that would be suitable. Sven was keen to get Nick's reply as he had eleven girls waiting to go, but his colleague in England had let him down. The moment Nick said yes, Uri interrupted and, after congratulating him, said he was taking him out to have some fun at one of the clubs he owned.

Ten minutes later Nick and Uri were leaving after thanking Sven for his hospitality.

The club Uri took him to was full of young girls that he could do whatever he liked to. After Uri confirmed that Nick liked to get rough, he told him to pick a girl.

Scanning the room, Nick pointed to a very young girl; she looked to be about fourteen. Uri called her and another girl over, and then along with Nick took them to a room under the club. It was like a dungeon, badly lit. There were shackles hanging from the walls and a selection of whips and torture implements were housed on a wooden table. The only normal thing was a bed with black satin sheets on. Uri could tell by Nick's face he was going to enjoy being there. Uri flattered him by saying the room was only for a privileged few. In there they could do whatever they liked, but should Nick's girl die, he would expect him to pay for her. The price was twenty thousand in English money. With a smirk, Nick told him not to worry, he wouldn't kill her.

Within minutes both men were slapping the girls around. Uri was as much an animal as Nick, dragging one of the girls and forcing her onto the bed, where he ordered her to blow him. While doing what he'd ordered, he told Nick to fuck her. The other girl huddled in the corner of the room absolutely terrified. When they finished with the first girl, Uri ordered the other girl to join them. The two men continued to torture them as they drank vodka and snorted coke. Pitifully the girls begged them to stop. Nick punched one of them in the face and ordered her to stop fucking whining. Then he dragged her to the bed with the other girl. Within minutes both girls were handcuffed and gagged while the two men raped and beat them.

It was three hours later when they finally stopped. One of the girls was barely alive by the time the two men left and returned upstairs.

Back in the club, Uri called a woman over. She was about fifty, heavily built with a hard chiselled face. She stood in front of them and nodded as Uri told her to tend to the two girls downstairs. Without answering him, she nodded again and left.

Uri poured them a drink while they talked about business.

"I want to make it clear Uri," said Nick "if I agreed to work with you it would be entirely down to me. None of my associates back in England are to know about it."

"That is your business Nicolai, we just send the girls. Maybe you see one you like as a replacement for Maria. You were very stupid to gamble with her!"

Nick assured him Maria wouldn't be a problem, she knew better than to tell Jimmy anything. With an air of arrogance, Uri said he wasn't worried, but she was a problem that needed to be dealt with and there were people in England who had expressed their concern to him. He had assured them Nick would deal with her.

They drank heavily that night, finally leaving the club around half four in the morning. As the driver pulled up at Nick's hotel, Uri said they would pick him up the next day at eleven thirty. Sven expected them at midday and he would not tolerate them being late.

KAREN CLOW

CHAPTER 7

At Jimmy's apartment, Gladys and Maria were getting along just fine. She had really warmed to the elderly lady. Gladys had a sort of grandmother thing going for her, with grey hair and a plump, happy round face; she made Maria feel very comfortable. They chatted about her husband Arthur, who was approaching his seventy eighth birthday. Maria noticed the look of love and pride every time she spoke of him and her family of three daughters and grandchildren, all of whom she loved dearly and saw regularly.

Gladys took a sip of her tea and asked how long she'd known Jimmy, but quickly added she had known him since the day he was born. She could remember his father being thrown out of the hospital for being drunk. He was a dreadful man; she didn't know how Jimmy and his mum survived the terrible beatings. When she asked if Maria knew his mum had committed suicide, Maria shook her head, she had no idea. She didn't know anything about his past, she only knew him through her ex-boyfriend.

"Oh yes him" said Gladys raising her eyebrows. "Jimmy told me you had a bit of a falling out when he rang me; but looking at your face it looks a bit more serious than a lover's tiff! I hope you're not thinking of going back to him love?"

Maria shook her head.

"Well thank God for that, you're better off without him love. Fifty years I've been married to my Arthur and he's never so much as raised a finger to me, God love him."

Unsure of what to say, Maria just smiled and listened as Gladys chatted on about blokes who hit women and how, in her opinion, they weren't worth a pint of cold piss. One thing Maria had learnt in the short time she had known her was she was honest, down to earth and she certainly didn't pull any punches. If Gladys thought it, she said it. Maria afforded herself a smile when Gladys said she should find a nice boy like Jimmy, he was the salt of the earth, they didn't come any better than her Jimmy. Like with her doing his cleaning, she knew he didn't need her because he kept the place clean and tidy, he only kept paying her because he didn't want to hurt her feelings. Gladys giggled and said she didn't really need to work as Arthur got a good pension from the railway after he'd worked there for forty eight years. Maria giggled when, after asking why she didn't quit, Gladys said it was because she didn't want to upset Jimmy either and the extra money paid for her bingo.

They both chuckled. Maria suddenly jumped as the front door opened. Gladys could see that she was nervous so in a calm voice said it was the lads returning. They waited for the lounge door to open.

"Alright girls, has Gladys talked you to death yet babe?" said Jimmy laughing as he entered the room.

"Cheeky devil, take no notice of him Maria!"

Jimmy walked over to Gladys and putting his arm around her shoulders said she knew he loved her really and she should put the kettle on. He kissed her on the cheek as she stood up. Gladys offered to make them a drink but she wouldn't stay, she needed to get back home, Arthur would want his dinner. After putting the kettle on she returned to the lounge.

Telling Maria she hoped to see her again and she should keep away from that ex-boyfriend as he was bad news, Gladys left. Mickey noticed how much calmer Maria seemed. He asked how she was feeling. Maria smiled, she felt better.

Talking to Gladys had obviously been good for her, but he didn't want to start questioning her straight away about her time at Nick's. For the time being he thought it was best to wait, his theory being the more comfortable she felt, the more she would tell them.

Jimmy came in from the kitchen carrying three mugs of tea. Placing them down, he asked Maria how she'd got on with Gladys. Both men grinned when she said Gladys was lovely and she'd enjoyed listening to her talk about her family. Jimmy asked if she'd managed to get a word in edgeways. Shaking her head she giggled. She hadn't minded though, the last three years of her life she'd been a prisoner, so she had nothing to chat about anyway. They both noticed she looked tearful. Jimmy tried to cheer her up by saying she didn't need to worry about the last three, but look forward to the next three. His words seemed to have the desired effect as she nodded her head and smiled.

They talked about Gladys for over an hour. Mickey could see a change in her as she chatted. Thinking to himself, apart from Shaun's wife Ann, Gladys was probably the only female she had actually talked to for the last three years. Jimmy could also see she was looking and acting more relaxed, that was until he changed the topic.

"Right then babe, as all three of us are here maybe we should talk about Nick."

Immediately her whole demeanour changed. Mickey noticed and suggested they left it for another time, after all Nick was out of the country so there was no hurry; they had a few days grace. With a look of relief, she smiled and nodded her head. Fifteen minutes later Mickey had to go as he had a court case first thing the next morning.

It was usual for the two men to go to Dixie's the following night, but with her staying there Mickey wasn't sure if their plans would change.

"I'll probably give the club a miss tomorrow Mick, I'll have the night in with Maria now she's actually talking to me!"

Despite grinning, she stated she would be fine on her own so he didn't have to change his plans for her. If he had no objections, she would use the time baking. He was happy to give the club a miss and for her to do some baking, but he did need to pop out for an hour about eight. Regarding her baking, if she wrote him a list, he'd be happy to get her whatever she needed.

Mickey asked where they were going at eight; he wasn't surprised when Jimmy said he needed to pop over to the Paradise Club. Mickey knew he was referring to Alfie Stubbs.

"Fuck me Jimmy," laughed Mickey "for Christmas I'll get you a fucking cape and a mask, you're becoming a right fucking super hero!"

They all laughed.

Laughing, Jimmy told him to piss off; he couldn't let Alfie get away with hitting Simone.

Noticing that Maria was looking at them, Mickey said "It's alright babe, like you, one of the girls down the club is having a bit of ex-boyfriend trouble. It must be the fucking week for it! So shall I pick you up about half seven then Jimmy?"

Jimmy nodded and said he just wanted a friendly chat with Alfie.

"That's what worries me," joked Mickey, "I'd best go with you, just to be on the safe side."

Five minutes later Mickey left.

Jimmy explained to her about Simone and the trouble she was having with Alfie. Maria smiled and said Simone was lucky to have him as her boyfriend. She felt secretly relieved when he said he hadn't had a girlfriend for over a year and Simone only worked for him. Judging by the look on her face she was happy he was single. In fact he was really beginning to notice how she had come out of her shell; maybe she was beginning to trust him.

By the time they turned in for bed, he had managed to get her to chat quite a lot. He deliberately didn't mention Nick, simply because he didn't want her to feel pressured. Her last words to him before saying goodnight were what would he like for breakfast in the morning. He was happy to reply, anything, but only on the condition she ate with him.

The following morning saw her cooking the breakfast. Since her arrival, with one exception, she always said she had eaten earlier. Jimmy's theory on that was she probably hadn't eaten at all. So from that morning on, he would make it clear he would like her to join him for breakfast.

After breakfast, he asked if she'd like to go out somewhere that day as she'd been cooped up in his apartment for days. He thought she might fancy going out for a drive or something, just to get some fresh air.

Without replying she started to cry as she stood up to clear the table and said she'd rather stay home if he didn't mind. Reaching out, touching her hand he told her not to get upset, it was just a suggestion. Trying to smile, she nodded her head before heading for the kitchen. Wishing he'd never mentioned it, he followed her.

Aware she was crying as she stood at the sink, he walked up behind her and placed his hand on her shoulder, but before he could say anything, she turned and hugged him. Totally surprised by her reaction, he reciprocated the show of affection. Pressing her head into his chest, she sobbed and sobbed as she tried to tell him she'd never be able to leave the apartment. Reassuring her she would be able to once everything had calmed down; he held her close as he waited for a reply.

"Nick has people everywhere Jimmy. I could never risk going out, but it doesn't matter because I like being here, I feel safe."

In that moment he felt an overwhelming desire to kiss her. Gently placing his hand at the back of her head, he leaned forward and pressed his lips against hers. Unsure of what her reaction might be, he removed his hand and placed it round her back. They kissed for several seconds before she pulled away.

"Please don't Jimmy, we cannot do this!"

Turning away from him, she began washing up. Gently he took her arm and pulled her back round to face him, but she couldn't look at him. Raising her chin with his hand, he apologised, stating he shouldn't have kissed her. With a look of sadness, she confessed she'd wanted him to, but if Nick found out he would kill both of them.

Tenderly he kissed her on the cheek and assured her, Nick wouldn't find out, but he would wait until she was ready.

Walking back to the table, he sat down. Whilst she made them a coffee, she thought about what had happened. Her mind was in turmoil, she had wanted to kiss him; yet she'd found herself gripped with fear when she had.

The day passed quickly with her baking and him making calls. Neither of them mentioned the earlier incident. Jimmy got ready for his trip to the Paradise Club as the time approached seven that evening. Twenty five minutes later they heard Mickey's car horn outside.

After waving to them from the window, she set about baking some cakes. Expecting them to be gone two or three hours she was surprised when just over an hour later the two men returned. They explained that Alfie hadn't been working that night so they would have to wait until Thursday to speak to him. Mickey only stayed until half ten then went to Dixie's.

Jimmy had smelled the cakes when he returned home so he asked if he was allowed to sample one.

Instantly she went into the kitchen, returning a few moments with a plate of cakes and scones. Complementing her on her cooking success, he ate almost half of them. They watched a film before finally turning in around one o'clock.

KAREN CLOW

CHAPTER 8

Time passed quickly in the Ukraine. Nick had now been there for six days. He'd had another meeting with Sven earlier that week after accepting his business offer.

During his stay, he'd begun to realise his new business associates were not to be messed with, but as always he was arrogantly confident he could fit in with them. Nick liked the idea of making large sums of money, along with power. The Russians would also make good allies should he ever need their services back in England. The girls who were to be sold meant nothing to him, they were purely a means to make money. One thing was clear though; the Russians were far more ruthless than any bosses back in England. With a very corrupt police force, men like Sven and Uri could virtually get away with anything, although fear played a large part in their success. Everyone knew if an individual stood up to them not only would they be eliminated, but their entire family too. The Russians were brutal that was for certain, with connections all over the world, buying and selling children and teenage girls from many countries.

The more time Nick spent with them, the more aware he became that the poorer the country, the easier it was to obtain the merchandise, especially places like the

Philippines and Thailand, there poor families would readily sell their children. They were easily deceived into believing the child would actually have a better life. In many cases they would sell them for as little as the equivalent of a few English pounds, which in their country would take them several years to earn. Most of them came from small villages with no formal education and the most basic of living conditions and like the Ukraine, the police could be easily bought for little money. Sex trafficking was big business with big money to be had and Nick wanted a bite of that cherry.

Most of his time there had been spent with Uri who had taken him to several brothels and strip joints. It was obvious Uri was second in command, Sven was the big boss. That particular day, Nick would see first-hand just how powerful the Russians were.

Uri and his driver, who was also his personal body guard, had picked Nick up just before midday and taken him to a small restaurant. As soon as they walked in, Nick could tell it was somewhere that business took place. At every table there was a boss with at least two body guards. Nick watched as Uri kissed several of them on each cheek, but he didn't introduce Nick to anyone.

A large fat man came out from the kitchen to speak to Uri; he was the chef and owner of the restaurant. Uri stood up and after kissing him they spoke in Russian, although Uri did introduce Nick to him in English before adding he was the best chef in the Ukraine. After the chef had returned to the kitchen; a young waiter came over with a tray of drinks. Nick noticed that Uri put an envelope on the tray; his instinct told him it was money.

Twenty minutes later as they were eating their meal, two men came into the restaurant and walked over to Uri's table. Standing up, Uri embraced the boss before kissing him. The man's bodyguard stood behind him. He was huge, at least six feet six inches tall with enormous biceps bulging through his shirt. His boss was small by comparison, barely five feet nine with a large rounded belly. Nick wasn't introduced. He just watched as the man walked away and sat at a table a few feet away from them. Nick had a strange feeling that something wasn't quite right, but he put it down to not understanding their language. They continued to eat their meal. It was as they finished their dessert Uri stood up and told Nick to stay at the table while he sorted out some business. He headed towards the kitchen. Uri's bodyguard stayed and talked to Nick, despite his English being far from good they managed to communicate, be it only about the meal.

Within five minutes, Uri came out of the kitchen accompanied by the chef. Nick was surprised when they walked past him and headed over to the table of the man with the huge bodyguard, the man who Uri had kissed and spoken to less than thirty minutes earlier. Suddenly without any warning, Uri took out a gun with a silencer attached to it and shot both the man and his bodyguard. Two clean shots within a split second of one another straight in the men's foreheads. Neither of them had seen it coming; the bodyguard didn't even have time to draw his gun.

Nick just sat there silently as the chef clapped his hands together to summon some men from the kitchen before walking over to the dead men. No one in the restaurant moved or spoke, even when the chef spat on the dead boss's body and said something in Russian, everyone in the restaurant just carried on eating. Uri walked back to their table and told Nick they were leaving.

By the time Uri had embraced and kissed several bosses, the bodies had been taken away and the table cleared. It was as though it had never happened. Nick waited until they were in the car before asking Uri what it was all about. When Uri stated the man was a pig who had no respect, Nick knew at that point he shouldn't ask any more questions, but he wanted to impress Uri and convince him he had a no care attitude so, with a laugh, he said the man had eaten like one!

Uri asked what he would like to do that evening, as it was his last night Nick could choose, but Sven had invited them to a private party. Asking Uri to thank Sven and tell him he'd love to attend. Uri knew a very good strip club he would take him to first then on to Sven's party. Nick would pack that afternoon as his flight left at two o'clock the following afternoon and it sounded as though it would be a late night.

CHAPTER 9

Since Maria had been staying with Jimmy he hadn't gone out so much in the evenings, so he was quite looking forward to that evening when he would go onto one of their clubs after he'd spoken to Alfie Stubbs.

With every passing day the transformation in Maria had been remarkable. The more she opened up to him, the more amazed he was as to how she'd managed to survive her time at Nick's and remain sane. No doubt a lesser person would have given up long ago. He understood that it was her belief in God and an inner strength she seemed to possess which had brought her through it; although it was obvious the past three years had a devastating effect on her. She still flinched when he raised his hand quickly and she jumped every time the phone or doorbell rang. Something else bothered him; he couldn't get used to the fact that she constantly cleaned the apartment and waited on him. If he suggested them having a cup of tea, she would immediately jump to her feet to make it and if he said he would do it, she would look tearful as if she'd done something wrong. One thing was clear though; she was now more comfortable talking to him. He was also aware that she thoroughly enjoyed seeing Gladys and because the place was spotless they had time to just sit and chat. Maria loved listening to her talk about her family and Jimmy. Gladys had actually commented to him that there was nothing for her to do, so she didn't expect him to pay her. His response had been that her visits were worth every penny because they were having a good effect on Maria.

The time was approaching seven that evening. Jimmy was waiting for Mickey to turn up when his phone rang, he knew from the ID it was Shaun.

"Alright Shaun, what can I do for you mate? Or did you want to speak to Maria? I've only got five minutes; I'm just waiting to be picked up."

Shaun had only called to warn him that Nick would be home the following night. Jimmy joked that with any luck the plane would crash.

"Aye," laughed Shaun "but knowing his luck he can probably fucking fly!"

They both laughed.

As the two men talked, Jimmy could see her watching him and she'd gathered from the conversation that Nick was coming home. Noticing she looked worried, he smiled at her before telling Shaun she would like to speak to him.

Before Shaun could reply, he heard Maria say that Mickey had just pulled up. Knowing Jimmy had to go; he would call Maria straight back on the house phone so they could have a good chat. Jimmy ended the call and told her what Shaun had said. He could hear the house phone ringing as he left the apartment.

On the way to the Paradise Club, the two men talked about Nick coming back. Mickey said he'd been asking questions about Maria and according to Tony, he thought it was Maurice who may have initiated her going to Nick's. Jimmy nodded and asked if Tony had said anything else.

"I've asked him to dig around for me Jimmy, but he won't dig too deep for obvious reasons; although there's no love lost between him and Nick, he is loyal to Maurice. When I thought about it, Maurice had a falling out with Nick around the time she moved in, now I'm curious as to whether she had something to do with it? Let's face it; we know Maurice didn't meet his Russian boy at a club. Perhaps that black bastard is not just buying kids; he's fucking selling them as well. Anyway, Tony might come back to us on that. Now let's sort fucking Alfie Stubbs out, we can worry about Nick when he's back as no doubt the fucker will contact us."

When they drove past the club they could see Alfie and another doorman chatting. There were only a few punters going in because it was early. They parked just round the corner and walked back to the club. They were both familiar with John the other doorman. As they approached, John said hello and asked what had brought them to the Paradise Club. When Jimmy said he'd come to have a word with Alfie, John looked concerned; he knew it wasn't a social call. Trying to make light of it he laughed and looking at Alfie asked what he'd been up to.

Alfie shrugged his shoulders and smugly said he had no idea, but it looked like he was just about to find out. Jimmy walked over to him, leaving Mickey talking to John.

"What's the problem Jimmy," said Alfie, arrogantly.

"I'm hoping there won't be a problem Alfie, but I need to speak to you about Simone."

"What's she been fucking saying the bitch?"

"Fuck me Alfie she didn't have to say anything; the bruises you gave her said it all!"

Alfie could see by the look on Jimmy's face that he meant business, but being as cocky as he was, he wasn't about to back down and say nothing.

"Fuck me Jimmy did you drive over here because of that fucking whore. I wouldn't have thought she was worth the petrol! Fucking cheeky cow, she let me take her out a couple of times then fucking blew me out! No fucking stripper is doing that to me!"

Jimmy could feel his temper rising as he listened to him. Trying to stay calm, he told Alfie to leave her alone; she didn't want to see him again. It's wasn't good for business with her covered in bruises, but there was no need for it to get nasty, so Jimmy suggested leaving it at that. Tactfully he added, he was certain Alfie had loads of other women so he didn't need Simone. Arrogantly, Alfie boasted he could have the pick and Simone was just a fucking stripper! Glad that Alfie seemed to see it that way; Jimmy walked over to Mickey and said they were leaving.

Once they were out of sight, Alfie told John he was going to teach Simone a fucking lesson she wouldn't forget. How dare she send Jimmy, who in his opinion was a fucking psycho, down to talk to him. John advised him to leave well alone, he'd seen Jimmy in action and in his opinion no bird was worth getting his head punched over, especially some stripper.

Driving back to their club, Jimmy asked if he fancied going to Sweet Cheeks to get a blow job. With a huge grin on his face, Mickey said "Why not!"

It was after two o'clock when Jimmy was dropped off back at the apartment, he entered quietly so as not to wake Maria.

Lying on his bed in the room next to hers, he thought about her and how much he liked her being there; she seemed to fit right in.

Alone in the darkness, he thought about making love to her and despite having had a blow job just a couple of hours earlier from one of the dancers, he found himself masturbating as he imagined having her.

CHAPTER 10

Two days after returning from the Ukraine, Nick made contact and arranged to meet them at Dixie's at four o'clock on Sunday.

Things with Maria had been going from strength to strength with every passing day and Jimmy didn't want that to change. It was that morning when he told her he was meeting Nick; she instantly begged him not to go, even stating she would go back to Nick rather than see him hurt.

Despite his reassurances, she got herself in quite a state, so much so he called Gladys and asked if she could come and keep her company while he was out.

Mickey sounded his horn outside the apartment at quarter to four, fortunately Gladys was already there. Before leaving, he told Maria he wouldn't be long and for her to stop worrying.

Gladys said to take as long as he needed, because her husband Arthur had gone fishing and wouldn't be back till the evening. Her last words to him were to sort Maria's ex-boyfriend out and tell him she didn't want him back!

Inside Mickey's car they talked about Nick as they drove to their club. If nothing else, the meeting would let him know that Maria wasn't going back.

Pulling in at the club they spotted Nick's car. Billy was waiting for them at the door.

Out of curiosity, Mickey asked why he was there. They laughed when he moaned that he'd left his jacket there the previous night. Then with a grimace, he told them he'd let Nick in, but was only waiting till they arrived in case they needed him. Thanking him, Jimmy asked who was with Nick. When he said just Shaun, they told him to go home and they'd see him later.

Entering the club they could see Shaun standing at the bar. Nick was sitting at a table just in front of him. Mickey called out hello. Jimmy simply said, "Shaun," then nodded his head to acknowledge Nick before asking Shaun to grab a bottle and some glasses.

Shaun poured himself a drink and then placed a bottle of scotch and three glasses on the table for them. Mickey was the first to speak, asking Nick how his trip had been. Arrogantly Nick said it had been good but he wasn't there to talk about his trip, he was there to take back what was his, namely Maria. Already pissed off by his attitude, Mickey instantly said they had a problem then, because she was no longer his, he'd lost the bet.

"Let's cut the fucking bullshit," said Jimmy looking directly at Nick "she's staying with me and nothing you can say or do is going to change that Nick!"

The tension between them was already heavy and even more so when Nick smirked and said she'd obviously gotten to Jimmy and had he fucked her yet.

Mickey knew if Jimmy lost his temper and gave him the impression that anything physical had happened between them, there would be hell to pay, so he quickly interrupted.

"Come on Nick, you worked her over real good, it's a miracle she can walk let alone fuck, but don't take my word for it ask Shaun, after all he brought her to Jimmy's."

"Aye boss she was in a bad way," said Shaun without hesitation "tell you the truth, I didn't think she would last the day."

His words seemed to have the desired effect and the situation calmed. Mickey asked if all this bad feeling was necessary, especially over a woman, after all they were all friends who worked together

Nick agreed, the whore wasn't worth it and like Mickey had said, he'd lost the bet, so if Jimmy just named his price they could all go home.

Aggressively, Jimmy stated she was staying with him.

Nick was furious; banging his fist down on the table he knocked a glass onto the floor smashing it. Trying to stop things from escalating, Mickey looked down at the shattered glass and told Nick not to worry about it. Nick arrogantly said he wouldn't, he was there to talk business, so he would ask again, what was Jimmy's price.

"You fucking deaf Nick or what?" snarled Jimmy "I've told you she's not for sale!"

"Everything has a price Jimmy and if I can't have her nobody will!"

Suddenly without warning Jimmy lunged at him. Shaun immediately grabbed him and told him to sit down as he didn't want to hurt him.

Nick nodded for Shaun to release him.

"I'll give you a few days to come up with a price, I will expect an answer. Don't fuck me about Jimmy I'm warning you!"

"Don't fucking threaten me you arsehole! I've told you she's not for sale!"

Nick stood up to leave then glancing back at Mickey said "Talk to your friend before someone gets hurt and call me, I have a job I want you to do next Friday."

Then he stormed out followed by Shaun.

After he'd left they talked about what had been said. It was clear to Mickey that neither man was going to back down.

"Maybe we will end up taking Billy up on his offer," joked Jimmy "especially if he can provide the boots!"

Although they laughed, Mickey knew Jimmy was seething, especially when he added that if Nick wanted a war, he'd fucking give him one!

"Calm down Jimmy. What we need is something to slow him down because I don't think there's a compromise. Do you think she's up to talking about it now? She might give us something we could use against the bastard?"

Jimmy would speak to her later as she was definitely more at ease with him now. It had finally sunk in he was trying to help her, only problem was she knew Nick wouldn't back down. She was obviously a threat to him which made Jimmy wonder if Nick would kill her.

Mickey wouldn't put anything past the bastard, but once they knew what she had on Nick they would know if they needed to worry about that. He asked how things were going with her on a personal level.

"I fucking fancy her Mick that's for sure, but she always looks so fucking scared. I've held her a couple of times without her pulling away and we did sort of kiss. Truth is if I keep lying there at night thinking about her I'll have to get a fucking support bandage for me wrist!"

They both laughed.

Back at the apartment Gladys had managed to keep her calm. Despite not really knowing the truth about Nick, she knew that Jimmy was meeting with him and that was why he had asked her to stay with Maria. They were just talking about her grandchildren when they were interrupted by the phone. Gladys noticed Maria looked edgy so she said she'd get it and it was probably Jimmy to say they'd be late.

When she picked up the phone an unfamiliar man's voice said "Oh good afternoon, I'm sorry to bother you but Jimmy said I could phone anytime to speak to my niece Maria."

Instantly Gladys said it was no bother, Maria was right there and she'd pass the phone to her. Maria asked her if it was Jimmy. When Gladys said it was her uncle, Maria felt sick to the pit of her stomach as a feeling of panic ran through her body. She didn't have an uncle, but she didn't want Gladys to think anything was wrong when she handed her the phone and left the room to make some fresh tea.

Maria put the phone to her ear and softly said "Hello." The moment she heard his voice, she knew it was Nick. Shaking from fear she just stood there, too scared to speak, but listening as he shouted "Now listen here you fucking bitch! If you know what's good for you and that bastard Jimmy you'll get your fucking arse back here! Who was the old witch who answered the phone?"

Barely able to get her words out, she stuttered that Gladys was the cleaning lady. Threateningly he called her a fucking whore and warned her not to say anything. Unable to answer him through sheer terror she was speechless. When she didn't reply he shouted down the phone.

"Do you understand you fucking bitch!"

In desperation she forced the word "Yes" from her lips as he continued to terrorise her.

"I'm not playing games bitch! I fucking own you and you know what I'm capable of, so fucking get back here! You've got till Friday, if you're not back by then some fucker's gonna die! Do you understand you fucking cock sucker?"

He slammed the phone down. Standing there frozen to the spot and shaking from head to toe, she thought she would pass out. Gladys appeared and sensing all was not well asked if she was ok.

Unable to speak, Maria placed her hand over her mouth and rushed towards the bathroom. Outside the door Gladys could hear her vomiting so she called to her but there was no reply. She was just about to call again when the bathroom door opened. Looking pale and shaking, Maria said she didn't feel very well. Gladys thought it may be something she'd eaten, or maybe some bad news from her uncle. Instantly Maria said it was probably the curry she'd ate the previous night.

"Perhaps you've got a touch of food poisoning love? That's the trouble with this foreign grub; I'm bloody sure half the time you don't know what you're eating. Like I always say to my Arthur, you can't beat good home cooking. Perhaps you ought to go and lay down love? I'll pull the bed back for you."

Maria simply nodded

Gladys assumed she was in the guest room. Entering the room she pulled the bed back for her and told her to rest. She asked if Maria wanted her to stay with her. Shaking her head, Maria told her she'd be fine so she could go home.

Waiting to hear Gladys leave, she sat on the side of the bed with her arms around her tummy and began to shake and sob uncontrollably, telling herself that she would have to go back; she couldn't risk anyone getting hurt, especially Jimmy, although she would need to convince him that she wanted to go back. Finally she lay down and drifted off to sleep, only waking when Jimmy returned and called out he was back. Hearing her call out from the guest room, he opened the door and asked why she was in there. Still shaking she explained she hadn't felt well and Gladys had assumed she was using that room.

"Yeah that sounds like Gladys;" he laughed "she's a regular old Florence Nightingale! So are you feeling okay now?"

Maria nodded; it was probably something she'd eaten.

"Well you've had a tough time babe; it's not surprising you feel a bit rough. I'll stick the kettle on. Oh and I hope you won't mind, but Mickey will be joining us for dinner tonight. I've asked him to bring something over from the restaurant. I thought we could go over what we discussed about Nick."

Immediately he noticed that with his words she looked uneasy and nervously told him they didn't need to discuss it because she'd made a decision. Looking confused he asked what decision and was dumbfounded when she told him she'd decided to go back to Nick's.

His expression changed to one of anger, he hoped she was fucking joking.

"No I'm not joking Jimmy and I don't want you to think I'm not grateful for all that you've done for me, because I am."

Raising his voice angrily, he asked what the fuck was going on.

Noticeably shaking and with tears now trickling down her cheeks, she said nothing was going on; she just wanted to go home.

"I don't fucking believe this Maria, something's happened I fucking know it has!"

Nothing had happened she just wanted to go home, back to Nick; she didn't belong there.

"So exactly what the fuck are you saying Maria, you fucking love him or what?"

"Yes that's it Jimmy, I love him."

"You're a fucking liar, he's fucking brainwashed you. Yeah that's it, you've been fucking brainwashed!"

Tears were now streaming down her face and she was shaking violently as she begged him to calm down and not be mad with her.

"Mad with you, that's a fucking understatement! To be fucking honest Maria at this precise moment I'm not sure who I want to fucking kill the most, you or fucking Nick!"

Terrified of what he may do to her, instantly she begged him not to hurt her.

Feeling anger as well as disbelief, he shouted and swore that he wouldn't fucking hurt her. Neither of them paid any attention when they heard the phone ringing until the answer machine cut in and a familiar voice said, 'Are you there Jimmy, its Gladys?' Welcoming relief from the ongoing argument between them, he walked out of the room and picked up the phone. Maria stayed in the bedroom.

"Sorry to be a nuisance Jimmy love, but I was a bit worried about Maria. I know she said it was because of something she ate, but I think it was something to do with that phone call she had from her uncle. I don't know if she mentioned it, but when you were out she had a call, he said you'd told him to call anytime. I know it's none of my business love, but I just had a strange feeling about it that was all. The poor girl she was as white as a ghost, not to mention sick as a dog!"

Jimmy realised immediately that the caller had been Nick. Thanking Gladys, he stated Maria was feeling much better and that Gladys was just an old worry guts.

Jimmy knocked on the bedroom door. Sounding nervous and tearful Maria asked him to come in. Hearing the fear in her voice, he knew she was afraid of him. Standing in the doorway looking down on her sat on the bed, he realised just how vulnerable she was. When he asked if she'd spoken to Nick, immediately she shook her head. Calling her bluff, he said she was lying because Gladys had told him. Looking distraught she said it didn't make any difference, she had to go back. Instantly he snapped, stating she didn't have to do anything because Nick didn't fucking own her.

For the first time she raised her voice slightly as she replied, "Yes he does! You know it and I know it, everybody knows it that's just the way it is!"

"You're wrong Maria I can't and I won't accept that, you said you had the means to put an end to all this and as far as I'm concerned nothing's changed!"

Hysterically she sobbed as she screamed that everything had changed when he called her, but Jimmy didn't understand. Not about to give up on her, he continued to shout until she finally broke down completely.

"If I don't go back Jimmy he's going to kill someone," she blurted out through her tears "I've got to return to him by Friday!"

Holding her tight, he kept repeating that he was sorry for shouting at her, but he had to know what Nick had said. She tried to tell him, but no matter how he much he tried to comfort her, she couldn't stop crying and shaking. In a last ditched effort to calm her down, he gently pushed her onto the bed then leaning over her kissed her on the mouth. Moving hesitantly at first, because he didn't want to scare her, then more passionately when she reciprocated. For a moment she seemed to calm down as she began to melt into him. Other than their brief kiss in the kitchen, it was the first time in her life she had felt a long tender kiss. Because she seemed willing, he gently probed her mouth with his tongue, when she reciprocated, he could feel his body responding. Never before could he remember a time when he had felt such overwhelming desire for a woman and he'd certainly had his fair share over the years. Maria was different, her innocence and vulnerability attracted him. He wanted to show her what real lovemaking was, not as she had known with Nick who had simply used her body anyway he wanted. As they kissed he wanted to fondle and kiss her all over, but he knew the time wasn't right. The Doc had said that she needed time to heal.

Like him, she felt confused as feelings she'd never experienced began flooding through her. Surprising herself she gently ran her hand up his back under his shirt. Her heart was pounding, this was new territory to her, but she wanted to feel him. She touched him as he undid the buttons on her blouse, slowly exposing her firm perfect breasts. Still tender from Nick's attack, a large bite mark was still visible beneath the bruising. Gently he fondled her, kissing her breasts, her nipples standing erect as if beckoning him to continue. Taking her nipple into his mouth, he gently flicked and sucked it. Her body was pulsing with anticipation. Slowly he made his way back up to her mouth, kissing her passionately, breathing heavily; their hot pulsing bodies wanting more.

"I want you so fucking bad," he said in a quiet whispering voice "but we must wait until you're well."

Bringing her mouth round to meet his as if to silence him; she fumbled to undo his trousers. Again he said they must wait, although by that point he was unable to bring himself to stop her because his body was crying out for her to touch him. The moment her hand caressed him, he released a shallow noise, a sigh of pleasure. Now he was powerless to stop her. Almost at boiling pitch, he kissed her neck and breasts, wanting desperately for her to continue. Slowly she moved her hand up and down him, arousing him more and more. Unable to hold back any longer he burst into orgasm.

Seconds later, he was gently resting his head onto her breasts then moments later they were kissing softly. He could see the tears running down her face so he asked what was wrong.

"Nothing's wrong Jimmy, it was wonderful. I never thought I would ever want to be with a man again, but you've made me feel whole. I always imagined it should be like that, but I never thought I would experience it."

Gently sweeping her hair back from her face, he said it had been wonderful for him too and they were going to work this out. There would be no more talk about going back to Nick. Looking afraid she made it clear she couldn't risk anyone getting hurt because of her.

"No one's going to get hurt babe; anyway we've got until Friday so cheer up and give us a kiss"

Their lips had just touched when they heard a noise. Jumping up, he stated it was the door. Scrambling to get dressed he emerged from the guest room tucking his shirt in. It was Mickey with their food. Having his own key, Mickey had let himself in and was heading towards the kitchen as Jimmy appeared. Looking a bit red faced he apologised, stating he hadn't realised the time.

"No worries Jim, I'm a bit early, how's Maria?"

No sooner had he asked when she came out of the guest room, clothes and hair looking rather dishevelled. Barely able to look at him and blushing profoundly, she simply nodded to acknowledge him as she quickly made her way into the bathroom. He didn't have to be a genius to work out what had happened.

Smiling at Jimmy, he winked and said things were obviously going ok between them. Jimmy replied they were better than ok as a cheeky grin came over his face as he called her name to say dinner was on the table. There was no reply, but they could hear water running from the bathroom. The two men talked while they waited. Mickey hadn't been sure what to get, so he'd left it up to their chef Luigi.

"Well the old Eyetie has done us proud Mick, this looks fit for a king. Come on Maria its getting cold."

Seconds later she appeared and said she was sorry, but she'd had a quick shower.

The table was laden with dishes full of Italian food. Maria giggled and asked Jimmy to choose for her as she didn't know what to have. Mickey looked baffled and asked if he'd missed something funny. Jimmy enlightened his friend to the fact that she had not been allowed to choose anything for herself and that it was driving him crazy. Mickey laughed, it was nice to see her laughing and how much better she looked; even her eye had gone down by the look of it. Thanking him, she felt a lot better.

Mickey expressed his happiness at her recovery, but they needed to talk about Nick. Concerned was how he felt when Jimmy enlightened him to the call she'd had and the fact they now only had till Friday then the shit was going to hit the fan. Instantly Mickey stated they needed more time.

Maria sat picking at her dinner while Jimmy told him about the phone call from Nick. Feeling a bit humbled knowing he'd probably made her feel bad about the time issue, Mickey looked at her, "Don't worry babe, we'll sort something out. They don't call me and Jimmy, Butch Cassidy and the Sundance Kid for nothing you know!"

They all laughed.

They were interrupted by Mickey's mobile ringing. The moment he answered it Monica's voice asked if he was standing her up again. Suddenly he remembered he was supposed to take her out that night. Apologising profusely, he said something came up and could they have dinner the following night? Monica agreed to dinner, but assured him if he stood her up again that would be it for her!

When he ended the call, Maria asked if the call was from his girlfriend, but before he could reply Jimmy laughed. Through curiosity she asked him why. Still laughing he explained that Mickey always stood her up, but she always came back for more. The fact she was a detective, Jimmy was surprised she allowed Mickey to get away with it.

Mickey tried to defend his actions; he didn't want Maria thinking he was a rat. Sounding sincere, he said Monica was a really nice girl. They had a great relationship, he just forgot some of their dates.

"Some of them?" laughed Jimmy "you mean most of them!"

"Ok sarky, now you've managed to pull my love life to shreds," joked Mickey, "shall we proceed with business? Perhaps you should just tell me what this information you have about Nick is Maria?"

Finishing her last spoonful of ice cream, she swallowed hard to clear her throat and began telling them how she'd noticed things about three months after she first went to live with Nick. She was never allowed to answer the phone or meet anyone who came to his place. He would tie her up and lock her in the spare room whenever he had visitors.

Mickey interrupted. He was curious as to how, at just fifteen years old, she'd come to live with him in the first place. Without any qualms and in a blasé manner, she told them it was Father O'Brien from St Augustus who had arranged it.

The two men looked at one another in disbelief before Mickey asked her to be more specific.

"We all thought it was strange at first, the meetings with different men at the church, but we had to go. Every few months some of the girls would be taken into the back of the church by Sister Marjorie, the head nun. It was normally off limits to us because it was Father O'Brien's private quarters. There would always be a man with the Father who would be introduced by a bogus name; I know that now because Nick was introduced as Malcolm Dalton. Father O'Brien would tell us that the man was a good friend of his and a wonderful benefactor to the church who was looking for a young girl to train as his housekeeper. He always said things like, 'it would be a wonderful opportunity for the right girl.'"

"Where did the girls come from, did they attend school there or something?"

"Oh no Mickey, we all lived there; in most cases we had always lived there, we were raised there. My mother abandoned me on the church steps when I was a baby. Anyway, every time a man came, he picked a girl. Before I was chosen I went to two previous meetings. The first time my friend Caroline was picked; the second time it was my friend Kate. I can remember helping Kate pack the day before she left, she was so excited thinking her new employer was really nice, not to mention very rich. We all thought she might travel and see the world. You see things like that were very attractive to us; we rarely left the convent, except for the odd trip. Sister Marjorie was very strict with us, always telling us that one day we would marry and have our own families and that it would never be appropriate for young Catholic ladies to date boys. It was strictly forbidden, even if we ever kissed or touched a boy, or one another, God would punish us because we were special and God would send the suitor he had chosen for us. We were afraid of Sister Marjorie. When she came into the dormitory in the mornings, if any of us had our hands under the covers she would beat us, but we never understood why. One night there was a terrible storm; my best friend Melanie was petrified so I told her to get into my bed. We never did anything wrong, I just held her. I was thirteen at the time, she was a year younger. We had planned for her to go back to her own bed when the storm passed, but we fell asleep. The next morning, Sister Marjorie caught us. It was terrible, she made an example of us; she said that we were like the whores of Babylon. No one was allowed to speak to us; we weren't allowed any food, only water for three days and she made us strip naked before she beat us in front of everyone. We all hated her, but we couldn't change anything. We had no families to defend us, there was no one."

Jimmy gripped her hand as she rested it on the table and fiddled with her rosary beads. They could see she was reliving the whole dreadful ordeal as tears streamed down her face. When Jimmy suggested taking a tea break, Maria simply nodded.

Five minutes later, Maria sat quietly sipping her tea while the two men discussed briefly what she'd told them.

Jimmy made Mickey grin when he said, "I think we should send someone round to visit this Sister Marjorie, I know a couple of people who wouldn't feel bad about belting a nun. Maria do you think you can carry on now babe?"

"Yes, I'm fine now. After each meeting one of the girls would leave and we never heard from them again. They would always promise to write, but they never did. Now I know why, they were prisoners like me. If we asked Sister

Marjorie about them she would just say, 'Oh I expect she's off on some yacht somewhere having far too much fun to write to the likes of you.'"

When Jimmy asked her to tell them what happened the day she had met Nick, they both noticed she started to tremble as she started talking again.

"Three of us were taken to Father O'Brien's quarters. Nick was introduced as Malcolm Dalton, he seemed really nice. Unlike the previous men, I thought he was handsome and he seemed to like me straight away. I can remember Father O'Brien telling him I was very bright and very spirited. Nick joked he liked girls with a bit of spirit. Then he asked me some questions, things like, had I ever had a boyfriend and how old I was and did I think I would like being his housekeeper, that type of thing. After talking to me for about an hour, he picked me. Melanie was quite jealous, but I promised to write to her. The following day I was taken to his penthouse."

Squeezing Jimmy's hand, she paused for a moment as though it was too painful for her to continue. Reassuringly he told her to take her time and she was doing great.

"That was the day I arrived in Hell. Gone was the nice Malcolm who I had met the day before, instead this horrible man named Nick was there. When I first arrived, he ordered me to sit down and listen to him very carefully. Then he slapped me round the face and said, 'if I ask you to do something you don't ask why, you just do it ok bitch, and from now on you can call me sir. You don't talk to anyone, you don't leave the apartment and you don't use the phone. You eat what and when I tell you to and don't ever think of trying to run away, because not only will I effing kill you, I'll kill your friend Melanie, or take her as your replacement!'"

Now the tears were flowing down her cheeks and she was shaking quite violently. Finally, after several minutes and verbal reassurances from the men, she regained her composure and continued by saying she wasn't sure what was worse, being left with Nick or realising the people who she thought loved her had actually sold her. Mickey asked how she was so sure Nick had bought her, had she actually heard them discussing it.

"No, Nick made a point of telling me, 'I've paid a lot of money for you bitch, so I expect a good return on my investment.' I can remember crying and him telling me to stop. I couldn't so he punched me in the face and said 'there, now you've got something to effing well cry for bitch!'"

The two men watched as her face relived every terrible moment of that first day at Nick's. Jimmy gripped her hand tightly and asked if she could continue.

"Yes," she replied wiping her eyes "after he punched me he dragged me to the bedroom by my hair. On the bed there were some women's clothes. I'd never seen anything like them before; it was a basque with stockings and a pair of high heeled shoes. He ordered me to put everything on. I had never undressed in front of a man before, I was terrified. He was so horrid, shouting at me, 'hurry up or I'll do it for you bitch!' When I was dressed, he slapped me and said I wasn't a virgin, but I was, he called me an effin…" suddenly she stopped. It was obvious to both of them that she wasn't comfortable using bad language, especially as she had said effing instead of fucking throughout their conversation.

"Don't worry babe," said Jimmy as he squeezed her hand "Mickey swears all the time, I'm used to it."

Smiling she knew it was his way of telling her that it was okay if she wanted to swear. Tearfully she continued, "He called me an effing lying whore. I pleaded and begged him to stop, but he was enjoying himself too much. Then he threw me onto the bed," she hesitated again and placed her hand up to her mouth as though she felt nauseous.

They could see she was too embarrassed to go on. Jimmy gently squeezed her hand again and told her to take her time, but it was important for them to know. Nodding her head with tears streaming down her face she took a deep breath. "Nick said 'you won't enjoy this you effing bitch, but I will.' Then he raped me. It was so painful I thought I would die. Most days after that were much the same. Some days were better than others, but the beatings and the deprivation got worse. Many times I thought he was going to kill me."

Mickey asked if she could remember anything else, especially regarding the meetings at the church. After thinking about it for a moment she nodded and told him that at every meeting there was also someone else there. The girls never saw him because he would hide behind a screen that partitioned off part of the room, even the men like Nick didn't know he was there. Mickey interrupted and asked if they never saw anyone how could she be so sure.

"Because he wore a strange perfume; it smelt like coconut. I remember once standing in front of the screen and smelling it quite strongly. When Father O'Brien realised where I was standing, he looked panic stricken and made me move. I didn't know what the smell was then, but I've smelt it many times since at the poker games. It's something Maurice uses on his hair. Another thing I noticed was that Nick always seemed uncomfortable when Maurice phoned him. I can remember one conversation; he didn't know I was listening, but it was definitely Maurice he was talking to. Nick shouted down the phone at him; 'don't think for one minute you can effing blackmail me Maurice, you effing cock sucking nigger. I'll take you and the effing church down with me, you black mother effer!' After that call, Nick phoned someone called Razor. I didn't hear all that was said, but I did hear him say, 'don't kill the effing nigger, just scare him, but find the pictures.' I think it was about three years ago. I hadn't been there long, but I could check."

With a look of disbelief, Jimmy asked if she'd kept some sort of record. When she nodded and having believed the fear Nick had instilled in her, instantly he questioned that surely she would be too afraid to keep records for fear of being caught. With a grin she said of course she was terrified, so that was why she hid it in the church. It was the one place Nick didn't go. However, the problem she had now was she couldn't go to the church. Jimmy grinned, they could send someone to get it, he just hoped it was still there.

"It's safe;" she replied confidently, "when I was living in the convent one of my duties was to clean the church after the Sunday morning service. I found a loose panel on one of the pews I used to hide things in from Sister Marjorie. After I moved in with Nick, I remembered names, dates and times in my head. Then when I went to church later that week with Shaun and Ann I would pretend to be singing, but I was actually jotting down the things that happened in my notepad, which was hidden inside my hymn book. Once or twice I thought Ann had seen me, although she obviously never said anything if she did."

Knowing they needed to get her notebook, Mickey grinned at Jimmy and asked when his last confession was and suggested maybe it was time for him to start practising his faith again. Maria was shocked when Jimmy told him to fuck off. Mickey knew he'd vowed never to set foot in a church again. When Maria asked if he was a Catholic, he said he was once but not anymore. She asked what had made him lose faith.

"Well let's just say babe I prayed to God day after day begging him to stop my father from beating up on me and my mum. Even in confession the priest would tell me that no matter what, he was my father and that God was watching over us. Like a fool I believed him, until the day I came home from school and found my mother dead. Where was God then, the same God she prayed to every day? I've not set foot in a church since."

Maria didn't reply she just looked at him as he suggested to Mickey giving Lenny Porter a ring. Curiously she asked who Lenny was. She wasn't surprised to hear he was an ex detective who now freelanced as a private investigator. Lenny was a good bloke who they'd used many times before. Mickey's mobile rang, interrupting them. Looking at the ID he told them it was Nick. Arrogantly Jimmy told him not to answer it, if need be Nick could leave a fucking message, they weren't at his beck and call! Mickey agreed and just let it ring.

Maria yawned, she was very tired. Realising it was gone midnight; Mickey suggested calling it a night. They could go over everything tomorrow. He was in court at nine the following morning, but in his opinion it shouldn't take long, it was just a greedy wife trying to screw her soon to be ex-husband over some property. He could be back round Jimmy's by midday, if that suited them.

"Yeah, that should be ok Mick. I can work from home for a couple of days. I've got a meeting at four o'clock with Tony; probably take an hour or so. Is there any chance you could stay on 'til I get back, just in case shit head decides to call again?"

Mickey welcomed spending time with Maria as they had lots to discuss. Maria would love to cook for them, but when Mickey reminded her he had a dinner date with Monica, she suggested doing them lunch instead.

The two men sat talking while Maria went into the kitchen to make them all a drink. Mickey was curious as to why Jimmy was meeting Tony the following day. He was even more so when Jimmy said it had been a surprise when Tony called him to discuss the Nick situation. Both men knew Tony hated Nick as much as them; their hope was he would help them.

Maria returned with the drinks. They continued to talk about Tony until Mickey finished his coffee. Five minutes later he was leaving.

After he'd gone, Jimmy looked at her and said she'd done really well and they were sure Lenny would dig up something on Father O'Brien. Maria spoke about Tony, she didn't really know him, only from the poker games, but he'd always been nice to her. Jimmy made her blush when he stated Tony had a thing for beautiful women. He hadn't expected her to say she knew, she'd heard him talking about his girlfriends and she felt sorry for his wife. Never having seen Tony's wife, she wasn't shocked when he said Isabella was a real beauty and regardless of his other women, Tony adored her, as she did him.

Seeing how tired she looked, he suggested turning in for the night. When she nodded and stood up he pulled her to him and kissed her softly on the forehead before bidding her good night.

Alone in the lounge, Jimmy poured himself a scotch and thought about the events of the last few days. What he'd said about Tony was true. They were tight, they'd been friends since Jimmy was a youngster and they'd worked together in the same crew for twenty years. Five minutes later he went to bed.

CHAPTER 11

Maria was up before him the next day. When he finally appeared in the kitchen she said good morning and asked if he'd slept well. She smiled when he said "Like a log."

Unfortunately, she hadn't been afforded a peaceful night, she'd laid awake for hours thinking of the phone call from Nick.

Putting his arm around her, he promised her everything would be fine. It had been a long time since she had trusted anyone, but something inside told her she could trust him.

Over breakfast they chatted and he told her Doc Daniels would be calling in to see her later that morning.

The morning passed quickly with him making several business calls while she kept out of his way by tidying the apartment and preparing lunch. Doc Daniels called in as expected. He was really pleased with how well she was doing and made a point of saying living with Jimmy was obviously doing her good and she would be back to health in no time.

Mickey arrived at about quarter past twelve. Maria served lunch ten minutes later. They talked over lunch with Mickey telling them he'd spoken to Lenny and he would contact them as soon as he had information on the priest.

Maria kept herself busy by clearing the dishes while the two friends talked. At half three, Jimmy left for his meeting with Tony, thanking Mickey for staying with her as he closed the door.

Tony had arranged to meet him at his gym; it was somewhere they could talk without being interrupted. Tony had only bought it because he liked to keep in shape.

When Jimmy entered the gym, he could see Tony working out with weights. Spotting one another, Tony indicated for him to wait where he was and he would join him. A few moments later Tony was standing in front of him. They made their way across the gym into his office. With the suspense killing him, Jimmy asked why he'd wanted to meet with him. Passing him a scotch, Tony asked him about Nick.

"What, other than the fact he's a fucking wanker?" said Jimmy arrogantly.

Despite agreeing with him, Tony advised him to be careful because he was a dangerous wanker. He'd heard about the beating Maria had taken, so he wasn't surprised when Jimmy said it was a miracle he didn't kill her. Tony asked what he intended to do after Nick had demanded she went back by Friday and Jimmy was adamant that wasn't going to happen. Tony knew neither man would back down; he just hoped Maria was worth it. Tony would do what he could to help him.

"I appreciate that Tony, but this is my fight. I don't expect anyone else to get involved."

"I know that, but that's why I like you Jimmy; you're a criminal with morals!"

They both laughed.

"We all know that sometimes in this game you have to pick sides Jimmy, I just wanted to let you know. So, what's the plan then?"

"Well we hope we can find something that will buy us some time. Maria knows a lot about his dodgy dealings, but it's gonna take time to put it all together. I don't want a war, but I'm not going to back down, so what we need is a compromise or at least enough time to come up with one. Trouble with Nick is, he always covers his tracks and we all know he doesn't like to get his own hands dirty."

"Leave it with me Jimmy; what you need is something that will take his mind off her for a while. I'll make some enquiries."

After thanking him, the two men shook hands and Jimmy left.

Driving back to his apartment, he thought about Tony. Both he and Mickey trusted him; he was popular within the crew, unlike his business partner Maurice. Most of the others simply tolerated Maurice because of business, but truth was they disliked him. Not regarding the way he ran his business, he was reliable, always making good contacts for the crew; it was because of his sexual preferences. They all knew he was a cruel sadistic bastard, although Tony seemed to block that out regarding their friendship. They had worked together for over twenty years and for the best part they got on well, but unlike Maurice, Tony is straight and proud of it. He loves women and brags about losing his cherry at the young age of fifteen to a girl of nineteen. Even now at forty six, he's still bedding beauties, despite his passion for his beautiful young Italian wife Isabella. God help any man who looks at her the wrong way. Tony makes sure he keeps her happy with a rich lifestyle and four young children to keep her busy. Everyone including his wife knows one woman will never be enough for him. He keeps a mistress and regularly sleeps with the dancers from the clubs, yet despite his weakness for women, he's a loving husband and father with three young sons, but the apple of his eye is his three year old daughter Sophia, a real daddy's girl. Tony is obsessed with looking good; strikingly handsome at six feet tall, with olive skin and dark hair, which is due to his Italian mother whom he adores. She raised him alone after his father died when he was just two. Tony is suave, sophisticated, educated and without a doubt a shrewd businessman. Having been introduced into organised crime by his Uncle Carlo, who had looked out for him like a father, until his own untimely death in a suspicious car accident when Tony was twenty nine. Jimmy knows there's no love lost between Tony and Nick, often known to disagree over business, but out of necessity they tolerate one another. It could even be said that both men have respect for what each has achieved. Fact is, Nick needs Maurice to run the blacks and Maurice is loyal to Tony, so it would not be in Nick's best interests to see that Tony met with an accident like his Uncle Carlo. Maurice is no fool, he knows he is the pawn between them and he uses this to his advantage, yet despite his loyalty to Tony and their mutual dislike of Nick, they're an unusual pair. Tony is well aware that Maurice has had a hard on for him since they first met as teenagers when Maurice came to Britain from the Caribbean, but being as shrewd as he is, Tony uses this to keep him on side, always treating him with respect; even asking his opinion on personal matters, but everyone knows if Maurice ever overstepped the mark, it would be his downfall. Tony is straight and a forty five year old black queen would never be in with a chance, but business is business and if Maurice ever dreamt for one brief moment that will ever change, he's most definitely kidding himself.

Back at the apartment things were going well. Mickey was really warming to Maria. He'd never really spoken to her at the poker games other than to say hello, but since spending time with her he could tell she was actually a very smart, gutsy lady. He talked about her notepad, stating if they played it right they could really do some damage.

As he waited for her to reply he looked at her. Jimmy was right, she was beautiful. Taking her time before answering, he noticed she looked worried, so he asked if she'd like to take a break.

"No, it's ok Mickey. I don't want you to think I'm not grateful, I know you're only trying to help, but I don't want anyone to get hurt over me, especially Jimmy."

Knowing she was genuinely concerned, he smiled and said, "Let me tell you something about Jimmy; he's just about the most decent bloke I've ever met. Despite his temper, which I must say has caused me some concern over the years, I couldn't wish for a better friend. I know he's doing this for you because he wants to, not because he has to. I know you really like him and he really likes you too, so let's not worry about whether or not anyone's going to get hurt; let's just concentrate on hitting Nick where it hurts. Now is there anything else you can remember that might help us?"

Just as she was about to answer, the door opened and Jimmy walked in. The first thing Mickey asked was how things had gone with Tony. Happy was how he felt that Tony was going to try and help them slow Nick down. Ten minutes later Mickey had to go because he was picking Monica up later.

"Oh yeah, she'll be pleased you remembered," said Jimmy laughing "say hello to her for me."

Calling him a sarky bastard, Mickey defended himself by saying he remembered most of the time! A few minutes later he left.

Alone with her, Jimmy put his arm around her shoulder and asked how she'd got on with Mickey. It was no surprise when she said he was really nice and the afternoon had gone well.

After eating a wonderful meal she'd prepared, they spent the evening talking and listening to music.

Across town Mickey was actually on time for his date, pulling up outside Monica's place just as she was coming out the door. Opening the car door, she grinned and thanked him for not standing her up again.

Apologising to her again, he said he'd been tied up with Jimmy.

"Sounds painful," she giggled "but if that's what rings your bell, why not!"

"Cheeky cow, a lot of things I might be, queer I'm not! So tell me how are things in the detective world babe."

Things were going well for her, especially after making a good arrest the previous week, which would no doubt look good on her record sheet should any promotions come up. He looked impressed as she continued that very day she'd received a hot tip from a reliable source. So in answer to his question, things in the detective world were going very well. Despite asking what the tip was, he was well aware she shouldn't tell him, but after he squeezed her knee and saying it was no big deal as he'd probably end up giving counsel to whoever it was, she relented.

"Ok Mickey; but not a word about it ok? The tip was about a local jeweller handling stolen goods and we have it on good advice that he's connected to a heist on a security van a few months ago. At the time the van was carrying several rare pieces of jewellery and up until now every lead we've had turned out to be a dead end, but this tip sounds kosher, those pieces will be moved. Our source said it will go down on Friday this week. It will look very good for me if I can nail them."

Mickey knew the heist she'd referred to was one they had given to Jacky Boy and Kevin, along with two of Nick's boys. He also knew that Friday was the day that Martin Blackwell, the local jeweller, had arranged a meeting with an overseas buyer for the rare pieces. Jacky Boy and Kevin were going along with Nick's boys to make sure the deal went down okay. Mickey asked who the grass was. Unfortunately, she had no idea as another detective got the information.

First chance he got, Mickey rang Jimmy to let him know what Monica had said about the jeweller's job. Jimmy's first thought was they'd have to let Nick know as two of their boys would be there. Mickey had thought the same, so if need be he'd arrange to meet with Nick. Mickey cut the call short because Monica would be wondering where he'd got to, he'd call round to the apartment in the morning.

Jimmy didn't sleep particularly well that night; things were heavy on his mind. It was the same for Maria in the next room; she tossed and turned for hours, finally dropping off around half three.

CHAPTER 12

Mickey arrived early at Jimmy's apartment the following morning. They discussed what Monica had said to him the previous night, both agreeing that they would have to tell Nick. The last thing they wanted was their lads getting caught. Mickey would call Nick later that day from his office.

Just over an hour later, he was leaving Jimmy's. He would call him later to let him know what Nick had said.

Thirty minutes later, Mickey entered his office. Jan his secretary told him a man waiting to see him. Despite having told him he needed to make an appointment, he'd been arrogantly confident Mickey would see him. He wouldn't give her a surname, even though she had insisted. He simply said to tell Mickey it was Nick. Assuring her it was ok, Mickey entered the corridor. He could see him waiting for him outside his office.

Mickey said hi and asked if he was alright as he opened his office door. Nick followed him in.

"No I'm not alright," said Nick arrogantly "are you deliberately trying to avoid me? I told you at Dixie's to bell me about a job; you didn't! Then I tried phoning you and had to leave a fucking message, but you still haven't called me! I hope this little problem with Jimmy isn't going to affect business?"

"You're getting paranoid in your old age Nick, it's just I've been busy that's all, in fact I was going to call you today, so what can I do for you?"

"It's about the job at Blackwell's on Friday. I'm not really comfortable about the boys handling it; you know what these overseas buyers can be like. I'd prefer you and Jimmy to do it."

Mickey had a bad feeling about the police tip, but he decided not to mention it, he would wait to see what Nick had to say first, because this was a big coincidence. In an effort to find out, he apologised but said Friday was a no go as they already had something on. Sounding more like an order than a request, Nick told him to fucking cancel whatever it was. Mickey could see he was agitated, which only convinced him that what Monica had told him was the reason why he was so adamant about them doing it.

"Sorry Nick, Friday's impossible. I'll give Martin a call and see if he can change the day or something."

Arrogantly Nick told him not to do that, he didn't want the buyers thinking something was wrong and showed his true colours when Mickey suggested Terry, Reggie or Maurice handling it. Looking quite aggressive, he snapped that he wanted him and Jimmy to do it! Mickey should stop giving him grief and fucking sort it out! Mickey was in no doubt he was up to something when, after telling him to calm down, Nick, totally out of character actually apologised and said the issue with Jimmy was getting to him. Being very shrewd, Mickey understood and said it was getting to all of them. Appearing calmer, Nick asked how Maria was. Without hesitation Mickey shook his head and stated he wouldn't be surprised if she didn't just go back to him once she was well.

Nick had one of those smirky looks on his face; he knew Mickey would say anything to help his friend, but how could he be sure he was lying.

"What has she said then Mickey?" he asked suspiciously.

"That's just it Nick, she doesn't say fuck all. All she does is cry, she knows this mess between you and Jimmy is because of her, maybe if you gave her time to recover she'll see sense."

"Jimmy has made this personal though."

"Leave him to me, I'm his best friend, I'm sure I could convince him to see sense if I had enough time."

For a brief moment, he thought that Nick was falling for his bullshit. To be a good solicitor you have to be good in the bullshit department.

Nick paused for a moment then in his normal arrogant manner said she'd had enough time, he wanted her back on Friday and it wasn't negotiable. With that he got up and walked out, slamming the door behind him.

Mickey made his way out of the office and back to the reception area. Jan smiled at him and referred to Nick sarcastically as being a real charmer! Mickey laughed and asked her to hold his calls as he needed to go out again. If anything urgent came up one of the clerks could handle it. If it was a matter of life or death, she could get him on the mobile.

From his car, he rang Jimmy to say he was on his way round and he wouldn't believe who'd just turned up at the office. Jimmy instantly said the name Nick.

"Fuck me Jimmy you should take up doing psychic work!"

They both laughed.

Jimmy asked him to collect his post and bring it up for him when he arrived.

Twenty minutes later, he was taking the mail out of the pigeon hole in Jimmy's apartment block. Curiously he looked at the plain brown envelope that simply had the name Jimmy typed on the front.

Maria opened the door with a smile and after letting him in, offered him a drink. Tea would be his choice.

Handing Jimmy his mail with the plain envelope on top, he looked questioningly at him. Jimmy opened it. Inside was a single photograph with a typed note attached by a paper clip. It read, 'This should buy you some time.'

After taking another look at it, he passed it to Mickey who was looking at it when Maria came in with his tea. Seeing the photo she cried out, "Oh my God!"

The photo was of a dead girl. It was obvious that she had been tortured and murdered. There were ligature marks around her hands and feet indicating that she had been tied up. Her naked body was covered in cuts and bruises and she had what looked to be the brand of a crucifix on her breast. There was another key factor; a man's hand could be seen quite clearly in the corner of the print. Whoever he was, the ring on his finger was a clue. Maria began to shake violently. Jimmy sat her down on the sofa and tried to comfort her.

Slowly she calmed down enough to tell them the girl in the photo was her best friend Melanie and the man was Father O'Brien. Questioning her as all that was showing was the man's hand, Jimmy asked how she could be so sure. With confidence she explained that all priests wore those particular rings, only Father O'Brien wore his on that finger instead of his wedding finger because his hands were crippled with arthritis.

Looking at Mickey, Jimmy smiled and simply said the name Tony. Mickey nodded; the photo could be just what they needed, especially as he'd just spoken to Nick at his office. Looking angry, Jimmy asked what he'd wanted. When Mickey explained he wanted them to handle the job on Friday because he didn't want to trust it to the boys. Jimmy smirked and, like his friend, believed it had some bearing on what Monica had told him. It was just too big a coincidence. They were being set up.

Ten minutes later, Maria was still sobbing over Melanie despite all their efforts to console her. She did stop briefly to ask Mickey if he thought Nick had killed her friend.

Replying truthfully he didn't know, but it was obvious whoever sent the photo thought it would have an effect. So they couldn't rule out that he may well have been involved, if not responsible.

"Melanie was so lovely," said Maria through her tears "she must have been picked after me. If Nick did do it, he didn't do it at his apartment because I was always there."

"Well, Father O'Brien knew," said Jimmy "if you're sure that's his hand."

Nodding her head she was positive.

Perhaps it was time they paid Father O'Brien a visit. Mickey thought it might be an idea to get some photocopies of the picture. Jimmy agreed and asked what they should do about the job on Friday.

"Well I think we can safely assume it's a set up Jim. I should have known, because the bastard actually apologised about giving me a hard time over it. Have you ever known Nick to apologise for anything and he was a little too insistent that we handled it!"

"Who the fuck does he think he is! I swear I'm going to have that mother fucker Mick; he's got it coming!"

They noticed that Maria looked dazed; the impact of Melanie's death was obviously taking effect. Combined with the added stress of seeing both men so angry was making her feel more responsible for what was happening.

Mickey told her to cheer up as he glanced over at her. Sobbing she said everything was her fault and Nick was trying to set them up because of her

"None of this is your fault babe," assured Jimmy, "it's because Nick's nothing but a mother fucker. The fact that he thinks he's set us up has got nothing to do with you being here, believe me he's an opportunist. He thinks that getting us stuffed will give him more power, but regarding you, it's purely a matter of his pride being hurt and that could well be his undoing because you know how the saying goes?"

When she shook her head, he grinned and said pride cometh before a fall and mother fucker Nick was about to take a fucking big fall!

"How about us paying a visit to Father O'Brien this afternoon," said Mickey "might be a good idea to give my old pal Jeff Black a ring first. Just to see if he knows anything about this Melanie. What was Melanie's last name Maria?"

"Humphreys," she replied tearfully "who is Jeff Black?"

Jimmy explained that Jeff was the big chief down at the nick. Mickey had been at university with him and it was one friendship that had come in very handy over the years.

Having rung through on Jeff's direct number, he was speaking to his friend seconds later. They bantered for a few minutes about family and work before Mickey asked if he could help him out with something. Instantly Jeff said he would if possible. Mickey asked what he knew about a girl named Melanie Humphreys.

"If memory serves me correct Mickey, she was a runaway from St Augustus, but it was a long time ago, about three years I think. I worked on the case; she turned up in a rubbish bin in an alley. I remember now, she was reported missing the same day we found her, it was pure fluke. The bin men were on strike at the time. Some kids were messing about; one of them threw another kid's bag in the bin, and bingo, instead of his bag he found a dead body. I interviewed some nun and a priest from the convent where the girl lived, found them a bit creepy and had my doubts about the pair, but nothing solid. What do you want to know about her for?"

"Not me, Lenny Porter asked me. I think he's working on an old case and her name came up. Cheers for that Jeff, I'll pass it on. We'll have to catch up soon for a drink, but got to go now."

Closing his phone he repeated to them what Jeff had said.

"Melanie could only have been fifteen," said Maria crying "if it was three years ago. After my first year at Nick's, I wondered why none of my friends were ever at the church when I went with Shaun, now I know why, like me they had been sold. It's no wonder Sister Marjorie avoided me like the plague when she saw me with Shaun, not once did she ask me how I was getting on."

The door to the apartment opened and the familiar voice of Gladys called out.

Entering the lounge she smiled and said it was a nice surprise to see Mickey there. Then she looked at Maria and commented on how much better she looked before saying she'd put the kettle on for a brew.

Jimmy declined the offer of tea, stating that they were going out on business. Before leaving he reminded the women not to answer the door, phone or the intercom, just in case it was Maria's ex- boyfriend.

KAREN CLOW

CHAPTER 13

Shaun was driving Nick to a meeting at one of his clubs; he'd been very cagey with the Irishman about it. As Shaun parked the car, he noticed a black MPV. Instantly, he recognised it as one of the vehicles that the Russians used. Nick got out and walked towards it, the passenger door opened and Uri got out embracing him. The Russian was flanked by three big mean looking Russian bodyguards. Shaun walked behind them as Nick unlocked the door.

Inside the two bosses sat at a separate table, leaving Shaun and the other bodyguards several feet away. Shaun tried to listen in on their conversation, but it was difficult, although he did hear the Russian say he had only arrived in England the day before. Then the other bodyguards started talking, making it almost impossible for Shaun to hear what was being said.

Over at Nick's table, Uri poured them a drink and asked if Nick had enjoyed his stay in the Ukraine. Nick nodded; he'd had a great time and was looking forward to doing business with him.

"Ah yes Nicolai, our business arrangement takes effect from tomorrow. The goods will be arriving at approximately ten o'clock tomorrow night. They are coming by private plane which will land in Kent; you will meet the delivery and take it to your designated place. The following day I will meet you and we will deliver the goods personally to the individual buyers. Just one other thing, do not damage any of the goods."

"As if I would," laughed Nick, "about the delivery Uri. How many packages, (girls) and when do I get paid?"

"Unfortunately there will only be ten items and not the eleven that we spoke of, one was so badly damaged we could not send it. When we meet I will pay you, also Sven has arranged for another delivery in nine days' time. I think I will enjoy working with you Nicolai, we make lots of money together."

As they continued to talk, Uri asked if he'd got Maria back, when Nick shook his head and said no but he would have her on Friday, Uri asked if she knew anything that could be bad for them.

Nick was only too aware that she probably did know things about him, but he needed to convince the Russian he had nothing to worry about. In an effort to convince Uri, he said even if she did know something, she wouldn't be stupid enough to open her mouth. It was obvious the Russian didn't share his trust in her keeping quiet.

"I think maybe you make sure she is quiet if she is risk to us. I get you another dog to fuck, it will be my gift!"

Thanking him for his generosity, Nick said it would be fine and he would keep her once she returned to him. Uri's thoughts on the matter were they should simply eliminate her, but he knew Nick liked this girl and that could be very dangerous for all of them.

"On this occasion, I give you the benefit of the doubt Nicolai, but if she is trouble I kill her myself and next time you think more carefully before playing poker. This man Jimmy, will he be a problem?"

Nick knew only too well Jimmy could be a problem and probably would be, but he couldn't tell Uri, Jimmy was just a fucking hot head; but he knew Nick wouldn't let him keep Maria. Uri suggested meeting Jimmy while he was in England and convince him to send her back

The last thing Nick wanted was for them to get involved, or for his crew to realise the depth of his association with them. Thanking him for the offer, but he was confident he could handle it; if things got out of hand he would let him know. When Uri nodded, Nick quickly changed the topic, he would take Uri out for something to eat, but it was too late for lunch and too early for dinner.

Uri was in no hurry to eat, he suggested they talked some more and then go out for dinner. Nick nodded.

"Is that your phone ringing Mick?" asked Jimmy as they drove to St Augustus church.

Turning the radio volume down, recognising the caller ID, Mickey answered the call. It was Jeff. The two friends talked about the case involving Melanie Humphreys. After Mickey had called him, Jeff's curiosity got the better of him so he'd been looking over that case and he'd found something Lenny might like to know. Melanie wasn't the only girl to go missing from St Augustus. Over a period of time, five others were reported as runaways. Jeff had looked at foul play, but drawn a blank, although in his opinion the priest was dodgy. Jeff had assumed Lenny would want to know about the other girls, so after telling Mickey to write the names down told him they were Caroline Bowen and Kate Fitzpatrick both fourteen. A few months later Maria Davis, she was fifteen. After her, two disappeared together, Louise Harper and Melanie Humphries. Thanking him, Mickey said Lenny would be grateful.

The moment the call ended and Mickey talked to Jimmy, they both agreed they should drop a few names and see what reaction they got from the priest.

Pulling into the church they noticed a hearse along with several parked cars. A group of mourners were standing around a grave listening to a priest conduct the service.

From the description Maria had given them and the finger the priest wore his ring on, they were in no doubt it was Father O'Brien. None of the mourners seemed to take any notice as they stood with them. That's the thing with funerals; nobody knows exactly who knew the deceased.

When the service ended and the mourners slowly made their way back to their cars, the two friends approached the priest. Mickey complimented him on a lovely service and asked if he could spare them a moment. Just as they'd expected the priest was polite and said of course. Thanking him, Mickey said they wouldn't keep him long, but they were investigating the disappearance of several girls from there.

Immediately the priest looked concerned and unlike his speech of a few moments earlier, stuttered slightly as he replied, "Sorry, who did you say you were?"

"Sorry," Mickey offered a handshake "Peter Taylor and my colleague is David Tyler."

Nervously, the priest asked who they were working for. Mickey, acting professional, apologised but said their client would prefer to remain anonymous.

"I don't think I can be of any help to you;" stuttered the priest "I told the police everything at the time. You must understand those young girls had been raised in a convent, so the outside world seemed very attractive to them. Once one of them finds the courage to run away, it unsettles the others."

With a look that told the priest he didn't believe him, Mickey sarcastically replied, "So you think they all ran away to see the world? That seems a trifle extreme, wouldn't you agree Father?"

Now visibly shaking, the priest began walking away, stating he couldn't answer any more of their questions, he had to attend the wake of the funeral. When Mickey apologised for coming at such a bad time, the priest looked relieved as he walked away.

"Just one last thing before you go Father, could you confirm for us that the girl in this photo is in fact Melanie Humphreys?"

A look of sheer panic appeared on the priest's face as he reached out and took the photo and glancing briefly at it instantly said, "Where did you get this?"

"Could you just confirm her identity please Father. Also the ring on the hand in the photo, we are correct in thinking it's the type of ring worn by priests?"

Visibly shaking and now sweating, the priest said he thought so, but couldn't be absolutely sure. Mickey questioned as to what he wasn't sure about, was it the ring or the girl.

"Yes I believe that could be the type of ring worn by priests, although I couldn't say for sure. I don't recognise the girl. Now I'm sorry, I really must go.

"Really, but you saw this girl on a regular basis Father, surely you must know? And the ring you're wearing today looks exactly like the one in the photo."

The priest retreated as he passed the photo back and repeated he had to go.

"Did you see the old bastard shaking when you gave him the photo," joked Jimmy on the drive back "he nearly shit himself! Oh and what was with Mr Taylor and Mr Tyler?"

Mickey laughed; they were the first fucking names that came into his head! Jimmy said next time he'd like to be someone with a bit more flair, to which Mickey laughed and said next time he'd introduce him as fucking Colombo. With a grin and referring to him as Theo, Jimmy said that would be fine. Instantly Mickey asked who Theo was. He couldn't stop laughing when Jimmy replied, "You know Mick, Theo Kojak. Who loves ya baby!"

The two friends laughed. They were still laughing when they parked at Jimmy's apartment.

They both noticed as they entered that Maria looked anxious as she asked how the meeting had gone.

Before replying to her question, Jimmy asked where Gladys was. Relieved that she'd just left, they talked about the visit to the priest. Jimmy referred to him as a fucking dodgy old bastard, who had nearly shit himself when they showed him the photo. Their guess was he would be on the phone to either Nick or Maurice by now. Curiously she asked what would happen now.

"Well the first thing we do is send a copy of the photo to Nick. Then we get your notebook from the church. I thought Jacky Boy could get it, his mum goes to that church and he can go with her. After all the shagging he does with Lisa, he could do with confession!"

They all laughed.

Mickey asked her for the exact details of where Jacky Boy could find it. Maria nodded and for the next couple of hours the three of them went over all the details. Mickey phoned Jacky Boy about going to church while Jimmy rang Lenny Porter to ask if he had managed to find anything out. He wasn't surprised when Lenny said he'd discovered that Father O'Brien had some very unsavoury friends who regularly made large donations to the church, via the priest. Two of them were Maurice and Nick. There were some names that he hadn't recognised, but there were two others that seemed familiar. He was certain Mickey would know one of them, it was the bigwig QC, Quinton Randal-Scott known in certain circles as a pervert who likes to fuck little boys. His preference was blond boys aged between twelve and fifteen. The other name was Uri Karpov. A known sex trafficker wanted by the police in several countries, he spent most of his time in the Ukraine and the Philippines catering for clients requesting children for sex. Originally from Russia, he was always well protected. He travelled under several aliases; a low life sadistic bastard with money and contacts.

"Fuck me Lenny you have been busy! We're lucky you still have your contacts. We'll drop your money round in the next few days."

Lenny told him to hang on to the money as he intended to keep digging up information. He believed what he might find could be very interesting.

Jimmy filled Mickey in on the information Lenny had given him.

"From what Lenny said Jim, this thing with Maria could be just the tip of the iceberg. We need to get our hands on that diary as soon as possible, but we can't do anything now, so if you two don't mind, I think I'll call it a day."

Agreeing there was nothing more they could do until they had her notebook, Mickey left.

Jimmy said he was sorry for not spending much time with her, but he was glad she had Gladys to keep her company when he had to go out. Although she smiled and agreed with him over Gladys, he could see how concerned she was about Nick. In an effort to lighten the mood he said he fancied a long hot soak in the Jacuzzi and jokingly added if she felt an overwhelming desire to come in and scrub his back, he would have no objections because despite being shy he would brave it for her. They both laughed. Despite being surprised when she said she might join him, he grinned and said great, in that case she could do with him as she wished.

They both laughed.

Twenty minutes later, she was lying in the Jacuzzi between his legs, resting her back against his chest. They could feel the tiny air bubbles bursting against their bodies. Wrapping his arms around her, he fondled her breasts. She could feel his erection against her back. Lying there, she was experiencing feelings she'd never had before, she so wanted to turn around and make love with him; she wanted to feel him inside her. Had she not have been raped so violently by Nick, she would have. Slowly she turned round to face him. Pulling her closer, he kissed her passionately as he held her in his arms. Kissing him made her feel alive. When she said she was upset they couldn't make love, she felt humbled when he replied he was sorry too, but the time would come when they could. In the meantime he was content just having her there and also flattered that she still wanted him after all that had happened to her.

Although she felt embarrassed, she wanted to explain to him how she was feeling. Snuggling her head onto his shoulder, she told him she had always imagined real love would be wonderful, but never thought she would experience it. She truly believed that one day Nick would kill her, or if she ever did manage to escape, all men would treat her badly. Spending time with Jimmy had changed that; with him she wanted to experience love. With sincerity in his voice he said making love was a good thing to do and if it was with the right person, it could be wonderful. Stroking his face gently, she looked deep into his eyes and told him she loved him then pressing her lips to his, they kissed passionately as the warm soapy bubbles flowed over them. Sliding her hand down into the warm soft water, she found his hardness, easily moving her hand up and down. Still kissing her, he laid his head back against the edge of the Jacuzzi and feeling totally relaxed, he climaxed within minutes.

Standing in the bathroom, he wrapped a towel around her. For the first time he could see clearly the terrible bruises and bites that Nick had inflicted upon her. Jimmy had believed her when she said she loved him, but he couldn't help but wonder if it was because he was being kind to her. Although she was an adult, it was clear to him she was extremely naïve about the real world. However, considering what she had endured she was remarkably normal. At first he thought she was offering to do sexual things to him simply because it was the only way she could repay him for his kindness; yet despite those thoughts, he knew that when she touched him it just felt so right, even allowing himself to think that, like him, she was getting some degree of pleasure from their sexual encounters. In a strange way he felt relieved that her injuries prevented him from having full sex with her, simply because he knew that once he could, he wouldn't want to stop. Never before in his life could he ever remember wanting a woman the way he wanted her.

Gently he dried her back as he kissed her neck. They retired to the lounge, his borrowed robe almost wrapping round her body twice. Minutes later they were sitting on the sofa, with her legs tucked up under her body and her head resting on his chest. Jimmy asked if she fancied watching a film. Nodding, she offered to make them a sandwich before they got comfortable.

Having gone along with her suggestion, he flicked through the TV channels. Several minutes later, she returned from the kitchen with their sandwiches, only to be told there was fuck all on telly, so he'd picked a DVD. The Shawshank Redemption, he asked if she'd seen it. Shock was his reaction when she stated Nick never allowed her to watch television apart from the odd time which had been rare.

"Fuck me babe, you mean you haven't seen anything for three years? You must have gone stir crazy."

"Not really; he did give me books to read."

"Oh that was very fucking decent of him I must say!" he replied sarcastically, "can we not mention him again tonight? I don't want to ruin what has otherwise been a great time."

Noticing she looked a bit upset by his remark, he squeezed her hand and apologising stated it wasn't her fault, but he fucking despised Nick.

Having eaten their snack they settled down to watch the film. They were about thirty minutes into it when he pressed the pause button and turned to look at her. Something was bothering him, he told her, she didn't owe him anything, which meant she didn't have to have sex with him, not that he was complaining, it was simply he didn't want her to feel he was using her.

"I do it because I want to Jimmy. Nick made me feel dirty; there were times when I thought he was right and I was a whore. Many times I did things with him that I hated, but I thought it might make him like me; or at least make him stop hurting me. I used to ask God for forgiveness when I had seduced him, but believe me Jimmy, I want to share my body with you. For the first time I know what it feels like when your body actually wants someone. In my heart I know no matter how much you say everything will be ok, Nick will make me go back, but no matter what he does to me, he can never take from me the love I have experienced with you. At least now if he kills me, I will have known what it was like."

"Don't talk like that babe; you're not going back. I want you here with me and don't think for one minute that without you here everything would be ok, because it wouldn't. Nick has got too big for his boots. For a long time we've thought he was doing things that could get us all killed and what you've told us has confirmed that. So we want to break away from him. It's just that when you said you loved me, I believed you Maria. What I'm trying to say is you don't have to say you love me just to feel safe with me."

Tears were rolling down her cheeks as she stated her love for him was real. Ironically, Nick would beat her until she said she loved him and then make her thank him for raping her.

Gently gripping her head in his hands, he kissed her. It was a long lingering kiss. Then he suggested watching the film before she used her womanly charms to seduce him,

Giving him a playful slap, she snuggled her head back on his chest. As he watched the film, she slowly ran her hands up and down his bare chest. Through the gap in his robe she could see that she was arousing him; so she slowly moved her hand down towards his cock. Gently squeezing her hand, he said she didn't have to do that.

Pulling her legs round, she lowered herself onto the floor and kneeling in front of him, she slowly began opening his robe before moving her head towards his now erect cock. Running his fingers through her hair in a gently voice he said, "Maria," but before he could continue, her mouth was over him. His heart was racing; his whole body was pulsing as she slowly moved her hand and mouth up and down him, rolling her tongue over him. Gripping her hair in his hands, now totally in her control he groaned with pleasure as he came.

"Oh God" he said, as he slumped down into the sofa, never before had his body been so in tune with a woman.

KAREN CLOW

CHAPTER 14

Maria was surprised to hear him up before her that morning. Finding him in the kitchen, she could see him frying something on the stove and judging by the amount of smoke, whatever it was, it was burning. Calmly she walked towards the cooker and looking at the pan, giggled and offered to cook it. Looking relieved, he stated he was no Jamie Oliver and scrambled eggs were his only successful breakfast second to cornflakes!

Looking closer into the pan; she tried not to giggle when she saw that half of the bacon was burnt. Not wishing to hurt his feelings, she discreetly wrapped it in a piece of kitchen roll before throwing it in the bin. Then she started again from scratch and within minutes they were tucking into eggs and bacon. Jimmy asked how she'd become such a good cook.

"We learnt some cookery at the convent and most of the books Nick let me read were recipe books. On rare occasions he would allow me to watch a cookery programme; but not very often and there would always be a price to pay. I suppose being able to cook helped me to survive; apart from my faith it was the only thing I had."

After complementing her on her culinary skills, he said he might have to go out later as he thought Mickey had arranged a meeting with Nick. He would ask Gladys to stay with her if he did go. The moment he'd mentioned the name Nick, he noticed her expression change and she instantly asked if he had to go. He needed to buy them time with Nick and meeting him was the only way to try and achieve that. Sensing she wasn't happy about him going, he quickly changed the subject.

"Maybe you could speak to Gladys before she gets here babe;" he said with a smile "get her to pick you up some shopping just in case you want to cook. Tell you what, why don't I ask Mickey to stay for dinner tonight, you can dazzle him with your cooking skills. If you're not careful we'll be calling you fucking Delia!"

From the books she'd read, she knew that he was referring to Delia Smith.

"Yes that would be nice. I don't mean calling me Delia," she giggled "I mean about inviting Mickey. Is there anything in particular you'd like me to cook?"

Just as Jimmy said she could surprise them, his mobile rang. It was Mickey. He wasn't impressed when Mickey said he'd arranged to meet Nick at one of his clubs, he thought it would have been better at Dixie's. Mickey disagreed and stated this was their way of showing Nick they were serious. He would pick Jimmy up at three. Before the call ended, Jimmy asked if he'd managed to get the photo delivered to him and would he like to stay for dinner that night adding, Maria was a cracking cook!

"Yes and yes please," said Mickey "actually he should have seen the photo by now. I would love to have seen the look on his fucking face!"

After Jimmy said Mickey would love to join them for dinner, he spent most of the next hour on the phone, the first call being to Gladys.

The moment he got through to her, Gladys said she'd be happy to pick up some groceries for Maria.

Having time to themselves; he suggested going onto the internet and ordering her some new clothes. She could choose whatever she liked.

For over an hour they looked at several different stores and although he noticed she went for styles that were baggy and quite frankly drab he never said anything, but he did think the women he knew would want to flaunt themselves if they had a body like hers.

The morning passed quickly. They were sitting chatting when Jimmy looked at his watch and stated he should get ready.

Half an hour later they heard Mickey's car horn outside. Jimmy was concerned and reluctant to leave because Gladys hadn't arrived. Maria assured him she'd be fine until Gladys arrived, but he was still reluctant to leave her alone. He signalled out of the window to Mickey that he would be a couple of minutes. It was then he noticed Gladys heading towards the building. Maria heard him mutter under his breath, "Fuck me Gladys hurry up, I've seen faster fucking snails!"

Still giggling she told him to be careful as he left.

Gladys stepped out of the lift as he got in it, thanking her before he closed the doors.

Approaching the car, he could see Mickey talking on his phone. When he opened the door, he heard him thanking Jeff and adding they'd catch up soon. Knowing Jeff had probably rung in connection with the missing girls, Jimmy asked if everything was alright.

"You could say that, we've had a result. That was Jeff on the phone; apparently Father O'Brien's been attacked, he's in the hospital. They're not sure if he'll regain consciousness. According to Jeff two men wearing balaclavas broke in; looks like they tried to beat him to death. At first the Old Bill thought the motive was robbery, but nothing of any value appears to have been taken. Sounds like someone wanted to shut him up. The nun who raised the alarm overheard the assailants say something to the priest like, 'Are you sure it was the fucking nigger who took the photo?' She also said one of the men had letters tattooed on his fingers. They're treating her for shock." Before he could say any more, his phone rang again. Assuming it was Jeff who'd forgotten to tell him something he didn't check the ID. The last thing he expected was to hear Nick's voice. He was even more surprised when after telling Nick they were on their way to him, Nick said he had to cancel, something had come up, but he would get back to them.

Nick hung up before Mickey could reply. When he told Jimmy that Nick had cancelled the meeting, both men thought it was likely to have something to do with the photo.

Mickey talked about the description the nun had given the police. When they thought of balaclavas and tattoos; Terry Clark and Reggie Swaine readily sprang to mind. They had been at the poker game the night Jimmy won Maria. They were a pair of real hard bastards who worked for Nick, mainly running the docks. At the game they had sat either side of Nick. Both men looked like British bulldogs, hard bastards with bad reputations. Terry is the one that Nick relies on to keep things running smoothly. Known for having a way with words, he could charm the knickers off a nun with his quick wit, and despite looking like a bulldog, with a shaved head and a menacing look, the ladies love him. At forty one and a confirmed bachelor, he looks like a big dumb fucker, but if anyone made the mistake of thinking he was one, it would probably be the last mistake they would live to make. Like all of the men at the poker game, Terry has a long and colourful history of violence. Between the age of eighteen and thirty, he had served a total of eight years in prison. Was well known to the police for fighting, especially when he worked the doors in the clubs, but for the last five years he'd managed to stay out of court, reason being working the docks instead of clubs presented less opportunity for trouble. He runs the docks like clockwork; nothing moves that he doesn't know about.

The man sitting to the other side of Nick that night had been Reggie Swaine, once regarded as one of the toughest men in London. Reggie is no stranger to trouble, only nineteen when he served his first sentence for GBH. Having been a bare knuckle boxer in his younger days, now in his late forties he carries the legacy of his violent past in the form of a cauliflower ear and a flattened pug type nose from having had it broken several times. There is also the occasional slow slurred speech that so often follows too many blows to the head. Nicotine stained fingers from being a chain smoker, along with years of heavy drinking have taken their toll, leaving him looking older than his years. Two bitter ex-wives and three grown up kids he never sees, the only important things in his life are his two Rottweilers, Zeus and Thor. Like him they're mean bastards, but he looks after them as though they were his children; even on poker nights they're left outside on the roof terrace of Nick's penthouse. No doubt about it, Reggie prefers his dogs to people, except Terry of course, they're tight. Back in his younger days everyone wanted to take a pop at Reggie due to his hard reputation. Despite the fact that then he mostly kept his aggression inside the ring there was always some young loud mouth who wanted to prove something. Usually trying to impress some young girl; they would goad Reggie into a fight. One such arsehole was young Johnny Dolan. Back then Johnny's family ran a small piece of the docks; rumour has it Reggie only hit him once to shut him up. Johnny never recovered, he's still a dribbling wreck confined to a wheelchair. The rest is history; Johnny's family wanted pay back, Reggie took the beating of a lifetime from five big dockers, which put him in intensive care and would probably have killed him had Terry not intervened. Since then Reggie is one hundred per cent loyal to Terry. Another thing they have in common is they like hurting people, which was why Mickey thought they were probably responsible for the attack on Father O'Brien.

"Well as we're already out," said Jimmy with a grin "we could always pop over to the club, Maria seemed happy to be left. I told them not to answer the phone or the door. Of course the alternative is, we go back indoors and listen to Gladys rabbiting on for the next two hours!"

Mickey agreed and suggested he gave Lenny a call to see if he was free. Lenny's phone rang until the answer phone clicked in. Leaving a voice mail, Mickey said if he was free that afternoon they would be at the club till about six.

Five minutes later, the two friends were entering their club Dixie's. Jacky Boy and Kevin greeted them. When Jimmy asked them if everything was ok, Jacky nodded but asked him what was happening about the job at the jewellers, only they'd heard through the grapevine that they were now going to handle it.

Jimmy explained that was what Nick wanted, but it wasn't going to happen and it was just Nick's way of trying to rattle them. Kev laughed and said they'd thought that too.

"Personally I can't stand Nick," said Kevin "the big headed prick. Still I'm sure he'll get his fucking comeuppance one day."

Affording himself a moment's indulgence, Jimmy smiled and said he could bet money on it, arseholes like Nick always did.

Just as they sat down Lenny arrived. Mickey said hello to him, then he asked Kev and Jacky Boy if they had work to do. Knowing he wanted privacy with Lenny, the two lads began walking away.

"Catch you later," said Jacky Boy "oh and by the way, thanks for the meal, the fucking grub was great. Lisa couldn't keep her fucking hands off me after our lovely romantic night out, even Kev pulled. He went home with her friend Mandy, the dirty bastard!"

They all laughed and Mickey said they could do it again soon.

"Yeah, but next time Lisa can bring another friend;" joked Kevin "that fucking Mandy nearly shagged me to death. She was like a fucking maniac, gagging for it!"

Everyone was still laughing as the two lads left.

Jimmy grabbed another glass and placing it in front of Lenny, asked him if he had any information for them.

They were surprised when he said he'd heard the vicar had been beaten up so he'd been over to the hospital to see if he could talk to the dodgy old bastard.

"Fuck me we've only just found out about that" stated Jimmy "and anyway he's a priest."

"Priests, vicars, they're all one and the same. Any bloke that wears a fucking frock in my book is a bit dodgy, and as for all that old bollocks about being married to God, it's not normal, men should fuck women!"

"No chance of you becoming a priest then Len," joked Mickey.

They all laughed.

When they asked if he'd found anything out at the hospital, he said no, but the priest had certainly taken a beating. In his opinion if he did survive he'd be eating through a straw.

When Mickey said they'd done the priest over good Lenny replied, "If you ask me they wanted him dead, but they got interrupted. Tell you something strange though, when I arrived at the hospital your mate was there, you know the black guy who hangs out with Tony. I can never remember his fucking name."

Mickey asked if he meant Maurice, when Lenny nodded he asked what Maurice had said to him.

"Nothing to me Mick; he was talking to a nurse, asking her if the vicar was likely to regain consciousness. Funnily enough, he went a bit pale when he saw me, excuse the pun, but you know what I mean, looked a bit put out that I was there."

Curiously Mickey asked if Tony had been with him. Shaking his head Lenny said no. He was going to take a trip over to the vicar's place that night and have a nose around, see if he could find anything. Jimmy joked and told him not to go getting himself into any trouble.

"Who me, never," replied Lenny with a broad grin.

They all laughed.

A couple of hours later, Lenny left after telling them he would call them. Jimmy phoned home to check on the ladies, the phone rang and rang. Several seconds passed.

"Fuck me," said Jimmy "why ain't they answering?"

"Because Colombo," replied Mickey sarcastically "you told them not to, remember? When the answer phone clicks in say it's you and tell them to pick up, bullet!"

Moments after he spoke into the answer machine, Gladys picked up the phone. When Jimmy asked to speak to Maria, she handed her the phone. He asked what time she wanted them back for dinner. Six thirty was her reply.

After closing his phone, he looked at his watch and informed Mickey that dinner was in three quarters of an hour. Pouring themselves another drink, they chatted over the events of the last couple of days. Jimmy reminded him that he needed to speak to Nick about the job on Friday. They had decided to tell him they had it on very sound advice that the Old Bill had been tipped off, leaving them with no choice but to call the job off. Mickey was still worried about Nick wanting her back and time was running out. Jimmy suggested lying to Nick, maybe telling him that when they'd returned that evening Maria had fucked off?

After Mickey said even Nick wasn't stupid enough to fall for that one, he wondered if they could tell Nick she'd collapsed and Doc Daniels thought it may be an internal injury? If need be, they could actually get her in the hospital, just for a few days and he was sure the Doc would back them up. Jimmy could see that would work, but would be concerned that Nick would go to the hospital and kill her.

"I agree Jimmy, but not if someone tipped off the Old Bill about a hit on the priest; the place would be crawling with coppers."

"What a devious mind you have Michael, but that might just work if we can't come up with something better."

The two of them finished their drinks and left.

Jimmy called out that something smelled good as they entered the apartment thirty minutes later.

Gladys appeared and with a smile told them they were in for a real treat, Maria was quite a cook. Gladys put her coat on stating that she would leave now they were back because Arthur worried about her being out at night.

"Quite right Gladys," said Jimmy as he threw his car keys at Mickey, "take Gladys home for us Mick. Arthur's got a point, so many fucking criminals in London it's just not safe!"

Gladys said there was no need as it was only a ten minute walk.

"Just get in the car Gladys;" said Mickey "you know you want all your neighbours to see us pull up so they think you've got yourself a rich toy boy. I'll take my car that should impress them."

"Oh love you're incorrigible," she giggled "but it would make 'em look, wouldn't it?"

Maria hugged her and kissed her cheek as she thanked her for staying with her. Within seconds of them leaving, Jimmy walked over to her and put his arms round her waist, and after calling her gorgeous, kissed her passionately.

She was shocked a few minutes later when she asked nervously what had happened at the club and he told her Nick had cancelled. Curiously and knowing Nick rarely cancelled, she asked why.

"Don't know babe, but I suspect it's something to do with the photo and the priest being done over."

Totally at a loss with what he talking about, she frowned and asked if Father O'Brien been beaten up or something. Apologising that she hadn't been told and trying not to upset her, he went over what had happened. Tearfully she asked what he was going to do. Despite saying he had a few tricks up his sleeve, he wouldn't really know until they'd spoken to Nick.

They heard the front door open and Mickey came in. Jimmy thanked him for taking Gladys home.

"Fuck me Jimmy, next time you can take her she never stops fucking talking!"

Although they all really liked Gladys, he did have a point and his comments made them laugh.

Entering the dining area, both men complemented her on how nice the table looked. Gladys had shown her where Jimmy kept the table napkins; after she had emphasised to Maria that he never used them. She also managed to find a couple of tea light candles. Maria looked quite humbled with their praise of the table.

Passing Jimmy a bottled of chilled wine from the fridge, she said dinner was ready. A few minutes later she laid the table with a wonderful meal.

The men ate every last morsel of both the meal and dessert. Finishing before her, they waited as she ate her dessert of mango sorbet. Mickey suggested when the trouble with Nick was sorted out, she could cook for them at one of their restaurants.

They waited for her to finish eating; she was slow because of her loose teeth, which Jimmy would get sorted out for her the following week. After complementing her again on a fabulous meal, they took coffee in the lounge. The evening seemed to fly by as they chatted. Mickey couldn't believe how quickly she'd healed and how it seemed like she'd been there a lot longer.

"Thanks Mickey, I know what you mean, it seems like I've been here for ages. I'm so grateful to everyone, it's the first time in years I actually feel safe."

"Good, then we'd better make sure you stay here. In fact I think I'll ring Nick now and break it to him that we're definitely not doing the jewellers job. I'll play it close to my chest about you Maria, leave the ball in his court."

Taking out his phone he rang Nick's number. When the answer phone came on Mickey said they couldn't make Friday and for Nick to call him back. Closing his phone he smirked and said that should get the bastard's attention.

Twenty minutes later his phone rang; anticipating that it was Nick, he was surprised to see Tony's name come up on the ID. Without chatting or explaining why, Tony said he was at Maurice's and they should get over there and make it quick. When Jimmy asked about the call, Mickey told him they needed to get over to Maurice's as something was up.

Jimmy was reluctant to leave Maria alone; he wouldn't put anything past Nick. Even though she assured him she'd be fine, he insisted they took her somewhere, although when he suggested Gladys's she blatantly refused stating it was too late.

Mickey said she could stay with his mum; it was his dad's card night which meant he'd be out till the early hours of the morning, if not all night. His mum would be only too pleased for some company; he would ring to let her know they were coming over. Maria felt embarrassed and stated she'd never met his parents.

"You'll love them babe," said Jimmy "his mum Mary is just like Gladys, you'll get along just fine."

Although she believed what he'd said, she still felt uncomfortable with the idea and asked Mickey if he was sure they wouldn't mind.

"I'm absolutely positive they won't. I've just spoken to mum while you two were talking and she's looking forward to meeting you."

Despite their reassurances, travelling to his family home she felt nervous. Jimmy squeezed her hand and told her to just go along with the ex- boyfriend story.

Twenty minutes later they dropped her off at Mary's, who quickly put her at ease when she opened the front door and smiling said, "Hello love, come in, I've got the kettle on."

Confident that the ladies would be fine, the men made their way to Maurice's. He lived in a converted factory unit. From the outside it looked like a regular building; inside was a different story. Lavishly modern, exquisitely furnished, although Jimmy always referred to it as a typical pimp's pad, the type you see in the movies.

Tony's car was parked outside next to Maurice's; there was another car which belonged to Hudson Leroy. Hudson worked for Maurice and was well known in the neighbourhood. Also of Afro-Caribbean descent, he worked as a debt collector and heavy, but not your run-of-the mill heavy, Maurice gave him respect. Hudson was a straight guy who loved women; his nickname was Humping Hudson, although no-one would have called him it to his face. He was a big black bastard and well known for fighting. He handled a lot of drug business, especially overseas. Taking his orders directly from Maurice although they were rarely seen together socially, but if anyone knew anything about Maurice, it was Hudson.

Jimmy pressed the intercom.

"Come up," said a deep male voice which he instantly recognised as Hudson's.

The lift was the type with the cage front that you had to manually shut before it would work. It was the only original feature Maurice had kept when the place had been converted. The lift came to a halt just inside the apartment lobby. Peering out through the mesh the two friends could not believe the scene. The place had been turned upside down. There was blood everywhere; it was like a scene from a horror movie. Tony was standing with Hudson waiting for them to enter.

At the far side of the open lounge there was a body lying on the floor. It was that of the Russian boy Maurice kept as a sex toy, he was dressed in only his boxer shorts. Half his head had been blown away. Blood, hair and brains were splattered up the wall and his hand was still clinging to the gun. There were lash marks across his back and a leather collar and leash was still secured to his neck. Just a few feet away slumped in a chair was the body of Maurice, stripped naked and covered in blood, his cock had been severed and put in his mouth.

"Jesus Christ!" said Mickey, "what the fuck is going on Tony?"

"Beats me; whoever did this wanted it to look like the boy did it then blew his own brains out."

"Maybe that is what happened, just look at the poor bastard; perhaps Maurice fucked and tortured him once too often, looks like they had a fight."

"Or that's what someone wants us to think?"

Before Mickey could reply, Hudson interrupted and said, "Come with me."

They followed him into the bedroom; once inside he pointed to the wall safe.

"Dead Russians don't break into safes," said Hudson "the boy certainly didn't need money where he was going. Someone wants us to think the Russian did it, but they were looking for something, and shoving his cock in Maurice's mouth like that tells us he's said or done something that's really pissed someone off."

Mickey asked if he knew what Maurice had kept in the safe. He wasn't surprised when told, due to the place being so isolated, Maurice only kept a few valuables there, but he did have a safety deposit box at the bank. Hudson had driven him there on several occasions, although they always stopped by the church first where Maurice would give Father O'Brien an envelope. They needed the key to that deposit box. Unfortunately Hudson had no idea where Maurice kept it.

"Actually I might," said Tony, "Maurice always wore that stupid locket thing round his neck; he always said the key to his heart was inside. I always thought it was a photo of one of his boys; you know how sentimental these queers can be. One thing's for sure, he never took it off."

They all looked over at Maurice's body and noticed the locket was no longer round the dead man's neck.

Mickey pointed to something lying on the floor in the blood. Taking a pen from his pocket, he hooked it through the object. It was the locket; obviously it had broken during the struggle. Wiping it with a handkerchief, Mickey undid it. There was a small key inside. Tony's first thought was now they needed to find a way to get to that safety deposit box. When Mickey grinned and said he had a few contacts, Hudson was quick to vent his feelings as to whether that was a good idea.

They took it that he was implying he didn't trust him, but they all knew it was because the box, in theory, could be worth a small fortune. Tony instantly vouched for Mickey, stating not only was he one hundred per cent kosher, but probably the only one who could do it.

"If you think that Tony" said Hudson "then it's good enough for me. Sorry Mickey, I didn't mean anything by it; I'm just looking out for Maurice."

Mickey hadn't taken offence; he'd have been the same if it had been Jimmy. He suggested they didn't talk to anyone about Maurice until they found out who was responsible. Despite agreeing with him, Hudson thought they should at least tell Nick. Mickey expressed that Nick probably already knew, and it would not be in Hudson's best interests to say anything to him, or anyone else.

"Mickey's right Hud," said Tony "and there'll be a big opening in the firm now with the demise of Maurice; but his replacement would have to know when to keep his mouth shut."

Hudson knew exactly what he was saying and he quite fancied taking over Maurice's action.

"We were never here;" he said with a grin "first I heard of it was when the Old Bill started asking me questions."

Jimmy smiled at the others and said he thought they may have found a replacement for Maurice.

They all nodded.

"It's probably a good idea if we keep out of each other's way for the next couple of days," said Mickey "I'll place an anonymous call to the Old Bill. We'll be in touch, let us leave first then wait ten minutes just in case anyone sees us."

Leaving Tony and Hudson in the apartment, the two friends left.

Back in the car they talked about Maurice. By the time they pulled up outside his parents' house, both men were confident that Nick was behind the hit.

Mickey told Jimmy to go and call for Maria because if they both went his mum would insist on them going in. Jimmy could simply say they were having a few problems down the club and Mickey was waiting in the car.

A few moments after he rang the doorbell, Mary embraced him and kissed him on the cheek as she asked where Mickey was. Going along with the plan Jimmy said he was waiting as they had to go to the club, but it was good to see her.

"And you love, you don't visit nearly enough. I'm always telling Mickey to bring you round for Sunday dinner. Den and I would love to see you, bring Maria with you, she's a lovely girl."

Jimmy had just nodded at her invitation to dinner, when Maria appeared in the doorway. Thanking Mary, they left a few minutes later.

Outside Jimmy's apartment, Mickey declined their offer of a night cap. He'd see them in the morning around eleven as he had a few things to do at the office first and some calls to make.

Inside the apartment five minutes later, Jimmy asked her how she'd got along with Mary.

"Oh Jimmy she was lovely; all she talked about was you two. Telling me what a lovely lad you are and that she wished you two would settle down. I got the impression she likes the fact that Mickey goes out with Monica, but she said she wants you to meet someone nice and not one of the old tarts who work in your clubs."

He laughed and referred to Mary as a cheeky cow. Then he surprised Maria by adding his days of dating old tarts were over, and it just so happened he'd found himself a really nice girl. Nervously, Maria said she'd not mentioned them to Mary. With a smile he said it wasn't a problem, Mary would know soon enough, because when the trouble was over he wanted to take her out and show her off.

The look on her face told him she doubted they would stay together, but she smiled and said she hadn't been taken out anywhere for years. She wasn't sure if she'd be able to do it. Reassuring her he said maybe their first date could be a foursome with Mickey and Monica. Instantly she smiled and said she'd like that. Reaching over taking her hand he stated they wouldn't be doing too many double dates, because he intended to wine and dine her alone by candlelight. Maria said it sounded very romantic. Grinning he confessed he was just an old romantic at heart, but she couldn't tell anyone as he had his reputation to think of.

"I think you're wonderful Jimmy."

"Wow steady on babe! I don't want people referring to me as humpty dumpty!"

"Why would they call you that?" she asked with a rather baffled look.

"You know babe, humpty dumpty had a big head!"

"Oh you're so funny. You make me happy Jimmy, but it's not going to last, is it? We both know Nick is never going to let me stay here, he'll see me dead first and I don't want anyone getting hurt. I'm not worth it."

"Don't talk like that babe; I've told you we'll sort it out. You're never going back and you are worth it. So don't let me hear you say that again; something will turn up, you'll see."

She asked if the meeting he'd had with Tony had been about her. Shaking his head, he filled her in with all the gruesome details and the belief that they thought Nick had been responsible. Their assumption was it was probably Maurice who had taken the photo of Melanie. Instantly she referred to what Nick was capable of and she really should go back as it would be better for everyone. He wasn't going to debate it again, so he said he'd sort it. Then he suggested them having a drink before turning in for the night. Shocked was his reaction when she asked if he'd sleep in the bed with her.

"Of course babe," he said with a huge grin "but I hope you're not trying to entice me so that you can have your wicked way with me?"

"Well you won't know," she giggled "until you're in there, will you?"

Jimmy was already in bed when she came out of the en-suite. Watching her as she walked towards him, he could feel himself becoming aroused, even with her wearing his large baggy pyjamas, she still looked sexy. When she got into bed he put his arm out to hold her and felt relieved when, without hesitation, she snuggled her head into his shoulder. Within minutes they were kissing passionately before she told him how sorry she felt that they couldn't make love properly. His response was it didn't matter; it was just nice having her there with him. Despite what he'd said he was desperate to have her. Slowly she made her way down his body, kissing him and touching him. Barely able to stand the suspense, he was secretly hoping that she would take him in her mouth rather than doing him by hand. A few minutes later she was sucking him. With his body responding to every movement of her mouth, it wasn't long before he was coming. Lying back down next to him she asked if he'd enjoyed it and had she done it properly. Curious as to why she'd asked, he told her it had been fantastic, but he would have thought she already knew that. Gently lifting her head, he asked her why she'd asked him.

With her eyes filling with tears, she looked embarrassed as she softly replied, "Until I lived with Nick I didn't know people actually did things like that. I felt sick when he forced me to do it. I never enjoyed it with him and he always told me I was useless at it before giving me a beating. One day he almost choked me, but said if I bit him he would kill me. I always hated it, but I couldn't understand that if I was so bad at it, why did he make me do it all the time?"

"The way you do it is wonderful babe. Nick knew that, but being an arsehole, he could never tell you. Not wishing to put too fine a point on it, I've had enough in my time to know when it's good and when it's not, and believe me, I've got no complaints. On a scale of one to ten you're definitely a twenty, but I do feel a bit guilty because I can't repay the compliment. When you're healed I'll make it up to you, I promise."

In her naivety, she thought he was referring to intercourse. She said she enjoyed everything they did and hopefully it wouldn't be long before she could please him properly.

"You already do babe, anyway it's not just about pleasing me, so stop worrying about it, although feel free to do whatever you like to me, I won't object!"

Pinching his thigh she giggled and said they should get some sleep.

CHAPTER 15

The morning came all too quickly for Jimmy. Feeling the empty bed next to him, he dragged his feet into the kitchen. Saying hello, he asked what the time was. With a beaming smile she said good morning and it was quarter past eight.

"Fuck me, no wonder I feel like I've been dug up; I've only had about four hours' kip!"

Ordering him back to bed, she stated she wasn't going to wake him till ten at which time she had intended to take his breakfast to him.

Just over an hour later she was knocking on the bedroom door telling him that Mickey was there.

While they waited for him to dress, she offered Mickey a drink. Readily he said tea would be great and he was sorry for arriving early.

Over tea he asked if she'd remembered anything else about Nick that might be useful. Nodding, she said there was something, but she wasn't certain it would be of use. She'd remembered the man who picked Kate had an accent. Mickey asked what nationality the man had been. Possibly German or Russian was her reply, but she couldn't be sure.

Jimmy's phone rang just as he entered the room and said hello to Mickey. Checking the caller ID he stated it was Nick before answering the call and arrogantly asking what he wanted.

Nick told him he had to go away on business again for a few days, but he didn't want him thinking he'd gone soft and he was having her back. Jimmy instantly said she wasn't for sale.

"And like I said before Jimmy, everything has a price. Let me put it another way; if I don't get her back I'll have to replace her."

"Fine you fucking do that!"

"Oh I intend to, matter of fact I've already got my eye on someone else, actually you know her she's a good piece of arse young and fresh, just how I like them."

Feeling his temper rising, Jimmy snapped and shouted down the phone how the fuck would he know who she was, he didn't fuck little girls!

Mickey and Maria had sat silently listening until then, but realising something was being said that involved young girls Mickey looked at Jimmy and held his hand out to take the phone. Jimmy frowned and shook his head.

There was a brief pause.

"Name of Charlie;" said Nick "apparently she loves her Uncle Jimmy."

Instantly Jimmy lost his temper. The others watched as his tone and body language changed to aggressive as he shouted down the phone, "You fucking sick twisted bastard! You so much as fucking look at her and I swear I'll fucking kill you!"

Mickey interrupted and asked what was going on. Ignoring him, Jimmy continued his conversation with Nick.

Having recognised Mickey's voice, Nick told Jimmy to put him on the phone.

Not having heard Nick's side of the conversation Mickey asked him what the fuck was going on.

With an arrogant tone, Nick said Jimmy could tell him later, he was only interested to know if they were all set for the job as he didn't want any mistakes.

"We told you the job's off Nick so you'd better let Martin and the buyers know!"

"I fucking warned you Mickey" shouted Nick "don't piss me about!"

"It's a fucking set up; the Old Bill is going to be waiting for us!"

There was a deathly silence.

"It's probably nothing;" said Nick "just another firm trying to muscle in."

"No it's for real Nick; I can vouch for my source. Whatever you think, we're not doing it! If you're that sure it's safe, get a couple of your boys to handle it or do it your fucking self, but we're out!"

"I'll call it off, but if you're winding me up Mickey!"

"No wind up, it's kosher."

With that Nick hung up.

Mickey instantly asked Jimmy who'd they'd been talking about as Nick wouldn't tell him. The moment he said Charlie, Mickey went ballistic. Jimmy was quick to say he'd fucking kill Nick if he so much as looked at her. Maria started to cry.

Mickey told them not to worry, he wouldn't let Nick get anywhere near Charlie. Tearfully Maria interrupted and said she must go back because it wasn't about her anymore. Nick was hurting innocent people and she couldn't allow that. For the first time, Jimmy seemed to lose his temper with her.

"For fuck's sake Maria" he shouted "I don't want to hear this again! You are not fucking going back, do you understand?"

Looking afraid she nodded her head.

With her now trembling Mickey tried to ease the situation by telling Jimmy to calm down as it wasn't her fault, it was Nick's. He was trying to get to Jimmy, but it wouldn't work. The only reason he said about Charlie was to fucking test them.

"Sorry Maria" said Jimmy "I didn't mean to have a go at you. It's just you seem to think if you go back everything will be okay, but like I keep telling you, it won't. Nick's gone too fucking far this time, he's crossed the line. If he wants a war we'll fucking give him one! What are we going to do about Charlie though Mick? We can't take the chance he's bluffing."

Mickey assured them he'd sort it out and Nick would never get near Charlie, he'd see him dead first.

For the first time Maria saw another side to both men. When Charlie had been brought into it, she saw a look of pure hatred in their eyes; it was the kind of look that told her they were both capable of murder. For one brief moment she had felt jealous of Charlie, because two people loved her enough to kill for her. Never in her life had anyone felt that way about her. Since the day she was born she had never felt loved; she had always been told what to do. Right up until she was sold, her only value in life had been how much money she would fetch. If Nick had killed her no one would have cared, no one would have come looking for her. Now for the first time she felt someone had genuine concern for her wellbeing. Convinced that God had sent Jimmy to her, she knew that if need be she would die for him.

Putting his jacket on, Mickey said he was going; he needed to sort the issue of Charlie. He knew the two of them were feeling bad over her.

They watched him get into the lift, before closing the front door. Feeling bad about the way he had spoken to her, Jimmy put his arms around her and told her he'd meant what he'd said, she was never going back to Nick's. It wouldn't help now if she did.

In her heart she knew he was right, but she still felt responsible and told him she wished he hadn't won the bet

"Well I'm glad I did and another thing, you know you asked God to help you, well he did. That was the first time in a poker game with Nick I've ever had a royal flush."

Tearfully she nodded and said, "Really Jimmy?"

"Yeah really, I've had a few in the past, but never at one of Nick's games. So you see babe, you're meant to be here. Now it might be a good idea to give Shaun a bell, see if he knows anything about Nick's trip."

Seconds later he rang the Irishman. When Shaun answered they bantered for a while before Jimmy mentioned Maurice's murder or whether Shaun knew why Nick had suddenly taken this trip. He was shocked when Shaun refused to talk over the phone and offered to meet him at Dixie's in thirty minutes.

Once the call ended, Jimmy looked at her and said he had to pop out for a while, but he'd bell Gladys and ask if he could drop Maria off at her place on the way. Maria instantly stated that with Nick away she would be fine to stay at the apartment, but he wasn't taking any chances so she was going to Gladys's and no arguments.

Twenty minutes later they arrived at Gladys's house. Jimmy thanked her as Maria walked through her front door and said he wouldn't be long.

Pulling up at the club ten minutes later, he had just turned the engine off when the passenger door opened and Shaun got in. Jimmy instantly noticed the black eye and facial bruises the Irishman was sporting. When he asked if Shaun wanted to go into the club for a drink, he shook his head and said he'd prefer to talk in the car because if Nick found out he was even talking to Jimmy, he'd have his tongue cut out.

As they talked Jimmy said he appreciated Shaun meeting him. This thing with Nick was getting out of hand and as lovely as she was he couldn't believe this was all about Maria.

Shaun said he was right. Nick was in over his head and the photo had stirred up a fucking big hornet's nest. He looked angry when in a blasé manner Jimmy said "So someone sent a photo, so what?"

When Shaun snapped and stated he knew exactly what photo he was referring to, Jimmy nodded and said so what if he did know about the photo.

"So what Jimmy? The fucking Russians, that's fucking what!"

With a curious look Jimmy asked what fucking Russians.

"The same fucking Russians that torture and murder people; the fucking Russians that Maurice introduced Nick to about three years ago. It was because of Nick doing business with them Nick and Maurice fell out. All I know is after he got that photo, Nick told me to go and frighten the priest, find out what he knew. I told him I couldn't do that, as dodgy as the fucking priest is I couldn't hurt him, not in the church. It put me in hot water with Nick, that's how I got this black eye but shit happens. Anyway he sent Reggie and Terry, they roughed the priest up, but he didn't tell them much. Next thing we know, four fucking big Russian bastards turn up at Nick's club and start throwing their weight about. There was lots of shouting and threats, something about that photo. It was the Russians who did the priest and Maurice. I tell you, Nick is scared. I'm not sure who the Russian boss is, I've only seen him a couple of times, think they call him Yory or some fucking Russian name. One thing's for sure, I didn't like him the first time I met him when he was friendly, and I sure as hell didn't like him this fucking time."

Jimmy explained he thought it was probably Uri Karpov, from what they knew he was a ruthless bastard. If Nick was working with him then Shaun was right, Nick was in over his head. Jimmy asked if he knew where Nick had gone. Shaun didn't, he'd run him to the airport but Nick hadn't said much because he'd talked on his phone most of the drive. Shaun had tried to listen to the conversations, one in particular he heard Nick say, 'well the fucking nigger won't be taking any more photos.' Nick also rang some upper class bloke, he'd heard the voice on the phone say 'This needs to be sorted; I can't afford to be associated with them.' He had a posh English accent. Shaun did know Nick would be gone for a few days. Jimmy thanked him and said he'd see what he could find out. As Shaun got out of the car he told him to be careful, those Russians were bad bastards.

Moments later, Shaun walked off.

Jimmy went into the club and looked round to see who was there. Jacky Boy was sorting out the bar when he spotted Jimmy and told him the thing he wanted from the church was in the office. Realising he was talking about Maria's notepad; he thanked him and asked if he'd had any problems finding it. He laughed when told it was easy and even Jacky Boy's mum hadn't seen him get it. They sat and chatted about the club before Jimmy left.

Driving home, he tried to call Mickey but his phone was switched off. When Jimmy arrived at Gladys's her husband Arthur opened the door and invited him in.

"Alright Arthur," said Jimmy "are the girls about or have they talked themselves to death?"

Laughing, Arthur said they were in the lounge and hoped he could stay for a cuppa. Jimmy noticed the look of disappointment on the old boy's face when he said he couldn't, which gave Jimmy a change of heart and he stayed for a quick one.

Following him into the kitchen, he waited while Arthur made the tea. Arthur said Maria was a good looking girl and if he was twenty years younger he'd give that ex-boyfriend of hers a run for his money.

"Twenty years Arthur?" laughed Jimmy "you dirty old bugger you'd still be old enough to be her granddad!"

They both laughed.

Arthur's advice to him was to get in with her before someone else had a chance. Winking at the old boy, he grinned and said he intended to.

A few minutes later the four friends drank their tea. Before leaving Jimmy asked Gladys if she and the family would be free one evening. He laughed when she said every night apart from her bingo night. Without hesitation he invited them all to one of their restaurants one night for a complimentary meal on him and Mickey. Gladys beamed as she thanked him for the lovely offer before saying Thursday would be a good night for them as the family don't do anything that night. Jimmy nodded and said he'd confirm the booking with the restaurant manager. They thanked him again as he left with Maria.

In the car, Maria said it was a nice gesture to treat Gladys and the family to a meal. She smiled when he referred to them as the salt of the earth and it was the least he could do. When he suggested them stopping for something to eat, she asked if they could have fish and chips.

"Fuck me babe," he joked "you actually made your mind up about something! Now are you sure you don't want me to pick something for you!"

"Very funny," said Maria "fish and chips just happen to be my favourite."

Thirty minutes later they were back at the apartment tucking into their fish and chips and drinking wine when he told her he'd got her notebook in his pocket. Taking it out, he opened it and flipping through the pages asked if she remembered any conversations Nick had with any Russians. Nodding she stated she'd written them down. She asked if Mickey was coming round that evening. Shrugging his shoulders, he explained that Mickey's phone was off, but no doubt he'd be in touch.

They sat and talked about her time at Nick's with her going into more detail about the way he had treated her. Jimmy was horrified when she said that Nick sometimes brought other women home and made her watch while he made love to them; he'd done it deliberately to upset her.

Knowing how she felt about Nick, Jimmy asked if it did upset her.

"Yes, but not because he had other women, but because he treated them well, he did things with them he never did with me. He didn't hit them or tie them up; he was loving and affectionate. In front of the women he would mock me and say things like, 'the woman deserved to be loved and to get such pleasure from him.'"

Jimmy could see she was tearful as she talked, but he asked her to go on. With the tears beginning to trickle down her cheeks she continued.

"Once I asked him why he did it; he said that they were real women and I was nothing but a dirty whore, who didn't deserve to know such pleasure. Then he raped and beat me until I lost consciousness. Perhaps he was right and I didn't deserve anything good. God had seen the things I'd let him do to me. Maybe in the eyes of God I am no better than a whore."

"It's not about God babe," he said clutching her hand "you couldn't be less like a whore if you tried and you do deserve pleasure. It's about Nick being a sadistic pig. He needed to make you feel bad so he felt empowered; he's just a sick twisted bastard!"

They talked for hours. For the first time she seemed happy to confide in him. They would have continued if, at eight o'clock, his phone hadn't rung. It was Mickey. Jimmy told him he'd been worried because he couldn't get hold of him and he needed to speak to him about Shaun.

"Everything's fine Jimmy, I just needed to sort a few things out. Can Shaun wait till the morning? I've been running about like a blue arsed fly. Thought I'd have a few drinks with Monica and then shag the fucking arse off her; apparently shagging is good for stress."

"I've heard that too Mick. I'll see you in the morning. Oh one thing before you go, Jacky Boy delivered that package today."

When the call ended, Maria asked if Mickey was ok. She felt relieved to hear he was, but shocked when with a grin Jimmy said he wasn't so sure about Monica. Her first reaction was to ask if something happened to her. Laughing he said no, but it was going to, because Mickey intended to shag the arse of her that night. Despite giggling she said that was a terrible thing to say and she hoped he'd never say that about her.

"Depends babe; for all I know you might say it about me. Who knows, when it does happen you may want to shag the arse off me!"

"Jimmy you're terrible, but there's only one way to find out; perhaps we should have an early night. Shall I run us a bath?"

Feeling aroused at the thought of sharing a bath, he asked if she was sure she was up to sex, especially after what the doc had said. Assuring him she was fine, she left to run the bath for herself after he declined, stating he wanted to read her notepad.

Watching her as she headed for the bathroom he thought about having her. His pulse was racing, he'd dreamt about this night since he'd first laid eyes on her, this was the night that she would know what it felt like to have pleasure. Trying to put her out of his mind he browsed through her notepad. The name Quinton was there several times, but no matter how hard he tried to concentrate, he couldn't get the thought of having her out of his head. Even her notebook had failed to distract him for more than a few minutes at a time. From where he sat, he could see her in the bath; her beautiful dark hair swept up on her head in an attempt to keep it dry. Watching her, he fantasised about having her that night and everything he wanted to do to her. Things she had been made to watch Nick do with other women, yet never been allowed to experience herself. Feeling aroused just thinking of her, he called out to ask how long she was going to be and anticipating having her when she called out that she was just getting out.

Knowing he was only moments away from having her, his stomach churned. Barely believing that any woman would have such an effect on him, he switched off his phone. There would be no interruptions that night.

Taking himself off into the kitchen while he waited for her, he poured two fresh glasses of wine, walking back towards the lounge with them just as she appeared.

Standing in his robe, with her hair swept up, she took his breath away. Placing the wine glasses down on the table, he pulled her to him, kissed her passionately and then removed the ribbon that held her hair. It fell down around her. Gently moving it off her shoulders he kissed her neck. Then undoing the belt, he slid the robe over her shoulders, it fell to the floor. Standing naked in front of him, he could see she was trembling. Her beautiful body still showed the bites and bruises, although they were now barely visible. They kissed as she undid his shirt buttons and then removed it, before moving her hands down towards his trousers. Stopping her he placed his hand on hers and whispered, "Tonight is your night babe."

Scooping her naked body up into his arms, he carried her through to the bedroom. Laying her gently on the bed, her hair cascaded around her. Her perfect firm breasts moved up and down in time with her heavy breathing. Quickly removing his trousers, he laid next to her.

Placing his leg over her, he kissed her passionately for several minutes, then moving slowly down her body he began kissing her breasts and sucking her nipples. She caressed his head and shoulders as he slowly moved further down her body, rolling his tongue seductively over her belly button. Responding to every touch and kiss, her body writhed in motion with his as he moved his body slowly over her, until he was lying between her legs. Kissing her thighs he could sense she was nervous; this was something new to her.

"Jimmy don't." she said holding his head.

Hearing the apprehension in her voice, he reassured her saying "Sshh babe it's ok."

Desperately she tried to relax; but her legs wanted to close, even though her body wanted him to continue. Many times she had been made to watch Nick doing this to other women, but never to her. Laying there her body trembling with anticipation, she felt his fingers touching her, now her entire body was desperate for him. Unable to remain silent, she gasped as he flicked his tongue over her. Suddenly her body jerked; a sensation she had never known before rushed through her body. "Oh God, Jimmy, stop!"

Knowing she was experiencing orgasm, he ignored her and continued pleasuring her. Pressing harder with his tongue, he could feel her body arching with every movement.

Now gripping his head tightly and pushing him harder onto her unable to control herself, her body jerking and writhing as she cried out his name.

Slowly regaining her senses, her breathing calmed. Still kissing her as he moved back up her body, her stomach, her breasts and finally her mouth, she could taste herself as he probed her mouth with his tongue. Moving her hand down to guide him into her, slowly at first then faster, wrapping her legs around him; pushing him deeper into her, raising her body up to his in perfect unison, they were moving together as one. A final thrust, he was coming as he called out, "God Maria!"

Her legs still wrapped round him, she held him close as his body gave a final thrust before he gently collapsed onto her. Moments later, he was looking down at her and gently stroking her face asking if she was ok. He hadn't expected her to burst into tears. Instantly he asked if he'd hurt her.

"No it was wonderful Jimmy. I don't know why I'm crying, but it's not because I'm unhappy, I've never been so happy. Thank you Jimmy, I love you."

CHAPTER 16

The next morning, she was cooking breakfast whilst he read through her notebook. Realising he hadn't turned his phone on, he checked it. There were two missed calls from Mickey. Immediately he rang his number. Mickey said everything was ok and he'd only tried to call to say he'd be round at lunchtime.

Having heard that Mickey would be coming round, Maria smiled and suggested they could eat breakfast and then shower together before he got there.

"I'm not sure babe," he said with a grin "if I keep letting you seduce me in the bathroom I could end up looking like a wrinkled prune!"

"Who said anything about sex?" she giggled "I simply offered to share a shower with you."

"Oh well, if you're not going to have your wicked way with me I may have to decline your offer!"

Over breakfast they chatted. She asked if Gladys was coming over as she needed a few things from the supermarket. Gladys wasn't due that day, but if Maria wrote a list he'd call one of the girls from the club who would shop for them, then Mickey could pick it up en route to them. After convincing her that Mickey wouldn't mind, he rang the club while she wrote the list. After speaking to one of the girls at the club about the shopping, he rang Mickey and asked him to call into the club for it. Jokingly Mickey said it was no problem as long as Delia invited him for dinner.

Noticing Maria was staring at him as he closed his phone, he asked if she was ok. Having heard him banter with the girl at the club, she said she thought it was strange that he hadn't settled down because women clearly liked him. He was handsome, sexy, kind and rich, so why hadn't someone snapped him up?

She smiled when he said maybe he just hadn't met the right woman. His first marriage had been a fucking disaster and to say it had put him off would be a fucking understatement. She asked what his wife had been like.

"Bossy fucking cow; Jimmy do this, Jimmy do that, she got right on my fucking nerves, although I was no angel back then, I was never home. We were both too young. I wanted kids she didn't, fucking unusual I know, but she was a career girl. Anyway we fought all the time; it just didn't work out. After the divorce she remarried, end of story."

"I would like children one day Jimmy, maybe four? I know I've only been here a little while and you think I love you because you've been kind to me, but you're wrong. I don't expect you to love me; it doesn't matter."

"It's a strange word love;" he said taking on a serious expression, "people say it all too easily. Not me, when I say it I'll mean it, so it does matter."

Sensing that she felt slightly humbled by his words, he had meant what he'd said. An hour later they were still talking about love, marriage and children when the front door opened and Mickey called out "Delivery boy."

Maria thanked him for getting the shopping and giggled when he said he hopes the delivery boy gets a cup of tea. Moments later, she left the two friends talking while she went to make tea.

The first thing the two men talked about was Charlie and the fact Mickey had managed to get her on a flight to America. She was going to stay with his sister Fay, just until things blew over with Nick. He'd spoken to her that morning but she was tired, probably suffering the effects of jet-lag. Confident that Charlie was safe, Jimmy passed him Maria's notepad. Mickey browsed through it and noticed the name Quinton kept appearing.

"Could that be our old friend Quinton Randal-Scott?"

"My very thought Mick, not exactly a common name is it?"

Mickey would endeavour to have a little chat with the Right Honourable Quinton Randal-Scott, although personally he couldn't stand the creepy old bastard. Jimmy didn't know him, but stated that in his opinion all judges were creepy bastards!

They laughed before Jimmy asked if there was any news on the safety deposit box. Mickey said he had an appointment that afternoon with his old friend Raymond Murray, aka the bank manager. There was a number engraved on the key which he hoped was the deposit box number.

Maria entered the room and asked what they'd like for lunch. Both men agreed that anything would do as neither was fussy.

Waiting until she was out of earshot, Mickey quietly asked how things were going with her. He felt happy for his friend when he said everything was great and she seemed to bring out the best in him, although he expressed his concern at her saying she was in love. With a grin Mickey assured him it was ok, Monica said it all the time. Jimmy couldn't help but doubt Maria. Mickey reassured him, stating he was bound to feel that way, best to just play it by ear.

"Only one problem Mick, I haven't told her but I feel the same way about her. I can't get enough of her. I can't imagine being without her now."

"Fuck me Jimmy, you have got it bad, and there was me thinking I was the soft romantic one! Still it's about time, it's a bit ironic really; the one girl you fall in love with comes with a fucking government health warning!"

The two friends were still laughing when she called from the kitchen that lunch was ready. Over lunch, Jimmy asked after Monica. Mickey said she was fine and sent her regards.

"Oh she's still got the strength to speak then?" said Jimmy sarcastically, referring to his friend shagging the arse off her.

Mickey looked a trifle embarrassed in front of Maria because he knew exactly what his friend was implying.

"Oh yes she still has the power of speech," said Mickey with a grin "I'm just not sure if she'll be able to sit down without the aid of a cushion for a few days!"

They couldn't contain their laughter, even Maria.

Mickey complemented her on the lunch and said if things had been different for her, she would have made a great cook. With sincerity in her voice, she said she loved to cook and her dream had been to own her own restaurant, not that she ever thought it would happen but it was a lovely dream.

"Never give up on your dreams babe; that's our motto isn't it Jimmy? We never thought we would own clubs and restaurants, but we do. I've got to go for my appointment at the bank. I shouldn't be too long, maybe an hour?"

They wished him good luck when he left a few minutes later.

Alone in the apartment, she asked what he thought Mickey would find in the box. Shrugging his shoulders, he had no idea, but whatever it was Maurice had been prepared to die for it. As the conversation ended, she asked if he would mind her going to lie down for a while, she felt so tired.

"It's all that shagging, it's worn you out babe. You should try and get a couple of hours kip, because we'll be doing it all again tonight!"

Despite her obvious happiness, he could see sadness as she replied that would be wonderful. Taking her hand, he told her not to look so worried as they didn't have to do anything if she didn't want to.

Too embarrassed to look at him, she hung her head slightly and, referring to oral sex, said he didn't have to do that if he didn't want to, although she'd really enjoyed it. She'd watched Nick do it to other women, but it had been a first for her with Jimmy. She still looked concerned even after he stated he loved oral sex. Snuggling her head into his chest, she asked if he thought she was stupid.

"Of course not and you don't need to be embarrassed because you've not done something. Like I said before, with the right person it can be wonderful. I just want you to enjoy it. If the way you were screaming was anything to go by, I would say you did!"

"Oh this is so embarrassing for me, but that was also the first time for me. I'd never had one before and then when it happened again a second time when you made love to me I still wasn't sure what it was. Now you know how stupid I am. Some of the girls at the convent used to say about things happening if you had sex, but we didn't really know what it was."

Lifting her chin with his hand, he kissed her and stated orgasms were great and she would be having lots more from then on. In fact he was feeling quite horny talking about it so he may just have to come to bed with her then, or maybe they could simply do it there in the lounge. Pulling her closer, he kissed and fondled her. Within minutes they were almost naked, but she felt uneasy knowing that Mickey could walk in on them at any given moment. Standing up Jimmy held out his hand to help her up and said perhaps they should go to bed.

They made love for over an hour. Afterwards she fell asleep snuggled up to his chest. Carefully he moved off the bed, leaving her sound asleep after their afternoon lovemaking. Quietly he returned to the lounge.

Mickey was gone for nearly two hours. Jimmy was beginning to worry when he heard the front door lock turn. Moments later Mickey appeared in the lounge. Jimmy asked where he'd been as he was getting worried, thinking he may have been mugged or something.

"Patience Jimmy, patience, these things take time. I had to convince Raymond that what I was doing was legal."

"And was it?"

"Course not, but everyone trusts a solicitor!"

"Dishonest bunch of bastards, present company excluded of course!"

They both laughed.

Mickey placed a small box on the coffee table. Whatever Maurice had thought was so important was about to be revealed as he removed the lid. Inside they could see a large stack of photographs, all of young boys and girls being sexually abused by men. Looking through them they found a photo of Nick standing astride a young girl urinating on her. Several more photos were of the QC Quinton Randal-Scott sexually abusing young boys. Mickey recognised several familiar faces from the legal world. Also in the box were handwritten receipts to Father O'Brien and Uri Karpov. However, the most interesting deposits were four DVD's. Jimmy loaded one into the DVD player; the images that came up on the screen were sickening. The first one was of the QC Quinton abusing a young boy. The boy was obviously begging for mercy, despite not speaking English possibly Russian. The QC was dressed only in his robe and his judge's wig as he abused him, whipping the terrified boy with a riding crop before buggering him.

They didn't hear Maria come into the room until she apologised for sleeping so long and offered to make some tea. Glancing at the TV, she saw the QC abusing the boy. Tearfully she exclaimed how horrendous it was. They could both see she was trying hard not to cry. When Jimmy suggested her making the tea, she nodded and left the room.

The next recording on the disc was of Nick and two other men. A young girl was being subjected to vile sexual acts by them; her hands were tied behind her back as they repeatedly raped and beat her while they drank vodka and snorted coke. They watched two more recordings, both of different men abusing young boys and girls. They had just started another recording when Maria came back in with the tea. Fumbling with the remote, Jimmy pressed the stop button, but it was too late. She had recognised the young girl on the screen; it was her friend Melanie. The colour drained from her face and tears began streaming down her cheeks. Despite feeling sick, she wanted to know what had happened so she asked him to leave it on.

Jimmy pressed play as she sat on the arm of his chair, gripping his hand tightly. Nick was beating Melanie and shouting at her that she was not a virgin, but a dirty worthless whore. Her beautiful blue eyes were swollen and bruised. Around her neck she wore a leather studded collar attached to a leash which Nick was holding in his hand. As the camera panned around the room, another man was sitting in a chair. Nick dragged the screaming girl across the room by the leash and then he ordered her to get on her knees and suck the other man's cock. Terrified she did as he ordered. Nick stood above her, pushing her head down harder. She was gagging and choking as he talked to his perverted accomplice. They clearly heard him say, 'What do you think Uri; she's no fucking virgin, no fucking innocent Catholic girl!'

The man who'd replied laughed and said 'she was just another cheap whore.' It was the Russian Uri Karpov.

When they had finished they dragged her to a bed and tied her to it, then took turns raping and beating her again, stopping only to snort coke and drink vodka. Nick beat her whilst sitting astride her and ordered her to call him sir. She was too weak to resist as he pushed a pillow onto her face. When he finally removed it, she was dead. The two men laughed as Nick said 'she's just another fucking whore who wouldn't be missed.'

Maria rushed into the bathroom and vomited. Jimmy stood outside the bathroom door listening to her sobbing.

When she emerged, he was there to hug her. Taking her back to the lounge, he looked at Mickey and suggested it would be a good idea to watch the rest at his place. Mickey nodded and said he'd record a couple of copies along with some copies of the photos. Having asked Mickey to pour her a drink, Jimmy took the glass of scotch from him and passed it to her as he sat down next to her on the sofa. The moment she sipped it she coughed and grimaced before handing it back to him.

Regaining her composure, she asked Mickey if the disc would be enough to send Nick to prison.

"Possibly babe, trouble is people like Nick can afford to hire the best barristers. It's unlikely the disc alone will be enough; it would only prove he had sex with a minor. The fact that she was dead at the time would be hard to prove; he could simply say she was unconscious."

"I want him to pay for what he did to Melanie."

"Oh rest assured babe he's going to. As the saying goes, there's more than one way to skin a cat."

Maria stood up and said she needed to prepare and cook the fish for dinner. As she went to leave, Jimmy pulled her down onto his lap and hugging her told her to cook plenty as he needed to keep his strength up. She blushed because knew he was referring to them having sex again.

With her in the kitchen preparing the meal, the two men continued to talk. Also in the deposit box was a wad of money. Mickey counted it; there was over three hundred grand. They decided it would be best if Mickey put it in his safe for the time being, along with the other items. Although they would need to tell Tony what they'd found he suggested waiting a few days. They had just finished packing away the contents when Maria came in and said dinner was ready.

They both noticed how quiet she was throughout the meal, even though the two men complemented her several times on the dish.

An hour later and after thanking her for a wonderful dinner, Mickey stood up to leave. When Jimmy asked if he'd be safe carrying Maurice's valuables, he grinned and nodded stating he'd be fine as no one knew he had them, but erring on the side of caution, he arranged to call them later to confirm he'd arrived home ok.

Alone in the apartment they sat together on the sofa. Holding her hand, Jimmy expressed how sorry he was about her friend Melanie. He was horrified when she said Nick would do the same things to her, putting a pillow over her head was one of his favourites. Not wanting to upset her, but allowing his curiosity to get the better of him, he asked if Nick had ever made her do things with other men. Instantly she said no, but now she was questioning why, especially having seen the disc.

"That's because he thought he owned you, he only wanted you for himself; he's a sick, twisted fucker who deserves a bullet to the head!"

Tears were streaming down her face as she asked him what was going to happen to them. Kissing her cheek and holding her tight, he assured her they would be fine. She wanted desperately to believe him, but stated Nick would kill her if he couldn't have her. With a grin he said they'd just have to kill him first, because he promised her they were going to stay together.

Later as arranged, Mickey phoned to let them know he was home. Everything was safely put away and he'd looked at the court lists for tomorrow. Quinton the QC wasn't in court until the afternoon so he suggested taking the photos round to show him in the morning. He would pick Jimmy up about ten.

Jimmy agreed it was a good idea and he'd get Gladys to stay with Maria

Maria talked about Nick and Melanie until they went to bed, where they spent several hours making love. The remainder of the night was spent just holding each other.

CHAPTER 17

It was just before quarter to ten the next morning when Gladys arrived. Jimmy thanked her for coming round early to sit with Maria.

Maria entered the hallway and after saying hello to Gladys, told him she'd heard Mickey's car horn.

Gladys called him a cheeky devil when before leaving he told them to behave themselves while he was out.

Mickey drove for thirty minutes before turning off the road onto a private estate which led them up a long narrow driveway to a manor house. Walking from the car to the manor house door, Mickey said he would do the talking as he rang the doorbell.

A maid answered. Mickey smiled, said good morning and politely asked if it would it be possible to speak to Quinton.

Shaking her head she said Mr Randal-Scott was taking a swim and did not want to be disturbed. From the doorway they heard the QC's wife call out to the maid, "Who is it Louise?"

Before she could answer, Mickey poked his head round the door and said, "It's me Cynthia, Michael Mann. We met last year at Hugo's retirement party, remember?"

"Oh yes of course, do come in Michael."

Thanking her, he introduced her to Jimmy and apologised for any inconvenience. Next time he would phone first. Smiling a false smile, she agreed but said now they was there she believed Quincy would see them. She disappeared for a few moments before returning and taking them into the drawing room. Offering them a seat, she said Quincy would be along any moment. They both declined her offer of refreshments.

"Can I assume you've come to speak with Quincy on a legal matter Michael?"

"Yes you can Cynthia, after all he is the best," said Mickey patronisingly trying to flatter her.

Sickeningly, she proudly stated they were right, he was the best. Quinton entered the room his hair still wet from his swim and asked Cynthia to leave them before asking Mickey what he wanted.

"It's a bit sensitive Quinton; my colleague here is working on a very sensitive case and asked for my advice. Naturally, when I read the file I said there's only one man who can give you the best advice concerning such a dreadful case and that man is you Quinton."

"What's the case about Michael?"

"Paedophiles, sick perverts, sex trafficking; you name it this case has it all. The reason we've come is because some photographs have come into my colleague's possession. Lewd photos," he said passing them to the QC. "There are some of men raping and buggering young boys and girls. We just need to know if they can be used as evidence in court. They're quite sickening; there are some real animals out there."

"Oh I know Michael; thank God I have the power to send these vile creatures away for a long time."

Jimmy clenched his fist; he so wanted to beat the pervert sitting in front of him to a pulp.

The four copies of the originals he handed the QC were all of Quinton abusing young boys. The moment the

QC looked at the first one, his manner changed and he demanded to know where they got the photos from.

Before Mickey could reply, Jimmy said sarcastically, "Does your wife know you like to fuck and torture little boys Quincy?"

The QC ignored the question and again demanded to know how they got the photos, but more importantly what did they intend to do with them.

"Well that's up to you Quinton, we need you to identify some other men for us. If you don't we will be sending these photos to every nick and every newspaper in London. Oh and I'm pretty sure dear old Cynthia will want a set to! Your choice Quinton," said Mickey, as he called out to Cynthia.

"I won't stand for it!"

Panic stricken and after stating it was blackmail, the QC said he'd do anything to keep it quiet. Moments later Cynthia appeared in the room and asked if Quinton had called her. Mickey apologised saying it had been him who called because he wanted a glass of water. Nodding and stating it was no trouble, Louise their maid would bring him one. Waiting until she left the room, he looked at the QC and said "What's it to be then Quincy?"

Looking quite pale, the QC stated it wouldn't appear he had any choice but to do as they requested. With a smug expression, Mickey nodded and passed him a photo of two men raping a young girl. The QC studied it, stopping momentarily when the maid came in with the glass of water for Mickey. After she left, the QC said he didn't know the man on the right; he'd never seen him before. The other one he'd met once at a private party.

"Would that be the type of party where animals like yourself torture and dick little boys?" said Jimmy.

The QC didn't answer until Mickey asked who the man was. All the QC knew was he was a Russian diplomat; possibly called Mikhel. Mickey passed him the next photo; it was of an old man dressed in bondage gear, holding a whip. A terrified young boy of about ten was cowering on the floor. Mickey watched him looking at it and asked if it was giving him a hard on. Ignoring his remarks, the QC stated he didn't know the man.

"You're a fucking liar Quinton; he's into the same perverted sick stuff as you. We know you know him, so you'd better talk!"

The QC looked intimidated as Jimmy glared at him and cracked his knuckles in the palm of his hand.

After several seconds of silence the QC finally said he couldn't tell them, if the man found out he would kill him.

"I can understand that," said Jimmy sarcastically "I've only just met you and I want to fucking kill you!"

Mickey demanded the QC tell them who the man was. Trembling and looking afraid, the QC said the man was an MP, very high up in the government. He was a very powerful man; more powerful than either of them could even begin to imagine. His name was Aubrey Morton-Smyth. When Mickey asked where they could locate Aubrey Morton-Smyth, the frightened QC asked why they needed to know that. He looked terrified when Mickey stated that sometime in the future, some friends of theirs may want to pay him a visit. They ordered him to write down the address and the address of the house where the orgies took place, along with the name of the person who sets them up.

"Make it quick," snarled Jimmy "my patience is just about to run out! You've got about thirty seconds before I beat you to death, you disgusting pig!"

Now shaking badly, the QC said it was Francis O'Brien who arranged them. His face was one of complete shock and horror when Mickey told him Father Francis wouldn't be arranging any more because he'd died the previous night. The QC instantly asked what happened to him.

"Let's just say there are people out there who don't like others talking about them, and I suppose you could say Father O'Brien had a big mouth. So remember to keep yours fucking shut; you can't even trust your friends. Now it's time for us to go Quinton, I've enjoyed our little chat."

Picking up the photos from the desk, Mickey looked at him and advised him not to go too far as they may need to speak to him again. The QC remained seated after Jimmy said they'd see themselves out.

As they emerged into the hall, Cynthia appeared and asked if they were leaving. Mickey, although smug, sounded sincere when he said unfortunately they were because Quinton wasn't feeling too well and they felt a trifle upset about it. Reason being they'd showed him some sordid photographs of the case his colleague was handling and although Quinton was extremely helpful the photographs had clearly turned his stomach. They both hoped they hadn't affected him too badly. Confidently, she assured them Quincy was used to that sort of thing and no doubt he would be fine. Mickey nodded and with a smile agreed that he did indeed see a lot of things like those. The two friends grinned at one another as they said their goodbyes then left.

In the car, Jimmy talked about what Shaun had said and how he agreed with him that Nick was in over his head. He just wondered how long it would be before the issue of Maria came up again. Mickey assumed it wouldn't be long, but for what it was worth, he thought her and Jimmy made a great couple and what a bonus she was such a great cook. He was right, most modern women couldn't even boil an egg and Monica was one of them. Regarding Nick though, he would worry about him when the time came.

Jimmy's phone rang. Checking the ID it was Jacky Boy so he answered it but before he had chance to say anything other than hi, Jacky Boy said they needed to come to the club then he hung up. They knew something was up because he'd sounded scared. They could be at the club in fifteen minutes. Mickey suggested giving Shane and Billy a call and ask them to meet them there, but to wait in the car park as it could be a set up.

Pulling up at Dixie's they noticed a black people carrier with tinted black windows and new plates. Making a note of the registration, Mickey asked Jimmy if he had seen it before. Jimmy shook his head. Reaching into the door side panels, Mickey took out a small baseball type club, while Jimmy took out a rubber truncheon from his side of the car. They hid them inside their jackets.

Just as they got out of the car, Shane and Billy pulled up. Shane asked what was up as he approached their car.

Pointing to the people carrier, Mickey stated they may have some uninvited guests. He asked them to go round the back and if they saw anything out of the ordinary, hit first and ask questions later.

Shane and Billy nodded. Neither man was afraid of a fight; late twenties to mid-thirties both heavily built and knew how to handle themselves.

When Jimmy and Mickey walked through the main doors, they could see Jacky Boy, Kevin and Lucy, one of their staff, sitting at a table with three heavily built men sitting in between each of them. Lucy was crying.

As they walked towards the table another man appeared. He was much smaller and they recognised him from the DVD's as the Russian, Uri Karpov. Speaking in Russian he said something to the three men sitting at the table. One of them got up and put more chairs around it. Moments later he ordered Mickey and Jimmy to sit down. They sat, but not before Jimmy gave him a look that said he was already pissed off with his attitude.

"You have something that belongs to us" said Uri "and it would not be in your best interest to fuck with me! Do not play games with me, or this pretty girl will not be so pretty."

He was referring to Lucy. As he'd spoken the big Russian sitting next to her had produced a knife and was pressing it against her cheek, she was terrified. Mickey said there was no need for violence and what exactly was it he thought they had. Uri referred to it as being something that belonged to the black bastard Maurice; along with some photographs of him and some of his comrades. They both knew that Quinton had contacted him as soon as they'd left.

Jimmy was really pissed off with the Russian's manner, especially as Lucy was petrified.

"We don't know what you're fucking talking about," said Jimmy arrogantly "we have nothing of Maurice's! Whoever took him out did the place over, so if anything is missing I suggest you talk to them! As for the photos, someone sent them to us, we don't know who, but it's obviously someone who doesn't fucking like you! We don't want any trouble; we just want Nick to back off!"

"Ah yes, Nick. That reminds me he wants the whore back!"

Jimmy could feel the anger raging within him when he snapped back saying he could tell Nick she was staying with him until she wanted to leave, if at all!

"I don't think you heard me; the whore goes back to Nick! I have offered to get him another dog to fuck, but for reasons best known to him he wants her back. I even offered him a good price for her, but he refused."

Feeling the tension, Mickey interrupted and told him Jimmy had won the game fair and square.

"So what?" said Uri, "no whore is worth dying for. Maybe I should fuck her, and then maybe I can understand why Nick allows her to get in the way of business! Or maybe I just shoot her and put an end to it! Now tell me where you got the photos or I kill one of your friends here!"

Mickey tried to reason with him but his efforts were futile. He knew he needed to come up with a name before someone got hurt. Thinking quickly he suggested that maybe it was Nick who had sent them the photos.

"You are really getting on my fucking nerves now, you are trying my patience! Why would he send you photos? You have thirty seconds to tell me, or your girlfriend loses her face!"

Lucy, looking terrified, begged Mickey to tell him. Reassuringly he told her it was ok and no one was going to get hurt.

"What makes you so certain that Nick isn't behind all this?" said Mickey "think about it. Nick has made this personal not us. Everyone at the game knew Jimmy won the bet fair and square. Nick will lose face if he cannot get her back, so he needs backup. Who better than you? So he sends us photos knowing that it will get back to you then you do his dirty work for him."

Instantly the Russian shouted that Nick would not dare to use him.

"Nick would use his fucking mother if need be. Think about it logically; we're probably the biggest threat to Nick. We're very successful and he makes no secret of the fact he wants Dixie's. With us out of the way he could have it. So he uses you to get rid of us, then if I know Nick he gets rid of you! Let me ask you something, why do you think we have whatever it is that belonged to Maurice?"

"Because I do!"

"Are you sure it's not Nick who has made you believe that?"

The Russian hesitated; it was obvious that what he had just heard had made him think, especially when he looked at Mickey and stated he was very clever trying to turn him against his friend.

Mickey assured him that wasn't the case and if Nick was in fact a trusted friend, he'd no doubt told him about Razor? The look on the Russian face was priceless when he stated he'd never heard of Razor. Mickey continued that Razor was a thug who Nick used to get information.

"What fucking information!" shouted Uri slamming his fist on the table.

"I have a written account of a conversation between Maurice and Nick a couple of years ago; Maurice was trying to blackmail him. We all know that the only true connection between them was the fact that Maurice knew all Nick's dirty little secrets, not to mention many others, you included. Just imagine the power Nick would have if he had evidence that high up powerful men were committing vile acts against children."

"Where can I find this Razor," snapped Uri arrogantly.

"Ah well you could have a little problem there, you see he met with a nasty car accident just a couple of days ago. I've only just found out myself, but you must admit, it's a strange coincidence."

"Enough of this bullshit; give me the photos now!"

Mickey put his hand into his inside pocket and passed him the copies of the photos he'd shown to Quinton. He hoped that would be an end to it for the time being, but he knew it wasn't to be when the Russian said, "You have tried to fuck me off; so now I must teach you a lesson!"

Uri nodded at the three heavies and one of them without any warning went for Kevin, punching him and sending him flying backwards. Immediately, Jimmy pulled out his truncheon and hit the heavy who was holding the knife at Lucy, forcing him to drop it. Within seconds a full scale fight was raging. The Russians did not anticipate Shane and Billy rushing in from the back after they'd waited and listened to the conversation just out of sight. Lucy immediately ran and hid behind the bar, narrowly missing being hit by a chair which hurtled past her before crashing into the optic bottles behind the bar. Mickey got a good hit against Uri; a full on blow to the guts from his bat. Winded and clearly in pain, Uri ordered his men to get out. Making their way over to the door, the Russian shouted at them it was not over.

Jacky Boy helped Kevin to his feet as Jimmy asked if everyone was okay. Shane was holding his hand as he grinned and said the Russian he'd hit had a fucking iron jaw! Mickey led Lucy out from behind the bar; she was shaking with fear. Reassuring her everything was ok; he sat her down and said they'd have a drink. Sitting together, Jacky Boy placed a bottle and glasses on the table. Mickey looked at Shane and Billy and stated the damage would have been a lot worse if they hadn't been here.

"Yeah you were like the fucking cavalry charging in" laughed Jacky Boy "and now you're here you can help us clean the place up!"

"I'll polish you sweep," said Billy "but just let me get me pinnie on first!"

Everyone laughed.

Mickey thanked them and said he would take Lucy home and she'd be taking a few days off. Jimmy would stay and help the lads; Mickey could pick him up his way back. Jimmy smiled at Lucy and jokingly said for her to make sure Mickey just dropped her off, because he may have trouble behaving himself if left alone with a beautiful girl.

"Don't worry Jimmy," said Lucy with a grin "my boyfriend's at home."

"Fuck it" said Mickey "that's just my luck!"

Unbeknown to them the Russians had only driven up the road before stopping. What had been said to Uri had left an element of doubt in his mind over Nick. Thinking about what Mickey had implied, he dialled Nick's number. When Nick answered the call and asked what he could do for him, Uri aggressively said he could meet him in five minutes at Jimmy's apartment as there was some business he needed to take care of. Despite acting calmly, Nick knew something had happened and quickly asked Uri what the hurry was because he'd assured him he would deal with Jimmy.

"Because today" stated Uri "an associate of mine was shown some photos which could be very damaging to our business! We believe they may have come from Maurice's safety deposit box. This Jimmy and his friend are involved and they must be taught a lesson! I will expect you there in five minutes, do not keep me waiting!"

Uri hung up. Nick pondered over the conversation he'd just had, the only photo he had was the one that had been sent to him but there was obviously something very wrong. He had a strange feeling that Uri had tried to intimidate him, almost like a warning. Grabbing his car keys he left to meet the Russian.

Having taken Lucy home, Mickey had driven back to the club to pick Jimmy up. Driving back to the apartment they talked about what had happened.

Jimmy complimented him over the twist regarding Razor and how, in his opinion, it was worthy of an Oscar. The reason he'd thought that was because only two days earlier they had learned the old time thug had been in a fatal car accident; there were no suspicious circumstances. He had been drunk at the time; running his car into the back of a stationary lorry.

Mickey grinned and said it came in fucking handy old Razor checking out like that and it had certainly planted a seed of doubt in Uri over Nick.

Reaching the apartment block they took the lift. With the doors closing, Jimmy said he hoped Maria had cooked something, because his fucking stomach thought his throat had been cut. Mickey agreed, stating he could eat a scabby horse and chase its fucking rider. They were laughing as they got out of the lift, until Jimmy noticed his front door was open. Quickly he prodded Mickey to alert him that something might be wrong. Both men took out their weapons from inside their jacket, before slowly pushing the door open and scanning inside the apartment. They could see Gladys lying on the floor; blood was trickling from her mouth. Mickey rushed over to her and tended to her whilst Jimmy continued to search the place. Certain that it was clear, he shouted to Mickey that Maria had gone.

Gladys began to come round. Mickey held her and asked if she was alright and what had happened. Regaining her senses she slowly explained that Maria's ex- boyfriend had broken in. It had all happened so fast, they didn't have time to call the police.

Mickey helped her up and sat her on the sofa before asking how she knew it was Maria's ex-boyfriend.

"Because she called him Nick; she told me before that was his name. It was awful. I tried to get him to leave, but he wouldn't listen and then the bastard thumped me one! I don't know what happened after that."

Jimmy entered and sitting next to her asked Mickey to make her a cup of tea. With his arm around her and aware she was still a bit shaky, he asked if she could remember anything Nick had said.

"It was awful Jimmy, Maria was screaming and begging him to leave, but the bastard laughed and said if she'd let you touch her she was dead! We were terrified. I tried to tell him that you'd just been looking after her, but he slapped her around and said terrible things to her, disgusting things. My Arthur would cringe if he heard me talk like that."

Jimmy knew she was old school and talk like that didn't sit well with her, but he had to know, so reassuringly he asked her to continue and of most importance was if she knew where Nick had taken Maria.

Despite her embarrassment at having to repeat what Nick had said she continued, "He said that if she didn't stop screaming, he would stuff his thing in her mouth. Then he added something vile like, he expects she's missed it. The dirty pig, even asked her if she'd sucked your thing. I can't say any more Jimmy, but it was disgusting things like that; he was a pig! I don't know where they went, but he did say he had some Russian friends who were waiting to see her. Now it's coming back to me and thinking about it, he did say something strange. He said he hadn't decided whether to keep her or not, that would depend on her; if she pleased him he might. When he finished hitting her, he dragged her out by her hair. She was screaming for you Jimmy. I tried to stop him, but when he punched me again I must have blacked out."

By the time she had finished talking, she was sobbing her heart out. Jimmy assured her they would get Maria back and she couldn't have stopped Nick because he was a psychopath. Mickey brought her tea in and passing her the cup asked if she felt better.

Still crying, she nodded her head before sipping her tea. Jimmy asked if there had been anyone else with Nick. Tearfully she told him she couldn't be sure as it happened so quickly and the bastard had thumped her. They offered to get their Doc to check her over, but she declined stating she'd be fine. All she wanted was to go home. Mickey rubbed her hand and said he'd take her, but asked her not to say anything to anyone except Arthur, just until they sorted things out. Despite agreeing, she suggested they should call the police. When Mickey explained that his girlfriend was a detective who would help them, Gladys seemed content with it.

By the time Mickey returned to the apartment, the anger Jimmy was displaying was frightening. Mickey had seen him in a rage many times over the years, but never had he witnessed such a display of aggression. Despite trying to calm him down, Jimmy punched the door putting his fist through it. Mickey shouted that his aggression wasn't going to help Maria and they needed their wits about them in order to get her back. Fortunately Jimmy agreed and said he'd save his anger for Nick. He had to get her back.

"Well let's look at what we know Jim. Nick wouldn't be stupid enough to take her back to his place, or to any of his clubs. He said he had friends who wanted to see her; the Russian bastards. They need somewhere quiet and isolated where they won't be disturbed. With the information we have, I would hazard a guess they've taken her either to the house where the orgies take place, or to the MP's house. Quinton said that the MP lives alone with only his housekeeping staff. Considering the photos that I gave to Uri, they wouldn't have any problems convincing the MP to let him take her there. Before we go charging off, we need to decide who to take with us; if the Russians are there we'll need to be prepared."

Jimmy said the lads had done well earlier that day; also Terry and Reggie were hard men. Mickey agreed about the lads, but thought Terry and Reggie may favour Nick. They both agreed that Tony would be a good choice and he'd made it clear if he had to pick a side it would be theirs. When Mickey suggested Shaun, Jimmy was quick to remind him that Shaun actually worked for Nick.

"I know that Jimmy, but we know he doesn't fuck young kids; that's one part of Nick's business that he stays out of. We also know how he feels about Maria and those Russian bastards."

"She feels the same way about him; she told me once he's her guardian angel."

"Not an easy image to conjure up, Shaun as an angel. Nevertheless, he would be a great ally to have. I think we should call him, test the water."

Pouring them both a drink, Mickey suggested calling the lads. Shaun was the first one that Jimmy called. The first thing he asked him was if he knew what had happened that day. He believed Shaun when he said no. Nick had surprisingly given him the day off so he'd spent it with his family. He couldn't believe it when Jimmy told him about the Russians and that Maria had been taken.

"Fuck me Jimmy I warned you; where's he taken her?"

Telling him they weren't sure but Gladys had heard Nick say he had some Russians friends who wanted to meet her. Shaun sounded concerned and asked if they had any idea where they may be. Jimmy said about the addresses the QC had given them; they were rounding up the lads to go with them.

"Best count me in then" said Shaun without hesitation, "another thing Jimmy, the Russians carry guns so make sure your boys are tooled up."

Relieved to have him along, Jimmy assured him they would see him alright. He was surprised when Shaun said after that night he'd need a new job. Without hesitation Jimmy said he was hired. The crew could always do with a good bloke like him, but he asked Shaun if he was sure about joining them as there were bound to be reprisals from Nick.

"He's a fucking wanker who dicks young girls; with any luck someone will get to him before we do. That's another reason why I want out, he's in over his head and people die Jimmy!"

Closing his phone a few moments later, he looked at Mickey and said Shaun was in and as of then was officially working for them now. He remembered to add the Russians would be armed. Mickey had expected as much so had told the lads he'd called to tool up. The last man he had to call was Tony. It rang several times before he answered and asked Mickey how things were going; he hadn't expected Mickey's reply.

"Not good Tony, we've had a bit of trouble today. That photo you sent us stirred up a real fucking hornet's nest. Also there were other photos in Maurice's deposit box. I was going to call you later and tell you about it. We had a run in with some Russian friends of Nick's; they came to the club and started throwing their weight about."

"Be careful Mick, Maurice told me about the Russians, they're fucking dangerous. He set up a couple of parties for them with Nick, but they were too extreme even for him; that's why he got himself some insurance with the photos. He said Nick and the Russians were getting involved with some very powerful people. Maurice was no fool; he gave me a couple of photos in case anything happened to him. I feel really bad about it now; maybe it's what got him killed but I just wanted to help Jimmy out."

"Believe me Tony, the photo he gave you was only the tip of the iceberg. It was the ones from the deposit box that got him killed. I'll tell you later, but there are more important things to sort out now. I'll be straight with you; Nick broke into Jimmy's today and took the girl."

"Fuck me Mickey; this is getting out of hand. He shouldn't have done that, not to one of us. Has Jimmy thought about just letting him have her back?"

"Too late for that, Nick is using the Russians as muscle, he's made it personal. Things used to run smoothly but Nick has got too big for his fucking boots. If we back down now he'll have the upper hand and none of us want that. In a nut shell Tony, I'm asking if you'll help us out."

Without a second thought, Tony was in. Mickey explained their plan and said he would call him when they needed him.

Mickey told Jimmy what Tony had said before saying he wanted to stop at his office and pick up some more photocopies, just in case they needed them. Before leaving the apartment they rang Shane and Billy to ask them to change the number plates on their cars so they could use theirs, simply because they drove Range Rovers and they blended in better than a Ferrari

They talked about arranging a meeting time for the others to pick everyone up. While Mickey made the calls to give everyone the details, Jimmy was removing the false floor from inside a fitted wardrobe in his bedroom where, along with several other illegal items, he kept his guns. There was a small armoury hidden there. Returning to the lounge, he passed Mickey a small handgun and a handful of bullets.

Twenty minutes later, Jimmy looked out of the window and told him the others were outside.

Five minutes later they were approaching Shane's motor where they spotted Tony sitting in the back.

"Good to have you with us" said Jimmy as they got in.

Shane raised his hand out of the car window to acknowledge the others, who had just pulled up behind them. When they asked where they were going Mickey gave directions to the MP's manor house. That would be their destination as it seemed the most likely place Nick would have taken her, but first he wanted to call into his office to collect the copies.

The five men travelling in Shane's car talked about the job. When Jimmy asked if everyone was tooled up Shaun opened his jacket and flashed a sawn off shotgun.

"Well I must say that is discreet" joked Jimmy.

"Fuck me;" said Shane "London's answer to Dirty Harry!"

Even Shaun laughed before saying he wasn't taking any chances, the Russians were ruthless bastards!

They had been driving for about forty five minutes. Pointing to a slip road, Mickey indicated for him to drive up it. About two hundred yards in, they spotted a sign. It read, 'No access to road users; private property, trespassers will be prosecuted.'

"Aye this looks like the place," said Shaun, "all these dirty perverts are tucked up out of the way. This fucking country should bring back hanging for these fucking low lives!"

"Well maybe we could suggest that to him when we get there," said Mickey "after all he is a fucking MP."

Everyone laughed.

When Tony asked what the MP's name was, he laughed when told it was Aubrey Morton- Smyth. He exclaimed that was a real mouthful so they should just refer to him as arsehole because it had a nice ring to it! The laughing stopped as Mickey indicated for them to be quiet because he could see the MP's manor up ahead. After pulling up, Mickey suggested him and Jimmy walking up to the house to see who was about. If they weren't back in ten minutes the others were to come and find them.

Billy pulled up behind them. Walking over to his car Mickey told them the plan.

Minutes later, Mickey and Jimmy approached the rear of the manor. They could see several parked cars; the black people carrier they'd seen at Dixie's was there, along with a Bentley and a Range Rover. Peering in through the window they could see four Russians, the three who had been at the club earlier and one other. The MP was chatting with them; but there was no sign of Maria, Nick or Uri.

"Fuck me," said Jimmy as something startled them, "it's a fucking dog!"

Just a few feet from where they were standing was a kennel with a big German Shepherd chained to it. One of the Russians walked over to the window to investigate the dog barking. Hiding underneath the window they heard the MP say, "Don't worry about Barkley; he's probably heard a fox or something."

They waited until the Russian moved away from the window.

Pointing to where they had left the others, Mickey indicated for them to go back. A few minutes later they were telling the others they believed Maria was there. Exiting the cars quietly they all began making their way up to the manor, only this time going to the front of the house so as not to alert the dog. Mickey rang the bell assuming that the staff had been sent home. He knew he was right when the MP answered the door. Instantly Mickey stuck a gun under his chin and signalled to him to be quiet, then he indicated for Jacky Boy and Kevin to stay at the door while the other men followed the MP inside.

Walking into the room where the Russians were, Shaun pulled out his shotgun and said, "If any of you Ivans wants to be a fucking hero, just say so now, if not, put your weapons on the table."

They all placed their guns down on the table and then sat back down. Leaving Shane, Billy and Shaun to watch them; the others went to look for Maria. As they made their way quietly up the stairs, they could hear laughter. They were thrown off guard by a Russian coming out of a room. Before they could silence him, he shouted something. Jimmy shot at him, hitting him in the neck. Hearing the shot, one of the Russians downstairs threw an ashtray at Shaun to distract him, while another Russian grabbed a gun, which was hidden inside his boot. Billy took a slug in the arm as the Russians tried to get their weapons from the table. Shaun fired, missing one of them by barely an inch. One rushed at Billy, who despite having been shot delivered a fierce right hook knocking the Russian on his arse. It was pandemonium; everyone was trying to hide behind furniture or shoot someone. The MP was cowering under the table.

Upstairs, having been alerted to trouble, Nick and Uri had begun plotting their escape. Within seconds of the three friends reaching the upstairs landing, Jimmy kicked the door with such force it burst open. A warning shot was fired from inside to prevent them from entering. Trying to look into the room without getting shot, Jimmy indicated to the others that he couldn't see anyone. Tony picked up a vase which was housed on a small ornamental table in the hall and threw it into the room. There was no response. Crouching down low he made his way in. The room was empty, but a door to an adjoining room was open, which was an indication there could still be someone there.

They could still hear shots being fired downstairs as they slowly made their way into the other room, scanning it for several seconds before they agreed it was empty. The window was open so they assumed that Nick and Uri had escaped. It was as they continued to look Tony noticed something out of the corner of his eye. On a large bed in the corner of the room was a naked body. Instantly he alerted the others.

"It's Maria," shouted Jimmy as he rushed over to the bed where her lifeless body was tied to it.

Fresh blood stains were visible on the sheets and she was covered in cuts and bruises, there were cigarette burns on her chest and a leather strap pulled tight around her neck. Frantically he tried to undo the bindings which were cutting into her flesh where they were so tight. Mickey quickly took a penknife from his pocket which Charlie had bought for him so he always kept it with his keys. Trying not to hurt Maria, he desperately tried to cut the neck strap.

At that moment Shaun and the others appeared. The MP was with them, Shane was pressing a small gun into his back. Billy was pale from his wound; but he was confident he would be okay once he received medical treatment. Seeing Maria, Shaun rushed over to help but Tony said they were too late, she was dead.

Jimmy was frantically screaming her name; Mickey grabbed hold of him and pulled him away from the bed as he shouted for Tony to cover her up. Jimmy was ranting hysterically that the bastards who murdered her were going to pay! Pulling away from Mickey he rushed out of the bedroom and down the stairs into the lounge, he could see the four dead Russians lying in different areas of the room.

Kevin was standing in the hallway just inside the front door. Jimmy ran towards him and asked which way they went.

He didn't know. When the shooting had started he'd stayed at the door in case anyone came that way. He was just going to look for Jacky Boy as he hadn't returned since he ran out to stop anyone from getting to their cars and escaping.

Suddenly from upstairs someone shouted, "Jimmy!"

Rushing back up to the bedroom taking the stairs two at a time, he called to Kev to find Jacky Boy. Entering the room he could see Shaun giving Maria CPR. Realising the impact of what he was witnessing, he hurried over to the big Irishman and, placing his hand on his shoulder, tried to pull him off her and shouting at him to stop as she'd gone.

"No she fucking well ain't," exclaimed Shaun "I've got a pulse!"

Immediately on hearing Shaun's words, Jimmy grabbed her and shouted at her not to leave him and fight! Although it was barely noticeable, he heard a noise. She was trying to breathe.

For a brief moment she tried to open her eyes as she raised her hand to touch his face. Begging her not to leave him, he whispered in her ear that he loved her just as her eyes closed and she drifted into unconsciousness.

"She needs to get to hospital now," exclaimed Shaun.

"You take her," said Jimmy "Shane can drive; you go with them Billy and get that wound checked out. "I trust you with her life Shaun. I need to sort things out here. That bastard is not getting away with this; as soon as I can I'll meet you there. Give Doc Daniels a bell on the way; we don't want any awkward questions at the hospital. He'll sort all that out for you."

Shane left to bring the car up to the manor. Jimmy gently wrapped her in a blanket and lifted her from the bed. Her body was limp; she was barely clinging to life. Tenderly he kissed her head and begged her to hang on because he didn't want to live without her, he loved her and he'd see her soon.

Shaun held out his arms and lifted her from Jimmy as he told him to find Nick and the Russians and make them pay for what they'd done.

When Jimmy asked him to look after her and not let her die because he loved her, Shaun replied "Aye Jimmy so do I."

Billy asked what they wanted him to do with the MP. Mickey said to tie him up. The MP winced as Billy tied his hands.

"Ops sorry did that hurt you? If it was up to me they'd be round your fucking neck!" said Billy as he pulled the straps tighter.

The MP was moaning and shouting they wouldn't get away with what they were doing.

"Shut the fuck up," said Billy as he pulled the MP's tie off and stuffed it into his mouth. "I only wish I could stay and watch my friends deal with you, but unfortunately I have to go. I'm sure by the time they've finished you'll be begging them to kill you! Frankly I hope they cut your cock off and leave you to bleed to death, you fucking dirty old pervert!"

Looking absolutely terrified, the MP made mumbled noises through the gag; beads of sweat were running down his forehead. Billy was just about to say something to him when Kevin shouted up the stairs that Jacky Boy had been stabbed!

When Kevin had gone to look for him, he'd had found him at the rear of the manor lying on the ground. Picking him up he'd carried him back to the house.

Shaun was already halfway down the stairs carrying Maria. He passed her to Jimmy who was right behind him. Shaun rushed to help Jacky; he could see his shirt was soaked in blood. Kevin was kneeling down next to him putting pressure on the wound with a table cloth he'd grabbed from a hall table. Shaun knelt down and slowly lifted the cloth off.

"He's lost a lot of blood; looks like a knife through the guts," said Shaun "keep up with the pressure Kev."

Jacky Boy was unconscious, drenched in blood and failing fast. Shaun knew he needed to get him and Maria to hospital quickly or they would both die. At that moment, Shane pulled up in the Range Rover. With not a minute to spare, they got in and sped quickly away.

From the car Billy called Doc Daniels to tell him they were on their way to the hospital and for him to meet them there. Jimmy and the others waited until they were out of sight before going back inside the manor.

His two friends kept telling Jimmy that Shaun would get there on time and that she would make it. He felt guilty he hadn't gone with her, but he had to find Nick before the fucker got away! He swore to his friends that Nick was going down that night.

The three of them made their way back up the stairs. The MP, still bound and gagged heard them coming. Terrified he began rocking the chair and mumbling. Entering the room they made their way over to the terrified man. Tony spat at him as he approached. Jimmy asked Mickey for one of the photos of the MP in his bondage gear. Mickey took one from his pocket and passed it to him.

Standing in front of the terrified MP and holding the photo up in front of him, Jimmy said "The gear you're wearing there, where is it?"

The MP shook his head and mumbled something, which indicated that he wasn't going to co-operate. Jimmy punched him full pelt in the face; blood gushed from his nose as Jimmy snarled and asked again if it was in the house. The terrified man nodded and flicked his head in the direction of a large walk in closet to indicate where it was. The MP was co-operating; his air of earlier defiance was gone. Tony walked over to check out the closet.

"Fuck me," he said as he opened it, "you two might want to see this."

Walking over to investigate what he was looking at, both men stopped dead in their tracks as they looked inside. It was full of adult costumes, ranging from Nazi SS uniforms to schoolboy clothes; there was even a priest's robe. The other side of the closet held all types of depraved torture implements which included nipple piercers, whips and vibrators with metal pins protruding from them.

"Quite a selection you have here Aubrey;" said Jimmy looking over at the MP, "do you use these things on little boys?"

Shaking and mumbling the MP shook his head.

"Oh please don't try and deny it" said Jimmy arrogantly, "you fucking sick bastard! We have a feature length film of you abusing young boys Aubrey. You are a fucking disgusting, poor excuse for a man! Oh look lads the poor old fucker's crying, he's scared. So you fucking should be! Pick something out for Aubrey to wear Tony."

"I've seen just the gear for him Jim."

Reaching into the closet, Tony pulled out a biker's full leather get up.

Jimmy said it was a good choice as he began to untie the MP. When he finished, he took out his gun and aimed it at the terrified man, threatening him that if he moved he would blow his bollocks off!

Shaking with fear the terrified man pulled the gag out of his mouth and begged them to let him go, stating he was very rich and they could take whatever they wanted. Jimmy told him to shut the fuck up and strip off. Too afraid not to, the MP began to undress, until he was standing in just his underpants. After Jimmy shouted for him to strip completely, gingerly the MP removed his pants and stood with his hands in front of his cock.

"Fuck me, don't bother covering that Aubrey;" said Mickey laughing "I've seen bigger fucking maggots!"

His friends watched as Jimmy chucked the gear at him and ordered him to put it on and to fucking hurry up about it.

"Please don't do this," pleaded the MP "I'm begging you."

"I fucking warned you if you said another word I'd shoot one of your balls off! Not that you'd notice if I did, from where I'm standing they look like two tiny marbles flopping about in a bag!"

Everyone except the MP laughed.

After the MP put the gear on, Tony wolf whistled him as he stood in front of them dressed in tight leather trousers, leather chest straps, biker boots and a little leather waistcoat, finishing the outfit off with a tiny leather cap. It was as much as the trio could do to contain their laughter. Had the matter not been so serious they would have prolonged the MP's suffering. Jimmy asked how old he was. In a shaky, nervous voice the MP said he was sixty three.

"Have you any idea how fucking ridiculous you look? Do dirty old men like you really parade around dressed like that? Does it give you a hard on, or do you do it to frighten little boys?"

"It's fucking frightening me Jim," said Mickey as he burst into laughter, quickly joined by the others.

"Strange thing is," said Jimmy, "in your film Aubrey you acted all tough and macho; not quite the image you're showing now, is it! What a fucking shame I didn't bring my video camera. Did it ever occurred to you that the young boys you fucked and tortured were probably feeling the way you are now? Well let me tell you this, unless you tell us exactly what we want to know, every day for the next twenty years you will know what it feels like to be raped and terrorised because we'll see to it that you go to prison. Oh and I know what you're thinking; you're an MP who carries a lot of clout, so you could avoid prison. Under normal circumstances Aubrey you'd be right, but these are not normal circumstances are they? Fortunately we have some very sick photos and recordings of other powerful men, men who I can guarantee will have no problem sending you down if it means us keeping quiet about them. Just out of curiosity Aubrey, have you ever had a ten inch black cock rammed up your arse? The reason I ask is a friend of ours by the name of Maurice was murdered. No doubt when his many gay friends in prison find out you ordered the hit I would imagine they won't be too happy."

"I had nothing to do with that;" stuttered the MP, "it was Nick and Uri!"

"Well I know that and you know that, but Maurice's friends don't and who do you think they'll believe, a dirty old pervert who likes to rape little boys or me?"

The terrified man begged them to tell him what they wanted from him. When Jimmy said they wanted to know where Nick and the Russian were, the MP swore he didn't know. Jimmy threatened him not to test his patience as he asked Tony to pass him a whip. Seconds later, he lashed the MP across the face and asked him again where Nick had gone. Again the terrified MP pleaded for him to believe he didn't know. He continued crying and begging and kept repeating he would give them whatever they wanted, if they just left him alone. Without any regard for his victim, Jimmy lashed him again and again as he stated that anything they wanted they would simply take. Finally Jimmy stopped and walked over to the closet, browsing over the torture implements before picking out the nipple piercers and walking back towards the MP.

"These are good," said Jimmy "I didn't realise the nipple rings are actually loaded into them. Looks like all I have to do is put your chosen body area in between the two edges and squeeze. So what do you fancy first Aubrey, nipple, cock, or maybe your lip, I'll let you choose."

As he moved closer to him, the MP tried to run but the others grabbed him, dragged him across the room and threw him onto a chair. Then with one either side of him they held him firmly as Jimmy placed the piercers over one of his nipples. Looking as though he would pass out as his nipple was pierced; the MP screamed and begged them to leave him alone.

"Shut the fuck up!" said Tony as he punched him in the face "if you don't tell us what we want to know things are going to get a lot worse, you fucking dirty pig!"

When his other nipple was pierced he did actually pass out. Jimmy slapped him hard round the face and said for him not to pass out again as the party was just getting started! Jimmy told the others to stand him up. They could see his legs were like jelly, he was barely able to stand.

"Right that's your nipples done," said Jimmy "and I must say Aubrey, piercings suit you, now get your cock out!"

When he refused, Jimmy picked up the whip and lashed him several more times, ripping through the flesh on his chest.

"Alright, alright!" screamed the MP hysterically, fumbling to undo the zipper on the trousers, "what are you going to do? Oh God please help me!"

"Isn't that half the fun of these sex games Aubrey, the adrenalin rushes, the anticipation of not knowing? Even God wouldn't help you, you disgusting fuck, now shut the fuck up! Tie him to the bed; we're just wasting time. Let's finish this!"

The MP kicked and screamed as they dragged him across the room being kicked and punched several times before he was secured to the bed. Terrified he laid there tethered, struggling frantically when Jimmy moved towards his cock and pinched some of his foreskin between the edges of the pincers. Screaming and thrashing about, he pleaded for them to stop.

"Shut the fuck up!" said, Jimmy coldly "how many fucking kids have you tortured? I bet they fucking begged you to stop, so I'll show you the same degree of mercy you showed them! Anyway it probably won't be that bad, because I don't want to touch your fucking cock. I know where it's fucking been! I'll probably only nip the tip!"

The others laughed until Jimmy squeezed down hard on the piercers. Screaming pitifully the MP pulled frantically at his ties.

"Fuck me that's making my fucking eyes water," said Mickey "rather you than me Aubrey."

The three friends laughed.

Eventually the terrified man stopped screaming. Although totally traumatised and in terrible pain, he was still reluctant to tell them where the others had gone. Jimmy took a large Cuban cigar and a book of matches from a box which was housed along with bottle of vodka on a table just a few feet away. Lighting the cigar, he took several draws on it before telling the MP this was going to be painful.

The MP begged and begged as Jimmy walked back towards the bed. Now completely devoid of any feelings or compassion Jimmy ignored him. He wanted to hurt him and make him suffer. The end of the cigar was glowing as he drew hard on the butt before removing it from his mouth. Then without a second thought, he held it on the MP's cock, pushing it down harder every time he screamed. The others just watched as he inflicted excruciating pain on the man. Mickey knew he wouldn't stop until the MP told him what he wanted to know; either that or he would kill him in the process. This was the dark side; the cruel merciless side of Jimmy that concerned him.

Struggling and screaming with pain the MP screamed, "Please God no more!"

"Come, come Aubrey, I'm sure you've done worse than this to your boys. I'm sure you must secretly be enjoying it? Just tell me where they've gone and I'll stop, all this can be over."

Aubrey could barely speak; he was obviously on the verge of passing out again when Jimmy reached over and grabbed the vodka bottle and poured it over the MP's face to keep him conscious.

"Please, please," screamed the MP "I'm begging you, no more please! In the name of God please!"

"Like I told you, God won't help you, but I'll stop when you tell me what I want to know. Now where have they gone?"

When the MP continued to refuse to tell him, Jimmy drew on the cigar again before repeating the torture. The

MP writhed and screamed in agony and screamed out for God to help him as he begged Jimmy to stop. Defiantly, Jimmy kept drawing on the cigar and told him all the pain could stop if he just told him where they'd gone. Unable to withstand the pain, the MP screamed out that he would tell him.

"Now that's better, you could have saved yourself all that suffering. Oh and before you confess Aubrey, I should tell you Tony will be staying here with you, just in case you lie to me. Once we've located Nick and the Russian, I'll bell him and he'll let you go. If we don't find them, he'll kill you. I'm not sure exactly how he'd do it; but let's just hope for your sake it's quick."

The MP was shaking and having difficulty speaking coherently as he asked how he could be sure Jimmy would keep his word and let him go.

"Quite frankly you can't Aubrey, but unlike your so called friends who fucked off and left you here, my word is solid. We know you can't go to the police; we have too much on you, so it would be in everyone's best interests to let you live. After all, there may come a time when we have a use for you. In fact, a good friend of ours would like to request this country bringing back the death penalty. Maybe when you're feeling better Aubrey you could look into that for him?"

The others were trying not to laugh.

Desperately wanting his torture to end, in a shaky voice the MP said he had no choice but to believe him, he was in a no win situation. He told them there was a small cottage on the estate. If they drove along the dirt track at the rear of the property for about a mile they would see it. Just past the lake on the right the track veered off, if they followed it for about fifty yards they'd find the cottage. That was where they were hiding. Jimmy said there was just one more thing he needed to know. When they were torturing and raping the girl, had he joined in or had he just watched. Professing his innocence, the MP swore he was downstairs with the others and had no part in it. It was down to Nick and Uri! He looked terrified when in an aggressive tone, Jimmy asked if it had occurred to him to try and stop them when he'd heard her screaming and begging for her life?

"I couldn't do anything," he said pitifully "they would have killed me!"

As Jimmy began to walk away from the bed, the MP called after him. Jimmy turned abruptly and said, "What?"

The MP stated he had helped them so he wanted him to keep his word and tell Tony to let him go once he had found Nick and Uri. Without saying a word, Jimmy pulled out his gun and aimed it at him. The MP screamed and in the name of God begged him not to shoot, stating he had helped them and Jimmy had given him his word.

"I lied," said Jimmy coldly as he pulled the trigger and shot him through the forehead.

Moments later they left the room.

Mickey made no bones about being happy that Jimmy had shot him. In his opinion the MP's days of dicking little boys were over and it was one less fucking pervert for them to worry about.

Tony agreed before saying he would go and get the car while they checked the house.

It didn't take them long to locate the house safe. Jimmy said it was a piece of piss and he'd be in it within five minutes.

Inside was about four hundred grand in cash and some jewellery, but the real find was a little red book. Written inside were the names of several prominent VIPs who were paying for sordid sex orgies, with their preferences to gender and age clearly written next to their names.

After putting everything in their jackets they stood at the door waiting for Tony. Moments later he pulled up. Jimmy took a can of petrol from the back of the car and, returning to the lounge, doused the carpets and furniture along with the bodies of the dead Russians. Then he walked out of the door and calmly striking a match threw it behind him into the doorway.

Within minutes the manor was ablaze.

Following the MP's directions they drove towards the cottage. After several minutes they could see a dim light in the distance, so they parked the car and continued on foot. Nearing the cottage they could see someone moving about inside.

"You two go round the back," said Jimmy "I'll take the front. Don't take Nick out. That pleasure is going to be mine."

Making their way slowly in the darkness of the country side, Mickey and Tony edged their way around the rear of the building where Tony signalled to him that he could see a light. With his gun in his hand, he made his way towards it, stopping only to wait for Mickey.

Looking through the window, Mickey could see Uri the Russian standing with his back to the window talking to Nick who was sitting at a kitchen table. Mickey had a clear shot of the Russian, so quietly he indicated to Tony that he was going to take him out. No sooner had Tony nodded his head when he heard the shot ring out. The bullet smashed through the window and hit Uri in the back of the head; he was dead before he hit the ground. With the Russian lying dead, Nick ran into another room, turning the lights out so as not to be seen.

Tony called out to Jimmy the Russian was dead. Hearing him, Jimmy called out for Nick to come out. The reply from Nick was "Fuck you."

Jimmy warned him if he wasn't out in thirty seconds, he would burn the fucking place down with him in it.

Nick knew he was in a no win situation, but he wasn't about to give up or go down without a fight. Typically he would try and talk his way out of it, or at least goad Jimmy into coming in to find him. His thoughts being if he was going down, he wasn't going alone. Someone, namely Jimmy, was going down with him.

"Was that fucking whore worth this Jimmy?" shouted Nick, "she was a whore Jimmy, that's why I had to kill her! She wanted to die; she asked me to kill her, but that would have been too easy, so I let the Russian have her. She left me no choice but to fucking kill her after that! Tell you the truth, I was glad to see her dead, she made my fucking head ache with all her fucking begging and screaming!"

Jimmy could barely contain his fury; he wanted to rush at the door and confront him. Had Tony not have appeared and told him to keep Nick talking because Mickey thought he'd found a way in round the back, he would have.

"What's the matter Jimmy," shouted Nick "are you upset that the whore is dead? I warned her if she ever let another man touch her I'd fucking kill her! So what does the fucking stupid bitch do, only fucking tells me that she let you fuck her. She said she loved you; signed her own fucking death certificate the fucking stupid whore! If only she had kept her fucking mouth shut I could have sold her to the Russians, they would have put her in one of their brothels; but all she kept saying was I love Jimmy! After all I'd done for her, the fucking ungrateful bitch! I fucking did her myself. I watched the fucking life drain out of her!"

Finally Jimmy answered as calmly as he could in order to rile him and give Mickey time to get in.

"Well you didn't finish it Nick, she's alive. Maybe for the first time in her life she had something to live for. Who knows, maybe it was her love for me that kept her alive?"

As he waited for Nick to answer, a gunshot rang out from inside the cottage. Jimmy rushed at the door, followed by Tony.

Inside, Mickey was standing over Nick, pointing his gun at him. He'd shot him in the arm. Only a minor wound which momentarily had forced him to drop his gun which was lying a few feet away.

Moments later, Nick was looking up at the three men and telling Tony he was surprised he got involved in the situation. With an air of arrogance, Tony told him he'd never liked him, a fact which he thought Nick had been aware of. His arrogance turned to hatred when Nick implied it was because Tony was jealous of him.

"Fuck off! Why would you imagine for one minute I'd be jealous of you," snapped Tony "you're nothing but scum! You know I always thought you were responsible for my Uncle Carlo's death. We were all young and ambitious back then, but you were brutal Nick; you wanted power and you didn't care who you killed to get it!"

"Oh yeah, that was so long ago I'd all but forgotten about poor old Uncle Carlo. I remember watching him after the accident when he dragged himself from the car. I can still recall the smell of his flesh burning as he begged me to shoot him. Of course me being so brutal, I couldn't do that so I just watched him burn! But like you said we were young then, just kids really."

Fuelled by hatred and anger, Tony kicked him in the face knocking him flat to the ground.

Jimmy snarled at Nick to get up and grabbing him by the shirt collar pulled him to his feet. Mickey picked up the gun from the floor, before he and Tony moved to the edge of the room. Nick immediately took a swing at Jimmy, but he wasn't quick enough and missed. Jimmy was raging with anger as he punched him several times with a series of blows to the face and body. With Nick momentarily dazed, Jimmy took pleasure in goading him.

"What's the matter Nick, don't you like it when someone hits back? Or is it only women and kids you feel tough around, especially when they're tied down. Does it make you feel powerful; you piece of shit! You're a sadistic bastard who thinks he's tough, so come on let's see what you've got!"

"Is she worth dying for Jimmy?" said Nick still trying to bargain "we could have everything, money, clubs, women, fast cars; she was just a little tart that I bought for ten grand. I should have sold her on once I fucked her, but that's me, I'm all fucking heart!"

Jimmy had heard enough, he let loose with a barrage of blows to his head. Blood was pouring from Nick's nose and mouth, until finally he hit the floor. Jimmy kicked him several times in the head before stopping. Nick was barely conscious when he looked at Mickey and asked why he'd got involved, Maria meant nothing to him she was just a whore. Mickey glared at him and said he'd crossed the line when he brought his daughter Charlie into it and made it personal!"

"Nice piece of arse that girl of yours Mick, I could have done things with her!"

Mickey raised his foot and stamped down hard on his face, feeling the bones crush under the impact.

"Like I said Nick," he said glaring down on him, "you crossed the fucking line!"

The three men had all but beaten him to death when Jimmy called a halt. Nick was lying in a pool of blood, his face was unrecognisable as the once handsome man he was. With his eyes so badly cut and swollen, he could barely make out the figures of the three men standing above him.

Jimmy asked Mickey to fetch the other petrol can from the car. While they waited for him to return, Jimmy continued to taunt Nick.

"So you thought the Russians would protect you Nick?" Just goes to show, you can't rely on anyone for protection these days. Just out of curiosity, did Maria tell you she couldn't get enough of me; she said I was a real man that satisfied her and that you were a lousy fuck!"

Nick was barely alive, but Jimmy knew he could hear him.

Within a few minutes, Mickey returned with the petrol can. He poured some over Nick before passing the can to Jimmy, who then poured the rest over the furniture and floor. Passing Tony a lighter, Jimmy thought the honour should be his for his Uncle.

"This one's for Uncle Carlo," snarled Tony as he threw the lighter onto him, "I'll see you in hell Nick!"

They could hear Nick screaming as they walked away. From the moment he knew Nick was as good as dead, all Jimmy wanted was to get to the hospital for Maria.

They could hear sirens and see the manor burning in the distance as they drove rapidly away.

"Do you reckon there'll be any retaliation" said Mickey "from the Russians?"

"Naugh" said Tony "they won't know it was us and due to the people they sold kids to we'd be the last people on their list. Compared to them Nick was small time, I doubt they'll even bother to look."

Twenty minutes later they were pulling up outside the hospital. Jimmy jumped out and ran through the main entrance doors. Just as he reached the information desk, he spotted Doc Daniels talking to Kevin and Shane. As he approached them he asked where Maria was and if she was going to be ok. Doc looked upset when he told him they weren't sure, she was in a bad way, there was some internal damage. They'd taken her to theatre and although the surgery had gone well, she'd slipped into a coma. With a look of desperation, Jimmy said she would be ok though. The Doc's expression was telling him it was hard to say whether she'd live or die, he just didn't know. Jimmy felt a glimmer of hope when Doc added that sometimes when a person suffers such trauma a coma was the body's way of giving it time to heal, but only time would tell.

Jimmy asked after Jacky Boy and Billy and was relieved to hear that Billy would be fine; fortunately the bullet had gone straight through missing his arteries. The news wasn't so positive for Jacky Boy. He'd been taken to surgery, it was touch and go because he'd lost a lot of blood. The surgeon had told Doc another ten minutes in the car and Jacky Boy would have bled to death.

Before he could say anything else, a surgeon from the emergency department walked towards them. It was hard to tell from his expression whether the news he had to tell them was good or bad. They were all relived and thankful when he told them Jacky Boy had survived the surgery and was a lucky man. Had the knife he'd been stabbed with been half an inch longer they would probably be having a different conversation. Now Jacky Boy's biggest risk was from infection as the surgeon had to remove one of his kidneys. He would be in intensive care for a while and then all being well they'd move him to a room. The surgeon contributed him surviving to the fact he was young and fit.

Shaking the surgeon's hand they thanked him. It was as he turned to leave, he looked back and suggested next time they were out drinking and a fight broke out they should simply walk away as they may not be so lucky next time.

Jimmy soon cottoned on that Doc Daniels had obviously told the hospital that they'd been involved in a fight.

Jimmy asked Doc to take him to Maria, he wanted to see her. Before the Doc could answer the other two appeared. Tony was moaning about how long it had taken to find a parking space. When Mickey asked how everyone was, Jimmy said Doc would explain, but first he was taking him to see Maria. As expected Mickey was going with him.

Leaving the others to talk, they left. Turning into a corridor they could see Shaun sitting outside her room. They both acknowledged him before Doc suggested them going for a coffee while he spoke to the surgeon to ask if Jimmy could see Maria.

Before they left, Mickey patted his friend on the shoulder and with sincerity said Maria would be okay.

Doc Daniels went into her room and spoke to the doctor who was tending her; moments later they came out. He stood quietly while the surgeon spoke to Jimmy and explained that Maria was unlikely to respond, but he believed she could hear them.

Entering the room, Jimmy was shocked as he looked at her lying motionless in the bed. Her face was swollen and bruised; he wouldn't have recognised her instantly had he not known it was her. All around the bed were tubes and wires attached to her via monitors. She looked so pale and fragile; he could not hold back his tears. Approaching the bed he noticed how badly bruised her neck was from were Nick had tried to strangle her with the leather strapping. Taking her hand in his, he tried to talk to her but was unable to stop crying. The entire length of her arm was covered in burns and human bites, just like the day she arrived at his apartment a few weeks earlier, only the new wounds now covering the last remnants of the old ones.

"Maria babe it's me," he said "don't leave me babe. No one is ever going to hurt you again, I promise. I hope you can hear me, because I want you to know Nick is dead; he can't hurt you anymore. I love you babe, I want to spend the rest of my life with you."

She didn't respond. It was as though she was in a deep sleep unaware of what was going on around her.

A doctor entered the room and in a kind manner told Jimmy not to expect too much as she could be like that for days and in some cases weeks or even months, they had no way of telling. However, he was happy to say the results of the tests they'd run showed there was no permanent brain damage. Now her body just needed time to heal at its own pace.

Jimmy took some comfort from the doctor's words. Before leaving he kissed her forehead, telling her to hang in there and he'd see her soon.

He met up with the others in the waiting room and instantly asked if there was any more news on Jacky Boy. He was happy to hear he was going to be ok.

Shaun asked after Maria before telling them he was going home.

Before everyone left, Mickey asked if they could meet at the club at midday the following day.

They all nodded.

Tony drove the other car, dropping Jimmy and Mickey back off at the apartment.

Back at Jimmy's, the two friends went over the day's events. Jimmy suggested sending out for takeaway as they were both starving. While they waited for their supper to arrive, Jimmy said he'd put the money from the MP's house in his safe. They talked about what to do with it. Mickey suggested giving the lads a bonus. The intercom rang just as Jimmy was about to reply. It was their takeaway.

Five minutes later they were eating and talking. Jimmy agreed that giving the lads a bonus was a great idea and asked Mickey what sort of figure he had in mind.

"Fuck me" he exclaimed and almost chocked when Mickey replied "What about twenty grand each, they earned it. The way I look at it is, all those boys stuck with us today and let's face it things could have been a lot worse. Jacky Boy lost his kidney; it could have been his life."

When Jimmy agreed and asked what they would do with the rest, Mickey grinned. He was sure they could find a good use for it. He already had a couple of ideas which they could discuss at a later date, but there was something else he wanted to ask him.

Jimmy nodded and said "What?"

"I've been thinking about the stuff in Maurice's deposit box Jimmy. Now Nick and the Russians are out of the way, maybe we could send it on. I think it's time the dirty perverts like Quinton were put in the spotlight. At the very least it'll stop perverts like him dicking kids. I thought maybe we could sort of drop them in Monica's lap. I know she wouldn't let anything go and she would have the resources to follow up on the other perverts in the photos. Personally I think we should just find them and cut their fucking knobs off! The other thing is the money; I don't think we really need to tell Tony; after all he certainly doesn't need it. Anyway think about it, we can talk tomorrow; I know you're worried about Maria."

With genuine remorse, Jimmy said he felt really bad about what happened to her; especially after he'd promised he wouldn't let anyone hurt her again. Reassuringly Mickey told him none of what happened had been his fault and if anything, he'd given her a reason to live.

"I hope you're right Mick, she deserves something. I'm not sure it's me though."

"Fuck me you are joking, she's nuts about you! And don't give me all that old bollocks about it's because you're fucking kind to her. I've seen the way you two are together; it's meant to be mate."

Taking comfort from his words, Jimmy thanked him and said he hoped he was right.

Fifteen minutes later after telling Jimmy to try and get some sleep and he'd see him the following day at the club, Mickey left. Jimmy thanked him for everything as he headed towards the door.

Taking his friends advice, Jimmy drank another scotch and then turned in for the night. Despite his tiredness, he tossed and turned all night, unable to get the image of Maria lying tied to that bed out of his head. It was more than he could bear to imagine what they had done to her. When they had found her, his first thoughts were all the Russians had raped and tortured her. He'd felt relieved when the MP told him they hadn't, but even knowing they were dead, he still felt such white hot fury as he thought about them. Gazing up at the ceiling he made a promise to himself, if she survived he would do something really special for her.

The entire night he tossed and turned, unable to drift off to sleep. Finally feeling frustrated with the fact he couldn't sleep he got up at first light. It seemed strange not having her there. Even though she had only been there for a short time, he enjoyed having her around. The apartment seemed empty without her.

At eight o'clock that morning he phoned the hospital. The sister on duty told him Maria had a peaceful night. When he'd asked if she had regained consciousness, he was disappointed when she said no. For the first time in years he was at a loss; it was too early to go out and he didn't want to go back to bed. Not wanting to stay in the apartment, he decided to go for a walk which was not something he would normally do. Although he wasn't going anywhere in particular when he left the apartment, twenty minutes later he found himself standing outside St Augustus church. Hesitating for a moment, he looked up at the church. It felt as though something was drawing him as he began walking towards the doors. He'd not been in a church since his mother's death; simply because he'd blamed God for letting her die.

Sitting down in the back row he thought he was the only person there. Briefly glancing up at the statue of Christ, he put his head in his hands and quietly said, "I'm not here for myself, I've come to ask you to let Maria live. I'm not a particularly good person, but she is and I think you owe her. You've let her down badly and she didn't deserve any of it."

Briefly he scanned the other pews to see if anyone had come in. Still believing he was alone he continued his prayer.

"This will be the only chance for you to prove to me that you care. If you want to punish someone, punish me not her. I promise if you let her live, I'll look after her and love her for the rest of her life."

He hadn't noticed the priest come in until he said 'good morning' to him and asked if he could help him with anything.

Looking up at him, Jimmy thanked him, but with a smile stated he was beyond help.

"Would you like me to hear your confession so God can be the judge of that?" asked the priest "if whatever you've done is that terrible perhaps we can ask God to forgive you?"

To the priest's clear surprise, Jimmy said he didn't need God to forgive him; he could live with what he'd done. Although he didn't feel like talking, Jimmy nodded when the priest asked if he could sit with him and offering his hand introduced himself as Father Thomas.

"Jimmy Dixon."

The priest asked if St Augustus was his parish and apologised for not knowing, but he had only been there a few days so he wasn't familiar with his parishioners. Shaking his head Jimmy said he didn't go to church, he was an atheist. With a frown, the priest questioned why he was there. Jimmy was quick to explain, he wasn't there for him but for someone else. The priest asked if it was a member of his family or simply a friend.

"Let's just say it's someone I love Father; someone who has made me want to love again."

"That's good Jimmy, love is a very powerful emotion."

Despite his hatred for the church, he actually found himself warming to Father Thomas. In fact, he thought in a different world they could actually be friends. Unlike the priests he remembered from his childhood who had all been old and set in their ways, Thomas was different. In his early forties, plump with a slightly receding hair line, he had a warm friendly attitude, the total opposite to the likes of Father O'Brien.

Now happy to talk, Jimmy asked him what had brought him to St Augustus.

"Unfortunately my predecessor Father O'Brien died. Apparently he had been here for years, although I never met him. There have been rumours about him, actually he was murdered; he died in hospital as a result of an attack on him. We thought the motive was robbery, but the police think he may have had dealings outside of the church."

Jimmy tried hard not to grin when he asked what sort of dealings.

"I really cannot say, but that's why I'm here; the church doesn't like scandal. Sadly since he died we'll never know, but I want to bring people back to the church. You see Jimmy I have never doubted God; my faith is as strong today as when I joined the church twenty four years ago."

The priest detected a hint of sarcasm as Jimmy replied, "So you believe God listens to you then?"

"Oh I know he does," said the priest with conviction.

Despite Jimmy's total lack of faith, there was something in the way Thomas had replied that made Jimmy want to believe. So much so, he asked him to ask God to help Maria. The priest smiled and after saying 'of course,' suggested they both pray for Maria.

Not wishing to offend the priest, he politely reminded him that he didn't believe. Father Thomas smiled, not because of Jimmy's reply, but because he had heard him praying when he'd thought no one could see or hear him. Jimmy smiled when the priest said it was ok if he didn't believe, because he had enough faith for both of them. The church doors would always be open to him and he would pray for Maria every day.

Standing up to leave, Jimmy said he would appreciate it.

CHAPTER 18

Mickey and Shaun were already at the club when Jimmy arrived, the others arrived ten minutes later. The six men sat round the table as Mickey poured everyone a drink and waited until everyone was settled.

"Right," said Mickey "the reason we've called this meeting is to tell you we managed to retrieve Maurice's safety deposit box, the contents were something of a shock to say the least. There were some very explicit photographs of kids being abused by very high profile men. Also DVDs of Nick and several other men torturing and, we believe, murdering kids. Now as you're all aware of the events of yesterday, Nick and his Russian friend won't be abusing anyone else."

"Fucking good riddance," said Shane "all animals like them should be fucking terminated!"

"I think we'd all agree on that, but back to business. I've discussed the contents of the box at length with Jimmy and after some thought we came up with the idea of passing it on to Monica, who, as you all know I'm seeing. Obviously it would be done anonymously; we don't want to draw any suspicion to us but I know she would do right by those kids. So can we have a show of hands of all in agreement with me passing it on?"

In principle they all agreed, the show of hands was unanimous. They talked about some of the people who were in the photos as some of them were known to them. Tony suggested it might be a good idea to keep the QC Quinton's film and photos back as there may be a time in the future when they needed his services. Having a judge in their pocket could definitely have its advantages.

Mickey stated they had both questioned whether or not to do that, but they didn't like the idea of the QC getting off scot free, especially as they knew what he did to kids.

"Why don't we just cut his fucking bollocks off and choke him with them," said Shaun "or just let the fucker bleed to death!"

"That's what I like about you Shaun," laughed Jimmy "you're such a sweet gentle soul."

Everyone laughed.

"Talking of people bleeding to death Shaun," continued Jimmy "I must say you were great yesterday; you really seemed to know what you were doing. We all thought Maria was dead; how come you know about that sort of stuff?"

The big Irishman felt slightly embarrassed but before he could answer, Mickey said he'd been a regular fucking Doc Martin.

They all laughed.

Shaun proudly stated it all came down to his eldest boy Liam being a paramedic. When he was doing his training he used to practice on Shaun and Ann.

Laughing, Jimmy said it was a good trade, one which no doubt they had supplied plenty of business to over the years. He was curious to know why Liam hadn't wanted to work with Shaun though. Shaun believed he did want to but his mother, Ann, wouldn't hear of it; she insisted all the kids had regular jobs. Mickey interrupted and after saying she sounded like a good woman, asked how long they'd been married. Shaun replied thirty two years and that Mickey had been right, they didn't come any better than his Ann. Tony joked and stated he would have served less time for murder.

Jimmy asked Shaun to tell them about Ann.

"Nought to tell really, I met her when I was eighteen. She was sixteen; a wee scrap of a lass back then, but I knew from the minute I laid eyes on her she was the girl for me. I married her when I was twenty. We've had our ups and downs over the years, but I wouldn't change a thing. It was love at first sight."

Thinking of the way he felt about Maria, Jimmy took heart from what he'd said, until Mickey interrupted his train of thought by stating they should get back to business. He suggested voting on whether to keep the QC or sell him out.

Everyone thought it would be wisest to keep him.

"The dirty old bastard will probably think twice before attending any more orgies," said Shaun "especially if we put the frighteners on him."

They all agreed.

So it was agreed. Mickey would give Monica the recordings and photos, even though they couldn't take any credit for it because she would receive them anonymously. It was as Mickey finished discussing business, Jimmy handed them all an envelope each and told them it was a bonus for the previous day and they'd all earned it. Kevin opened his and looking inside said, "Fuck me!" as he saw the wad of money.

They all laughed when Mickey said that should get him a few shags. They would keep hold of Billy's and Jacky Boy's until they came out of hospital. Shaun peered inside his envelope; being the newest member of the crew he hadn't expected anything, let alone the same amount as the others. With a look of genuine gratitude, he said it was very much appreciated. In all the years he'd worked for Nick he'd never had a bonus like that. Unlike Nick, they would look after the lads and now they'd be taking over

Nick's end of the business there would be more where that came from.

They were interrupted by Shane's phone. It was Simone, she could leave a message and he'd get back to her later. Jimmy told him to answer it as it might be important.

Shane answered the call and asked what she wanted. The others sat quietly as he listened to her. It was obvious all was not well when he asked if she was sure she was ok because she didn't sound it, he could barely make out what she was saying. He ended the call by telling her not to worry, as he was sure they could manage without her for a couple of days.

They all looked at him as he closed his phone and Mickey asked him if everything was ok.

"Yeah no worries Mick, Simone's had a bad fall, Sharon's been up the hospital with her. Thankfully there are no broken bones, but sounds like she'll be off for a few days. I'll sort out some cover for her."

It was Jimmy who asked if she'd said where it had happened. Shane wasn't sure, but from the sound of things it possibly happened when she left work because she hadn't got home from the hospital until six o'clock that morning.

Mickey said they'd send her some flowers then changed the subject and asked if they'd eaten. When they shook their heads, he suggested taking them for dinner at their restaurant.

Thirty minutes later they were sitting in the restaurant. As they ate their meals they talked about the events of the previous day.

"I heard on the radio the MP's manor burnt to the ground;" said Shaun "fucking good riddance, we should burn all the sick dirty bastards!"

The men all nodded in agreement with him.

When Jimmy finished his meal, he said he was leaving as he wanted to drop by the hospital to see Maria. Kevin asked if he could tag along as he wanted to see Jacky Boy. Leaving the others talking, they left for the hospital.

Twenty minutes later, Jimmy was sitting by her bed holding her hand, feeling sad and disappointed that there had been no change in her. Laying his head on the bed, clutching her hand to his face he told her he loved her. Staying with her for a couple more hours, he kissed her and said he would see her tomorrow then left.

Driving back home, he thought about her. He missed her terribly. Walking through his front door the place seemed empty without her.

After drinking a scotch he fell asleep on the sofa. When he woke around eight that evening, he called Mickey and asked him if he fancied going to the club that night. He was happy to be told that Monica was working and he would love to go. He suggested going to Sweet Cheeks and getting a blow job. That sounded good to Jimmy, so he arranged to pick him up at nine.

Later that night, Mickey was ready and waiting as Jimmy pulled up. Fifteen minutes later they were parking at the club. Shane was on the door. As they approached they asked him if everything was okay. Nodding his head he said, "Fine."

The three of them chatted for a while before Jimmy and Mickey made their way inside. They had only been there half an hour when Sharon, one of the dancers, came up to the bar for a drink. Jimmy placed his hand on her arse and gently squeezing her buttock asked how Simone was doing.

Both men noticed she looked nervous as she replied, "Yeah she'll be ok."

Jimmy could tell she was hiding something from him, so he asked how she'd had the fall and stating she must be in a bad way if she couldn't work.

"Oh Jimmy, Simone asked me not to say anything," she said as she moved closer to him "but I think you should know she didn't have a fall. It was fucking Alfie Stubbs; he turned up at her place after work last night. The bastard gave her one hell of a pasting, she's black and blue. She called me when he left and I went round to her place. When I saw the fucking state of her I took her straight to the hospital. I thought they were going to keep her in, but they didn't. He's a bloody psycho; she finished with him weeks ago. He just won't take no for an answer. I'm staying with her for a few days, just in case the bastard comes back! I told her to call the police, but she's too scared."

"Well tell her to get well, we need her here shaking her bits," said Jimmy jokingly.

With a giggle, she nodded as she took her drink and headed back to the dressing room.

Mickey could see by the look on his friend's face, he was seething so he asked him what he wanted to do about it. He wasn't surprised when Jimmy said he was going round to see her. Mickey had anticipated his reply and said he'd go with him.

It was just before eleven when they arrived at Simone's flat. They knocked on the door several times before she nervously called out to ask who it was. It was obvious she was afraid it might be Alfie. When she realised it was them she opened the door and invited them in.

"Fuck me babe," said Mickey as he looked at her face, both her eyes were black and her lips were swollen and split.

Seeing she was curious as to why they'd turned up, they explained that Shane had told them about her accident and just thought they'd pop in and see if there was anything she needed. Thanking them she said she was fine, Sharon had been shopping for her.

It was after she'd made coffee and they sat talking Jimmy asked her exactly what had happened the previous night. Trying to sound convincing, she said she'd left her bag in the car when she returned home from work. When she went out to get it she'd tripped and fallen down the stairs.

When Jimmy said it hadn't had anything to do with Alfie Stubbs then, she looked worried and knew by his face he was aware she was lying.

"I told Sharon not to mention it. I don't want any trouble Jimmy; I just want him to leave me alone. Please don't say anything to him, that's why he came round again because you'd spoken to him. I don't mean to sound ungrateful, but please, just leave it. With any luck he'll leave me alone now. He scares me, there's something wrong with him and the last thing I want is him coming to the club. I don't want to lose my job, I like working there and you two are good blokes, so please don't say or do anything."

They assured her Alfie wouldn't come to the club because deep down he was a coward and even if he did she wouldn't lose her job. Jimmy confessed and told her Sharon did the right thing telling them, but they couldn't just let it go, Alfie needed to be taught a lesson. He was only tough when he was hitting women so Jimmy wondered how he'd feel about someone his own size that hit back. In desperation, she looked at Mickey and begged him not to let Jimmy front Alfie. To her horror, Mickey touched her hand and said Jimmy was right. They couldn't let Alfie get away with it. If they did, he'd think he could just come round whenever he liked. Reassuringly he promised her Alfie would never bother her again after that night.

Jimmy asked if Alfie would be working the doors at the Paradise Club. Shaking her head she said it was his night off so he'd be playing pool down the Red Lion with his mates. Again she asked Jimmy not to go as she was sure it would only make things worse for her.

"Like Mickey said babe, don't worry about Alfie, fucking gob shite Stubbs, he definitely won't be bothering you again after tonight. I give you my word on it. Anyway look at it from our point of view; we can't have our best looking girl not working, we'll get grief from the punters who only come to watch you dance."

Wanting to believe what they'd said, she thanked them. Mickey put a roll of money in her hand as they were leaving and said for her to consider it sick pay; he grinned and added that if Jimmy wasn't there he'd offer to put it in her knickers! A broad grin appeared on his face when she told him to hold that thought until she was better.

She kissed them both on the cheek and told them to be careful as they left.

The time was quarter to twelve as they drove towards the Red Lion. Ten minutes later they were pulling in opposite the pub.

It went very quiet as they entered and walked over to the bar and Mickey ordered two drinks. As they stood facing the two pool tables, Alfie spotted them as he stood up from taking his shot. He didn't acknowledge them, he simply smirked. Jimmy put his drink down on the bar and walked towards him.

"I don't want any trouble," said the landlord to Mickey "I'll call the Old Bill."

Mickey assured him they hadn't come looking for any trouble.

The four players stopped playing as Jimmy approached Alfie. They just stood there with their pool cues in their hands. It was almost as if they were trying to intimidate Jimmy. They should have known by his reputation he was not that easily intimidated. Standing in front of Alfie, he just stared at him. Alfie was trying to act cocky in front of his mates, smirking at him.

"Fuck me, you must fancy me or something," said Alfie cockily "this is the second time you've come looking for me."

"And now I've found you," replied Jimmy menacingly "must be my lucky night! Do your mates know what a big tough man you are Alfie, or haven't you told them you like to beat up women?"

Feeling belittled in front of his mates, Alfie had to retaliate or lose face. Shouting aggressively, he told him to fuck off; she was just a fucking stripper who needed to be taught a lesson after she'd sent him to do her dirty work.

Mickey was surprised that his friend had managed to control his temper, but he knew any second it would all kick off. Walking over to Jimmy he said it wouldn't be a good idea for either of them to get themselves arrested. Jimmy nodded before he looked directly across the table at Alfie and said how about they settled it outside, man to man. His mates could even come and watch if Alfie was too scared to face him alone. After all everyone knew he preferred beating up women and just to make it easier for him, Jimmy would let him bring his cue as he was going to need it. It was obvious that Jimmy unnerved him when Alfie tried to act tough.

"You're fucking past it Jimmy;" he shouted hoping to impress his mates "I'll take you outside anytime!"

"Great, let's settle this tonight then and if you ever go near Simone again after tonight you'll be taking a fucking midnight dip, do I make myself clear Alfie? Oh, one more thing, if any of you boys feel the need to join in, feel free but just remember this, I will hold a fucking grudge and you won't always be with your mates! Now that's said, shall we take a walk over to the car park?"

Making their way across the road, Jimmy took his jacket off and handed it to Mickey.

Within seconds of entering the car park, Alfie took a swing at him with his pool cue. Jimmy grabbed hold of it, throwing Alfie off balance. Now with the cue in his hand, he snapped it in half and threw it down on the ground. Alfie ran at him. A fight raged between the two men. It didn't take Alfie long to realise he was no match for his opponent. Jimmy was beating the shit out of him. Even Alfie's mates declined from getting involved, possibly because Mickey also took his jacket off and placed it on the ground. Fifteen minutes of bare knuckle fighting was all it took for Alfie to say he'd had enough.

Jimmy helped him to his feet and said, "You took it like a man Alfie, so let's be clear, it ends tonight. You and your mates can just walk away. You put up a good fight and at least you lost to a bloke. There's nothing clever about hitting women, you just remember that."

Jimmy casually walked back towards Mickey, who was bending down to pick their jackets up. Suddenly Jimmy felt a searing pain across his neck. Alfie had grabbed another cue from his mate and hit him full pelt across the neck. The look on Jimmy's face as he turned round said it all. At the very least, Alfie had expected him to go down, most men would have, but not Jimmy; oh no he charged at Alfie like a fucking pit bull. It wasn't long before a couple of his mates put the boot in too, that's when Mickey joined in taking one of them down with a full throttle kick to the bollocks. One of Alfie's mates ran off, leaving the odds slightly more even at three on two, although the one Mickey had put down was still on the floor groaning. After ten minutes, the fight was all but over, Alfie was on the ground curled into a ball, while Jimmy kicked and punched him. He probably wouldn't have stopped had Mickey not said Alfie had enough and dragged Jimmy off him.

Two of Alfie's friends picked him up and tried to run away dragging him between them.

Jimmy called after them that next time the odds would be even, so they should think fucking twice before taking them on again. He couldn't help but add they were a bunch of wankers as he walked over and picked up their jackets.

"What a bunch of fucking pussies Mick, my mum hit harder than them!"

"Yeah and to think I was quite happy to watch," laughed Mickey "but I couldn't have them hurting you or getting all the thanks from Simone. I'm on a promise with her, remember!"

"You dirty bastard, after this I think I should be the one she blows!"

"No way, she prefers the more sophisticated man!"

"Bollocks," replied Jimmy with a laugh.

Back in the car, Mickey asked if he thought they'd hear from Alfie again as he started the engine. Laughing, Jimmy said even Alfie wasn't that fucking stupid and he couldn't believe the cheeky bastard had the balls to say he was past it. Mickey laughed with him and stated Alfie had a point as they used to fight in car parks when they were kids.

They both laughed.

Mickey dropped him off arranging to meet the following day after Jimmy had been to the hospital.

By the time Jimmy got to bed his head was thumping from the blow from the cue.

When he woke the following morning his neck was killing him. Before leaving for the hospital he took a couple of pain killers and the pain had eased off considerably by the time he saw Maria and spoke to the doctor as to whether there had been any improvement in her.

His heart felt heavy when the Doctor said no, but added it was early days yet. All he could say was for Jimmy to continue visiting her and keep talking to her because that was important.

CHAPTER 19

Jimmy never missed a day. For the next five weeks, he sat by her bed every day holding her hand and telling her how much he loved her. Mickey called as often as he could and Shaun visited almost daily. Despite the fact she never moved, or gave any indication that she could hear them, they never gave up hope. Although he never showed it Jimmy was becoming despondent.

One day when arriving at the hospital, he bumped in to Father Thomas.

"Jimmy isn't it?" said the priest "how is your friend Maria?"

Nodding at the priest, he told him there had been little to no improvement over the last five weeks. Father Thomas asked if he'd like him to visit with him. Jimmy thanked him and said he knew Maria would like that.

Father Thomas followed him to her room. Jimmy noticed Thomas looked sad as he sat looking at her. They sat opposite one another on either side of the bed, both men held her hands.

Thomas introduced himself to her and told her how he had met Jimmy and that she was lucky, because he loved her very much. When Father Thomas stood up to leave, he looked at Jimmy and asked if he could pop in and see her again as he was a regular visitor to the hospital. Nodding, Jimmy said he would appreciate that. They shook hands and the priest left.

Once alone, Jimmy held her hand and talked to her.

"Well babe," he said "now you've met Father Thomas. You'll probably find this hard to believe, but I really like him. I've got some more good news for you; remember I told you we sent the contents of Maurice's deposit box to Monica anonymously. Well I'm happy to tell you several high profile people have already been taken in for questioning, including Sister Marjorie. Word is a new nun has been put in charge of the girls; apparently she's young and the girls like her. Regarding Maurice, the coroner has finally released his body; his family are flying him back to the Caribbean. The irony of that is if Nick had simply shot him they would have released his body weeks ago, but because of the way he died they needed it for evidence. Not that it's done any good, the Old Bill still haven't got a clue who killed him. I miss you so much babe, I love you Maria, please come back to me."

Then he broke down in tears. It was as he laid his head on her chest, he felt her gently squeeze his hand. Trying to talk through his tears he told her to come back. Lifting her hand to his mouth, he kissed it several times before calling out for a nurse. When a nurse came, he excitedly exclaimed Maria had squeezed his hand.

The nurse left to fetch a doctor. Within minutes the doctor was there checking Maria and the monitors she was attached to. Jimmy noticed that one was making a bleeping noise; he hadn't heard it before.

Taking a hypodermic needle from a pack, the doctor scratched it across the bottom of Maria's foot and then gently pricked it. He smiled as her foot twitched. Taking her hand he squeezed it and asked if she could hear him. Feeling her squeeze his hand, he quickly asked the nurse to pass him a dose of a drug which he administered through the tube in her arm. With Maria lying deadly still, the

Doctor looked at Jimmy and told him all they could do now was wait. Clutching at hope, Jimmy asked if the Doc thought she'd be alright. The Doc was honest with his reply, stating it was too early for him to make a prognosis, but he was very hopeful. He asked Jimmy to stay and talk to her.

Feeling real positive hope for the first time in weeks, Jimmy quickly replied he wouldn't leave her. He wanted to be there when she woke up.

The Doc had a look of empathy on his face when he told him she may not wake up for hours, maybe days, or at worst not at all. What just happened may have been a false alarm. The Doc smiled when with an air of confidence, Jimmy assured him she would wake up because she knew how much he loved her and she wouldn't leave him.

For the next nine hours Jimmy sat clutching her hand and telling her over and over how much he loved her. Hoping against hope she would wake up.

As the hours passed, he began to think the doctor had been right and it was a false alarm. Feeling exhausted, he felt himself nodding off several times not because he didn't want to be there, it was through sheer boredom.

When the shift changed, a nurse came in and introduced herself as Ronnie. When she asked him if he would like a cup of coffee he nodded.

Five minutes later when she returned with his drink, he was asleep. His head was on the bed still clutching Maria's hand against his face.

Ronnie placed the coffee on the bedside cabinet and then quietly checked Maria, before returning to her station.

Jimmy slept for several hours, never stirring, even when Ronnie came in and checked on Maria.

Rousing from what he thought was a dream after hearing someone calling his name, he began to wake up. It was as he regained his senses he became aware that something was touching his face. Lifting his head from the bed, he felt Maria squeeze his hand and whisper his name. Jumping to his feet, he shouted for the nurse.

Ronnie appeared. "She called my name" he said excitedly.

Leaning over, he kissed Maria on the lips. Slowly she began trying to open her eyes. Ronnie left to fetch the doctor.

The Doctor heard Maria say Jimmy's name as he entered the room a few minutes later.

The Doctor asked Maria if she could hear him. In a weak voice she said yes. Jimmy could not hold back the tears when the doctor smiled at him and said she'd regained consciousness.

For the next hour the room was overflowing with doctors, nurses and physiotherapists. Jimmy tried to keep out of their way. Ronnie suggested he went and had a coffee while the doctors examined her. Jimmy liked Ronnie; she was a no-nonsense nurse, kind but firm. Doing as she asked he left, but not before telling Maria he wouldn't be long.

Once outside the hospital, he phoned Mickey and told him the wonderful news that Maria was going to be ok. Mickey was genuinely happy for them and asked if Jimmy needed him to go down. Thanking him, Jimmy explained there was no need as he would be going back into the hospital. Mickey said he'd let Shaun and the others know.

Walking around outside the hospital, he thought about Maria. Glancing at his watch, he'd lost all track of time and was surprised to see it was quarter past eight in the morning.

The hospital cafeteria was already full of people, so he gave up on the idea of coffee. Instead he walked to St Augustus, which was a just minutes from the hospital and, unlike before, he entered without hesitation.

Pleased to see Father Thomas making preparations for Mass, he called out to him. Thomas was clearly pleased and surprised to see him. After saying hello, he asked after

Maria. With a grin Jimmy said that was why he was there, to tell him she was going to be ok and to thank him for visiting her.

"No thanks needed;" replied Thomas "that's wonderful news. Tell her I'll call in to see her later. God knew she was in a dark place, but he also knew you were waiting for her."

"Whatever Thomas," grinned an ever doubting Jimmy, "I just wanted you to know."

Thomas afforded himself a smile as he noticed Jimmy dipped his fingers into the font and crossed himself as he left.

Back at the hospital, Jimmy was shocked as he entered her room. Some of the machines had been disconnected from Maria and she was sitting up, although supported by pillows. Still pale and looking drowsy, she smiled as he entered the room.

Ronnie was the first to speak to him, telling him Maria was still very weak, so if she wanted to sleep he must let her.

When Jimmy asked her what time her shift finished, Ronnie laughed and stated an hour ago, but she wouldn't leave until she knew Maria was okay because she had watched over her at night.

Finally alone with Maria, he held her hand and said he knew she'd wake up. Squeezing his hand she said she'd had a strange dream that Nick was dead.

Smiling, he gently stroked her hair and stated it wasn't a dream, Nick was dead. He would never bother them again. A tear trickled down her cheek. Wiping it away with his finger he told her he loved her.

"I love you too," she replied as she drifted off to sleep.

Gently touching her cheek, he waited ten minutes to see if she woke again. When she didn't, he took Ronnie's advice and went home to get some sleep, leaving her to rest. Before leaving, he wrote a note, which read, 'Back later babe, I love you J xx.'

KAREN CLOW

CHAPTER 20

Over the next few days, Maria slowly improved. Although still unable to walk on her own, the physiotherapist assured them that it would only be a short while before she was strong enough. She was eating small amounts of food which had to be mashed to a pulp. Everywhere you looked in the room there were bouquets and baskets of flowers, two dozen white roses from Mickey took pride of place on the window sill. The card read, 'To Delia, get well soon darling, I miss you and your cooking, love Mickey xxx.'

Doctor Cairn told them if she kept improving the way she was, she could probably go home in a couple of weeks. Jimmy couldn't wait; he knew Mickey would take care of business and Gladys would be only too happy to clean and stay with her should he need to go out.

It was twelve days later when she was finally discharged from the hospital. Jimmy made a donation of ten thousand pounds to the hospital fund. He also left a note for Ronnie which said she, along with a guest, could have an all-expenses paid weekend trip to Paris, plus a meal at any of their restaurants. She just had to call him to arrange it.

CHAPTER 21
(Eight Weeks Later)

After only two months of being home, Maria was almost back to her old self.

Over lunch that day, he asked if she felt up to going out at the weekend as it was her birthday. Excitedly she said she would love to but she didn't really have anything to wear.

She looked curious as he stood up and walked over to the lounge cabinet and took out a large, expensive looking gift wrapped box.

"I hope it fits," he said handing it to her, "Charlie helped me choose it when she got back from America. Which reminds me, never let a fifteen old girl talk me into taking her shopping again!"

Maria laughed at what he'd said; but accepting presents was not something that came easily to her. Slowly she removed the beautiful bow from the box and lifted off the lid; inside was something black. Carefully unfolding the tissue paper, she lifted out the contents and began to cry. Placing his arm around her, he said if she didn't like it they could change it. Instantly she stated it was beautiful and thanked him.

Taking it out, she held up a stunning black evening dress. Jimmy suggested her giving him a demo, just to make sure it fitted. After carefully placing the dress back in the box, she headed for the bedroom. A few minutes later, she called to him to help her with the zipper.

Kissing the back of her neck as he zipped her up, she turned to face him and asked him what he thought. She loved it and had never owned anything so nice.

"You look absolutely stunning babe. God I'm a lucky man, but you'd better take it off or I won't be responsible for my actions!"

"Well I'm hoping by the weekend," she giggled "I'll be feeling a lot better; especially after an evening out and maybe then it'll be me who won't be responsible for my actions!"

Pulling her closer to him, he kissed her and said he'd missed her.

Saturday evening finally arrived. Jimmy was waiting for her to appear from the bedroom. Several minutes passed so he called out impatiently "Babe you ready?"

Maria appeared. Jimmy was speechless; she literally took his breath away. Apologising for keeping him waiting, she explained that when Monica had showed her how to put some make up on earlier in the week, it had seemed a lot easier. Gazing at this stunning young woman standing in front of him, he reassured her she hadn't needed to put any makeup on because she was already beautiful.

Outside a limousine was waiting for them. Sitting in the rear, she asked where they were going. It was a new restaurant that had only opened that evening. Nervously she asked if it was posh, only she'd never eaten out before.

"It's the best babe, and you'd better get used to it; because from now on you will be eating out at posh joints. Don't worry about this place tonight though, I've got VIP membership, I know the owner."

The limo stopped after twenty minutes. Before getting out, he asked her to give him her hand. Holding out her hand, he handed her a small box. Carefully she opened it. Inside the box was a key. Curiously she asked what it was for, to which he replied she was just about to find out but as it was a surprise, she had to close her eyes.

Carefully, he helped her from the limo and walked her forward a few feet before saying she could open her eyes. Looking straight ahead, she couldn't believe her eyes. There in front of her was a fabulous restaurant; the sign above it read 'Maria's.'

"It's yours babe," said Jimmy "happy birthday, you can see why I couldn't wrap it!"

"Oh Jimmy," she said as tears trickled down her face, "I don't know what to say. I never expected this thank you so much; I love you."

"Good, because I love you too, now stop crying or you'll ruin your make up. Shall we see if the key fits?"

Her hands were shaking as she put the key in the lock and opened the door.

Inside was stunning with beautiful furnishings. It was the type of place she had only seen in books. A chef appeared with a waiter. Jimmy introduced them to her and explained they normally ran one of their other restaurants, but they were on loan to her for the evening.

She noticed one table had the candle burning; it was set for six diners. A bottle of champagne was chilling in a silver ice bucket on a stand next to the table. When she asked if he was expecting guests, he said just a couple of friends who he'd asked to join them. In fact they should be there any minute.

Just as they sat down, the door to the restaurant opened and in walked Mickey and Monica, followed by Shaun and his wife Ann.

They all kissed her and wished her a happy birthday. Shaun handed her a gift box. Inside was a solid gold cross and chain. It was obvious by her face and the tears in her eyes that she loved it.

"I didn't have a clue what to get you babe" said Mickey handing her an envelope, "I hope you like it. It's dated for three months, so you've got time to get a passport."

Even Jimmy looked baffled. Nervously she opened the envelope. Inside there were two airline tickets and a receipt for an all-expenses paid luxury seven day stay in Venice. Momentarily lost for words, she just stared at the tickets. Jimmy could see she was totally overwhelmed so he thanked him saying it was a great gift.

They lifted their glasses and Mickey made a toast to wish her a happy birthday.

They chatted for hours after they ate. Maria got quite tearful when she spoke about how romantic Jimmy had been, especially with the key in a gift box.

"Steady on babe," joked Jimmy "you're ruining my bad boy reputation!"

Everyone laughed.

Ann asked if she'd thought the key box had a ring in it. Blushing Maria confessed she had. Jimmy interrupted and asked what she would have done if he'd given her an engagement ring.

"I would have been very happy to accept," she replied without hesitation.

"Good job I brought this then!"

Her heart was pounding and her hands shaking as he took a small box from his jacket pocket and handed it to her. Everyone watched as she opened it. Inside was the most exquisite diamond ring. Slipping it onto her finger, she began to cry as she said it was perfect. Reaching over the table, he held her hand.

"I wasn't sure whether it was too quick," said Jimmy "but it was something Shaun said a few weeks ago that convinced me the time was right. I know you've had a rough time babe and it will take time for you to adapt to things, but there's no rush, it can be a long engagement."

With his curiosity getting the better of him, Shaun asked what he'd said. Jimmy enlightened him to a conversation they had where Shaun had said it was love at first sight for him with Ann and he knew she was the girl for him.

"It was the same for me Jimmy," said Ann "he was a rough diamond that's for sure and my dad wasn't happy about it, but when your heart tells you something's right; you have to follow it. I couldn't imagine being without the big ox now, although there are times when I think about trading him in for a younger sexier model!"

Everyone laughed.

"Aye well," said Shaun "let me tell you something darling, these young blokes are ok for a quick shag but when it comes to it, a virile man in his prime like me is a much better bet!"

"I wouldn't argue with that darling," said Ann, "you're the only man for me, that's for sure and as they say, better the devil you know."

"Aye you're right darling and of course there's the other minor detail you've missed out. If some young stud did ever try his luck I'd have to break both his arms and legs before I ripped his head off!"

"Now everyone can see why I love you," laughed Ann "you're such a big old softie!"

They were still laughing as Mickey asked everyone to raise their glasses in a toast.

"To the happy couple and let's hope all your future children look like Maria!"

Everyone laughed, especially when Jimmy called him a fucking cheeky bastard!

It was turned two o'clock when everyone finally went home. Maria had made a point of telling them all before they left that it had been the best birthday she'd ever had and with the exception of Jimmy winning the poker game, the best night of her entire life.

When they arrived back at the apartment, Jimmy poured them a drink and said what a great night as he passed her glass. He noticed she looked as though she would burst into tears, when she stated it was the best night and she'd never imagined anything like that happening to her. Telling her to cheer up he suggested them turning in as they had a lot of catching up to do and he wanted to do disgusting, but wonderful, things to her. When she asked him to give her a few minutes because she wanted to change, he grinned and told her not to bother because he'd waited two months for this night and he intended to ravage her body. Her answer to that was, in that case five more minutes wouldn't make any difference would it.

Kissing her passionately, he ran his hand up her leg and into her panties. Pulling away from him, she grinned and told him to go to bed; she would join him in a moment.

Eagerly he lay in the bed waiting for her after she went into the spare room to change. The suspense was killing him. Then from outside the bedroom door, she asked him to close his eyes. Less than thirty seconds later, she entered the room and said he could open them now. Jimmy felt his heart skip a beat as he looked at her standing in the doorway wearing a leopard print basque, stockings, suspenders and high heels.

"Fuck me babe," he exclaimed "you make me so fucking horny! I could come just looking at you!"

Seductively she walked towards him and giggling said she was rather hoping they'd come together. Throwing the duvet off him, she looked at his cock and grinned. Pulling her onto him, he kissed her wildly as he fondled her breasts and she took his cock in her hand. The passion between them was electric as she moved over and knelt on the bed resting on her elbows over the pillows. Without wasting a second Jimmy was mounting her from behind and thrusting into her, holding her firmly by the hips only moving to fondle her breasts.

"Don't stop Jimmy, I'm coming!" she screamed as he thrust harder into her.

Moments later, he'd rolled her over so she could straddle him, taking him deep into her. Kissing her breasts and sucking her nipples as she rode him. Then suddenly she leaned forward and went down hard on him as she cried out "Oh Jimmy!"

This time he held her tight and moved in sync with her.

"Christ babe, don't stop!" he gasped.

Powerfully he gripped her hips as he came. Finally collapsing onto him; lying along his body she kissed him and said it had been fantastic. Their bodies entwined, within minutes they fell asleep.

KAREN CLOW

CHAPTER 22
(Two Years Later)

Jimmy could smell freshly made toast as he made his way to the kitchen. "Morning gorgeous," he said as Maria put the scrambled eggs onto the plates.

Walking towards him with their breakfast, she leant over and kissed him as he asked what her plans were for the day. She was going to the restaurant to run a couple of new recipes past chef, after that she was going to see Father Thomas to speak with him about the wedding arrangements. Jimmy nodded and said "Ok babe."

Over breakfast they chatted about the restaurant and how it had become one of the most popular restaurants in London.

"I never doubted it would be;" she giggled "with your contacts and my culinary talents, we couldn't fail. Now don't let your breakfast get cold."

Looking at her he never imagined he would love any woman the way he did her. During the last two years since he won the bet at Nick's, his life had changed so much. His love for her had grown stronger with every passing day, as did hers for him. Jimmy always vowed he'd never marry again after his first marriage had ended in a bitter divorce, but it was different this time. Despite never appearing too excited, secretly he couldn't wait for their wedding day although he had left all the arrangements to her and Monica. Often he would joke with them and say things like 'you two sort everything out, have whatever you like; I'll just pay for it all and turn up on the day.'

Glancing over at him, she could see his thoughts were miles away. Curiously she asked what he was thinking about.

"Nothing really, just that I'm a lucky man and how much my life has changed for the better babe."

"I'm the lucky one Jimmy. I love you so much and I thank God every day for sending you to me. Oh and while we're on the subject of God, Father Thomas said it would be really nice to see you in church on Sunday, especially as we're getting married in eight weeks' time."

She wasn't surprised when he asked her to apologise to Father Thomas for him and explain how busy he was. In an effort to get him to the church, she said he could go with her that day. She grinned when he told her Mickey was picking him up around half ten because they had to call into Sweet Cheeks. Apparently Shane and Billy had a bit of trouble with some Jamaicans down there a couple of nights ago and they needed to check everything was ok. Looking worried she asked what sort of trouble. Just as she'd expected, he made light of it stating it was nothing, just a group of Jamaicans who got a bit out of hand with a couple of the dancers.

Despite his cool manner, he had a bad feeling about the incident. He didn't really warm to the Jamaicans, they often brought trouble with them. The locals were okay, they never gave any bother, but this group was different. Shane had told Mickey they had caught one of them trying to sell drugs but when he'd ordered him to get out, the Jamaican had said something to the effect that they would be back. Maria could tell by the way Jimmy had spoken there was more to it, but she knew he wouldn't tell her.

Still talking about the club, Maria said she couldn't understand how the dancers did what they did; she could never flaunt herself in front of strangers.

"It's just a job to them babe," he said "anyway we look after our girls, we never allow overzealous men to get out of hand with them. Some of the girls are doing it to pay their way through university; a couple of them are single mothers who need to work. The fact is on a good night they can earn in excess of three hundred quid, they see it as a good career move."

Hearing about some of the dancers' backgrounds and how much money they earned shocked her but regardless, she knew she'd never be able to do it.

"Shame," he laughed "with a body like yours the punters would be gagging to stick a twenty pound note in your knickers!"

Slapping him playfully, she told him to behave and how would he really feel if she did do it. His look told her before he said he'd hate the thought of other men ogling her. Truth was he'd probably lose his temper and end up thumping someone. Leaning over the table, she kissed him and said she'd never need another man.

"Good," said Jimmy "then we're both in agreement on that score, because I never intend for us to be apart. The way I see it, you're stuck with me forever."

Standing up she moved towards him and sat down on his lap, within minutes they were kissing passionately, their hands were all over each other as they frantically undressed. Still sitting on the chair she straddled him; seconds later they were making love. The passion between them had grown stronger; their bodies seemed to be in perfect sync with one another. Their love making was adventurous and exciting, filled with passion and desire.

Maria glanced at the clock on the wall and stated they should take a shower as it was a quarter to ten and Mickey would be there soon.

"Yeah I know," he grinned "you've got to stop keep seducing me babe, I've got things to do; so I'll only agree to share a shower with you if you promise to keep your hands off me."

"Perhaps we should abstain from sex until after the wedding," she joked "especially as you have so many important things to do?"

Laughing he grabbed her and said, "If that's the case, the fucking wedding's off!"

They both laughed.

Less than five minutes after taking a shower and dressing, Mickey's car horn sounded outside. Jimmy grabbed his jacket and kissed her on the cheek. Opening the front door, he turned and told her to give Shaun a ring so he could drive her to the restaurant and the church. After they said they loved each other, she heard the front door close behind him.

Pouring herself another coffee, she sat in the kitchen and pondered over the trouble he'd mentioned. Undoing the top button of her blouse, she held the cross hanging round her neck that had been a birthday gift from Shaun and Ann. Gently rubbing it she asked God to watch over Jimmy and to keep him out of trouble. In the two years since she'd lived with him, she had come to realise there was a side to him that concerned her. On several occasions, he had returned from the clubs with black eyes and bruises and despite his reassurances that it was always someone else who had started it, she knew it probably wasn't. Although her love for him was paramount, there were times when she felt uneasy, knowing just how many questions she could ask before he would lose his patience and become angry. There was a point which she would go to, but know when to stop. Not that he'd ever laid a finger on her in a violent manner, hitting women wasn't in his character, but her track record with Nick was enough for her never to take the chance. In many ways she wished he was more like Mickey, always the diplomat, never rushing into things, weighing up certain situations carefully before deciding what action to take. Jimmy would just wade in regardless of the consequences, although like Jimmy, Mickey was known to have a temper, but he seemed to have control and she was grateful he helped to keep Jimmy out of trouble. As she thought of Mickey, she felt blessed to have him, not only for Jimmy, but for her; he was always there for her. Like the times when she was worried over things Jimmy had done, he would always reassure her that everything would be fine.

Outside in Mickey's car, Jimmy asked about the trouble at the club. In his opinion it had sounded like the Jamaicans were too cocky by far. Mickey felt the same, his experiences over the years with Jamaicans was they often spelt trouble. Pushing drugs and having scant respect for women, in fact he found them quite abrasive.

They both agreed the Jamaicans they'd grown up with were good blokes, so they wouldn't tar them all with the same brush.

Pulling in at the club, they noticed a young woman talking to Shane. When they approached, Shane pointed at them and told the woman they were the people she needed to speak to. "What's up Shane?" asked Mickey.

With a grin, the big bruiser explained the girl was looking for a job. Mickey asked her name, age and what she could do regarding working for them.

Looking confident, she said her name was Max, short for Maxine. She was twenty five. She'd worked in bars and restaurants along with doing nude modelling for a college art department so she didn't have a problem with stripping. She'd never pole danced, but was happy to give it a try.

Jimmy asked why she needed the job and stated she didn't look like the type they'd expect to want to work in a club, and definitely not as a pole dancer, she was very attractive and seemed bright. He was a bit put out by her attitude when she said her reasons were personal.

"Fair enough" said Jimmy "but if you're doing it to fund a drug habit, you'd best go elsewhere."

"Let me assure you I've never taken drugs," admonished Max "nor do I intend to start!"

"Ok, well as we're both here you can try out now if you like."

Max smiled and nodded as she followed them into the club, but when she looked at the three poles on the stage, they noticed she didn't look quite as confident as a few minutes earlier. Shane said another dancer, Sharon, was there practising some new moves. He would take Max to the dressing room and introduce her.

Fifteen minutes later, the three men were sitting at a table waiting for the two girls to perform.

"What the fuck's taking them so long," said Mickey "they've only got to strip off!"

Shane stated that Max had seemed a bit nervous when he'd taken her backstage to meet Sharon. They all agreed she didn't seem the type, but she was good looking with a fit body and she would appeal to the punters.

Back in the dressing room, Sharon was trying to get her to relax by telling her the club was ok and the doormen never let the blokes get out of hand. Max asked how much it paid.

"Depends, if I'm dancing a couple of hours on week nights I get ninety in cash and a couple of hundred on Fridays and Saturdays. Weekends are always busier and we get to keep whatever the punters give us. On the best nights, I can turn over anything in excess of four hundred in tips."

Max was clearly shocked by the amount and readily stated she needed to earn that kind of money, but she wasn't actually sure she'd be able to do it.

"Course you can do it," laughed Sharon "it's easy. Just watch what I do and remember it's nothing to be ashamed of. You've got a good body so why not use it? Come on let's get out there and shake our booties!"

Suddenly Max felt less enthusiastic, but Sharon just peeled off her tight fitting top exposing her bare breasts, leaving her in just a skimpy pair of knickers. Gingerly Max undressed until like Sharon, she too was standing in just her knickers.

"Nice tits," said Sharon, "you'll be popular with Shane, you're just his type. He's the big guy who brought you in, he's the manager come doorman; lovely bloke. If I wasn't already engaged I'd be in there like a shot."

Max giggled and after agreeing that Shane was indeed tasty, asked if Sharon's boyfriend had a problem with her dancing for other men. Shaking her head, Sharon surprised her when she said he actually thought it was cool that other men fancied her, but he was the only one who got to shag her. Under no circumstances would he ever share her. For him, like her, the money was the big attraction because they wanted to travel. In a year or two once they'd done all their travelling and settled down, Sharon would return to her career as a primary schoolteacher. Sharon asked her if she had a career.

"I wanted to be a doctor, but things didn't quite go to plan," said Max "I had to drop out of medical school after the first year. I hope one day I'll be able to continue. I was pregnant and the baby's father wasn't the man I thought he was, but please don't say anything, let's just see if I get the job first."

Sharon smiled and said it was in the bag, the job was hers. Max smiled back and thought how much she liked her; she knew that if she got the job they would become friends.

"Fuck me girls!" said Mickey with a laugh as the two girls appeared "we were beginning to think you'd fucked off home!"

"You should be grateful you're getting a private show," laughed Sharon "and that at half eleven in the morning two beauties are willing to shake their bits for you!"

"She's got a point Mick," laughed Jimmy "stick some music on for them Shane."

Sharon told Max to watch her and join in when she felt comfortable, which judging by the look on Max's face and the fact her arms were folded across her breasts, would probably be never. Sharon moved towards one of the poles. Soon as the music started, she started gyrating up and down the pole. Max thought she moved very seductively and elegantly. After several minutes she called for Max to try. Slowly she dropped her guard and tried to look as elegant and seductive as her mentor, although for the first five minutes she was anything but. However, once she began to feel more at ease, it seemed to come quite naturally to her. When the music finished, the three men clapped. Mickey said that with a bit of work, he reckoned she'd do okay. The others agreed.

They decided to give her a try out on one of the quieter nights and asked if she could work that Tuesday with Sharon. When she nodded and thanked him, he said in that case it looked like she'd got herself a job if Tuesday went ok. Sharon could show her the ropes.

After the two girls dressed they joined the men for a quick drink before leaving them to discuss business.

Once alone, the men talked about Max, with Shane telling them she's a bit tasty and he wouldn't mind giving her one. It was unanimous; they all thought she would probably work out ok and Mickey, like Shane, wouldn't mind giving her one either! They all laughed when Jimmy warned him not to let Monica hear him say things like that because she'd chop his nuts off!

"Not me Jimmy, you're the one getting married," said Mickey "although I must say Monica's help with the arrangements is having an awkward effect on us; all she keeps fucking talking about is getting engaged! So let's change the topic and talk about business."

They all laughed.

Jimmy asked Shane to tell them about the Jamaicans.

"Big bastards with fucking dreadlocks," said Shane "fuck knows what women see in them. There were five of them, not your run of the mill clubbers, suits, money and plenty of gold jewellery. They tried to talk to some of the dancers, one of them really seemed to take a shine to Simone but she made it obvious she wasn't interested. Then Billy saw one of them trying to pass some dope to one of our regular punters. When we told them to leave they gave us a bit of lip; with all that crap talk, you know, 'yeah man, no man, ya be sorry man;' all that load of old bollocks! Truth is we didn't really take much notice 'til I spoke to Simone when we closed. Apparently they'd said she'd soon be working for them, because they were going to be the new owners of the club. Simone didn't think anything of it until they mentioned you two by name and made reference to other things. Like how you and Maria sort of got together because of a bet."

"Fucking cheeky bastards," snapped Jimmy "what else did they say and are you sure they're not local boys?"

"Definitely, even their accent is pure Jamaican; my guess is they're looking to make a name for themselves. They never said much else, except they'd be back."

"Well they picked the wrong fucking manor if that's the case!" said Mickey "I'll give Lenny Porter a bell, see what he can dig up and maybe a word with Hudson wouldn't be a bad idea. He's well in with the Jamaican community. In the meantime, we'll send over a couple more boys just in case they do come back and give us any grief. Maybe Terry and Reggie, I'm sure they could spare us a couple of nights. We all know Reggie's well known for hating the blacks and especially Jamaicans. Right, now business is sorted we can have another drink."

Shane asked Jimmy how the wedding plans were going. With a grin Jimmy said he hadn't had a lot to do with them, Monica had been a diamond with the time she'd put in helping Maria. According to the girls everything was running smoothly. Shaun's two granddaughters had agreed to be bridesmaids; along with Mickey's daughter Charlie.

When Shane asked Mickey if he was looking forward to being Jimmy's best man, Mickey grinned suspiciously and raised his eye brows.

They all laughed.

They had one more drink then the two friends left. Fifteen minutes later, Mickey dropped Jimmy off.

Jimmy called out "Hi babe" as he entered the apartment, but there was no reply, she was still out. While he waited, he called Terry. Just as he put down the phone after talking to him, Maria walked in and after saying hi, said Father Thomas sent his regards and hoped to see him in church one Sunday.

Quickly changing the subject, he nodded and instantly asked her what Leon the Chef thought about the new recipes. He could see the excitement on her face as she told him Leon loved them and they would be on the menu within a week. Before he had time to congratulate her, she asked how things had gone at the club. Knowing she would worry if he told her the absolute truth, he played it down and said it had simply been a couple of Jamaicans acting up with a couple of the dancers and it was nothing to worry about.

"So why were you asking Terry to work the doors for a couple of nights then Jimmy?"

She had obviously heard the tail end of his telephone conversation. Well aware she would want to find out more, he was relieved to be interrupted by his phone. It was his friend Martin Blackwell the jeweller calling to tell him their wedding rings were ready and for them to pop into the shop to check the fit.

They arranged to meet that afternoon. Maria felt excited and giggled when he said she would need to feed him before they left otherwise his ring might be too loose.

"It wouldn't hurt you to lose a few pounds," she said playfully patting his stomach "especially as your wedding suit had already been tailored!"

"If anything I need to eat more to keep my energy levels up babe because of your constant sexual demands on me!"

Blushing she giggled as she walked off into the kitchen.

While they sat eating their lunch, she chatted about the wedding plans. Simply from the enthusiasm in her voice he could tell she was excited with the whole thing, but he asked if she had any second thoughts. With a beaming grin she replied "None."

It was the same for him; he couldn't wait to marry her. Casting his mind back, he remembered the frightened young girl who had been brought to his apartment just two years earlier after he'd won her in a poker game. It was obvious since that time she had grown into a confident young woman, barely resembling the same girl who had prayed to God to let her die. Gazing lovingly at her, he remembered the terrible pain and cruelty she had endured at the hands of Nick. The sheer fact she survived was a testament to her character and faith.

After lunch they drove to the jewellers. He talked about the new dancer they'd taken on called Max and how she didn't seem the type, although they all thought she'd do ok.

Maria's thoughts on Max were simple, perhaps she wasn't really comfortable doing it but she needed the money badly.

Martin greeted them as they entered the jewellers and then suggested going through to the back of the shop. They followed him to a small room where there was a ring display board on the table. Taking the two rings from it, he passed them one each. Both were a perfect fit. When Jimmy asked how much he owed him, Martin smiled and said there wouldn't be a charge. Instantly Jimmy said he couldn't agree with that, it was far too generous.

"Consider them my wedding gift, you've given me a lot of good business over the years Jimmy, it's the least I can do and anyway I can afford it," joked Martin as they shook hands before Jimmy passed the rings back to him and asked him to keep them. They would pick them up nearer the day.

Jimmy asked Maria if there was anything else she wanted from the shop. Shaking her head she didn't think so. Martin suggested that they go back into the shop so she could have a look around. The two men chatted while Maria browsed.

"That's pretty," she said as she pointed to a gold necklace with a gold initial hanging from it "shall we buy the bridesmaids and Monica one as a token of our gratitude?"

Jimmy nodded and asked Martin how much they were. He didn't flinch when he told him they were two hundred and thirty five pounds each but of course he'd give them discount.

Jimmy made it clear that wouldn't be necessary as he'd already done too much.

They both thought it would be a good idea to buy Mickey something from there as well. Martin had some new stock which had only come in that week and he had just the item for Mickey, some gold cuff links with three small diamonds in one corner.

The moment Maria said, "Oh they're lovely."

Jimmy said, "Sold!"

They told Martin what initials they wanted on the chains, although Jimmy had momentarily forgotten the names of Shaun's grandchildren, Megan and Chloe, who were to be their bridesmaids. Ordering one for Maria as well; he paid in cash and said he would collect them with the rings.

It was turned four o'clock by the time they got home. Jimmy offered to take her out to eat, but she declined stating she wanted to try a new recipe on him that evening.

"Sounds good," he said with a sexy grin "you can try anything you like on me, including dinner!"

Knowing he was making a reference to sex, she grinned and told him to go and put some music on and relax while she prepared the food.

Listening to the music, he was dozing off when his mobile rang. It was Mickey who, in a whispered voice, asked if Maria could hear him. Jimmy said no she was in the kitchen and why was he whispering.

"That secret project of yours Jimmy, I've just had Justin on the phone. He needs to run a couple of things past you before he can move forward on it. I told him you'd pop over sometime tomorrow. One more thing, I thought tonight we ought to go to Sweet Cheeks; just to check up on things. You can pick me up around half nine."

Maria appeared in the lounge and asked who was on the phone. When he said it had been Mickey because he wanted him to go to the club later, she asked why he'd said she was in the kitchen, had Mickey asked him.

"Yeah that's right babe, he did ask where you were. Just Mickey being nosey I suppose."

"If I didn't know better Jimmy Dixon, I would think you two were up to something."

"Who me, no" he replied trying not to look guilty.

Changing the subject he told her the dinner smelled great and asked what it was. With a grin she stated it was a surprise and he'd have to wait an hour because it had to slow cook. Patting the arm of his chair, he asked her to sit with him. She placed her arm around his neck as she sat down. It wasn't long before they were kissing and fondling one another.

Knowing he was thinking did they have time for sex and not wanting to disappoint him, she moved her hand down his body and undid his trousers. Then she knelt down on the floor between his legs. His pulse was racing; the anticipation was as much as he could stand. Gripping her head firmly in his hands, he groaned as she took him into her mouth.

"Christ Maria, stop babe!"

"What's wrong, I thought you'd like that?"

"Like it, that's a fucking understatement, but I want to fuck you."

Lying down on the floor she began to unbutton her blouse. Kneeling in front of her, he lifted her skirt and pulled down her panties. Desperate to be inside her, seconds later he entered her. She was surprised at how forceful he was, but she put it down to his overwhelming need for sex which, despite the lack of foreplay, she was ready for. Within seconds their bodies were moving together, the pace of their love making getting faster and faster with every thrust. Pinning her arms to the floor, he needed to be in total control of her. She could sense that nothing was going to stop him. For the first time in almost two years, she felt she had no control over their love making, and although she'd felt like that with Nick and hated it, she felt differently with Jimmy. At that moment she wanted him to take control; to dominate her. There was nothing she wouldn't do with him, she trusted him completely.

"God Jimmy, don't stop," she cried out as he thrust deeper into her.

With one final thrust they were coming. Moments later he lowered himself onto her. The moment he released her arms, she threw them around his hot pulsing body.

"God Maria," he sighed "you do something to me!"

"It's the same for me Jimmy, but now I need to check the dinner."

Moments later she called from the kitchen for him to lay the table and open a bottle of wine as their dinner was ready.

Although it looked delicious, he stated he didn't recognise the dish.

"It's a vegetarian dish," she said with a grin "Leon has been saying he's asked more and more about vegetarian dishes, so I'm trying a few out."

Despite being a bit put out that there was no meat, he was happy to try it to please her. Gingerly he put a fork full in his mouth. As he chewed he couldn't believe how tasty it was.

With sincerity, he told her it was delicious and he couldn't believe something with no meat could taste that good.

The evening passed quickly.

As Jimmy got ready to meet Mickey, she told him to invite them over for dinner one evening the following week. Jimmy was certain they would accept the invitation. Before leaving he told her not to wait up for him as he'd be late.

"Ok just be careful Jimmy and no fighting!"

"Yes boss!"

They kissed tenderly at the door and she told him again to not to get in any fights as he left. She waved at him from the window as he pulled away.

Mickey was speaking to someone on his mobile when Jimmy pulled up ten minutes later. Finishing the call, he got into the car and told Jimmy it had been Shane on the phone; apparently the Jamaicans were at the club.

"I'm looking forward to meeting these fucking Jamaicans!" said Jimmy arrogantly as he pulled away.

Arriving at Sweet Cheeks they could see Billy and Reggie standing at the door. Reggie's dogs were sitting a few feet away. Although Mickey wasn't particularly fond of the dogs even he had to admit that they were immaculately trained. If Reggie told them to sit, they sat. If he said stay, they stayed. In fact every command he gave them, they obeyed.

Exiting the car, they approached the club doors. Mickey nodded at Billy and asked if anything had happened with the Jamaicans.

"No I warned them on the way in Mick; if we have any trouble with them they're out!" said Billy "cheeky bastards said they didn't want any trouble they just wanted the club. I just laughed and said in your fucking dreams you cheeky bastards!"

They all laughed.

Walking into the club they nodded at Shane who was standing just inside the door. Jimmy grinned and asked where their Rastafarian friends were.

With a smirk, Shane nodded toward the seating area. The Jamaicans were sitting at a table watching the dancers. Terry was standing at the end of the bar keeping a close eye on them. Mickey walked over and spoke to him while Jimmy stayed and talked to Shane. Eventually the two friends sat together at the bar.

Sue the barmaid chatted to them as she poured their drinks. Jimmy glanced towards the Jamaicans and looking quickly back at Sue asked if everything had been ok. She told them it had been quiet earlier; but the last hour had been busy. She grinned when she added that one of the Jamaicans had asked her what time she finished because he wanted to take her out.

Both men laughed because they knew she wouldn't give anyone, especially a Jamaican, a second look. She had been happily married to Nigel for thirteen years. Another factor being her sister Tracy had lived with a Jamaican for three years; he used to beat the crap out of her and her kids. Shane and a couple of the lads had sorted him out for her as a favour to Sue. She was one of the best barmaids they'd ever had; very attractive with a bubbly personality, great with the punters and the staff. Good at her job, honest, reliable and she didn't take any shit from anyone.

As they bantered with her, she discreetly told them that one of the Jamaicans was heading towards them. Standing next to Jimmy the Jamaican ordered four double Bacardi's. Turning round, he offered Jimmy his hand.

"I am Damon," he said "ya must be Jimmy?" They shook hands, "and ya must be Mickey," he said as he offered his hand again. "I like ya club, I wanta buy it."

"It's not for sale mate," replied Jimmy.

"I dan't think ya understand me man. I said I wanta buy ya club!"

"We heard you," snapped Mickey having taken an instant dislike to him, "but like we said, it's not for sale." Damon seemed undeterred and offered to play poker for it. It was when he added 'or was it just their women they played for' Jimmy knew he was making reference to Maria.

"Now listen hear you black mother fucker," snarled Jimmy aggressively "the club is not for sale! Now you can either leave or be thrown out, the choice is yours!"

"Dare is no need for ya ta be like that man, we is all business men here, ya don't want any trouble man, it's bad fa ya business. Ya have other clubs; I hear ya very successful, so do ya selves a favour and sell me dis club."

"Are you fucking deaf or what?" said Mickey, "the fucking club's not for sale! So drink your Bacardi and either go back to your mates or fuck off!"

Taking on an aggressive stance, the Jamaican snapped back and warned them they were making a big mistake. His boss wanted the club and he wouldn't like being told no, he would cause them trouble! Jimmy's answer to that was his boss could go fuck himself! Almost as though he was goading Jimmy, the Jamaican said he knew he was getting married in eight weeks and it would be tragic if Maria became a widow, although he was certain his boss would look after her because she was young and beautiful.

Jimmy couldn't hold his temper another second. Grabbing the Jamaican round the throat he pinned him against the bar. Instantly the three other Jamaicans rushed over. Terry picked up a baseball bat from behind the bar while Sue pressed a bleeper to alert Billy and Reggie.

Now standing around the bar, one of the Jamaicans put his hand inside his jacket, Terry lifted the bat and said, "I wouldn't do that if I was you mate!"

Terry looked menacing and whatever the Jamaican was reaching for, he changed his mind. Billy and Reggie were by then standing just a few feet away. Jimmy still had a firm grip on Damon. Holding him with one hand; he smashed a glass on the bar and held it to his throat.

"Now you listen to me, you black bastard" snarled Jimmy "if you so much as say the name Maria again I will fucking kill you, do you understand man! And if your boss is looking for trouble, he's come to the right fucking place! Now take your fucking shoe shine boys and fuck off back to Jamaica!"

Throughout the incident, the dancers had continued to dance; fortunately the music had drowned out most of the noise.

They followed the Jamaicans out of the club and watched them get into their car. It was as they pulled away the passenger side window rolled down and Billy shouted, "Gun!"

Suddenly a spray of bullets hit the pavement outside the club. The men ran for cover inside.

Once they were sure the Jamaicans had gone they checked the damage. The only noticeable damage was a few holes in the outer door. It wasn't until the group calmed down they realised one of Reggie's dogs was whimpering.

"Those fucking black bastards have shot my dog," shouted Reggie to the others as he bent down to tend the wounded dog. "I want them fucking dead for this, you fucking find out who they are!"

Minutes later, he was cradling the wounded animal in his arms as Billy drove him to the vet's. Fortunately no one outside had seen or heard the incident. The last of the queue had been let in just a few moments earlier. There were a few people walking nearby, but it was all over by the time they'd realised what might be happening. Despite no one inside having any idea as to the attack, Mickey and the others decided to close the club early, just in case the Jamaicans came back. He would use a gas leak as the reason for shutting.

When the club was finally empty they sent the dancers home. Jimmy phoned Maria, he knew he'd woken her up and she was curious as to why he'd called. It was when he said everything was alright, but they'd had a bit of trouble at the club and he was just checking she was ok; she knew something really bad had happened. Her fear was made more real when, before ending the call, he told her to go back to sleep but she was not to answer the intercom or door. Telling him he was frightening her, he told her not to worry; he'd be home in a couple of hours. Knowing she wouldn't be able to sleep, she said she'd wait up for him.

With the last of the dancers and bar staff gone, Shane locked the outer doors. The men sat in the club having a drink. Mickey talked of the urgency in finding out who the Jamaicans were and who they were working for. Looking aggressive Jimmy assured him they would find them.

Billy returned. Using his keys to get back in, he joined the others. Mickey asked after Reggie's dog.

"He'll pull through" said Billy "according to the vet the bullet narrowly missed all its vital organs. They're going to remove the bullet once the dog's anesthetised. The vet said the x rays looked good and that the dog would probably be fine in a couple of weeks. I'm not so sure about Reggie though, he's gone fucking psycho. He wants the fucking Jamaicans' blood!"

Mickey nodded and after telling Billy to get a drink, said he thought everyone should go home. He would call them the next morning to let them know what was happening.

Mickey and Jimmy left, leaving the others to lock up. Jimmy dropped him off and then drove home. Maria was waiting up.

Despite his reassurance to her that everything was fine, she was not so easily convinced. Concerned she asked him exactly what had happened. Although he did technically tell her the truth he left out the shooting part, simply because he knew how much she would worry, but he also knew it would only be a matter of time before someone would let it slip. His theory on that being he would worry about it when it happened.

For most of the night he tossed and turned. He kept trying to make the connection between the club and the Jamaicans. Every thought he had seemed to lead back to Maurice. Despite the fact that Maurice had worked with them, it was no secret that he had kept some very dodgy company. It didn't make sense though, if it was about Maurice why now; he was murdered two years earlier which technically they had nothing to do with. It was down to Nick and the Russian, but maybe the Jamaicans didn't know that. Finally he dropped off to sleep.

CHAPTER 23

Over breakfast Maria noticed Jimmy was unusually quiet, but when she asked if he was ok he simply said he hadn't slept very well. When he'd finished eating, he phoned Mickey to see if he'd heard anything. Like Jimmy he hadn't, but he had arranged a meeting with the lads at midday. He would pick Jimmy up en route.

No sooner had Jimmy hung up when his phone rang, it was Terry who told him Reggie had a visit from the Old Bill after the vet reported the dog had been taken in with a bullet wound.

"So what did Reggie say then Terry?"

"Well they didn't get any joy from him that's for sure Jim. He said he was walking his dogs on the common and totally out of the blue someone took a pot shot at them. They asked if he saw the shooter, I nearly fucking pissed myself laughing when Reg said, 'No I fucking didn't, I was more concerned over me dog than looking to see who'd done it!"

"Yeah that sounds like Reggie, do you reckon the Old Bill believed him?"

"I know they didn't, because they asked him about the club. Apparently some good citizen called them about a disturbance. They heard gun shots and what may have been an injured dog. God bless neighbourhood watch hey! It was probably some nosy old fucking do gooder who had nothing better to do with their time. Still at least the dog's going to be ok. Can you imagine how Reggie would be if it had died!"

Jimmy laughed and said it didn't bear thinking about. His first thought was to phone Mickey again, but he didn't want Maria to know about the shooting so he decided to wait until they met later. Looking at Maria he asked what she had planned for the day. With a grin she told him not to be nasty when she said Gladys was due round and he instantly said he had to go out. She knew Gladys drove him mad but since she'd given up doing the cleaning, she missed having something to do and Maria enjoyed seeing her when she popped round at least once a week for a cuppa and a chat.

Taking a twenty pound note from his wallet, he handed it to her and told her to give it to Gladys; she could treat herself to a night at bingo.

Despite his kind gesture, she still knew he was keeping something from her, especially when he reminded her not to open the door to anyone while he was out. Deciding not to question him, she nodded and smiled. Before leaving, he said he'd grab something for lunch while he was out with Mickey but she could cook them something delicious for dinner as there was a good chance Mickey would join them.

By half twelve everyone was at Dixie's. Everyone except Hudson, no one had seen or heard from him in days.

Mickey asked Tony what was going on with Hudson. He was surprised that Tony had no idea, but said for some unknown reason he seemed to be keeping a low profile. At first he'd thought it might be because a jealous husband was looking for him, but a couple of weird things had happened in the last couple of days. Jimmy asked what sort of weird things.

A buyer had approached Tony after being unable to contact Hudson. The buyer had ordered a Mercedes and a Porsche. Tony had seen the lads in the chop shop working on them and he knew they were ready. The buyer had expected a call from Hudson, but it never came, so Tony had dealt with it. He'd asked around the workshop, but none of the lads had seen or heard from Hudson. He'd even checked out a couple of Hudson's regular girlfriends thinking they may know, but even Tina who Hudson shagged at least twice a week hadn't heard from him. It was as if he'd vanished into thin air.

"Sounds like it," said Mickey "something definitely ain't right."

Mickey looked over at Jacky Boy and Kevin. Knowing they were well in with the black community, he told them to poke around, ask questions and see what they could find out.

They both nodded.

They spoke about the Jamaicans, all agreeing the only obvious link would be Maurice, based on the fact the Jamaicans seemed to know a lot about Jimmy and the business, and they could only have got that type of information from one of the crew. Whatever their reasons for wanting to make trouble, the priority was to find out who they were working for and how far they were prepared to go to get what they wanted. Jimmy referred to the shooting outside the club and told everyone they should expect a visit from the Old Bill as some nosy bastard had called them, but as far as everyone was concerned, Reggie wasn't at the club when it happened. He'd been walking his dogs on the common.

Everyone laughed as Reggie grinned and nodded. Jimmy continued that whether the Old Bill believed them or not, it was their word against the police and the fact that Mickey was there at the time of the shooting his word should be enough to sway it. He suggested that if any of them were asked about any trouble with the Jamaicans, they should simply play it down and say things just got a bit out of hand with a couple of the dancers. Shane could speak to the girls and tell them what to say.

They all nodded.

With the meeting concluded, Jimmy suggested they eat. Mickey laughed and said all he did was eat and he wondered if he had worms.

"It's Maria's fault, she can't leave me alone," said Jimmy "if I don't keep my strength up I won't be able to keep up with her!"

"Oh you poor bastard, my fucking heart breaks for you. It must be hard for you having to give her good sex all the time!"

"You've got no fucking idea what I have to put up with Mick, its sex, sex, sex all the fucking time!"

Everyone laughed.

Jimmy rang their restaurant in the hope of getting a table. When the waiter said they were packed to capacity, he asked them to send some food over to Dixie's.

The men chatted about the Jamaicans while they waited for the delivery. An hour and fifteen minutes later, Adam, the waiter from the restaurant turned up with their food. Jimmy joked and said if they'd have waited much longer they would have died from starvation! Adam laughed, but the restaurant had been heaving and Luigi the Chef hadn't been impressed with them asking for such a large order right in the middle of the rush hour. Jimmy grinned and asked him to tell Luigi, the miserable old eyetie, that he'd get a good bonus at the end of the week.

Jimmy handed Adam a twenty pound note and thanked him for bringing it over. The young lad looked well chuffed, and with a huge smile on his face thanked him.

They had just finished eating when the door opened and in walked the Old Bill, two regular coppers and Detective Samuels, or as Mickey referred to him, slimy Samuels. Having met him several times at different social functions with Monica he couldn't stand him, but he always remained friendly and polite for Monica's benefit and also because he knew what an arsehole Samuels was, he certainly wouldn't want to make an enemy of him.

"Well this is quite a gathering," said Samuels in his normal arrogant, sarcastic manner "I didn't expect to see you here Mickey, or could it be that you're representing one of them?"

"I'm a partner in this club," replied Mickey "my friend Jimmy is getting married so we're going over the wedding plans. I'm the best man; there's nothing illegal about that is there Detective?"

"No nothing illegal, but I'm curious as to why these others are here. Or could it be that they're the bridesmaids?"

Shane glared at the detective. Mickey could sense an atmosphere mounting, so thinking quickly he told Samuels they were there to arrange the stag night. Samuels asked what they'd decided on. In an arrogant tone, Jimmy stated they had been about to decide when he'd interrupted them.

Samuels went on to ask them questions about the shooting. They all stuck to the plan as earlier agreed. Samuels was well aware that no one was going to tell him anything. Telling them the investigation was ongoing, Samuels said he may need to speak to them again. Smugly he added, considering there were bullet holes in the main door, he was surprised no one saw or heard anything. Mickey agreed and said they were just lucky.

Just as Samuels turned to walk away one of the policemen whispered something to him. Instantly Samuels turned and looked at Reggie.

"My colleague tells me it was your dog that was shot."

Reggie nodded.

"And you're sure you were on the common when it happened?"

Again Reggie just nodded.

"Is there a problem with that" said Mickey "only I feel as though you're implying something Detective, so let's get something straight. He was walking his dog on the common, ok and several people will confirm that. So is there a problem?" Samuels knew Mickey was clever and pressing the subject would get him nowhere so he shook his head and promptly asked after the dog.

"Yeah he's doing ok;" said Mickey "hopefully he'll make a full recovery. What bothers me is that somebody shot it in the first place. There are some sick bastards about; it's coming to something when you're not even safe to walk your dog. I hope you catch whoever did it soon Detective, because next time it could be a child. Maybe you would do better to take your investigation to the common and ask the people there if they saw anything. Can't have people running about with guns, can we? That's the trouble with London now, so many nutters. It used to be great living here but it's changed. It's quite worrying when you think about it. Anyway, I won't keep you, good luck with your investigation, hope you catch them soon."

Despite hoping that would be the last they'd hear from Samuels that day, no one was surprised when, as he started to leave, he turned back to face them and said he wanted to ask one more thing, who was working the door that night.

Shane said he was, but he hadn't seen or heard anything. Chances were he'd been in the toilet or something, but the music was really loud, so it was no wonder really. Aware he was lying, but unable to prove it, Samuels left.

"He's nothing but a jumped up little shit," said Mickey "he's always on Monica's case trying to better her. When she received the contents of Maurice's box he was really snotty about it; the fucker even implied that she must have known who'd sent it. I'd love to see him get his comeuppance; he's such a fucking arsehole! We need to keep him at arm's length, he could be dangerous."

"It might be an idea to keep Reggie and Terry working at the club for a while," said Jimmy "we can always get cover for them down the docks if need be. Shaun I'd like you to keep an eye on Maria for me. I know it's unlikely anyone would target her, but let's err on the side of caution. Maybe for the next few days you could run her about, just to be on the safe side. So now our number one priority is to find Hudson."

When they finished discussing business, Jimmy asked what they had planned for his stag night.

"Fuck off," laughed Mickey "we hadn't thought about planning anything that was just for Samuels benefit!"

"Well if that's the case you miserable bunch of bastards, you can all fuck off home!"

They all laughed.

The moment Jimmy walked into the apartment; Maria asked how the meeting had gone. He had just said fine when his phone rang. It was Mickey who asked if he'd forgotten something. Jimmy stated no and what the fuck was he talking about as he had just left him. Mickey said the name Justin.

"Oh fuck me Mick; I completely forgot. Tell him I'll be there in fifteen minutes!"

Closing his phone, he glanced at Maria and apologising said he had to pop back out for half an hour, as he'd forgotten to do something. When she asked if he would like her to accompany him, he was quick to say no because the bloke he was going to see was a nutter and nine times out of ten he was abusive. Nervously she asked if he would be ok. With a grin he told her he went back a long way with the bloke and he knew better than to upset him. Maria knew there was no point in pursuing it when he said it was nothing to worry about, just something he should have done on the way home.

Driving to meet Justin, he was annoyed with himself that he had forgotten about seeing him, which had meant he'd had to lie to Maria but he convinced himself she would love him for it in the end when she saw the surprise.

Justin walked towards the car as Jimmy pulled up outside a large house. Justin apologised, but said it was difficult to get hold of him in case Maria overheard them.

Maria was busy in the kitchen stirring something on the stove when he returned. Walking up behind her, he wrapped his arms around her waist, gently kissing the back of her neck as he apologised for having to go back out.

"If you weren't always so keen to have sex Jimmy Dixon," she giggled "I might think you've got another woman!"

Instantly he said he'd never need another woman and she should know that. Looking lovingly at him, she nodded then asked him to lay the table.

"What's that babe;" he joked "you want me to lay you on the table because you're ready!"

"You've got a one track mind," she giggled "I said lay the table stud!"

"If that's the case I'll just have to have you for dessert then!"

During dinner they chatted. Maria asked him if he thought it would still be so good between them in ten years' time.

"Without a doubt," he replied "truth is babe I can't imagine being without you now, and the sex just gets better and better. I never thought I would feel this way; no woman has ever made me feel like this. I've even surprised myself. If I'm honest, before I met you I had a few dates, but once I'd shagged them a couple of times I was bored. Not with you though, all I seem to do is think about having you. Maybe God got it right this time babe, perhaps we are a match made in heaven?"

"You might just be right Jimmy. I never thought I'd fall in love or have anyone desiring and loving me the way you do. I can't imagine how I would feel if you never wanted to make love to me."

"Well you needn't worry yourself on that score babe, because it won't happen; so hurry up and eat your dinner, I'm ready for my dessert!"

Forty minutes after they had eaten their meal, the table was cleared and she was lying face down, spread eagled over it. Jimmy was getting his dessert.

Later that evening, he went back down the club with Mickey just to check on things. Shane greeted them when they arrived and said there had been no sign of the Jamaicans, the club had been quiet, but that was normal for a week night. Max had done well for her first night, the punters seemed to like her and there had been no shortage of money being put in her knickers! With a huge grin, Mickey suggested them going over to watch her for a while.

Minutes later they were watching her dance. Both men agreed she could be quite an asset to the club. Shane joined them and talked as they watched her dance. They weren't surprised to hear that he'd asked her out and she had sort of said yes, but had made it clear to him that just because she danced without clothes on, she wasn't easy.

"Fuck me;" said Mickey "she's cottoned on quickly to you being a dirty bastard! So what did you say?"

"You know me Mick; I don't give up at the first hurdle. I like it when they play hard to get. I said the offer stands if she changes her mind. Oh yeah and I told her I'd behave myself! Then she said if I fancied taking her out for a drink or dinner one night, she'd be only too happy to go. I wasn't surprised though, like I said before she just didn't seem the type, but you know me, I like a challenge! I'm taking her out for dinner on my night off."

Jimmy told him to take her to Maria's restaurant on the house. Thanking him, Shane left to check around the club.

Jimmy left around twelve thirty, leaving his friends drinking.

Maria was asleep on the sofa when he got home; despite him trying not to wake her, she stirred and asked him what the time was. It was one o'clock and he was just going to make a drink if she fancied one. She replied she would love a cup of tea.

Fifteen minutes after finishing their tea, they were in bed cuddled up together fast asleep.

The following morning he was woken by her shaking him. His phone was ringing, it had rung five times previously and whoever it was hadn't left a message.

Reaching over to the bed side cabinet, he grabbed his phone, recognising the caller ID as Mickey he answered it and asked what was up.

"Morning Jimmy thought you might want to know a body turned up floating in the Thames this morning. It was Hudson and before you ask, yes I'm positive, Tony had to identify the body."

"What happened to him?"

"Not sure Jim, but Tony said he was cut up pretty bad. The coroner thinks he's been dead about a week. I've told Tony we'll meet him in an hour, so get your arse in gear. I'll pick you up in forty five minutes.

Maria looked concerned and nervously asked what had happened. Horrified was her reaction when told they had just fished Hudson's body out of the river. Jimmy knew she was worried, so making light of it he said it was probably down to some irate husband who'd caught him shagging his wife. Trying to sound convincing, he told her not to worry as it probably hadn't got anything to do with them.

"Stop worrying! Remember I know what you do Jimmy; you get involved with bad people. Sometimes I wish I was marrying a baker!"

"That's a fucking dodgy profession, baking; all too often you hear that some poor baker has fallen into his oven!"

Trying not to giggle, she playfully slapped him and asked him to be careful because she planned on him living long enough to see their future children grow up. With a grin he said so did he.

Just over thirty minutes later, they heard Mickey's car horn outside. Jimmy grabbed his jacket, kissed her quickly and said he wouldn't be long. Moments later she was waving to the two friends as Jimmy got into the car.

Driving to the club they talked about Hudson. Mickey was convinced that one way or another, he was involved with the Jamaicans. Tony was already at the club with Shaun when they arrived; they were standing at the bar talking to Kevin. They acknowledged them as they walked past and sat at a table. Kevin carried on with his work stocking the bar but Tony and Shaun joined the others at their table.

"Hudson had been tortured," said Tony "even though he'd been in the water for days the wounds are still pretty clear. His left ear had been cut off along with three of his fingers; they're all classic features of torture. Whoever's responsible I'm convinced he would have told them whatever they wanted to know."

Mickey asked him if he thought Hudson's death was connected to the Jamaicans.

"I wouldn't rule it out; I know some of Maurice's family were heavily into drug dealing. Over the years he told me several times that they had been keen to do business in the UK, but he put them off. He didn't really want them here. Maybe with his demise they thought they could muscle in?"

Mickey suggested they look into that possibility. If they were over here from the Caribbean they had to be staying somewhere, so the first thing they needed to do was find them. Tony could check out all the hotels within five miles of the club, they knew it was a long shot but he might just get lucky.

Just as he was about to continue, his phone rang. It was Lenny. Mickey asked if he had any information for them.

"That's why I'm calling Mick. I've been nosing round and apparently you're not the only ones who are having trouble with Jamaicans. Big John Duggan down at the Cove had a run in with them a couple of weeks ago. Same type of thing, they wanted to buy his place, but like you he wasn't interested. Then a couple of nights ago they turned up, gave him some grief, wouldn't take no for an answer, he had to throw them out. According to my source, two of John's doormen got a bit carried away; beat the shit out of one of them. I've tried to find out where they're staying, but the one that was injured never went to hospital which means they have someone treating him. Other than that, there's not much else I can tell you."

Thanking him, Mickey closed his phone and he repeated to the others what Lenny had said before asking Tony what sort of relationship, if any, Maurice had with John Duggan.

"They were friends Mick; John was quite a frequent visitor to one of his brothels, because of that they had become friends. Maurice would have known a lot of personal stuff about him."

Thinking that was interesting news, he suggested Tony having a chat with John; maybe Shaun could accompany him as he was friends with a couple of the doormen at the Cove. Shaun nodded and stated he used to drink with a couple of John's lads. The two friends agreed to go to the Cove that evening to see what they could find out.

After leaving the club, Mickey and Jimmy spent the rest of the day checking in on their other clubs. Although Dixie's was their favourite, Sweet Cheeks and their other club, Lazer, actually brought in more money. Lazer catered for the younger generation. People would queue for hours on Friday and Saturday nights just to get in. Mickey and Jimmy rarely went there other than to discuss business. They didn't really like the music that was played, plus the fact it was packed with kids aged around eighteen. Not really their scene, but the young punters loved it. Twins

Simon and Steve Turner had run the club for the past eight years. They had grown up in the same street as Jimmy and like him were no strangers to crime. One of the reasons they let them manage the club was simple, they wouldn't want them as opposition. The twins were well known and well liked. They were given a free hand in making decisions concerning the club, unless of course it needed the owner's approval. It had obviously worked because Lazer was raking in plenty of money and there was rarely any trouble. Simon and Steve handpicked all the staff, most of them being tough, which was probably why there was rarely any trouble.

As they drove home, Mickey said he was seeing Monica that night and he would try to prise some more information out of her about Hudson.

Having mentioned Monica reminded Jimmy that Maria told him to invite them over for dinner one night.

"Tell Delia we'd love to;" grinned Mickey "I'll leave Monica to arrange it with her."

"What's the score with you and Monica, I mean with you being a solicitor as well as a club boss. She must be aware that you're not strictly kosher? Do you think you'll ever marry her?"

"She knows I'm dodgy," laughed Mickey "but she has to turn a blind eye or she'd have to finish with me. How would it look if she admitted going out with a criminal? Slimy Samuels for one would have a fucking field day! Anyway you know what they say Jimmy, you can't help who you fall in love with and she loves me. She knows I'm not kosher and if she ever asks me I'd probably tell her, but I know she'll never ask. Our relationship is great so why rock the boat. Maybe one day I suppose we might marry. I know she'd like kids, but I've been there, done that and at my age I'm not really sure if I want to be a dad again. Don't get me wrong Charlie is the love of my life, but would I want to do it again, probably not!"

"Fuck off you're a great dad and you're not too old; anyway you cheeky bastard, I'm the same age as you and I can't wait to have kids with Maria!"

"That's great, I'll tell you what, you have loads of kids and me and Monica will help you look after them, save us having any."

"You're on mate!"

When they arrived at Sweet Cheeks, Shane said that everything was fine so they only stayed for one drink then went on to Lazer.

As they walked into the club they could see the managers, Simon and Steve, sitting with a couple of young girls. The twins spotted them and asked the girls to leave, but only after telling them they would see them later. Jimmy said hello to who he thought was Simon, only to be told it was Steve. He asked how anyone ever told them apart and laughed when Steve said that was easy; he was the good looking one with the big cock!

"You wish bro!" laughed his brother Simon.

Mickey asked the twins how things were going.

"Great" replied Simon, "one of the perks of running the club is all the young totty; they just can't get enough of us!"

They all laughed.

Mickey asked after the two girls who they spotted with the twins when they arrived and how they looked a bit young for them. Simon said they were eighteen and hopefully a right pair of goers, which with any luck they'd find out later after the club shut. Jimmy laughed and asked the twins how old they were. When they said thirty seven, he said maybe it was time they thought about settling down.

"Fuck off Jimmy," said Simon, "who wants to end up with some old wrinkly when you can have prime totty every night!"

"You'll end up with galloping knob rot the way you're going! One day you'll both meet Mrs Right, God help the poor cows!"

They all laughed.

They could see why the young girls liked them, they were good looking, tall, blonde, blue eyed and their characters were likable.

When Simon congratulated Jimmy about the wedding, Mickey told them Maria was a real cracker. Steve nodded and said maybe she should meet him before she committed to marrying Jimmy?

"My Maria wouldn't look twice at either of you pretty boys," said Jimmy "she needs a real man. She can't keep her fucking hands off me!"

"Before you get Jimmy on the topic of sex and marriage," said Mickey "we came to ask you if you've had any trouble with any Jamaicans."

They both shook their heads. Simon said they get a few regular Jamaicans in, but they didn't give them any grief. Out of curiosity he asked why they'd asked.

They explained what was going on.

"We heard something about it," said Steve "but we didn't realise how bad it was. Hudson the poor bastard, now there was a man who liked to fuck! Let us know when the funeral is, we got on ok with Hudson, he was alright. We'll listen out for any news on the grapevine about the Jamaicans and we'll let you know if they show up here."

They thanked the twins then left.

In the car Jimmy suggested them having dinner with them that night as well as later in the week. Maria would be well chuffed to have them on both occasions as she was trying out some new recipes for the restaurant and needed more guinea pigs.

"As long as it's ok with Maria, I'd be only too happy to be her guinea pig and I've got no qualms whatsoever that Monica will be happy about it too."

Jimmy called Maria to check it was ok and just as he'd assumed she was thrilled they were coming, dinner would be served at eight.

Ten minutes later Mickey pulled up to drop him off. Before getting out of the car, Jimmy asked him not to mention the shooting at the club, only he hadn't told Maria yet. Grinning Mickey nodded.

Maria was in the kitchen as he walked in. Putting his arms around her, he kissed her neck and thanked her for letting him invite their friends. With a sexy grin, she said she was really happy they were coming as the basque she'd ordered for under her wedding dress had arrived and she'd really value Monica's opinion.

"I'll give you my opinion if you want to slip into it now?" said Jimmy with a sexy grin.

"Not a chance, you'll have to wait 'til our wedding night, but now you had better take me shopping, because I need some bits and pieces for the meal tonight."

He had never been keen on shopping but as he'd suggested having dinner guests, he felt obligated.

Fortunately the shopping trip didn't take very long; they were home within an hour. While she sorted out the meal she instructed him to lay the table for three courses and to chill some wine.

Time passed quickly. At quarter past seven she asked him to watch over the cooking while she quickly washed and changed. Just as she disappeared into the bathroom, his phone rang. There was no caller ID, the number had been withheld. "Jimmy," said a voice he recognised as Jamaican "da dog was just a warning, next time it'll be one a ya!"

Jimmy shouted down the phone, but the caller hung up. Maria appeared from the bathroom and asked if it had been Mickey who called. She knew he was lying when he said "Wrong number" because she had heard him shouting, but she decided not to ask simply because their guests were due to arrive at any minute.

Throughout the meal she noticed Jimmy seemed a bit edgy, even Mickey asked if he was ok. Trying to play it down he said he had a headache.

"This meal is fantastic," said Monica "I wish I had your culinary talents Maria."

"So do I!" joked Mickey.

"We've all got different talents!" snapped Monica as she pinched him playfully.

He didn't argue with that, although he did have to agree Maria certainly was a great cook. Monica looked excited when Maria said she'd be happy to give her cooking lessons.

They sat chatting while they drank their coffee after the meal. Talking mainly about the wedding with Monica dropping several hints about how lucky Maria was and that she wished it was her. The two men brought up the subject of Hudson in the hope Monica could tell them something. Their plan worked when she said there wasn't much evidence to go on because the body had been in the water a long time. Her colleagues had interviewed several people, but apparently no one saw or heard anything. Unaware the men wanted to hear what Monica had to say, Maria asked if they could change the subject and not talk about dead bodies. She wanted to show Monica the underwear she'd bought for the wedding.

The two girls left the men talking and went off into the bedroom and not a minute too soon for Jimmy; he wanted to tell Mickey about the anonymous phone call. Mickey listened to him and said perhaps whoever it was had simply done it to frighten them.

"I couldn't swear to it Mick, but I think it was that Damon who made the call; can't be absolutely sure because all Jamaicans sound the fucking same! As a precaution I think we should call the clubs, just to check on things; also we need to call Tony to see if John Duggan told him anything."

Between them they rang the clubs and Tony. To their relief everything at the clubs was fine, there had been no sign of the Jamaicans. Tony said John told him it was the same as with them, the Jamaicans wanted to buy his club; when he refused, they got punchy. Tony wasn't sure how Shaun was doing with the doormen, he would try to find out and ring back.

"I'm beginning to think the Jamaicans want to muscle in on our manor," said Mickey "could be they're looking to take over some business Jimmy."

"Over my dead body Mick, we've worked too long and too fucking hard to let a bunch of fucking Jamaican bastards take over!"

"I agree and business is good especially from the clubs and we rarely get any trouble with the Old Bill. I work hard to keep things looking kosher. Too much trouble with the Jamaicans could have them poking around, which could be dangerous."

The girls returned from the bedroom whispering and giggling. When Mickey asked if everything was ok, Monica giggled and said Jimmy's in for a real treat and of course he could be too, if they were getting married. Everyone was aware she was dropping yet another hint. They talked about marriage and Jimmy assured her that one day Mickey would make an honest woman of her. With a giggle she agreed, but added she hoped she would still be young enough to walk up the aisle without a Zimmer frame.

The four friends laughed.

They continued to talk about the wedding until Monica realised the time. It was quarter to one and she had the early shift in the morning.

At the door they thanked their hosts for a wonderful evening. The two men arranged to talk the following day before Mickey and Monica left.

With their friends gone; Maria was just about to suggest them turning in for the night when they heard a loud bang like a car back firing. They wouldn't have taken much notice had it not have been instantly followed by yelling. Jimmy rushed over to the window and looked down into the street.

"Fuck me Maria," he shouted "phone an ambulance, something's happened down stairs!"

Within seconds he was running out of the front door, not waiting for the lift he took the stairs.

Just outside the main door he could see Mickey crouched down over Monica. Moving closer, he could see his friend was covered in blood. Instantly he asked if she was ok and that an ambulance was on its way. Monica had been shot.

Mickey held her in his arms; she was breathing and trying to talk. He told her to just lie quietly until the ambulance arrived.

Maria appeared and, seeing her friend lying on the ground covered in blood, the colour drained from her face as she started crying. Then they heard the siren.

A crowd had gathered in the street and the Old Bill had arrived. Two paramedics put Monica onto a stretcher and gave her some air through a mask. Mickey travelled with her in the ambulance repeatedly asking the paramedic if she would be ok, but the paramedic danced round the question without actually giving him an answer.

When they arrived at the hospital a team were waiting to take her to the operating theatre. Two nurses pushed the stretcher bed through the swing doors. A doctor told Mickey to wait outside. Moments later a nurse came over and took him to a waiting area, stating that someone would come and see him when they'd finished. Thanking her, he explained he was expecting his friends to join him and he'd need to let them know where he was. Reassuringly she said she would bring them to him.

Ten minutes later she returned with his friends. Maria just threw her arms around Mickey and sobbed. Jimmy said he'd go and find a coffee machine. Looking at him over Maria's shoulder as they embraced, Mickey nodded.

When Jimmy returned with their coffee, a doctor was talking to Mickey. They were going to try and remove the bullet; the procedure could take several hours. When Mickey asked if she would be ok, the Doctor said he was sorry but it was too early for him to make a prognosis, but he would have a nurse keep them informed.

Time dragged, Mickey kept looking at his watch. They talked about Monica.

"It's not until something like this happens," said Mickey "you realise what someone means to you. I do love her; I just wish I'd told her more often."

Jimmy tried to comfort him, telling him he knew exactly how he felt because he'd thought exactly the same when Maria was in the coma. Monica was a tough cookie though and he was sure she'd pull through.

Another nurse came in to check on them. Mickey asked if there was any news. Shaking her head she said they were still working on Monica, but she would let them know as soon as she could. Before leaving, she asked if she could get them anything. The two men shook their heads, but Maria asked if she could use the chapel.

With a smile the nurse said of course, it was just along the corridor and she would show her where. Maria knew where it was but felt she would like the nurse's company, so she just nodded. Jimmy knew that it was her way of dealing with things. After she'd left, Mickey said at times like these he wished he had half Maria's faith. Jimmy simply nodded.

Four hours had passed when a doctor finally entered the waiting room, he was still wearing his blood stained surgical gown. Mickey stood up desperate for any news.

"We've successfully removed the bullet, however there were some complications," said the surgeon; "we had to perform a hysterectomy because her womb had taken the bullet's impact. It was the only way we could stop the bleeding."

Looking desperate Mickey asked if she'd be ok. The surgeon said she'd lost a lot of blood so she'd have to stay in intensive care for several days, but her chances were better than average. Mickey thanked him and asked when he could see her.

Seeing the anguish on his face, the surgeon stated it would be several hours before she came round but if he wanted to have a brief moment with her that would be alright.

Following the surgeon, they headed for the intensive care unit where Monica was lying peacefully wired up to several monitors. Gently taking her hand, he kissed her forehead before telling her he loved her and he'd see her when she woke up.

Outside the hospital his friends were waiting for him. Jimmy suggested him staying the night with them as it probably wasn't a good time for him to be alone. Mickey nodded and, thanking him, said he'd appreciate the company. It was half five in the morning when they arrived back at the apartment. Maria made coffee and asked if they wanted breakfast. None of them had any appetite. Jimmy suggested Maria going to bed to try and get some sleep; he would stay up to talk to Mickey.

Before going to bed, she kissed Mickey on the cheek and told him she would pray for Monica. Leaving them talking she headed towards the bedroom. Jimmy asked him exactly what had happened.

"We were just leaving the building Jim when a car drove past. We didn't take any notice at first until it slowed down, next thing we knew someone shot at us!"

"Did you get a look at them?"

"Oh yeah I fucking clocked him, it was a fucking Jamaican! The car was a black BMW, but I didn't catch the registration."

"We'll make these fucking Jamaicans pay for what they've done! I'll bell all the lads in a couple of hours and tell them what's happened. Fancy another coffee?"

Mickey nodded.

Returning from the kitchen with their drinks a few minutes later, he could see that the full impact of the shooting had just hit Mickey. Sitting with his face in his hands, Jimmy could hear him crying. He passed him a mug of coffee. Wiping his face, Mickey took it and said he was sorry about crying. Jimmy said it was a normal reaction, one he'd gone through many times when Maria was in the coma.

"When I thought she was dead, I realised I wouldn't know what to do without her. I didn't always treat her right Jimmy. I was always standing her up and sleeping with the dancers from the club. Once I even forgot her birthday. I did make it up to her, but I feel so bad about it now. No matter how bad I treated her, she was always there for me."

"It's normal to feel like that Mick, sometimes it takes a tragedy like this to make people realise what someone means to them, but sometimes if you're lucky like us, you get a second chance. I always remember how badly my father treated my mum, yet when she topped herself my old man cried for days. At the time I never understood why, but I do now."

Jimmy suggested they should try and get some sleep as there was nothing they could do for a few hours.

Mickey nodded and said he would call Charlie's mum later that morning and ask her not to let Charlie come over at the weekend, just until things had settled down.

It was just after nine when Jimmy surfaced later that morning. Believing he was the first one up he walked into the lounge. Mickey said good morning and that the kettle was on. Jimmy wasn't surprised to hear he hadn't slept, due to the Jamaicans laying heavy on his mind. His theory was they had meant to shoot him and Monica had simply got in the way. Jimmy thought the same. Mickey looked angry, they'd gone too far and he would make them pay for what they'd done.

Maria joined them and after saying she must have dozed back off, offered to cook them breakfast.

When Mickey said he really wasn't hungry, she insisted he ate something. Finally after they both nagged him, he agreed to have scrambled egg.

"So are you going to tell me what's going on and don't lie to me Jimmy," said Maria, "I know something is. I'm not stupid."

"She's right Jimmy. We should tell her" said Mickey "before someone else does."

Sitting quietly, she listened as they went over the full story about the Jamaicans. Despite being angry they hadn't told her sooner, she knew Jimmy was sincere when he said he hadn't wanted to worry her and especially with their wedding only weeks away. Knowing how excited she was about getting married, Mickey felt quite humbled when she offered to put the wedding on hold until Monica was better. Thanking her, he said there was no need as he felt confident Monica would be well on to the road to recovery by then. He'd called Charlie's mum earlier that morning, she was going to tell Charlie what happened to Monica. She even offered to run her over so she could visit because she knew how much Charlie liked Monica.

Maria smiled and said that was nice of her.

"Funny thing really," said Mickey "we get on better now as friends than we ever did as man and wife. I also called Monica's family; her parents are going to drive up from Devon today. They probably won't get here till late evening. I'm going to book them into a hotel near the hospital. It's probably not a good idea for them to stay with me, just in case we have any more trouble. Fortunately she's an only child, so I know there are only her parents and a couple of aunts and uncles. Her parents were frantic when I told them. They did feel a bit better when I told them the nurse said she was comfortable and she's being taken off the critical list."

"Oh that's good."

"Yeah, but she also said I would be the only visitor allowed in to see her today. I explained that her parents would be here this evening; fortunately she said it would be ok if they wanted to go with me. Cheeky bloody cow did say she'd prefer them to leave it until tomorrow though. I can just see them agreeing to that, wild horses couldn't keep them away. She said it would be better for me to leave visiting for a couple of hours as Monica's not really awake yet, she's been heavily sedated."

Mickey's phone rang, it was Charlie. Her voice sounded tearful as she asked if Monica was going to be alright. Reassuringly he repeated what the nurse had said earlier and that from the sound of it, Monica would be fine. Charlie sounded disappointed when, after asking if she could see Monica, her dad said probably not for a few days, but he would let her know.

They chatted for a few minutes. Charlie wanted to know all the details, but Mickey tried to play it down by saying it was just a random drive by shooting because he didn't want to worry her. Calling her princess, he said he loved her and would talk to her again later. She told him she loved him too and to give her love to Uncle Jimmy and Maria before he ended the call.

When the call ended he relayed her love to Jimmy and Maria. He wasn't surprised when Maria said Charlie was a lovely girl and she'd often said how she wished her dad would marry Monica because she really liked her.

Mickey knew he was lucky that the two most important girls in his life got on so well. Perhaps Charlie was right, maybe he should marry Monica. Yesterday's incident had certainly made him realise just how much she meant to him.

Maria said maybe they should have a double wedding, Mickey shocked them when he said if Monica was well enough and if she accepted his proposal they were on.

Leaping to her feet, Maria flung her arms around him and stated that would be wonderful and she knew exactly what dress Monica would want as she'd picked it out when they were shopping for hers.

"Fuck me Mick," laughed Jimmy "now we're going to have this for the next seven weeks!"

"Yeah," said Mickey "but unlike yours, ours won't be a long engagement! Maybe after yesterday she won't want me?"

Maria laughed and said there was no chance of that; she was absolutely besotted with him.

Mickey said he'd have to go home; he needed to shower and change his clothes. He'd call back round after he'd seen Monica.

As he left they told him to give their love to Monica and they'd see him later.

CHAPTER 24

When Mickey arrived at the hospital, he was surprised to see the slimy Detective Samuels waiting outside intensive care. When Samuels tried to ask him some questions Mickey was quite standoffish with him, telling him he'd speak to him after he'd seen Monica. Leaving the detective standing at the door, Mickey entered the unit. A staff nurse stopped him and said that Monica was still very drowsy but the doctor was very pleased with her. She'd need lots of rest over the next few days.

Mickey thanked her and asked if she was aware a detective was waiting outside to speak to Monica. He grinned when she abruptly replied that yes she did know but like she'd told him earlier, she was in charge so he'd be in for a long wait, Monica needed rest not questions.

Mickey nodded; it was obvious she wouldn't take any crap from Samuels. Moments later he was sitting by Monica's bed gently holding her hand. Slowly she opened her eyes and said hello to him.

"You had me worried there for a minute babe."

"You won't get rid of me that easily," she replied before she drifted off momentarily.

Leaning over he whispered something in her ear. A few seconds passed then slowly she opened her eyes again and asked him to repeat what he'd said. Although drowsy from the drugs, she smiled when he said he'd asked her to marry him.

"I would have got shot years ago if I'd known you'd propose," she said before she drifted off again.

Mickey stayed with her for another hour until the nurse said it was better if he left her to rest. Just as he was about to leave, she woke up and asked if she'd dreamt him proposing. Taking her hand, he said he had asked her, she smiled and accepted. Seconds later she dropped off again.

Outside Samuels was waiting for him. He asked a nurse if there was a room they could use. Checking that one was available, she showed them in.

"Monica's a lucky girl," said Samuels "could have turned out a lot worse. Have you any idea who did it?"

Mickey shook his head and stated that everything had happened so fast he didn't get a good look at the gunman, although he thought he was black, maybe Jamaican.

"That's interesting" said Samuels smugly "as I hear you've been having a few problems with some Jamaicans?"

"First I've heard about it," replied Mickey sarcastically "we had a couple of Jamaicans who got a bit too friendly with a couple of the dancers, but not really trouble. I certainly wouldn't assume that the two incidents were connected."

"That's why you're a solicitor and I'm a detective Mickey. I assume everything."

"Yes, Monica's often said you're very good at making assumptions and let's be honest here, she is a first class detective."

Samuels knew he was referring to the anonymous gift Monica had received in the form of Maurice's deposit box, so changing tactics he said he just hoped Monica remembered something when she woke up. Then he asked Mickey exactly where he was the previous night. Mickey said they'd been dinner guests at Jimmy's.

"Ah yes him, the chap who's getting married. I've looked up his file, quite a criminal in his younger days. I'll be popping round to have a little chat with your friend Jimmy."

"I wouldn't waste your time detective, they didn't see anything and for the record he's a legitimate business man. In fact a very successful business man with several clubs and restaurants to his credit that no doubt costs him a small fortune in taxes."

The tension between the two men was growing stronger by the second and even more so when Samuels sarcastically said, it was tax payer's money that paid him to keep the scum off the streets. Mickey had more than enough of the slimy detective so he told him he had to go as he needed to double check the hotel reservations for Monica's parents. His actual destination would be Jimmy's, but he wasn't about to tell Samuels that. Mickey simply nodded as he walked away and Samuels said he may need to speak to him again.

Back at Jimmy's apartment, they were thrilled to hear that Monica was doing well. Maria was preparing them yet another lunch.

"If I keep eating here," joked Mickey "I'll have to start paying housekeeping, although I must admit it's a pleasure, you're such a great cook."

Jimmy's phone rang; it was Tony calling to tell them they may have struck lucky. He'd been checking out the local hotels and 'Flanders Hotel' just off the high street had five Jamaicans staying there. When Jimmy asked if he thought they were the same Jamaicans, Tony was in no doubt as they'd signed in under the name Damon Sinclair. Thick bastards used the same name as they knew them by. He thought they should meet up to talk about it.

Jimmy suggested he came round as Maria was just doing lunch and he could eat with them.

Jimmy ended the call and told them what Tony had said and how he hoped Maria didn't mind that he'd invited Tony to lunch.

"Well it's a bit late to ask now as he's on his way," giggled Maria, "but as it happens I've got plenty."

"That's why I love her Mick," said Jimmy with a grin "she never moans about anything."

Twenty minutes later the intercom buzzed, it was Tony.

Maria opened the door to him and after telling him how nice it was to see him, offered him a drink.

He said coffee as he kissed her cheek then he thanked her for inviting him for lunch. After taking their drinks, she left the three men talking business and returned to the kitchen.

Tony began telling them what he'd managed to find out.

"I know the owner of Flanders Hotel, which is very handy. The Jamaicans checked in six weeks ago and checked out after four, but another interesting fact is around the time that John Duggan's boys got a bit out of hand with one of the Jamaicans, a doctor came to the hotel and it was several days before the staff saw one particular Jamaican. So I think we can assume he was the one that was injured. When he did come out of the room, he had a large gash down the side of his face that would fit in with what John told me about the incident at the Cove."

When Mickey asked if they'd left a forwarding address Tony shook his head, but stated he didn't think they'd gone far because every week one of them called round to pick up any post. So far he'd always called on Thursday afternoons.

Mickey suggested calling Lenny Porter. He could go round to the hotel then, if the Jamaican turned up, he could follow him. None of their boys could do it because the Jamaicans knew them but they wouldn't notice Lenny, he blended in.

They all agreed it was a good idea just as Maria called to tell them lunch was ready.

Mickey told Tony about his encounter with Samuels at the hospital and how in his opinion the Nazi party had lost a good man when Samuels left and joined the police force! He told Jimmy to expect a visit from Samuels, but to watch him, because he knew they'd all stuck to the same story and no doubt he would be hoping someone would slip up.

The conversation moved onto the clubs with Mickey saying they should check in on them later. He asked if Tony could check Lazer for them.

"No problem," grinned Tony "even though it means I'll have to watch all that young totty wriggling about in their miniskirts I'll grin and bear it!"

They all laughed.

"Yeah," said Jimmy "we can see how much you'll hate that Tony!"

Everyone laughed except Maria. She knew Tony was a player, yet his wife Isabella was beautiful and she adored him. Jimmy could see the look on her face, so in an effort to change the topic he asked her if she had anything planned for later. She said she'd like to pop down to the restaurant at some point as they had a new waiter starting that night. Leon had interviewed him, but she felt she should go and introduce herself. It would be nice if Jimmy went with her. Mickey saw the look of disappointment on her face when he said he couldn't, but he would get Shaun to take her, so he quickly suggested the three of them eating at the restaurant, then the two men could go on to the club afterwards. Leon or Shaun could always give Maria a lift home if she wanted to stay late.

"Good idea," said Jimmy "once all the trouble passes you'll be able to come to the club with us babe."

"That would be nice," said Maria.

It was unusual for club bosses to take their wives or regular girlfriends to the clubs because most of them would have a girl on the side, but not Jimmy. He loved showing her off and he would never do anything deliberate to jeopardise their relationship. Before the trouble she would often join him at Dixie's, although she never really felt comfortable at Sweet Cheeks. Truth was she found it quite embarrassing watching the dancers. Despite being friendly with a couple of them, especially Simone who she got along really well with, Maria found it degrading. She was just about to ask when they would be able to visit Monica at the hospital when the intercom rang.

Jimmy answered, it was Samuels. At the same time back in the lounge, Mickey had a call on his phone; it was Monica's dad confirming they had arrived in London. Mickey arranged to meet them at their hotel.

When Jimmy called out that Samuels was on his way up Mickey quickly looked at Tony and said they could leave via the stairs before he got there. Tony instantly stood up.

They kissed Maria quickly on the cheek before they left.

As the detective walked out of the lift, he noticed the stairway door close, just missing whoever it was by a whisker.

Jimmy opened the door and invited him in. Maria offered him a drink. Declining her offer Samuels scanned the apartment. Telling them he was there to discuss the shooting, he asked if they could remember anything about the incident. Jimmy shook his head and stated the first he knew about it was when he looked out of the window and saw Mickey on the pavement holding Monica. It was then he'd shouted for Maria to call an ambulance.

"Do you think the attack has any connection to any of your business interests? Only Mickey believed the shooter to have been black and rumour has it some Jamaicans have been causing you a few problems lately?"

Jimmy acted very cool shook his head and looking surprised said, "No detective, as far as I'm aware a couple of Jamaicans got a bit rowdy with a couple of our dancers, but there's nothing unusual about that. As you know most of the blokes are married men just out to have a good time, but sometimes they have too much to drink and get a bit over zealous."

Samuels nodded then looked at Maria.

"I've heard about your restaurant, I've been told the food is excellent. Unfortunately on a detective's salary I doubt I could afford to eat there which is a shame, because it's my sister's birthday next week and I always take her out for dinner."

Knowing that Samuels was fishing for a free meal, Jimmy interrupted and suggested Samuels took his sister to Maria's with their compliments. If he let Jimmy know which night, he would reserve them a table.

The detective was used to being offered perks; it came with being an arsehole, although he knew that Jimmy would not have offered had there been any strings attached. The only reason he had done it was to impress the detective that he was a shrewd business man with many assets. Regardless of his reasons, Samuels was only too happy to accept and stated he'd be taking her out the coming Monday.

When Maria said she would book a table for two for eight o'clock, Samuels said that was perfect. Then he talked about her getting married, even offering his congratulations, but before she could thank him, he said he wasn't sure about the men who were arranging the stag night, they seemed quite a bunch and was she sure her future husband would be safe with them.

"On the contrary detective," she replied, not about to let him run their friends down "with people running around London shooting innocent bystanders, I will be only too happy for them to take him on his stag night, especially as the police don't seem to have a lot of luck in catching the criminals who are responsible for such terrible things!"

Jimmy afforded himself a smirk. She certainly caught on quick. Samuels smirked as he stood up and said he may need to speak to them again.

"We're always available;" said Jimmy "I hope the police soon find the people responsible for the shooting. It simply isn't safe to walk the streets anymore and after all, that is part of what we pay our taxes for."

Samuels knew he was taking the piss, but there was nothing he could do or say. Samuels left.

Jimmy put his arm round Maria and said, "Thank fuck he's gone! Oh and I liked what you said about my stag night babe, that shut him straight up!"

"I wasn't even aware you were having a stag night, but I suppose if you are Simone and a couple of the girls from the club would be only too happy to do something with me. They keep mentioning it. The last time I spoke to Simone she mentioned something about male strippers who are at the Denbigh that week?"

From the minute she said it, it was obvious to her he wasn't keen on the idea when he quickly said it wouldn't be her scene and she probably wouldn't enjoy it. She knew what he really meant was he didn't want her to go. In the two years they had lived together she had never really gone anywhere without him, except for the odd shopping trip, or lunch with Monica or Simone. With a giggle she said if she didn't know better she might think he was jealous. Despite wanting to convince her he wasn't; truth be known he was.

"Don't get me wrong babe," he said "you'd probably enjoy a night out with your friends. I just think strippers are not your cup of tea, you'd be better off taking the girls for a meal at one of our restaurants and then going onto one of our clubs."

"Oh Jimmy you're so funny, do you really think I'd want to go and watch other men strip off when I have you. I've already asked Monica and a couple of the girls if they want to go out to eat then on to the club, but if I thought you didn't trust me I'd be so angry."

Feeling bad that he didn't want her to go, he tried to redeem himself by stating it wasn't her he didn't trust, but he knew how blokes thought and they'd be round her like bees round a honey pot! Despite what he'd said, he knew in his mind the reason their relationship was so good was simply because he called all the shots. Many of the girls he had dated in the past would often go out drinking and clubbing with their friends but Maria was different, for the first year she had rarely left the apartment without him. Then as her confidence grew, she started wearing makeup and clothes that showed off her figure and more recently she'd started accepting invitations from Monica to go out shopping and for lunch. Even on those rare occasions, he would always ask her where they'd been and how long they'd been out; did they see anyone he knew, or did they chat to anyone. Monica would often joke with him and say 'we only went for lunch; it's like the Spanish inquisition!' Always he would try and joke about it, but they knew he was insecure about Maria being out without him.

Maria was annoyed with what he'd said about men being like bees round a honey pot and she was about to let him know.

"You should know I'm totally faithful Jimmy and it takes two to tango! So even if another man did hit on me, you know I'd tell him in no uncertain terms I wasn't interested!"

Looking a bit sheepish he said he hadn't meant her, he just knew what men were like when they saw a beautiful woman. Despite trying to justify what he'd said, he knew she was right; the very thought of any man hitting on her made him feel sick to his stomach. His dark side was always lurking just under the surface. He would rather see her dead than with another man. He remembered how he had loathed Nick because of how he had treated her, yet for that brief moment he had become him.

Watching him she could see his body language change, there was something about him that made her feel uneasy. What had started out as a silly game was beginning to send alarm bells through her head. In two years she had never really seen this side to him, this controlling jealous side and quite frankly she didn't like it. There had been times when they were out that he would make it quite clear to other men she was with him. She'd also noticed that when he came home after a fight he would always want sex, but he had never hurt her, nor had he ever implied that he didn't trust her. She had never wanted to go out without him, now she was beginning to realise that if she did, he wouldn't like it. She found this infuriating, because she had never so much as looked at another man, let alone fancied one.

Feeling the tension growing between them and hoping to change not only the subject but the atmosphere that was developing, he pulled her to him and kissed her.

"Don't imagine you can win me round so easily," she said pulling away from him "you've upset me Jimmy, I feel very hurt that you don't trust me!"

Unexpectedly, he grabbed hold of her and shouted at her.

"Yes ok Maria, you're right, but I know how easy it is to trust the wrong people and I have never said I don't trust you! Truth is I would die without you, and yes I'm a jealous bastard, but if I didn't love you so much, I wouldn't fucking care! If you want the truth I would kill any bloke who touched you, so now you know does it make you feel better?"

Shocked by his outburst, she burst into tears and apologising told him she had only been joking but now they were arguing about it. He said he was sorry too, but he couldn't help the way he felt about her, she was the most important thing in his life.

They began to kiss passionately, within minutes they were naked. Pushing her up against the lounge wall, she wrapped her legs tightly around his body. Seconds later he entered her with such force and passion she groaned with every thrust of his body. When he'd finished they lay down on the sofa, their bodies wrapped around one another. Still breathing heavily, she gently stroked the side of his face.

"See what you do to me babe, you bring out the jealous angry man in me, which even I don't like but when I'm around you I can't help myself."

She didn't say anything; she simply kissed him softly on the lips. Within minutes they were cuddled up together asleep. They were woken by his phone ringing. It was Mickey.

Jimmy asked how Monica was on answering the call. He was pleased to hear she was doing really well and Maria would be able to visit her the following day. Mickey continued and told him he'd arranged for Lenny to go to the hotel where the Jamaicans stayed. The call ended when Mickey said he had to go and he'd see them at the restaurant at ten that evening.

When Jimmy repeated to her what Mickey had said, she was thrilled about seeing Monica but suggested Jimmy calling the restaurant to reserve them a table. Chef Leon would probably blow a gasket because it was such short notice.

After sweet talking the chef, Jimmy managed to book a table.

As usual he was ready before her, but as always she was worth the wait. She looked stunning when she finally emerged from the bedroom. Wearing a white figure hugging dress, her hair was swept up and the tasteful jewellery he had bought for her finished everything off perfectly.

"You look beautiful babe," he said "this is why I'm so jealous, you're without a doubt the best looking girl in London; if not the world!"

"Oh stop it Jimmy," she giggled.

Thirty minutes later they were entering the restaurant and instantly he was aware of the other diners looking at her, especially the men. Jeremy the new waiter greeted them.

"Good evening madam, sir, do you have a reservation?" he asked politely.

"You must be Jeremy," said Jimmy offering his hand "I'm Jimmy and this lovely lady is Maria, we own the restaurant."

Jeremy apologised for not realising who they were and said it was a pleasure to meet them. After taking their jackets, he showed them to their table.

Once they were seated, Jimmy ordered a bottle of wine and their choice of meals. Jeremy returned to the kitchen with their order.

Jimmy grinned at Maria and stated that Jeremy was definitely an iron hoof. Looking shocked she said she wouldn't have assumed that and how did he know he was gay. With a grin, he stated that was easy to answer. When they'd arrived every man in the restaurant had looked at her, every man except Jeremy and he eyed Jimmy up.

Giggling she joked and said if he'd been alone without her, he might have pulled.

"Let me tell you something babe, if anyone like Jeremy ever so much as implied that he fancied me, I wouldn't have a problem beating him to death!"

"Oh Jimmy you're so old fashioned, being gay is considered quite normal nowadays."

"Sticking your cock up another man's arse is not fucking normal and never will be!"

She knew he would never change his opinion on gays, but as long as he was respectful and polite to Jeremy, he was entitled to his opinion.

They chatted as they enjoyed their meal. Jeremy came over to ask if everything was alright. Maria said the meal had been superb and they'd like to order two coffees. Before he left, she asked if he could make a reservation for two on Monday evening at eight in the name of Samuels; it would be on the house. Jimmy asked him to give Mr Samuels and his guest a bottle of champagne and to wish the lady a very happy birthday on their behalf.

Jeremy said he would make the booking, but he'd actually already taken a complimentary booking for two on Monday after a gentleman telephoned to make reservations. It was made in the name of Bridger. Jimmy nodded and said both bookings were fine and would Jeremy also include a bottle of their best wine for Mr Bridger and his guest.

When Jeremy returned to the kitchen, Jimmy explained that Shane was taking Max out on his night off so he'd told him to bring her there, but he didn't think for one minute Shane would get anywhere with Max, although maybe after bringing her to such a fine establishment he'd be one step nearer to the bedroom.

She pinched his leg under the table and said he had a dirty mind!

"Yeah and as they say babe, a dirty mind is a terrible thing to waste!"

They didn't realise how quickly the time had passed, until Mickey showed up to join them at quarter past ten. After introducing him to Jeremy, Maria asked if he'd eaten. When he shook his head, she insisted he had something and promptly ordered him a steak.

They talked about Monica and how she'd surprised everyone at the hospital with her recovery. Mickey's theory was she was willing herself better because of his wedding proposal.

They all laughed.

They chatted while he ate his meal. When he finished he suggested him and Jimmy leaving as it was almost half eleven. They could drop Maria off on the way to the club to save Leon having to take her home when the restaurant closed.

Half an hour later they were pulling into a reserved parking space at the club. After talking to the staff at Dixie's, they were happy to hear that there had been nothing out of the ordinary happening so they went on to Sweet Cheeks.

Shane was on the door when they arrived, he told them everything was good and the club was busy. They'd had a couple of Jamaicans in, but they were regulars and never any trouble, although he thought it was strange how the troublesome Jamaicans seemed to have given up. It had been days without any sign of them.

"I don't doubt for one minute they'll be back," said Mickey "although I'm surprised too with the sudden quiet, but they're devious bastards who no doubt are planning something. With any luck, Lenny will have news on their whereabouts within the next few days."

Jimmy talked about the restaurant booking for Monday and how Max was still keen to go with him. They laughed when Shane said he thought Max was secretly gagging for him and just playing hard to get.

Shane looked surprised when Jimmy said Samuels would be there and why they'd invited the detective to dine there. Having no love for the detective, Shane was quick to joke and say he hoped he didn't put him off his fucking dinner.

Mickey suggested that under the circumstances, it might just be best if Shane kept out of his way but if Samuels did ask him anything, just for him to go along with what had already been said.

"No worries Mick. Having said that, Samuels will be off duty on Monday, so in theory if he does get lippy I could belt him one if I felt the need."

"As tempting as that might be Shane, I think you should save it for another time. Now tell us how Max is getting on."

"She's doing really well with the dancing. I've got to know her quite a bit; she's even talked to me about her past. Did you know she wanted to be a doctor and there's a kid, she's got a son of twenty months. Her parents look after him while she works but they think she works in the club bar. She never really talks about the father, but from the few things she has said, he's bad news. Her and the boy are better off without him."

They all agreed she was different, definitely not your average pole dancer.

With things running smoothly at the clubs, Mickey said he was going home as he was meeting Monica's parents at their hotel at ten in the morning. Jimmy said he would go home too as he was knackered. After saying goodbye to Shane and the other doormen they left.

Maria was fast asleep when he got home. Standing quietly in the bedroom, he looked at her; she was so beautiful, with her hair cascading across the pillow and part of her naked body showing where the duvet had slipped off. Slowly he got into the bed next to her. She stirred.

"Sshh, it's only me babe," he said as he placed his arm around her and fondled her breast. Then gently moving her hair he began kissing her neck and back. Moving his hand up and down her body, she began to wake up. Slowly she turned to face him, but he wrapped his arms tightly around her so she couldn't roll over.

"Stay the way you are babe," he said "I want to take you from behind."

Moving his hands up and down her body, he wanted her more and more as she pushed his hand down onto her, arching with pleasure every time his fingers touched her. When the time was right he entered her, still stimulating her with his fingers.

He remembered how jealous he had been earlier; he would never let another man touch her. Even as he thought about it he thrust himself harder into her. Making love to her this way he felt he had total control over her, be it all for only a short while.

As they lay holding each other afterwards, Jimmy apologised for the jealous way he'd behaved earlier.

"It's okay Jimmy, I like the fact that you feel so passionately about me. It was only because I thought you didn't trust me I made an issue of it."

They kissed and cuddled for ages before they finally settled down to sleep.

Over breakfast the following morning, Maria said she'd been thinking about the possibility of them having a double wedding with Mickey and Monica. Jimmy nodded and knowing Mickey as well as he did, he thought it could definitely be on. Maria stated they should let Father Thomas know and hopefully he could arrange it, should Mickey take up their offer.

"Tell Thomas we'll make a donation to the church for any inconvenience babe. I can't see it being a problem if it does happen. The guest list wouldn't change very much, the only extras would be Monica's parents and a few of her work friends. All of Mickey's family will be there anyway; even Fay and her family are coming over from the States. So as far as I can see a double wedding wouldn't cause any hassle at all and I'm sure the hotel would welcome some more guests at a hundred and fifty quid a head."

She nodded just as his phone rang. It was Tony calling to let him know the coroner had just called him to say Hudson's body had been released and he'd asked who was going to arrange the funeral. None of Hudson's family overseas was going to pay; they weren't even going to come over although they were all hoping he made a will the cheeky bastards!

People like that were worse than fucking vultures in Jimmy's opinion, so it looked like they would have to pay the bill. He'd leave the arrangements to Tony.

Maria was looking forward to seeing Monica later that afternoon. When she asked if they could stop off at a florist on the way to the hospital and get her a bouquet, Jimmy nodded and said of course.

While she busied herself, he called Mickey to tell him about Hudson and the fact that they were paying for the funeral.

"What with weddings and now funerals to fucking pay for Jimmy, perhaps we should put our protection fees up just to cover the expenses!"

They both laughed.

Mickey arranged to meet them at the hospital at two as Monica's parents were going to visit her again later that evening.

Maria had asked Jimmy to go with her to see Father Thomas before they went to the hospital, begrudgingly he had agreed as it was en route. Father Thomas was very pleased to see them when they both walked into the church later that day. Maria kissed him affectionately on the cheek before Jimmy shook hands with him. Maria told the priest that it was likely to be a double wedding. She wasn't surprised when Thomas said that would be wonderful and perhaps both men could attend a Sunday service soon. Looking less than enthusiastic, Jimmy nodded and said he'd speak to Mickey about it.

After talking to Thomas for almost thirty minutes, Jimmy smiled and stated they couldn't stay much longer as they were meeting Mickey at the hospital.

As they left, Thomas said he would continue to pray for Monica and he hoped to see them all soon.

When they arrived at the hospital, Mickey was waiting for them. Jimmy said he'd expected him to be in the room with Monica.

"I was, but I came out to warn you that the nurse on duty is a right old battle axe. You'll have to tell her you're Monica's brother and sister; otherwise she won't let you in to see her."

"Neither of us looks fuck all like her!" laughed Jimmy.

"That doesn't matter, but just in case the nurse smells a rat, just say you're her brother from your mother's first marriage and Maria is the child from your dad's second marriage."

"It's true what they say about solicitors, their nothing but a bunch of devious bastards!"

They all laughed.

As they approached the intensive care unit the nurse appeared from a small office. Instantly she looked at Maria carrying the bouquet and stated flowers were not permitted in ITC, but Maria could leave them there and when Monica moved to a private room she could have them.

Maria thanked her and with a grin asked how her sister was doing. The nurse said she was doing well.

After the nurse returned to her office, Jimmy pinched Maria's bum and said she'd go straight to Hell for lying. With a grin she stated she wouldn't because she'd ask Father Thomas to square it with God for her.

They all laughed.

They were all surprised to see Monica sitting up in bed smiling. Maria kissed her on the cheek and asked how she was doing. Monica was happy to tell her she felt better and it was only painful when she moved or coughed; otherwise it wasn't too bad considering she'd been shot.

When Maria talked about the possibility of a double wedding she noticed that her friend looked quite sad, so she asked if she would be ok with it.

Hoping the men wouldn't hear her as they were talking, almost in a whisper Monica admitted to her she was worried that Mickey had only asked her because of what had happened. Maria dismissed that thought by stating he loved her.

"You don't have to talk about me as if I'm not here babe;" said Mickey taking Monica's hand "you only have to ask me."

"More than anything Mickey I want to be your wife; only things are different now. I'll never be able to give you children, so I need to be sure we're doing it for the right reasons and not because I got shot and you feel obligated."

"I love you babe, when I thought I could lose you I realised I should have asked you a long time ago. As for children, that isn't a big issue for me, but if you really want them we could adopt."

Then to everyone's surprise, he went down on one knee and taking her hand asked her to marry him.

Tearfully she nodded and said "Yes."

Maria also had tears in her eyes, she knew he was a smooth operator, but she never realised how romantic he could be. Reaching over, Maria squeezed Jimmy's hand

Jimmy quickly reminded her they were supposed to be brother and sister and the nurse was watching them from her office.

"Thank God she didn't see us last night then!" said Maria giggling.

CHAPTER 25

No one was surprised when, over the next few days, Monica continued to improve. Within a week of being shot, she was moved to her own room.

Everything on the Jamaican front was quiet; no one had seen or heard anything. Tony had arranged Hudson's funeral, he was to be cremated that week with a wake being held afterwards at one of their restaurants, probably Satins, because it was closest to the crematorium.

Mickey was uneasy about the Jamaicans since a full ten days had passed and no one had seen or heard anything. Lenny hadn't had any luck at the hotel the first week, but he was going there again that Thursday.

Monica was getting stronger by the day. She had arranged to stay with Maria when the hospital released her. Mickey was pleased about it, because once her parents returned to Devon, she would have no one except him to look after her and he did have his law firm to run as well as other things. Another bonus was it meant that he would get to eat Maria's cooking every night.

It was the evening before Hudson's funeral, Jimmy's phone rang. It was Lenny Porter to tell him he'd been at the hotel waiting for the Jamaicans. He thought it was going to be like the previous week with no one showing up, but then out of the blue one of them turned up to collect a parcel. Lenny had followed him to an apartment just ten minutes from the hotel. He could see the other Jamaicans inside, but he'd wanted to get a closer look so he'd climbed onto the balcony so he could hear what they were saying.

"Great work Lenny, we've got the fuckers now! I just hope the hotel didn't think you were a peeping Tom!"

"No one fucking saw me, but the traffic made it difficult for me to hear. Now here's the good bit, I did hear one of them make reference to Hudson's funeral. The problem was I couldn't hear what he said, a fucking great lorry went past, so I'm going to stay here and keep watching. I'll try to bug the apartment if they leave."

Jimmy told him to be careful and it was a great feeling to know the ball was back in their court.

Immediately after the call ended, he phoned Mickey to tell him the news. He suggested now they knew the Jamaicans were still in London, maybe they ought to tighten security at the clubs especially while they were at the funeral. Even though the clubs would be closed, the Jamaicans might see it as an ideal opportunity to do something if they thought no one would be there. Jimmy said he would phone round the boys and get cover for the ones who were going to the funeral, especially Shane and Billy as everyone knew they'd be going.

When the call ended, Jimmy called Shane first and told him what Lenny had found out.

Shane was confident getting cover wouldn't be a problem; they had some good blokes who worked for them on a casual basis who would be only too happy to hold the fort while they were at the funeral. He offered to call Billy and let him know what was going on.

Jimmy said he'd see him the next day at the funeral before ending the call.

The time was after midnight when Jimmy finally went to bed.

Over breakfast the following morning, Maria asked if she had to attend the funeral stating she'd never been to a cremation, Catholics were always buried. She'd never been to a funeral either, but she'd seen hundreds conducted over the years at St Augustus. Jimmy wanted her to go with him as a sign of respect. Although she'd only met Hudson once or twice she would be expected to attend. Wanting to please him, she agreed to go.

Mickey had arranged to meet them so they could drive to the funeral parlour together; from there they would follow the hearse. The cremation was to be held at two o'clock. It was a little after half nine that morning when Jimmy's phone rang. It was Lenny to tell him he'd successfully planted a bug at the Jamaicans and while listening to their conversation from the night before, he thought there was something Jimmy should hear.

They arranged to meet at his office in half an hour after he'd picked Mickey up.

Less than an hour later, the two friends were sitting in Lenny's office. Mickey joked and asked how he ever got any clients as surely the state of the place would put most people off. The office resembled somewhere that had been burgled.

"People aren't interested in my office," grinned Lenny "they want to hire the best PI London has to offer and that's me!"

Both men agreed with that statement.

There were piles of old newspapers, empty coffee cups and take away dishes everywhere. It could certainly be said if anyone needed a cleaner it was Lenny, although any cleaner who took his office on would certainly have their work cut out. Jimmy suggested the person he needed to get the place ship shape was Gladys, she'd soon fucking sort him out. Jimmy guaranteed that within a week she'd have Lenny house trained!

"I'd never get any work done," said Lenny "she never stops fucking talking! Anyway I know exactly where everything is, thank you!"

They all laughed. Neither of them could deny the fact that he was in a class of his own when it came to finding anything out. Lenny placed the tape in a machine on his desk and told them it was the recording he wanted them to hear from the Jamaicans apartment.

They listened as the Jamaicans talked about hitting the funeral party at the restaurant. From the sound of it they intended to wait in the alley at the back of Satins restaurant until everyone was inside. Lenny stopped the recording and said the rest of the tape was much the same with the Jamaicans laughing and saying things like, 'they won't know what hit them.'

"Instead of risking any of our lives why don't we let Samuels earn his money for a change," said Mickey. "If we place our own people in the alley it could leave us vulnerable at the clubs, and judging by their arrogance on the tape someone is bound to be seriously injured or killed, not to mention the fact that a shootout in broad daylight would take some explaining. We'd have a hard time convincing the police that we knew nothing about it. An incident like that could open up a fucking big can of worms!"

"Those fucking Jamaicans are getting out of hand Mick," snapped Jimmy "especially as it doesn't sound like they're worrying about it being in broad daylight. What do they think; they're fucking invincible or something?"

Mickey agreed and suggested he would go and see Samuels. He'd tell him someone put the tape through the letter box of his office that morning. That way it became Samuels problem.

They agreed it was a good idea.

Lenny wiped the outer casing of the tape with a handkerchief to remove his finger prints and then handed Mickey the tape stating his prints should be on it.

Taking an envelope from his inside pocket, Mickey handed it to Lenny. Knowing it was cash, he told him to keep it as he was still working the case. He wanted to find out more about these Jamaicans. They'd get his bill when he'd finished. When Mickey told him to take it and consider it a bonus, Lenny thanked them and said it was appreciated.

Five minutes later they left and drove to the police station. Jimmy told him to watch Samuels because he was like a fucking bad penny that kept turning up.

"Yeah I know and Samuels is about to find out that I'm a bad penny too!" said Mickey "I'll be back in time for the funeral."

Forty minutes later, Mickey was walking towards the desk sergeant at the police station; he was familiar with him having seen him a few times. Smiling at Mickey, he asked how he could help him. Mickey expressed an urgent need to talk to Detective Samuels.

The officer phoned through to Samuels office and explained that Michael Mann was there to see him. Samuels told him to send him through.

After knocking, Mickey entered Samuels's office and smiled smugly as Samuels said he was surprised to see him and he hoped it was because he'd remembered something about the shooting.

Not wishing to spend a minute longer with the detective than necessary, Mickey said he was there on another matter as he handed him the tape and fed him the bullshit line that he had just received it at his office. Curiously, Samuels asked what was on it. When Mickey suggested he should listen to it, Samuels stood up and walked over to a filing cabinet where he took an old tatty tape recorder machine from the top of it. While the tape played, he kept looking at Mickey.

"And you've got no idea who sent you this?" said Samuels sarcastically when it finished.

Mickey shook his head and said he hadn't got a clue.

"Really Michael and I suppose you're still going to tell me that you're not having any trouble with any Jamaicans?"

"No that's right."

"So why then, if that's the case, would anyone send you this tape because it's obvious that the voices on the tape are Jamaican?"

"Beats me," said Mickey shrugging his shoulders "your guess is as good as mine."

"If you want my opinion Mickey, I'd say the tape is nothing more than a wind up."

"I wouldn't think anyone would go to so much trouble just for a wind up. In my opinion detective, the information on the tape seems genuine. They appear to have all the details of Hudson's funeral; surely such details would not be important unless they intended to do something? Can you imagine how it would look if you didn't take it seriously and something did happen?"

"So assuming you're right Mickey, why would someone send you the tape?"

"I wondered that myself and came to the only logical conclusion, it's probably something to do with Hudson. Maybe someone who intended to attend the funeral knows something about his death and they're concerned for their own safety? However, that's purely a guess on my part."

"Perhaps you're right, so I'm going to take the tape seriously. I'll send some officers to check things out; perhaps a police presence will be all that's needed to deter them, should any Jamaicans turn up. It will also give me a chance to speak to some of the people at the funeral."

Mickey knew that he wouldn't get any information from anyone, but if it meant the Jamaicans would back off, they would tolerate Samuels being there. After giving him the details of the funeral, he shook hands with him. Just as Mickey opened the door, Samuels called to him and asked how Monica was and if she'd remembered anything about the shooting. Mickey said she was recovering well, but he doubted she'd ever remember anything. With that he left.

Back at Jimmy's, he went over what Samuels had said and suggested that perhaps it would be safer to leave Maria at home, just in case there was any trouble.

"You're right Mick, but what if the Jamaicans are watching the restaurant they'll soon realise she's not there, which could also be dangerous. I doubt they'd have the balls to come here, but I don't fancy chancing it."

When the two men discussed whether they should take her to Mickey's parent's house or to Gladys's, Maria interrupted and stated she wasn't going anywhere and more to the point she was perfectly capable of making her own decisions. If they really didn't want her to attend Hudson's funeral, she would go and visit Monica at the hospital. Afterwards she could go to the church and see Father Thomas.

"It's only one fucking afternoon Maria, and for what it's worth, I'm not happy about you going anywhere on your own!" snapped Jimmy aggressively "for all we know the Jamaicans could be watching the apartment!"

"I appreciate that, but I'm not a child Jimmy."

"Ok then, just for talking sake how would you cope if when you left the church for instance, two big fucking Jamaicans pulled up in a car and dragged you inside? What exactly would you do about it? Or if they turned up here and burst into the apartment!"

Thinking about it for a moment, she knew in reality she would be no match for one Jamaican, let alone two. They were right and she knew that they had her best interests at heart so she reluctantly agreed to go to Gladys's, providing she could phone her first and check it was ok.

Jimmy apologised but stated they couldn't take the chance of her being hurt. He suggested telling Gladys she simply didn't fancy going to the funeral.

Maria understood, but said she wasn't sure if it would be a good idea to bring children into that type of environment as she would never allow her children to be put at risk.

Mickey could see by the look on Jimmy's face, what she had said had hit him like a thunder bolt. In the hope of reassuring her, Mickey said things like that were usually a one off.

Looking unconvinced, she quickly reminded him that not long ago, he'd had to send Charlie off to the States to protect her from Nick and the Russians.

With Mickey momentarily stuck for words, Jimmy interrupted and said the issue with Charlie was just a precaution. He could tell she was not convinced, but then was not the time to debate it so he told her to call Gladys as they'd have to leave soon.

Mickey suggested it might be a good idea to let the others know about the police. Jimmy agreed and told him to make some calls while he rescued Maria from Gladys who would no doubt keep her on the phone chatting.

He entered the room just as she ended the call, she smiled when she said Gladys had been fine about it and she'd be happy to see her.

After dropping her off they drove to the funeral parlour. During the drive Jimmy told him that what Maria had said earlier about kids bothered him, especially as he knew how much she wanted kids. He was worried she might change her mind about marrying him now.

"We all know how dangerous our way of life can be Jimmy. In some ways I believed Charlie was safer because she lived with her mother, but everybody's children are at risk one way or another; especially with the way our laws treats paedophiles and other high risk individuals. In my opinion dirty bastards are given a free hand to abuse kids and in most cases get away with it because some fucking high up judge tells us it's the law. Believe me; if anyone ever touched my girl I'd fucking kill them myself! I certainly wouldn't leave it to the justice system, no way! They'd find little pieces of them all over London. Well apart from his cock, I'd have that stuffed and mounted on my lounge wall! Don't worry about Maria mate; she's fucking crazy about you."

When Jimmy said he was crazy about her, Mickey laughed and said he was just fucking crazy full stop.

They both laughed.

From the funeral parlour, Tony and Shane travelled in the first funeral car following the hearse. Strange thing about funerals, even those with grudges would turn out; it was a sign of respect. Funerals were one of the few places where even enemies would tolerate one another. You could spot the bosses at a glance; they always had at least two big burly hard men with them.

When the hearse drove into the crematorium, they could see Samuels standing with two plain clothed detectives, anyone in the crime game could spot them a mile off. Samuels nodded to them later as they followed the coffin into the chapel.

A reverend said a few words about Hudson, including that he must have been well liked because so many people had attended his funeral which was a testament to the man he'd been. Jimmy looked at his friend and grinned, they knew that probably thirty percent of the so called mourners couldn't stand Hudson; they were simply there out of respect for them.

After the service the mourners stood around outside while some of the women read the cards on the flower wreaths. John Duggan walked over to Mickey and Jimmy and asked what Samuels was doing there. He couldn't help but add it was a fucking shame it was Hudson in the incinerator and not Samuels.

Mickey explained about the threat from the Jamaicans, just before Samuels walked over to them.

"Where's the lovely Maria then?" asked Samuels looking at Jimmy "I would have expected her to be here today."

"Yeah she was coming," said Jimmy "but she's not feeling well."

"Oh dear, perhaps it's because of the threat from the Jamaicans?"

They all knew he was implying that both men knew exactly who the Jamaicans were and that they did have it in for them.

"Like we said before, we've never had a problem with any Jamaicans," said Mickey "even the ones who got a bit out of hand with our dancers were really no bother. Thinking about it, perhaps this thing today is nothing more than a hoax."

"On the contrary Mickey," smirked Samuels "my officers almost nabbed four Jamaicans less than an hour ago. A suspicious BMW was seen parked in the alley behind your restaurant. The car was black, could be the same one you saw the night Monica was shot."

Mickey said it could have been, but then again, London was full of black BMWs, he'd had one himself a few years ago.

Samuels was well aware he knew more than he was saying, so he went on to say he was in no doubt it was the same car because his officers had run a check on the plates and they were false. Mickey asked if anyone had been arrested. According to Samuels when his officers had tried to speak to the Jamaicans they'd driven off. They had radioed a patrol car which was in the area, which had quickly pursued the BMW but because of the lunch time traffic, along with hundreds of pedestrians, it had been too dangerous for them to get involved in a high speed chase. Unfortunately they'd lost them, despite every effort on the officers part.

"Shame," said Jimmy sarcastically, "It would have been nice to find out exactly who these Jamaicans are, especially as you seem to think they have it in for us."

Mickey made their apologies, but stated they had to leave to get back to the restaurant for the wake, he added maybe they would see him there.

Back at the wake, they mingled with the guests and asked if anyone had heard anything about the Jamaicans. Most of them said they hadn't, only what was going on with them and the incident at their club. The one person there who may know something was Tina, she was probably as near to being Hudson's regular girl as was possible and looking at her that would come as no surprise. Half Malaysian, strikingly beautiful, from a good back ground and well educated, not the normal type of girl that Hudson would date. Tina was definitely up market.

She had always liked Jimmy so when he spoke to her she readily chatted and said she'd help him if she could. He asked her why she hadn't spoken to Tony when he was asking around.

"I'll tell you why Jimmy, when Tony spoke to me I could feel him undressing me with his eyes. I've never really warmed to him but I feel very comfortable with you, we go back a long way."

Long before she became Hudson's girl, she knew Jimmy. When she'd hit a tough patch some years earlier, he had given her a job at Dixie's serving behind the bar. Truth was she had a bit of a soft spot for him; especially as it was him who got her and Hudson together. Touching her hand reassuringly, he asked if she could tell him. Without hesitation she said some Jamaicans were giving Hudson a hard time, but he'd never actually spoken to her about them. They'd turned up at his place once when she was there and she'd overheard their conversation. They had been throwing their weight about, trying to intimidate Hudson. Jimmy asked over what. He was surprised when she said the places him and Mickey owned, the clubs and restaurants. The Jamaicans wanted to know how many they owned and how good business was, that type of thing. They'd asked Hudson to join them. She remembered hearing them say something like 'us brothers have got to stick together,' but Hudson wouldn't have any of it. They also mentioned Maurice's name several times, but she hadn't heard what was said only his name.

Jimmy asked if she was certain and if she could tell him anything else.

"Yes I'm positive," she replied "it was the last time I saw Hudson, he was going to take me out for dinner that night. He'd arranged to pick me up at eight, but at seven thirty he called me to say he'd be late and could I rebook the table for nine. When I asked him why, he said the Jamaicans had asked him to go somewhere with them. I told him to be careful, but he said they were backing down, even considering returning to the Caribbean and with any luck that evening would see the back of them. He promised me he wouldn't be late because they only wanted him to take them to another club, not one of yours. Once he had dropped them off, he would see me. That was the last time I spoke to him."

"Why didn't he say anything to us about the situation?"

"I asked him that very question Jimmy, but he said he would handle it and then tell you; maybe he thought it would get him a promotion? Hud was funny like that, but I loved him. I knew about all the other women. It did bother me, but he always came back to me. He rarely wined and dined any of the others; they were just dancers from the club, he'd simply take the other women home and sleep with them. It was different with me; he was loving and caring by far the best lover I've ever had. Always buying me jewellery and flowers, in fact, if it wasn't for the other women he would have been the perfect man and for what it's worth Jimmy I really did love him."

Jimmy could see she was getting a bit upset, so he called the waiter over and ordered her another drink. They continued chatting about Hudson as he said he honestly believed Hudson had really loved her too and that one day he'd have married her. If she ever needed anything she could always call them.

Tearfully thanking him, she squeezed his hand and said Hudson had a lot of time for him and Mickey. Then she asked if it was true that he was getting married.

"Yeah it is babe, who'd of thought it hey."

"Shame, because now Hudson's gone I'm available; so if you change your mind about tying the knot, give me a call. Take care Jimmy," she added as she leaned over and kissed his cheek "I hope the future is good for you and your lady."

When the last mourner finally left, it was almost eleven o'clock. Samuels had left around ten, although he left two officers watching the restaurant. There had been no sign of any Jamaicans. Mickey had called the clubs throughout the evening and everything was fine. The time was around half eleven when Jimmy said he was going to collect Maria from Gladys's then call it a night.

Mickey agreed it had been a long day, the chat Jimmy had with Tina being of the greatest value. First thing tomorrow morning they would send her a bouquet. He suggested calling them a cab and picking the car up from the funeral parlour in the morning as they were both well over the legal limit and the two officers had seen them drinking.

They gave the cab driver Mickey's address and dropped him off first. Then Jimmy gave Gladys's address and picked Maria up. Sitting with her in the back of the cab, he noticed that she seemed a bit quiet. Putting his arm around her, he asked if she was ok. Nodding she told him she was just tired.

Ten minutes later when they entered the apartment, she said she was going straight to bed. Jimmy was surprised that she didn't ask how the funeral had gone and for the first time in two years she didn't kiss him goodnight.

"Don't I get a kiss then," said Jimmy.

Without replying, she walked over and kissed him on the cheek said goodnight and walked away. Sensing that something was very wrong he pulled her back to him and asked what was going on. She repeated that she was just tired, but added they could talk about it in the morning. With an aggressive tone told her they could talk about it then as he took a firm grip of her arm to prevent her from going.

"Let go of me Jimmy you're hurting me!"

"Don't do this Maria, fucking tell me what's going on!"

Pulling her arm away she began to walk towards the bedroom, but he grabbed hold of her again and angrily shouted at her to tell him what was wrong. Trying to keep him calm, she said she wasn't discussing anything that night because he'd been drinking and he sounded aggressive.

Taking a firmer grip of her arm, he said whatever it was she could fucking discuss it with him then.

Not believing what he was hearing when she said she wanted to postpone the wedding, he grabbed her other arm and pulled her round to face him.

"You had better fucking explain to me what the fuck you're talking about Maria."

Desperately she tried to reason with him, begging him to leave it until the morning but he was adamant and aggressive stating she could fucking tell him then.

"Ok, it's because of your life in crime Jimmy. I will always live in fear that our children will be at risk."

"That's a load of bollocks Maria," he shouted with a menacing look on his face "you know I would never let anyone hurt you, or our children!"

Still trying to reason with him, she started crying. He was shouting at her as she tried over and over to explain how she felt, but he just wouldn't listen to her and she was aware that he was becoming more and more aggressive. No matter what she said, he was adamant that the wedding was going ahead. She pleaded with him to listen to her.

Finally she said it wasn't just the threat to their children, she didn't want to be a young widow!

"That's just a fucking excuse!"

"No it's not Jimmy. I've been talking to Gladys; she told me how many times you've been injured over the years!"

What she said enraged him and he shouted that Gladys was nothing but a fucking interfering old bag! Maria had never seen him in such a bad temper with her, but she knew he was just being nasty about Gladys.

"Gladys loves you," she said in an effort to defend the elderly lady, "that's why she mentioned it to me. Over the years she's been concerned about you," sobbing she added, "I'm going to bed, if you prefer I can sleep in the guest room."

"You're not sleeping in the fucking guest room! I want you in our bed! As for Gladys, you can just fucking forget about what she said, the wedding is going ahead as planned!"

Wishing at that point she hadn't mentioned it, she just wanted to go to bed. Her thoughts being hopefully they could discuss it in the morning when he was sober. She had only been in bed ten minutes when he came in. She pretended to be asleep when he got into bed, because she didn't want to continue the conversation with him, especially as he'd reacted so badly and lost his temper quickly because he'd been drinking. Although he wasn't really drunk she knew he wouldn't listen to reason. When he kissed the back of her neck, she didn't respond. Hoping that he would fall asleep, she just laid there silently. Then he began to run his hands up and down her body. Maria told him to leave her alone as she was too tired.

For the first time since she had been with him she didn't want sex. Not being the type to give up, he removed the duvet from her and started kissing her body. Tearfully she pleaded with him to wait until the morning. Ignoring her, he continued to kiss her, moving further down her body, pushing her legs apart he began kissing her intimately. Although she'd asked him not to, her body was responding to him. At that moment she hated herself for wanting him, but despite how she felt about marrying him, truth was she loved and desired him the same as she always had. It wasn't long before they were making love, but she noticed he seemed more dominant than usual, fortunately drink had never affected his performance. When he'd finished, he just collapsed onto her, he was almost asleep as she rolled him over. Maria did not sleep as soundly as him. Most of the night she laid awake thinking about how much she loved him. However, loving him was not enough for her to live in fear with their future children. Truth was the more she thought about it, the more she thought how difficult it would be to live without him. Without question she loved him with all her heart and soul, but was it enough? Lying there in the darkness she remembered how she had lived in fear of Nick every day when she'd lived with him. Many times she had wondered if that day would be the day he would kill her. She also knew men as ruthless as Nick would have no problems hurting a child, especially if he wanted something badly enough, and men like Nick were the sort of men Jimmy did business with.

Maria was up long before him the following morning. Finally he emerged from the bedroom and walked into the kitchen. When she said good morning and added she'd just made a fresh pot of tea, he didn't reply.

"What do you want for breakfast Jimmy?"

Without answering her, he just shook his head. Pouring him some tea, she sat at the table with him; the atmosphere between them was heavy.

"How long do you intend postponing the wedding," said Jimmy, breaking the silence "or do you want to call it off indefinitely?"

Looking at him, she could see that he was absolutely shattered; she had never intended to hurt him. Close to tears she tried to discuss it with him, but he obviously wasn't prepared to discuss anything.

"I told you last night," he said arrogantly "I don't want to discuss it! I just want to know where I stand."

Unable to hold back her tears, she started crying. This was not the reaction she had anticipated from him. Again she tried to talk to him, but he stood up abruptly and looked to be crying.

"Just tell me the fucking truth Maria, is it over? I'm the man I am and there's nothing I can do to change that, it's all I've ever known, but I can understand if you can't hack it. I told you when you first arrived here I didn't own you, it's the same now, although under the circumstances I feel it'll be easier if I leave, because I wouldn't want to live here without you anyway. So you can stay until you sort yourself out. I'll leave you to cancel everything as I haven't got a clue what you've ordered."

Feeling terrible along with shocked by his coldness, she looked at him as she cried and asked him not to do that.

"Do what Maria? That's my point; I haven't done anything except love you! I feel as though my fucking heart has been ripped out! I wish I could change the way you feel, but I can't! I'm sorry babe, but with me what you see is what you get, but for the record, I couldn't have loved you anymore. I'm not about to beg so the way I see it, there is no compromise. I can't give you what you want, so you see babe I don't have a choice. You know I would never let anyone hurt you or any children we may have had, but it's not enough, is it? So I'll be a man about it and walk away. Just one last thing, don't ever come into any of the clubs with another bloke, I couldn't handle that. Now if it's alright with you I'd like to be left alone!"

Turning he walked towards the bedroom. Feeling desperate, she called after him. Coldly, he glanced over his shoulder to briefly look at her before continuing towards the room. Feeling helpless; she sobbed. Stopping again, he just stood there staring at her as she tried to tell him how sorry she was.

"Me too babe," he said as he went into the bedroom, shutting the door behind him.

This was the side to him she knew she would never understand. Last night, he had refused to even talk about her reasons for wanting to postpone the wedding, now he was telling her it was over. Her logic was telling her he must have thought about it after she got up. In her heart she knew he couldn't change his life and more to the point, he didn't want to, which had left him with no choice but to end it. She knew he loved her, but his pride would not allow him to try and find a compromise, a compromise which they both knew didn't exist.

Standing in the lounge, her stomach was churning. She had never intended for it to be this way, she had never doubted his love for her, or hers for him. At that moment, she realised she would be making the biggest mistake of her life if she simply let him walk away. He was the best thing that had ever happened to her, he couldn't change and she knew that, but the way he had handled the situation had left her feeling so terrible.

In those moments since he had gone into the bedroom, she knew that she would rather be dead than without him. Hoping it wasn't too late and believing in her heart that their love was strong enough to survive, she knocked on the bedroom door. Several seconds passed before he told her to come in.

Nervously she entered, her stomach was churning and she could feel herself trembling. Not really knowing what to expect, she was surprised to see him sitting on the edge of the bed wearing just his boxer shorts. His eyes were red and swollen from where he'd been crying. Sitting down on the bed next to him, she reached out to hold his hand but he didn't reciprocate. Coldly he just looked at her and asked what she wanted.

"I want you Jimmy, I'm begging you, please forgive me" she sobbed "I would rather be dead than without you. Please believe me; I want to marry you more than anything."

"Why are you doing this Maria? I can't give you what you want, or what you deserve, so please don't make it any harder for me than it already is. What the fuck are you playing at, are you aware of what you've done? I was ready to walk away. Nothing's changed; I'm still in organised crime."

"Please listen to me Jimmy, I never meant to hurt you, but when Gladys told me how many times you'd been hurt, it scared me. I remember how you were when Nick threatened Charlie and because I knew the Jamaicans may have hurt you at the wake I just couldn't stand it. I worry about you all the time and if we had any children I would be afraid for their safety every day, but please believe me when I say nothing could ever feel as bad as you walking away from me like you did a minute ago. Without you I have nothing precious in my life, I tried to imagine my life without you in it, but knowing you would never hold me, kiss me, or make love to me again made me feel empty, so please Jimmy, can you just forget what I said last night?"

"You need to be sure of what you're saying Maria, because we will never have this conversation again. I felt as though my whole fucking world had crashed. I can't change my way of life. Since I met you, I've felt like my life was on a roller coaster, never before have I loved anyone or anything as much. I wanted so much to marry you and have kids, but this is the only life I can offer you. I understand how you feel, but I can't change that. I would give my life to protect you and our children, but this is a onetime offer, once we're married that's it. I will never discuss it again. Just one more thing, if you think for one minute I would ever let you leave me once we're married, you're wrong, so you need to be certain that you can live the only life I can offer you, for the rest of your life. Marrying me is a one way ticket, do you understand that?"

Despite her concern over what he'd just said and the conviction with which he'd said it, she snuggled her head into his chest and told him she loved him. Lifting her head with his hand, he kissed her and said he loved her too, but he needed an answer.

"I can't live without you Jimmy; you're the most important thing in my life. I never intended to hurt you; I just felt worried about our future. I know you will always protect me, but there are bad people like Nick in the world, and it scares me."

"I can understand that but I don't want to talk about it anymore, as long as you're sure about staying and the wedding's still on, we'll forget this conversation ever happened."

Sitting there next to him and in the hope of proving to him just how much she loved him, she said she couldn't wait to marry him.

When he just stared at her without replying, she found the stony silence very intimidating. With her still sitting on the bed, he leaned over and opened the bed side cabinet. She watched silently as he took out a pair of stockings and holding them in his hand looked at her.

"Strip off," he said. It was more of a command than a request.

This was unusual for him as he would normally undress her. When she was naked, he pushed her back onto the bed; then taking her arms he tied her wrists to the head board with the stockings. She had always hated this type of sexual role play with Nick, yet over time with Jimmy she had found it very erotic, possibly because she knew he would never hurt her or do anything she didn't want him to. This morning was different; in the past they had only used the stockings as a fun thing before, never doing them tight, only using them as a visual stimulant. She felt concerned that he hadn't spoken to her once whilst tying her up. Normally, he would kiss her and joke about all the things he was going to do to her. As he pulled the stockings tight around her wrists she felt a little nervous and uncomfortable. Whenever he had tied her up before he would fondle her and always practise oral sex on her, but not that morning, there was no passion or tenderness; he just took her without any foreplay.

Maria groaned as he entered her, but he paid no attention to it. Realising he was oblivious to her feelings, tearfully she asked him not to be so rough as he was hurting her.

Her words fell on deaf ears. Instead of showing her love and affection, he grabbed her head and kissed her hard on the lips whilst thrusting into her. Beginning to feel scared and totally helpless, she begged him to stop. Frantically she tried to pull her hands free, but he had tied them so tight her effort was futile.

Even when she pulled her legs up in an effort to lessen his thrust, he wouldn't stop. Despite her repeatedly begging him to, he wouldn't. In her heart, she believed he wouldn't really harm her; it was as though he was trying to regain his control over her having felt powerless just an hour earlier. Sucking her breast and biting her nipple so hard she winced, he thrust himself harder into her and groaned as he came, biting her neck at the moment of orgasm. When he finished, she was lying there with tears streaming down her face. Without saying a word he coldly got off her. Sitting on the bed with his back to her, he lit a cigarette which was unusual as he rarely smoked and never in the apartment. He was a social smoker at poker games and such like. Watching him as he drew hard on the butt, she could sense the tension coming from him. Lying there silently, she waited for him to finish his cigarette, finally he stubbed it out.

"Please untie me Jimmy," she sobbed.

Turning his head he looked at her, hating himself for the way he had just behaved. She looked so helpless, so fragile. Gently he undid the ties and scoped her into his arms and begged her to forgive him. They held each other tightly as they lay back down together with her head on his chest.

Stroking her hair, he said she'd made him feel so angry; he'd wanted to punish her. For the first time he actually wanted to hurt her for rejecting him. Still crying she kissed his chest and said she knew it was her fault.

Rolling onto his side to face her, he assured her it wasn't her fault and he felt ashamed for the way he'd acted.

"You scared me Jimmy."

"I know and I'm sorry, but when I thought you were going to leave me I wanted to kill you. I couldn't bear the thought of you being with another man, and knowing my way of life isn't something I can change, I felt gutted."

Jimmy loathed himself for what he'd thought and for what he'd just done to her. The anger and fear he'd experienced had left him without any control over the situation and he hated it.

"I love you Jimmy, the reality of losing you terrified me. Perhaps it would be a good idea if we just forget about the whole incident and pretend it never happened."

"Let's do that babe, because it'll never happen again. If you ever mentioned anything about leaving me again, I'll just shoot you," he joked "because I'm never going through this again."

Although she laughed with him, she felt that somewhere under his humour, he'd meant what he said. They snuggled down together in the bed and fell asleep. Jimmy woke three hours later because she was kissing his back and gently running her hands over him.

The next morning, he said he'd had a terrible dream about them, he'd thought she was going to leave him. With a grin, she said it wasn't a dream but a nightmare as she would never leave him, especially as they were getting married in a few weeks' time.

They both grinned and then they kissed. His hands were all over her as he whispered in her ear that he loved her.

After telling him she loved him too, she gently pulled herself onto him and straddled his stomach. Lifting his arms up she tied him to the head board with the stockings which were still hanging there. Giggling she looked at him and said, "Pay back is a bitch Jimmy!"

"Be gentle with me babe," he laughingly replied "I've had a rough night!"

With him firmly tethered to the bed she rode him like a wild mustang. This one was for her, although there certainly weren't any complaints from him.

It was two o'clock that afternoon when they finally left the bedroom to shower. Jimmy was ravenous, stating all the shagging she'd made him do had given him an appetite.

"I made you do?" joked Maria "I didn't hear you telling me to stop!"

"Nor will you. Shall we eat out and then go shopping I want to buy you something nice."

Remembering back to the previous night, she didn't argue with him, although he insisted on buying her a gift even after she said he didn't have to.

While she went to get ready, he phoned Mickey and told him he just wanted to check everything was ok so he could take Maria out to lunch. Mickey could sense that something had happened by Jimmy's tone, so he said everything was fine and they should go and enjoy themselves. He even suggested him taking the night off too, stating there was no need for him to come to the club as he could check them out if Jimmy wanted to stay home with Maria. With Monica in hospital, he'd got nothing better to do.

Jimmy thanked him and told him to ring him if anything cropped up. They arranged to meet up at Dixie's the next morning before ending the call.

Maria appeared and asked where they were going as she was ready. She smiled when he said he'd like to take her to Shades restaurant. They both really liked eating there. Maria particularly liked Hugo the chef and Jason the head waiter, she'd missed him since he moved from Jimmy's restaurant Satins to Shades about a year ago, when Jason moved in with his girlfriend Lorraine. The apartment they rented was only a ten minute walk from the restaurant, so when he had asked if he could change restaurants, they were only too happy to oblige. Shades did a good regular trade, every lunch time it was packed with high class executives who worked in the nearby office blocks.

A moment later, Jimmy was on the phone to Jason asking if they could book a table.

Jason said the restaurant was quietening down a bit now, but he would tell Hugo they were coming because he normally stopped serving around half three.

Forty minutes later, they were sitting in the restaurant chatting to Jason while they waited for their meals. When she asked after his partner Lorraine, she was thrilled to hear he was going to be a dad. Lorraine was three months pregnant. They congratulated him and she asked if he knew what sex the baby was.

"Nope, we don't want to know; as long as Lorraine and the baby are both ok that's all that matters."

Maria liked Jason from the first day she had met him. Not particularly handsome, what you would call average in height and looks, but he was a nice man, in his late twenties, a good worker, very solid and reliable.

Hugo the chef waved out to them as he called Jason over to collect their meals.

By the time they had eaten they were the only people left in the restaurant. Hugo had left after cooking their meals, but he would be back by six as Saturday night was always the busiest.

As they were leaving, Jimmy handed Jason five twenty pound notes and told him to buy something for the baby.

Jason said it was very much appreciated, especially as Lorraine had seen several things she wanted to buy.

Maria kissed him on the cheek as they left.

As Jimmy drove home, she said it had been a lovely gesture to give Jason the money.

"When we have kids they'll want for nothing babe, I just wish it was the same for everyone. When Lorraine has the baby you can go out and buy it something nice."

This was the Jimmy she loved; despite his dark angry side, he would always be her hero.

CHAPTER 26

The weekend seemed to fly by; they'd been shopping which saw Jimmy buying Maria several gifts including some sexy underwear that he'd chosen. By Monday evening it was as though they had never argued, everything was back to normal. He'd arranged with Mickey to call in on the clubs, more specifically Dixie's and Sweet Cheeks, as they had asked Tony to check in on Lazer.

Shaun's wife Ann just happened to call and ask if she could visit that evening to run over some details about the bridesmaids. Maria knew it was a set up and that Jimmy had arranged it through Shaun, because he still wasn't happy about leaving her alone knowing that the Jamaicans were still a threat. Maria didn't mind, she really liked Ann and secretly she could ask her how she had coped being married to Shaun, considering he was more or less the same as Jimmy.

Mickey's car horn sounded outside just as Ann arrived. As he made his way out the front door, Jimmy called out that he'd see them later and he should be back by midnight.

During the drive to the club, he briefly told Mickey about the argument he'd with her. Mickey could see why she would worry about kids, but he told Jimmy he was sure everything would be ok now.

Reggie was at the door of Sweet Cheeks, they chatted to him for a few minutes before going inside. Entering the club they walked over to Jacky Boy and Kevin and asked where Shane was. Jacky Boy reminded him it was Shane's night off and he'd taken Max out.

"Oh yeah Max," said Mickey "are they taking bets on whether or not he'll shag her?"

"Of course," laughed Kevin "I think she will, Jacky Boy thinks she won't, we've got a pony on it!"

They all laughed.

There had been no sign of the Jamaicans, so they had a couple of drinks then went onto Dixie's. It was the same there, all quiet on the Jamaican front and Tony called in to tell them that everything was normal at Lazer.

They talked about Monica and the shooting with Mickey saying her parents would probably be going back to Devon now she was doing so well. Despite him agreeing when Tony said they seemed like nice people, secretly he would be glad when they left. Not that they'd asked him for anything, but he felt obligated to take them for dinner and spend time with them.

They left the club just before midnight. Jimmy suggested he came for dinner the following evening as they would need to check the clubs again. He dropped Mickey off en route to his apartment.

The girls were still chatting when Jimmy walked in, although he did notice how quiet it went as he had entered. Despite sensing they had been talking about him, he just shrugged it off.

"Alright girls, I hope you've been behaving yourselves."

"Would we dare do anything but" said Ann with a giggle.

Walking to the window and looking out, Jimmy said Shaun had just pulled up. Ann asked him to signal to him that she was on her way down; it would save him coming up.

Kissing Maria on the cheek, she thanked her for a lovely evening then left. Jimmy watched from the window as she got into Shaun's car, before he poured himself a glass of wine, Maria declined as she'd already had several with Ann. She was just about to ask him how things were at the clubs when his phone rang. It was Shane. Jimmy asked him what was up. Shane apologised for calling so late, but he had to wait until he'd taken Max home. Jimmy commented that he thought he would be home with her and giving her one!

"Yeah I'd imagined the fucking same!" said Shane "we had a great time, but it's going to take me several nights out before I get into her knickers! I rang to tell you that something weird happened with Max when she saw Samuels at the restaurant. It would be easier to talk about it tomorrow, it's a bit involved. What are the chances of you and Mickey meeting me at the club in the morning, around ten?"

"Yeah that'll be fine Shane, so is there anything else, because unlike you, I will be getting laid tonight!"

"I didn't say I wouldn't get laid tonight," laughed Shane "I just said I wouldn't be shagging Max!"

"Dirty bastard, happy shagging, I'll see you tomorrow."

As he closed his phone, Maria asked if everything was ok with Shane. She looked curious when he said he wasn't sure, after Shane had said something about Max and Samuels. He was meeting him in the morning to find out more. He suggested her going with him. Nodding she joked that at least he wouldn't have to get Ann over to babysit her. He simply grinned.

They continued to talk; she said that while he'd been out Leon had phoned to ask if they had anyone who could cover tomorrow night at the restaurant. Jeremy's mum had been rushed to hospital with a suspected heart attack. They just needed someone to cover the bookings and greet the diners, take their coats, show them to their table, that was all. Maria had told Leon she could do it if he was really stuck. Jimmy didn't look happy and expressed his feelings by stating he didn't want her going anywhere on her own at the moment, not until they knew what was going on with the Jamaicans. It would be different if he could go with her, but she knew he had things to do. There must be someone else Leon could ask.

Maria was quick to say Leon wouldn't have phoned her if he had someone else. Ann had said Shaun would be available to run her, should she need to go. Seeing he wasn't keen, she stated that it was her restaurant and at least he wouldn't have the problem of getting her a baby sitter! Snapping at her, he told her to cut the fucking sarcasm and he'd only agree because Shaun was available to take and bring her back, but he didn't want her making a habit of it, even if it was her restaurant.

Thanking him, she would let Leon know first thing in the morning. Changing the topic, she said if he wasn't too tired, she'd like his opinion on the underwear he'd bought her at the weekend.

With a grin, he stated he could stay awake long enough to do that. Smiling she asked him to wait while she went and put it on.

Within minutes she was standing in the doorway seductively posed with one leg bent resting her heel up the door frame and her arms behind her back as she leaned against the door frame. From the moment he saw her, he could feel himself becoming aroused. Standing there wearing a dark mauve basque, complete with stockings, suspenders and black high heeled shoes she looked so sexy.

Rising to his feet, he moved towards her, grabbing her and pushing her against the door. With burning desire for him she fumbled to undo his fly. Unable to wait, he picked her up and carried her into the bedroom, gently throwing her onto the bed.

"Jimmy go steady I don't want you tearing it," she said as he yanked at the straps so he could pull the top down to expose her breasts.

"I'll buy you another one," he said breathlessly "Christ I want to fuck you so bad!"

Moments later, he was ripping her knickers off, leaving just the basque and stockings on. Kissing her passionately, he held her hair and thrust himself into her. She knew he wasn't going to last long from the sheer eagerness and passion at which he'd entered her. They made love which was hot and passionate, until finally falling asleep.

The following morning when she woke up, she was still wearing the basque and stockings, all that was missing were her knickers.

Later that morning, he was sitting at the table with his tea mug in his hand, he looked so tired. She had let him lay in until nine o'clock, only calling him then because Mickey was due round just before ten. Looking at him, she said he didn't look too good, his eyes were bloodshot. She giggled when he said he felt like he'd been dug up, but said she had no sympathy. It was his fault for wanting sex half the night!

"Me! It was your fault, seducing me with your womanly charms!"

Suggesting he took a shower while she scrambled him some eggs. Too tired to argue with her, he moved towards the bathroom. Emerging some twenty minutes later, looking much more human.

Finishing his breakfast only minutes before Mickey pulled up, he asked her if she was ready.

"I've been ready for the last hour," she giggled "remember some of us have great stamina and still get up early, even after having sex half the night! Come on lightweight, we don't want to keep Mickey waiting!"

Grabbing her arse with a grin he said he'd deal with her later and then they'd see who was a fucking lightweight!

"Promises, promises" she giggled "maybe you had better have a sleep this afternoon then if you're serious?"

"Get in that lift before I give you a good seeing to before we go!"

They both laughed.

They would have to take Jimmy's car because Mickey's only had two seats. When she apologised to Mickey for having to change cars because of her, he smiled and said it wasn't a problem, he liked being chauffeured about.

Shane was waiting for them when they arrived at the club; he was surprised, although happy, to see Maria. If she wasn't Jimmy's girl he would have hit on her long ago. Smiling at them as they approached, he told Maria how nice it was to see her.

"Thanks Shane, nice to see you too, but I've only been invited so Jimmy doesn't need to get me a baby sitter;" she replied with a giggle.

Shane frowned from curiosity as Jimmy joked back and said if she didn't behave herself he wouldn't let her work the restaurant that night.

Inside the club they sat at a table and Jimmy asked him what was so important he needed to see them.

"It's fucking weird Jimmy. Last night when me and Max were at the restaurant, Samuels spoke to her as if he knew her. When I questioned her about it, she was too afraid to talk to me. I was suspicious so I wouldn't let it drop, eventually she gave in and said if Samuels found out she'd said anything, he'd kill her. It was when we left I finally got her to open up. In the car she told me her ex-boyfriend owed Samuels money, when he didn't pay up Samuels threatened him. According to Max he sold drugs for Samuels, but a big deal had gone wrong. The buyers had taken the drugs and the money, two hundred and fifty grand in total. I reckon she's telling the truth, she was petrified; she begged me not to tell Samuels where she worked and for me to say she only knows me through a friend."

Mickey said they'd need to have a chat with her; they weren't surprised when Shane said he'd thought they would so she was on her way there.

Maria had sat silently and listened to what had been said, she knew what it was like to live in fear of someone. If Max was telling the truth they should feel sorry for her. She asked Jimmy to go easy on her as she knew it wasn't easy to open up to people. Jimmy promised her they wouldn't upset Max.

Ten minutes later, Max walked in. They all noticed how embarrassed she looked. Although she had never met Maria, she knew it was her from the way Shane had described her, there was also the fact that Jimmy was sitting next to her with his arm around the back of her chair.

Mickey thanked her for coming and asked her to sit down. Shane poured her a drink.

After reassuring her it was safe to talk, she repeated the same story she'd told Shane. Mickey asked where her boyfriend was now. He wasn't surprised when she said she didn't know and more to the point didn't care, she wanted him as far away from her son as possible. Mickey nodded and continued by asking if she was certain Samuels was the dealer.

With conviction, she was absolutely positive; he'd turned up at her flat and threatened to take her son if she didn't tell him where her boyfriend was. That was why she needed the job; she was trying to pay off some of the money her boyfriend owed him. Tearfully she said Samuels called round for the money on Thursday mornings, her mum picked her son up before they got there.

Mickey instantly questioned why she'd said they and not him.

"At first it was just Samuels then four weeks ago, he brought some Jamaican blokes with him; they smashed my flat up and threatened me. After that I never allowed my son to be there. If Samuels finds out I've said anything to you, he'd kill me and take my son!"

Jimmy asked why the boy's father hadn't dealt with it. Sounding angry, Max said because he was a fucking coward, cheat and a liar who had put their son in the situation.

Mickey reassuringly patted her arm and told her not to worry they would look after her, but they'd need proof that Samuels was dirty. Out of curiosity, he asked how her boyfriend got mixed up with Samuels in the first place.

"It was through some bloke called Maurice," said Max "I never met him; I only spoke to him over the phone. I had no idea my boy's father was a drug dealer; he told me he worked at the airport and I had no reason to question it."

Maria could see that Max was getting tearful, so caringly she reassured her that everything would be ok and for the record, she didn't like Samuels either.

They talked about Samuels and his extra income as a drug dealer.

"I always knew he was dirty," said Mickey "Monica's always said he's bent. She was right; so let's deal with him. Max has just given us an angle so let's use it. In the meantime Max, it's probably not a good idea for you to work at any of our clubs, Samuels could walk in at any time, as could the Jamaicans, which brings me to ask did Samuels ever call any of the Jamaicans by name?"

Max nodded and said she remembered last week when he'd called for his money, he called one of them Damien or something like that. Feeling fearful, she begged them to let her carry on working at the club, because if she didn't pay, Samuels would hurt her son. Mickey assured her they wouldn't let anyone hurt her or her son.

"But if I can't work, I can't pay. Please Shane tell them!"

She felt humble when Mickey said they would continue to pay her the amount she gave to Samuels every week.

Once it was sorted out she could come back to work. Instantly she stated she'd only taken the pole dancing job to pay the debt, once he left her alone she wouldn't do it, she'd find a regular job. Smiling, she thanked Maria when she said there would always be a job for her at one of their restaurants if she needed it.

Mickey waited for the two women to stop talking before telling Max he'd arrange for someone to bug her flat so they could listen to what Samuels had to say and make sure he didn't hurt her.

With tears welling in her eyes, she stated Samuels would hurt her if she didn't pay. Mickey gave his word that Shane would bring the money round to her every week.

Looking confused, she asked why they were helping her, after all they didn't really know her and she'd only worked for them for a short time.

"Let's just say we have something in common. Like you, we hate Samuels and just to see him take a fall would be worth it. So unless you want to tell us anything else, Shane can take you home."

Ten minutes later she left with Shane, leaving the three friends talking about what Max had told them. It was clear they all believed her, especially with the way she'd reacted every time she spoke of the danger to her son.

"Samuels has got it coming," said Jimmy "who the fuck does he think he is! Fucking little shit house! Well the bastard's going to pay for all the trouble he's caused, not to mention almost killing Monica! Thinking about it Mick, it makes sense why she took the bullet and not you, Samuels knows what a good detective she is, so it would make sense to get rid of her."

"My thoughts exactly Jimmy, and you're right, he's going to pay big time, but first we need to find out exactly how corrupt he is, and if it was him who ordered Hudson's execution, and how he came to work with the Jamaicans, who are obviously members of Maurice's family. I know from Monica that Samuels had contacted

Maurice's family after his death; maybe he saw it as an opportunity to broaden his own business interests, bringing in new people not locals to do his dirty work for him. I'll speak to Monica at the hospital maybe she can help; she's got some good friends in the department; perhaps they could find out a few things for her. One thing we do know, Samuels is a slimy bastard and he won't leave anything to chance and no doubt he'll work it so he'll never be implicated. If he finds out Max has talked to us he won't hesitate to kill her, so we really need to play along with the fact that she didn't know Shane had a connection with the club. It might be in Max's best interest to play it down a bit with Shane, let Samuels believe she wasn't really interested in furthering the romance. I'll bell Lenny and get him to bug her flat. I'll try and arrange it for this afternoon."

When Shane returned from taking her home, they filled him in on the details of their discussion. Thanking them for helping her, he stated she was absolutely terrified of Samuels. He'd suggested her staying at her parents for a while, but she was afraid Samuels would hurt them. Of course there was the other option that Samuels could meet with a nasty accident for which Shane would volunteer his services for free!

Jimmy joked and said if it did come to that Shane would have to join a fucking queue as there would be no shortage of people who would pay to see Samuels taken out!

Mickey didn't think taking Samuels out was the best way; he wanted to see him go down if possible. Although a midnight dip was attractive as there were dozens of people in prison because of him. He was well known for planting evidence. Samuels didn't care how he got a conviction; he just needed to look good. Trouble with the Samuels of the world they could always get people to get them off the hook. With so many corrupt coppers, it would be hard to bring them all to justice. That was why they'd kept

Quinton the QC, he did come in useful. Several times during the past two years, Quinton had helped a couple of their boys walk away from potential prison sentences, although a high ranking detective was different to a petty criminal. He suggested they should tell the others about Samuels that afternoon. They'd only need to visit a couple of places as word would soon get round.

Jimmy nodded and said he'd take Maria with him. She reminded him they needed to be back home by four o'clock, she didn't want to be late going to work at the restaurant that evening. With a grin he promised they'd be back by three. When she asked if they'd have time to pop in to see Monica, he said he couldn't guarantee it but promised he would take her the following day if not.

"I'll tell Monica, she'll understand," said Mickey "one thing I can guarantee, she'd want to see Samuels get his just desserts even if it means having no visitors."

Before they left, everyone agreed to meet back at the club later that night.

It was almost four o'clock when Jimmy finally took Maria home after making several business stops. They didn't have time to see Monica. As soon as they arrived back at their apartment, she asked what he wanted to eat although she was already running late so it would be a snack at best. Feeling bad about being late home, he told her not to worry he would get something later with Mickey. When he asked what time she would be home, she shrugged her shoulders and said around midnight, but she wasn't really sure.

"If I'm not here when you get back babe, ask Shaun to wait with you. Actually I'll bell him, I need to tell him I'll be running you to the restaurant so he'll only have to pick you up later."

Five minutes later she was standing in front of him dressed for work and asking if she looked ok. With a sexy grin he said she looked great, a regular maître de! Wearing a black skirt suit, with a crisp white blouse, heeled shoes and her hair pulled back at the sides.

"You look very professional babe; did I ever tell you I've got a thing for woman in suits?"

"No, but I can tell what you're thinking by the look on your face. Sorry but you'll have to fantasise until I get home later; I don't want to crease my clothes."

When he suggested her taking them off, she giggled and told him to forget it as she was already running late.

After making the last few adjustments to her hair, she was ready.

Jimmy closed his phone from the call he'd made to Shaun and grabbing his jacket said they should go.

Arriving at the restaurant, Leon apologised for bringing her in at such short notice. They asked after Jeremy's mum and were pleased to hear she was doing slightly better, but Jeremy would be off for a few days. Leon had managed to get cover for those days, all except Thursday. Without thinking, Maria said she could cover Thursday. When Jimmy glared at her, she knew instantly he would prefer her not to work so she made a joke and said it would save him having to get a babysitter!

Noticing Leon looked confused, Jimmy explained it was a private joke; one which Maria obviously thought was funny. Begrudgingly, he agreed to let her do Thursday.

A couple of minutes later he was leaving. Kissing him goodbye, she whispered in his ear and asked if he wanted her to keep her suit on until he got home later.

"Definitely," he replied with a grin.

Although the trade was steady at the restaurant, Tuesday night was normally average; she enjoyed having the time to talk to the customers. Time seemed to fly by with the last couple leaving at half eleven. Leon told her that she had been excellent, which was quite a compliment coming from him, everyone knew he was a no nonsense type of chef who ran a very tight ship. Thanking the staff as they left, he poured Maria and himself a drink. They sat and chatted while she waited for her lift home.

The door opened just as she finished her wine, it was Shaun.

"You ready me darling?" he said with a smile.

Maria nodded and said she was unless Leon needed any help before she left.

The chef thanked her, but said he was going to lock up and then go home himself. Telling her again she had been great for stepping up to help and he'd see her on Thursday.

While Shaun drove, she thanked him for picking her up and apologised for Jimmy being so paranoid. Leon would happily have given her a lift to save Shaun having to come out.

"I'm only too happy to pick you up darling. I know Leon would have dropped you home, but I prefer doing it myself that way I know you're ok. That reminds me, Jimmy called me, he'll be home by half twelve at the latest so he might already be there."

When Shaun pulled up outside the apartment block they could see Jimmy standing by the window looking out for them. Maria invited Shaun in for a drink, but he declined the offer stating that Ann would probably be waiting up for him.

She kissed him affectionately on the cheek before she got out of the car. Waiting until she entered the building, within minutes she was waving to him from the window.

Jimmy asked if she'd had a busy night as she walked into the lounge and sat down. Yes it had been busy, but she'd enjoyed it. Her feet ached due to not being used to standing for that length of time. Pointing to a glass of wine she asked if it was for her, he nodded and said he thought she may need a drink.

Relaxing back onto the sofa, she sipped her wine as he knelt down on the floor in front of her and took off her shoes. Massaging her feet, he asked if that felt better. Nodding, she said it was lovely and thanked him.

Still kneeling in front of her, a few moments later he leaned over and slowly began undoing her shirt buttons. When she giggled and stated she hadn't even finished her drink, he said he couldn't wait, he'd been imagining this moment all evening. All he'd thought about was having her, it was the suit. Telling him she ought to freshen up first, he leaned forward and licking her cleavage said she tasted great to him.

By the time he'd undressed her, they couldn't keep their hands off each other. Within minutes she was lying back on the sofa with his head between her legs giving her tongue.

"Oh God, Jimmy, don't stop!" she cried out as she pushed his head harder onto her.

"Bend over the sofa babe," he said as he pulled her down onto the floor.

Eager to please him, she turned around and rested her arms onto the seat whist still kneeling on the floor. Within seconds he was inside her, pushing her body down harder into the seat with every thrust. Grabbing her hair, he pulled her shoulders up and pushed himself against her back as he moved deeper into her. Reaching round behind her, she frantically tried to hold his buttocks as he fucked her. She knew when he let go of her hair and cupped her breasts tightly in his hand he was coming. Lying along her back with his hands still holding her breasts, he kissed her neck and said "Fuck me babe, was that good or what!"

They kissed passionately before she asked him to pass her wine.

Lifting it from the coffee table, he moved his hand towards her, but as she moved her hand to take it, he pulled slightly away and proceeded to dip his fingers in it and gently rub them around her nipples. Taking the glass from him as he sucked her, she dipped her own fingers in the glass and proceeded to drip more onto her nipple for him to lick off. It was twenty minutes later when they finally got up to go to bed.

While in bed cuddling him she managed to persuade him to visit Father Thomas with her the following morning, suggesting they could see him on their way to the hospital. Finally they fell asleep their bodies entwined.

Over breakfast, Maria said she hoped he hadn't forgotten he'd promised to visit Father Thomas with her that day.

"After the way you made love to me last night babe, I would have agreed to anything!"

Just over an hour and thirty minutes later, they were walking into the church. Father Thomas was pleased to see them, especially as the wedding was getting nearer. They talked about having a rehearsal and if Maria had decided who she wanted to give her away. She nodded and said, although she had considered asking Gladys's husband Arthur, her heart had opted for Shaun.

Jimmy knew she held a genuine affection for the big Irishman, and like Thomas, he thought she'd made the right choice. Both men were certain Shaun would be delighted when she rang him later to ask.

Twenty minutes later as they were leaving, Thomas said it had been good to see them and he hoped to see Jimmy in church on Sunday. With a grin Jimmy said he'd try.

From the church they drove to the hospital to visit Monica. They were both astounded by the recovery she appeared to be making. The two women talked about the prospect of a double wedding, with Maria saying she would be happy to go and buy the dress that Monica had liked.

"I really like the idea of a double wedding, but I don't want to take anything away from your special day," said Monica "especially as you've been planning everything for months."

"Don't be daft;" said Jimmy "I think it's fitting that me and Mickey get married together; especially with two beauties as our blushing brides."

Thanking them both, she said she'd best hurry up and get well as she didn't fancy being pushed up the aisle in a wheel chair! Accepting Maria's offer, she said it would be great if she could get the dress for her in a size twelve. They could sort out paying for it once she was home.

At that moment Mickey entered the room and after saying hello to everyone, he walked over and kissed Monica.

He asked what they'd been talking about before he arrived. When Monica said weddings, he grinned and looking at Jimmy said it was time to find a coffee machine.

They all laughed.

They left the girls chatting as they went for coffee.

Maria asked her what she thought about Samuels being corrupt.

"I'm not surprised I always thought he was; only up until now I could never prove anything. I can't wait to see him take a fall, especially as he thinks nothing about framing innocent people. Several cases I've worked on with him I've suspected foul play, but Samuels is a clever bastard. Still if it's ever proved that he's dirty maybe the legal system will look into a few cases he's handled, especially the ones where evidence may have been planted."

The two men returned with the coffee.

After finishing their drink, Maria said they should go so Mickey could spend time with Monica. Jimmy nodded and asked Mickey if they'd see him later. Shaking his head, Mickey said probably not as he was going to bring Charlie over to visit then take her out for dinner, but as it was a school night it wouldn't be a late one. He would see them the following day. He added he'd be happy to check in on the clubs that night after he'd dropped Charlie home, if Jimmy fancied a night in with Maria.

Maria thanked him and suggested to Jimmy they pick up a couple of DVDs on the way home and maybe order a takeaway to save her cooking.

"Looks like I'm having a night in," laughed Jimmy "cheers mate, but if there's any trouble at the clubs just bell me."

Mickey nodded. They kissed Monica then left.

On the way home, Maria asked if they could stop at the bridal shop so she could get the dress for Monica and if they didn't have her size they could order her one in.

Jimmy nodded and said she could sort out the dress while he chose the DVDs, then he'd meet her back at the shop.

At the bridal shop, Maria was disappointed that they didn't have a size twelve although the shop assistant said it would only take ten days to get one in for her.

Back at the car, she asked him what DVDs he'd bought. A night in with Al Pacino and Marlon Brando wasn't exactly what she'd hoped for when he said the box set of the Godfather.

Just as they arrived back at the apartment Jimmy's phone rang. It was Lenny calling to tell him the bug in Max's flat was working fine so he suggested they met up after Samuels had called round for his money. Jimmy agreed.

When he finished the call, she asked if he thought she should phone Shaun about giving her away. He nodded.

Jimmy watched as she spoke to Shaun, he could tell from her face, along with her replies, he'd been right, Shaun was chuffed.

When she ended the call she excitedly told him that Shaun had been quite overwhelmed that she'd asked. He'd actually said he'd be honoured!

By the time the takeaway arrived Maria was dozing off. Having sat through the first Godfather DVD, she tried hard to stay awake through the following two films. She was actually quite relieved when Jimmy woke her up to say the films had finished and that they should turn in for the night. After making love they both slept soundly until eight the following morning.

CHAPTER 27

It was almost midday when Lenny rang to tell Jimmy he wouldn't be disappointed, he'd got some interesting news from the bug at Max's flat. Jimmy was intrigued and said they'd meet him at the club in one hour. As the call ended he called Mickey and arranged to pick him up. They weren't surprised to see him ready and waiting as they pulled up outside his place thirty minutes later.

Lenny's car was already in the car park when they arrived at the club. Shane, Jacky Boy and Billy were inside.

Mickey asked Shane to get everyone a drink before they started talking to Lenny.

Lenny placed a tape recorder on the table and told Shane to hurry up as he would want to hear the tape. Shane placed the glasses and bottle on the table and sat down. Lenny assured them they'd find the conversation on the tape very interesting. They all sat quietly as he pressed the play button. Samuels' voice was instantly recognisable when he asked Max if she had his money. Sounding nervous, Max had said yes, she'd got four hundred pounds. They assumed that she'd handed him the money when Samuels said that was good, four hundred is ok and Max said he didn't have to count it. Typical of Samuels he replied he couldn't be too careful. Then he mentioned

Shane and asked how she knew him. Trying to sound uninterested, she said she didn't really know him; it was a friend who'd tried to fix her up with him on a blind date.

"My advice to you on that score would be keep away from him;" said Samuels "in my opinion he's bad news."

"Don't worry I've already decided I don't want to see him again, he wasn't really my type. I enjoyed the date, but I won't be seeing him again."

Then Samuels became smutty to her when he said she'd made a wise decision but if she ever needed a good fuck, he'd be only too happy to help her out.

It was obvious from the noises on the tape that he had tried something on with her, especially when she raised her voice and shouted at him to take his hands off her. Arrogantly Samuels stated she should be grateful he was allowing her to pay off her debt in instalments, and she could pay it quicker if she was nicer to him. With an adamant tone, she assured him that was never going to happen and he'd get his money every week. It was what he said next that really interested the men.

"You should think yourself lucky I'm asking you Max, if it was up to my friend Damon here, he would just rape you."

"If I fucked you bitch," said Damon's voice "you'd never want a white man again!"

There was the sound of a struggle and Max shouting for him to get off her, followed by the sound of someone being hit.

Samuels ordered Damon to leave her, stating she was no good to them dead and he didn't have to remind her that he could make her son disappear and adding he may even lead the investigation into his abduction.

Sounding distressed, they could hear Max crying and begging him to leave her son alone! Smugly he said all the time he got his money her son was safe. He would see her the following week unless she changed her mind about paying off some of the debt by other means; in which case he would call round one evening. Max repeated that wouldn't happen so he'd get his money Thursday. It was just as they were leaving she called him by name when she said, "Detective Samuels please don't hurt my son!"

Lenny pressed the stop button.

"Fucking cheeky bastard," snapped Shane "talking about me like that, and as for that black mother fucker saying about her never wanting a white man, maybe he can ask her that after she's had me!"

Everyone laughed.

"Good work Lenny," said Mickey "the tape is very incriminating. Trouble is on its own I doubt it would be enough to prosecute him. Samuels is dangerous and in my opinion he's in over his head with the Jamaicans. Shane, give Max a bell, check she's okay. Tell her well done for naming Samuels on the tape, she's a clever girl."

Maria never said anything, she felt so sorry for Max, knowing exactly how it felt to be so vulnerable. As she'd listened to the tape she had gone quite cold when she had heard Samuels and Damon threaten to rape her. Often when she lived with Nick the fear of thinking he was going to rape and hurt her was worse than the real thing. She wanted to help Max but she decided she would speak to Jimmy about it when they were on their own. Lenny had just put the tape recorder away when the door to the club opened and in walked Samuels, he was on his own.

Shane could feel his anger rising through his chest; he so wanted to thump him. Mickey asked the Detective if they could help him. When he replied that he was simply in the area so he'd popped in to see if anyone had remembered anything about the accident, Mickey was quick to say he would hardly call what happened to Monica an accident. Someone had tried to kill her. He went on to ask if they were any nearer to catching whoever it was, because he found it unusual that no one saw anything.

"Yes I'm also surprised that nothing significant has come to light, but we'll continue with the investigation," replied Samuels before he glanced over at Shane and asked, "did you enjoy yourself at the restaurant?"

Shane nodded and said the food was cushty.

"Quite a coincidence that I knew the woman you were with. Don't mind me saying but she's a bad lot, I would think you could do better."

Shane could not stand eating humble pie, regardless of Samuels being a detective and instantly sprang to her defence telling Samuels he disagreed. In his opinion Max was a lovely girl who seemed decent. He was only sorry she didn't fancy him. Aware that Shane didn't like him Samuels smugly implied how he wouldn't have thought Shane was the type to worry about a woman turning him down; he would have assumed that working in clubs he could take his pick.

Mickey could sense the tension mounting between the two men, so he decided to intervene before the situation got out of hand and Shane said something they all might regret.

"He's only pissed off detective because he didn't get into her knickers," said Mickey. "Thank fuck the meal was on the house otherwise he'd have really felt cheated!"

Everyone laughed, even Shane forced a grin.

Sarcastically, Samuels said Shane was lucky to have friends who owned restaurants. Telling them he'd be in touch, Samuels left. Waiting until they were certain he'd gone, Shane apologised for fronting Samuels, but he just couldn't agree with him, and in truth he would love to have taken a fucking swing at him because he was a slimy bastard! It was as much as he could do to control himself.

Mickey told him it was ok and he'd done the right thing speaking up for Max. Shane knew Max was a decent sort and if Samuels ever touched her, he would deal with him.

"You may well get the chance" said Mickey, "but until then you can't let it get personal. Samuels is a tricky bastard, it wouldn't take too much for him to smell a rat. Under the circumstances, it would probably be best if you simply kept out of his way."

Maria reminded Jimmy she was working at the restaurant again that evening and she didn't want to be late because Thursday's were always busy. Before they left, Jimmy arranged to pick Mickey up later at nine thirty so they could check the clubs.

Back at the apartment, Maria hurried to get ready, making them a quick sandwich. Even though he was eating at the restaurant he still managed to eat a snack with her.

Leon greeted them as they arrived at the restaurant. It wasn't long before Maria was busy working while Jimmy sat eating. From his table, he watched as she greeted the customers, she was very good with them. Gone was the shy timid girl that he had rescued two years earlier. Maria had blossomed into a confident, articulate and bubbly young woman. No woman had ever made him feel insecure, but he wasn't too happy about the way some of the men looked and talked to her; although the same could be said for the women that they were with, it was obvious they were jealous of her.

Before leaving the restaurant just after nine to pick Mickey up; Jimmy made a point of kissing her in full view of everyone. Maria asked him to behave as she was working and it wasn't very professional in front of the customers. Arrogantly he stated they owned the place so he could do whatever he liked. Knowing it was just his way of letting everyone know she was his, she just grinned. The last thing she wanted was a scene in front of everyone. Before he left, he checked with her again that Shaun was definitely picking her up. When she assured him for the third time, he kissed her and left.

Just like Tuesday, time at the restaurant seemed to fly by. The staff had been run off their feet all evening. It was quarter to twelve by the time everyone had left and Leon appeared from the kitchen. He looked exhausted.

Maria poured him a drink and said he looked shattered so he should get off home. Sipping his drink, he asked if she needed a lift and looked relieved when she told him Shaun was coming for her. When he suggested staying with her until Shaun arrived, she wouldn't hear of it, he needed to go home and rest. Finally she convinced him she would be fine and Shaun would be there any minute, so she insisted he went home.

Thanking her, he told her to lock the main door behind him as he'd already locked up out the back. Before he left, he thanked her again for standing in for Jeremy and added that he wished she could work every night as she was a definite hit with the customers.

Leon had only been gone five minutes when she heard a noise outside, it sounded like glass breaking. Just as she stood up to go and investigate, the lights went out. Suddenly she felt panic; her first thought was she wished Shaun was there. She walked towards the light switch, hoping that the lights would come back on if she pressed it. Then she noticed the lights in the kitchen were still on so she felt a little reassured that maybe it was simply a fuse or the bulb. Standing there alone in the dark she felt a little scared. Then suddenly someone grabbed her. Terrified she looked up in the darkness and saw a large Jamaican man standing in front of her. Immediately she tried to run, but there was another man blocking her escape. Frantically she tried to get away, but as she screamed one of the men punched her in the face, knocking her to the floor. Still dazed he dragged her up and pushed her across a table. When she tried to scream again, he put his hand across her mouth to silence her.

"If ya boyfriend wasn't such a dumb fuck," said the Jamaican grabbing her hair to stop her from getting up "dis wouldn't be happening! Ya give Jimmy a message, tell him unless he sells us da club, something bad will happen!"

Desperately she tried to get free, but the other man was holding her down. In the half light from the kitchen, although still dazed, she could make out the man standing over her. Despite her vision being blurred from the punch she'd taken in the face, she became aware that he was undoing his trousers. Desperately she struggled, but they were large men and she was powerless to stop them and unable to scream for help as his hand was still firmly over her mouth. Only seconds had past when she felt someone ripping at her clothes, followed instantly by the pressure of the man on top of her. One of them was going to rape her. Removing his hand from her mouth he tried to kiss her, she could taste his stale breath on her lips from where he had been drinking and smoking. Frantically she tried to scream as she kicked out with her legs, but again came another heavy blow to her face from his fist. Trying to stay consciousness she could hear them laughing, she also heard them say Jimmy's name again. Just as she felt the Jamaican start to penetrate her, there was a loud bang. Suddenly the Jamaican holding her down released his grip as she felt the other one quickly scramble off of her.

Falling from the table onto the floor and still in a daze, she heard the familiar voice of Shaun. From where she was lying she could just make out the figure of the big Irishman, he was holding something. Slowly she began to focus, it was a sawn off shotgun. Her head was spinning as she laid there, she wanted to say something to Shaun, but she couldn't get any words to come out of her mouth. Trying hard to stay conscious, she could hear the two Jamaicans begging him not to shoot after Shaun had ordered them to lay face down on the floor with their arms out stretched in front of them. On the verge of passing out, she became aware that Shaun was talking to Jimmy on his phone. Moments later he was covering her with his jacket and placing a folded table cloth under her head. He left her lying on the floor; he couldn't risk the Jamaicans escaping if he tended to her. Maria passed out.

Sometime later, she began to come round to the sound of Jimmy's voice. Reaching out to hold him, she burst into tears as he knelt down beside her and placed his arm under her neck. His voice was full of concern as he asked if she was ok. Shaking from shock, she sobbed as she asked if he'd caught them. Relieved when he said they had, she snuggled her head to his chest and sobbed.

Tenderly he removed Shaun's jacket then pulled her blouse across her chest, the buttons had been ripped off. Comforting her, he gently pulled her skirt down after the Jamaican had hoisted it up to her waist then he pulled her panties, which were torn back up over her. He asked again if she was hurt and if she needed a doctor. Still traumatised, she shook her head and said she just wanted to go home.

Lifting her from the floor, she clung on to him as he told her Shaun would be taking her home. Sobbing she said she wanted Jimmy to take her.

"I know babe, I'll be there before you know it, but first I'm going to have a chat with those fucking black bastards!"

Still shaking, she just sobbed as she clung to him. A few moments passed and then she felt Shaun's arms lifting her up.

"Come on me darling," he said "let's be getting you home. Jimmy will be back with you in no time."

Feeling as safe with him as she did with Jimmy and too dazed and traumatised to argue, she hung her arms round his neck as he carried her out through the back of the shop. As they approached the door, she spotted Mickey. He was holding Shaun's shotgun. On closer inspection, she could see the two Jamaicans lying face down on the floor with their hands tied behind their backs. Unable to bring herself to look at them, she just snuggled her head into Shaun's chest as Jimmy kissed her head. As they left the restaurant, Mickey said he'd see her later. Jimmy thanked Shaun and told him to look after her.

"I will," replied the big Irishman "don't worry about my lassie here, she'll be fine. I'll stay with her until you get back, all night if need be."

The moment she was out of sight, Jimmy grabbed one of the Jamaicans by his hair and calling him a fucking black bastard, dragged him up.

The Jamaican began to say something but Jimmy kicked him in the face. Then he grabbed the other one by his hair, now he had a firm grip on both of them. Mickey was still holding the shotgun on them. Pulling them to their feet, Jimmy started shouting at them that if either of them said one fucking word, he would put them down right there, right then. Shouting, he asked if they understood.

"Yah man we understand," said one of them nervously.

Instantly Jimmy smashed his head against the door frame and stated he'd warned him to keep his fucking mouth shut! When Jimmy told anyone to shut the fuck up, he meant fucking shut up. Again he asked if they understood. Neither spoke, they simply nodded their heads.

"There see," snarled Jimmy "now you're fucking catching on. There's a man waiting for you down the docks, he wants to talk to you about his dog!"

Hearing him say that, they tried to pull away from him, but he was having none of it. Without hesitation he kicked one of them as hard as he could in the knee. The Jamaican screamed out in pain which saw Jimmy telling him to shut up and stop screaming like a fucking pussy.

They bundled one of them into the car boot, while the other one was made to kneel on the floor in the back. Mickey sat with his foot pressed down on the Jamaican's neck and the shotgun resting on his head as they drove. Jimmy called Reggie and told him to open up the old warehouse down by the pumps. They would be there in five minutes and they were bringing him a present.

Minutes later they were pulling into the docks. Reggie was standing at the gates with his dogs. He didn't notice the Jamaican on the floor of the car until Mickey got out and with a grin told Reggie they'd brought something for his dogs.

Reggie deliberately let the dogs get into the car to sniff the terrified man. The Jamaican frantically struggled as he repeatedly begged him to call off his dogs.

"Get out you putrid streak of piss!" laughed Reggie "stop your fucking whining, my dogs won't hurt you until I tell them to! Now fucking get out, you fucking ugly black bastard!"

Jimmy walked round to the boot. As he opened it Reggie walked over with his dogs that readily jumped up at the other Jamaican before standing like statues at Reggie's command. The Jamaican could see and hear a low growl rumbling from them as he tried to push himself further into the boot. Reggie called his dogs back and ordered him to get out. Jimmy wouldn't wait. Grabbing him by the hair, he dragged him out. Unable to steady himself because he was tied up, he hit the ground with a loud hard thud, landing on his face.

"Oops!" said Jimmy sarcastically and much to Reggie's amusement.

They made their way through the docks where they were joined by Terry, who told them the warehouse they wanted to use was unlocked and ready. Everyone from that side of the docks had gone home so they wouldn't be disturbed.

"Cheers Terry," said Mickey "just to bring you up to speed, Shaun's taken Maria home but as a precaution Jimmy's phoned Shane and Billy to watch the apartment, just in case someone goes round there once they realise these two black bastards are missing!"

Inside the warehouse, Terry and Reggie tied the two men to a metal girder which was bolted to the floor. Terry picked up a baling hook and holding it against one of the

Jamaican's face menacingly asked who'd sent him to the restaurant.

Despite the fact that they knew it was Samuels, they needed to hear it from them.

"If I tell yah," said the Jamaican "I'm a dead man; ya have no idea who ya're dealing with."

Jimmy walked over to the Jamaican and taking the hook from Terry hit the man with full force in the leg, leaving him screaming in agony as it ripped through his flesh and blood began to gush out.

"I don't think you heard my friend," said Jimmy arrogantly, "he asked you a fucking question!"

Reggie's dogs became excited and started barking, stopping instantly when Reggie commanded them. Intimidatingly, Jimmy smirked and told the Jamaicans it was because they could smell blood. Then to the Jamaican's terror, he told Reggie to bring the dogs over, stating that they deserved some retribution, especially the one who had taken the bullet.

They just stood and watched as his dogs began to gnaw and rip the Jamaican's leg. Screaming in agony, the petrified man screamed out and begged them to call the dogs off.

In a cold calculating manner and without any emotion, Jimmy ignored their pleas and asked again who had sent them. "Ok! Ok!" screamed the Jamaican "I will tell ya. Samuels, his name is Samuels!"

Condescendingly, Jimmy smiled and said they already knew it was Samuels, what they needed to know was how the Jamaicans became involved with him.

With Reggie's dogs just a few feet from him and blood pouring from his leg, the Jamaican looked terrified and told them that when Maurice was murdered, Samuels had contacted them. Jimmy ordered him to continue as he kicked the man's leg.

The Jamaican had started to tell them that Samuels had flown to the Caribbean after Maurice's death, when the other Jamaican interrupted and told him to shut the fuck up and not tell them anything. Mickey shouted as he hit him across the mouth with the butt of the shotgun and said he was the one who needed to shut the fuck up.

Jimmy ordered the first man to carry on, stating that he had their attention.

They listened with disbelief as the Jamaican said Samuels had told them Mickey had ordered the hit on Maurice because of a dispute over money. Samuels had promised them if they came to England and worked for him, they could get even with Mickey and also earn big money.

"So all this is because you dumb fuckers believed a fucking low life like fucking Samuels!"

Bleeding profusely from his wound and stuttering to get his words out, the man was terrified as he said Samuels had assured them he could protect them and they would make big money running clubs and whore houses. Jimmy asked why they'd killed Hudson and what Samuels intended to do next.

While Jimmy listened to the Jamaican talk about Samuels and how he'd murdered Hudson because not only had he refused to work for him, but he was going to expose him to them, all Jimmy wanted to do was kill him, but he contained his anger as the Jamaican continued and said Samuels intended to plant drugs at their club. Again the other Jamaican shouted out that if his friend told them what they needed to know they would kill them.

Jimmy stepped forward and kicked the Jamaican in the balls, leaving him screaming in agony as he vomited.

Mickey asked how Samuels intended to plant drugs; he knew that if a single Jamaican set foot in their club they would deal with them.

Now fearing for his life, the terrified man said that Samuels intended to do it himself. Being a detective no one would think twice about him going into the club.

"Oi gob shites," said Jimmy as he kicked the other Jamaican "you've had plenty to fucking say, do you want to add anything?"

In an act of defiance the man said it didn't matter anymore because they were dead men!

Jimmy told Reg and Terry to get the Jamaicans up onto their feet. Standing was difficult for the one the dogs had mauled, but Jimmy didn't care, he ordered him to stand. Once on their feet, Jimmy glared at both men and aggressively ordered them to tell him which of them had hit Maria.

They both remained silent.

Standing directly in front of them; Jimmy punched them both in the gut. The injured one slid down the girder, but Jimmy dragged him back to a standing position. Still winded from the blow, the Jamaican gasped for breath. Waiting for a reply Jimmy asked them again. The defiant one just stood there, the injured one could not withstand any more pain and shouted out it wasn't him but the other man who'd hit her. Instantly the other man ordered him to shut up before he got them both killed. Jimmy kicked him and told him to shut his fucking mouth. With him now silent, Jimmy looked menacingly at the injured one and asked which one had raped her.

Neither one of them would answer; so without a second thought, Jimmy hit the non-co-operative one in the arm with the baling hook. They all watched as it ripped through his flesh.

"It was him," screamed the other man, clearly fearing the baling hook; "he did it!"

With the hook still embedded in his arm, the man shouted again for his accomplice to shut up. Unlike his friend, he was defiant. Jimmy could tell he wasn't going to say anything, but he was not going to let him get away with what he had done to Maria. Grabbing his hair, he pulled his head up then looking right at him said he knew it was him who'd raped her. With total defiance, the Jamaican spat in his face and said he was going to give her the best dam fuck she'd ever had and she would have begged him for more!

Jimmy was seething with anger; he could feel a rage, an uncontrollable rage surging through his body. How dare he talk about his beautiful Maria like that? Without a second thought he pulled down the Jamaicans trousers and boxer shorts exposing his cock before asking Reggie to lend him his knife.

The Jamaican watched the knife get passed from one man to the other; he hoped that Jimmy was bluffing in an effort to get information. Despite trying to remain defiant the man screamed in agony and begged Jimmy to stop when he ruthlessly pulled the hook from his arm. His early display of defiance was gone. Using the baling hook, which moments earlier he'd pulled from the same Jamaican's arm, Jimmy lifted the petrified man's cock up. He struggled frantically to try and free himself as Jimmy ordered the others to hold him. Snarling at him and calling him a mother fucker, Jimmy said he would never rape another woman again.

With the Jamaican screaming and begging, Jimmy just looked at him, then without any hesitation or empathy, he sliced off his cock with one flick of the knife. The screams from the man were pitiful before he passed out. The warehouse floor was covered in blood. The other Jamaican vomited.

Near to death, the Jamaican tried to say something. Jimmy bent down in front of him and said he couldn't hear him and he should open his mouth when talking to him.

Again the Jamaican mumbled something as he lay in the pool of his own blood. Still holding Reggie's knife, Jimmy sadistically placed the blade between the Jamaicans teeth and pushing against it, cut the Jamaicans mouth open.

"There now that's better," said Jimmy smiling "I told you to open you're fucking mouth when you speak to me!"

Moments later, Terry told him the Jamaican was dead.

"Good," replied Jimmy as he kicked him, "that's one less fucking bastard to contend with! Put his cock in a bag Reggie, we'll send it to Samuels as a present."

When Mickey asked if that was really a good idea, Jimmy just looked at him. Mickey knew at times like these it was best not to argue with him; he also knew, although they were best friends, Jimmy had an unhealthy liking for this type of violence. On occasion it had bothered him, knowing Jimmy was capable of such cruel, sadistic, violent acts without ever so much as a second thought. However, under the circumstances, he decided it wouldn't do any harm to send the severed cock to Samuels. Maybe it could be seen as pay back for Hudson, there was also the fact that Samuels could never prove who sent it. Yes, perhaps on this occasion he would agree with Jimmy.

As Reggie walked towards the body, Mickey told him to be careful and wear gloves when he bagged it, then he suggested driving at least thirty miles from there before sending it.

With his leg still pouring blood and his friend's cockless body slumped just a few feet away, the other Jamaican begged for his life. Coldly Jimmy turned to Reggie and said "Let your dogs' finish him off, I've had my fun."

Reggie didn't need asking twice as he pointed at the Jamaican and said "Kill!" Immediately the dogs were ripping at the Jamaican's throat, he was dead within seconds.

When Jimmy told them he needed to get back to Maria Terry said they would clear up and get rid of the bodies. Within an hour it would look like the Jamaicans were never here.

Mickey said he would drive him and then first thing in the morning he'd have the car cleaned. Jimmy told him to get rid of it; he didn't want Maria to get in it again.

"We were lucky tonight; things could have turned out a lot worse if Shaun hadn't turned up when he did" said Mickey as he drove, "and just for the record Jimmy, I think you've got a serious problem when committing acts of violence. If I ever piss you off just fucking tell me ok!"

They both laughed.

When they pulled up outside the apartment, Mickey asked if he wanted him to go up with him. Shaking his head Jimmy thanked him, but said he'd be fine.

Exiting the car he could see Shane and Billy sitting in Shane's car watching the apartment. Walking over to them, he thanked them and said they could go home. Mickey would contact them in the morning.

Noticing the blood on Jimmy's clothes, Shane asked if he was hurt. With a grin Jimmy said it wasn't his blood and he'd see them the following day.

Going up in the lift, he looked down upon himself; he was literally covered in blood. His thoughts were as soon as he'd spoken to Maria and Shaun he'd take a shower.

The moment he turned his key in the lock, Shaun called out. Acknowledging him, Jimmy made his way to in. When he entered the lounge, Shaun had the same reaction to the blood as the lads and asked if he was hurt. Quickly explaining it wasn't his blood, he asked where Maria was. Shaun pointed over to the sofa where she was asleep. He'd tried to get her to go to bed, but she wasn't having any of it, she'd insisted on waiting for Jimmy.

"No problem Shaun, thanks for staying with her. Those fucking black bastards won't be causing us any more grief. Sorry you've had to stay so late, and I mean it Shaun, thanks for all your help it's appreciated. Things could have turned out very differently if you hadn't turned up at the restaurant."

"No need to thank me, I'm just glad I got there before the bastard raped her."

With a look of shock, Jimmy asked if he was certain she hadn't been raped. Shaun was positive, although had he turned up ten seconds later it would have been a different story.

"Thank fuck for that," said a relieved Jimmy "one thing for sure, he won't be doing it again, I cut his knob off!"

"Ooh, bet that made his fucking eyes water!"

They both laughed.

Five minutes later Shaun left. Jimmy had just locked the door behind him when he heard Maria call out to him. Walking back into the lounge with a smile he asked if she was ok.

Seeing the blood on his clothes, she looked terrified and asked if he was ok and what had happened. She rushed over to him after he said he was fine.

Holding her in his arms, he apologised for having to leave her earlier, but he'd needed to deal with those bastards. Tears were welling in her eyes as he looked at her beautiful face, all bruised and swollen. Gently he kissed her as she cried and told him how terrified she'd been and still was in case they came back.

"They won't bother you again babe, in fact right about now they'll be on their way to Davy Jones locker, with the help of a concrete block courtesy of Reggie and Terry."

Although she hated violence, a part of her was relieved to hear that. Now a little calmer, she spoke about Shaun and how wonderful he'd been. She'd always regarded him as her guardian angel and never more so than that night.

"I'm glad you think that babe, because I've been thinking, until this mess with Samuels is sorted out perhaps it would be a good idea if Shaun was your personal body guard. I'm sure he'd love to do it for two reasons. The first being he loves you like a daughter and the second because he loves to eat, so you can try out all your new recipes on him!"

After what had happened, she knew if Jimmy couldn't be there with her, she'd feel safe with Shaun.

They sat together on the sofa talking, she was curious as to what the Jamaicans had said to him. Deciding to tell her everything, he gave her all the details. Including the way in which they had died. Watching him as he talked, she noticed he didn't flinch or show any emotion, even when he described the torture he'd inflicted on them. In her heart and because of her faith, she knew she should have felt some compassion, but truth was she didn't, she was glad they were dead.

Despite his tenderness towards her, she noticed his expression change when they talked about Samuels and how he intended to set them up by planting drugs at the club. Fearful of Samuels, she asked what they were going to do about it. Jimmy was going to meet up with the others to discuss it, but under the circumstances he wanted her to go to Gladys's. He didn't want to leave them alone in the apartment. Instantly and without questioning his request, she agreed.

Looking at her, he could see just how badly the incident with the Jamaicans had affected her, she looked pale and exhausted.

He suggested them taking a shower and then getting some sleep. When she told him she'd showered while Shaun was there to get the smell of the Jamaican off her, he grinned and stated her pyjamas were covered in blood from where she'd hugged him. Looking distressed as she looked down and saw the blood, she began tearing at her clothes in a panic to get them off. Quickly he embraced her and told her to calm down as she was becoming hysterical.

For the next few minutes she sobbed uncontrollably; the impact of what happened earlier had suddenly hit her. Leading her by the hand into the bathroom, he stripped off with her then they got into the shower together. Holding her close as the water cascaded over them, gently he sponged her down. Slowly she began to act more rationally.

Tenderly he dried her trembling body before wrapping her in the towel and carrying her through to the bedroom where he laid her gently in their bed. Pulling the cover over her; he kissed her forehead and told her he would go and make them both a hot drink. Tearfully clutching his hand, she begged him not to leave her. Calming her down, he reassured her he would only be a few minutes before kissing her head and leaving the room.

While he waited for the kettle to boil, he picked up all their clothes and put them in a black bag; at the first opportunity he would burn them.

Maria sat up in the bed as he passed her the tea before getting in beside her. After placing her empty cup on the dresser; she put her arm over his chest. Holding her close to him, he could feel her trembling as she told him that she thought the Jamaicans were going to kill her and at that time all she could think about was him. Caringly, he told her not to think about it, she was safe now and they should get some sleep.

They snuggled down together as she said "I love you more than anything in the world Jimmy; I wouldn't want to live without you. I'd rather be dead."

Pulling her closer, he said he wasn't planning on going anywhere for a long time and he loved her too, so she was stuck with him.

Lying next to her, he knew he felt the same way, the very thought of her not being there was incomprehensible to him. Tenderly he stroked her hair until she fell asleep.

Other than a few isolated incidents when he had lost his temper with her, he had always been caring, kind and compassionate. Yet just a few hours earlier to the Jamaicans, he had been a sadistic, evil bastard, bereft of any feelings.

CHAPTER 28

The time was a little after ten that morning. They had just begun to stir when they heard the door lock turn, followed by Mickey's voice calling out.

Jimmy called back and told him to get the kettle on as he'd be out in a few minutes. A few minutes later he emerged from the bedroom, said good morning and curiously asked why Mickey hadn't phoned first.

Mickey explained he'd taken Jimmy's car to be crushed at Sam's scrap yard and as his place is only ten minutes from there he'd come straight round. Mickey passed him a carrier bag with his personal items in from the car.

After thanking him for sorting it out, Jimmy asked after Sam. They had all been friends for many years, having used Sam's crusher on many occasions. Sam was a good bloke and, more importantly, someone they all trusted. He never asked why they wanted it crushed, he knew better than to question what people like them did. Mickey nodded and said Sam was fine, although he'd nearly cried when Mickey told him to crush the car. They knew he'd always liked Jimmy's car, but despite this, he never asked why it was being crushed. By the time Mickey left, the car would have fitted into a shoe box. At some point Jimmy said he would need to sort out another car.

"Funny you should say that, I've seen just the car for you; it's on the forecourt of Baxter's Autos. It's right up your street Jimmy, metallic silver top of the range Mercedes convertible."

They were still talking about the car and how Jimmy liked the sound of it, when Maria appeared. Mickey stood up and walking over to her; hugged her as he kissed her cheek and asked how she was feeling. He smiled when she thanked him and said she was fine.

Calling her princess, he told her to sit down as he was making the tea as he headed off towards the kitchen. Jimmy sat down beside her and kissed her on the lips, but he was surprised when he felt her slightly pull away from him. Squeezing her hand, he asked if she was sure she was okay.

The expression on her face was one of sadness, she looked as though she was about to burst into tears. Putting his arm around her, he held her tight.

"Perhaps it's not such a good idea for you to go to Gladys's babe," he said "maybe it would be better if you stayed here and rested. I'll ask Shaun to stay with you."

Too tearful to reply, she nodded her head just as Mickey appeared with the tea. Passing Maria hers first, she sipped it slowly, only stopping to ask what the time was. Jimmy stated it was almost midday. He'd left her sleeping when he got up because she had looked knackered last night. When he asked if she wanted something to eat, she shook her head. Mickey suggested her going back to bed as she didn't look to well. Again she simply nodded as Jimmy stood up, held out his hand and said he'd tuck her in.

In the bedroom, he noticed she seemed distant as he spoke to her. He was concerned about her, something wasn't quite right. Making sure she was comfortable, he kissed her head and told her he was only in the next room if she needed him. Without replying, she just snuggled down under the duvet.

Back in the lounge the two friends talked.

"I think you should ask Doc Daniels to take a look at her," said Mickey "I can take care of business if you want to stay home with her today. I'll call round later after I've spoken to the lads."

"I'd like to have gone to the meeting, but I think you're right Mick, I ought to stay with her. Can I ask another favour? Can you call into Baxter's and buy the Mercedes for me; a new car might cheer her up. If need be I can sort out the paper work over the phone. Baxter knows me well enough to know I'm good for the cash, so there won't be a problem. Another favour mate, I've put our clothes from last night in a bin bag, can you take it and burn it for me?"

Mickey grinned and stated he thought he could manage that.

Ten minutes later he left.

Jimmy checked on Maria. She was asleep, so taking his friend's advice he phoned Doc Daniels. Fortunately, he had just finished a morning surgery so he told Jimmy he would call round within the hour.

Forty five minutes later, Jimmy was just about to wake her when the intercom buzzed; it was the Doc. As he entered he said he was surprised and asked why Maria needed to see him. Shock was the Doc's reaction when told she'd been assaulted the previous night. The first question he asked was if it had been sexual. Jimmy said yes, but he was stopped before he raped her. Doc wasn't surprised to hear the assault hadn't been reported to the police because they were going to sort it out themselves. One thing Doc had learnt over the years was not to ask questions, so without further discussion, he suggested seeing Maria.

Following Jimmy, they entered the bedroom. Maria was stirring when Jimmy said the Doc had popped in to see her.

Looking surprised, she smiled as Doc sat down on the bed and asked how she was feeling. Before she could reply she burst into tears. Doc held her hand and told her not to get upset. Aware that she was worried as to how much the Doc knew, he said Jimmy explained to him that a man had assaulted her. Jimmy interrupted and quickly stated he hadn't given the Doc any real details, he thought he'd leave that to her. She knew what he'd said was his way of letting her know the Doc knew nothing about the Jamaicans and Jimmy wanted it to stay that way.

After Doc asked her a few questions he left her some pills, they would help to calm her down. Looking at the bruises on her face they didn't appear to have done any serious damage. Smiling he said he was confident that by the time she walked up the aisle they'd have disappeared and she'd be a stunning bride, then he suggested her trying to go back to sleep.

Nodding, she thanked him as he left the room.

"She's suffering from stress Jimmy," said Doc once in the lounge "it's obviously brought on by the recent trauma. I expected this from her years ago when she lived with Nick; I'm surprised it hasn't happened sooner."

Jimmy found it hard to understand what the Doc was saying, he could have understood her being stressed before she moved in with him, but now she knew she was safe.

"You're right Jimmy, she's more settled now than at any other time in her life. In a few weeks she's going to marry the man she loves; but weddings are actually very stressful events; she looks to you for her strength. I never imagined that after just two years she would be the confident young woman she now is. This attack simply made her realise just how vulnerable she really is, you weren't there to protect her and her mind is having trouble dealing with it. She will get over this, but my advice to you would be spend as much time with her as possible, especially over the next few days. Hopefully you'll see an improvement by then, but you'll need to be patient. Any problems just call me, if not I look forward to seeing you at the wedding."

Jimmy thanked him and said how much he appreciated him coming so quickly.

Jimmy returned to the bedroom after the Doc left. Maria was still awake, so he lay down on the bed and wrapped her in his arms, telling her he loved her so much and how really sorry he was about what happened to her.

"Would you still have loved me if I'd been raped?" she asked in a quiet quivery voice.

"I'd love you exactly the same, I always will."

Finding comfort in his words, she snuggled her head to his chest. Within minutes she'd dropped back off to sleep. Without disturbing her he got up, he wanted to make a couple of calls.

It was six o'clock that evening when Mickey phoned to say he was on his way over and did they want him to pick something up for dinner. Stating that Maria hadn't eaten all day Jimmy said fish and chips would be great as it was her favourite.

Gently waking her five minutes later, he said Mickey was on his way round with fish and chips so she had to get up. Opening her eyes, she looked at him and said she wasn't hungry. When he said she must try because she hadn't eaten since the previous day, she simply nodded.

Thirty minutes later Mickey arrived, letting himself in and headed for the kitchen with the food, just as his friends were making their way through the lounge. Following him, they all sat at the table. Mickey suggested eating it out of the paper like when they were kids, although then it came wrapped in newspaper. Jimmy said it was a fucking shame everything had to be politically correct nowadays; he couldn't ever remember anyone catching any disease from eating out of newspaper. Mickey agreed, stating the fucking country had gone mad with all the old bollocks about, 'you can't do this and you can't do that.'

Maria just smiled and nodded her head.

While the two men tucked into their meal, she just picked at hers.

After they had eaten they took their tea through to the lounge. Knowing they were going to be talking about business, Jimmy said she didn't have to sit and listen to them if she didn't want to, she could always lie in bed and watch the telly or a DVD. Telling him she felt tired, she suggested watching a DVD then if she dozed off she could rewind it. Standing up he held out his hand, moments later they were heading toward the bedroom. Jimmy called over to Mickey to pour them a drink while he settled her down.

After putting her chosen DVD in the player, he handed her the remote control. Just as he was about to leave, Mickey knocked on the bedroom door then entered carrying a hot cup of tea which he placed down on the dresser and jokingly said it would help put the colour back on her cheeks.

Thanking him, she giggled and stated she'd have to be ill more often, having two handsome men looking after her.

"Steady on babe," said Jimmy "you'll ruin our hard men reputations!"

She blew Mickey a kiss as they left the bedroom.

Things took on a more serious theme once the men were back in the lounge as Mickey told him that Lenny was going to bug the offices at each club; simply because they couldn't assume Sweet Cheeks would be Samuels's choice for planting the drugs. Lenny would place a camera in the office light fittings, that way they'd have total surveillance of each office. Once Samuels had planted the drugs, they'd simply remove them. Jimmy thought it sounded great and asked if there was any other news. Both men knew that regarding the Jamaicans and the attack on Maria, everyone was sticking to the same story; there never were any Jamaicans at the restaurant. Without proof, Samuels could never involve them.

"Lying bunch of bastards!" said Jimmy with a laugh.

"All the lads have an alibi for last night. Shaun is simply going along with the original arrangement, he picked Maria up from the restaurant around midnight and dropped her back here, came in for coffee before going home. Me and you were at the club 'til around half one, ok? One last thing, regarding the restaurant, Shaun blew a fucking great hole in the ceiling! I've sent some builders round; hopefully they can fix it without shutting the place. Fortunately it's at the back, so if anyone asks it was a burst pipe, ok?"

Jimmy thought it sounded as though Mickey had covered everything and humbly expressed that he wouldn't know what to do without him. They continued talking about what happened to Maria as Jimmy tried to explain to him what the Doc thought she was suffering from.

Mickey was certain the Doc was right, what with the wedding, Monica being shot and then the fucking turn out with the Jamaicans, it was no wonder she was suffering from stress. He told Jimmy to give her a few days; he could take care of business. If anyone outside the crew asked where Jimmy was, he would simply tell them he had the flu. He would also inform the lads to say about the flu in case Samuels asked them about Jimmy.

Later that evening around quarter to eleven, Mickey got ready to leave. He would check in on the clubs before going home.

Just as Jimmy went to close the door behind him, Mickey turned and stated he'd almost forgotten to tell him that the Mercedes would be ready in a couple of days. One of Andy Baxter's boys would drop it round for him. Andy had said they could sort out the money when he saw him. Although Mickey had offered to pay him, he'd said there was no hurry.

After Jimmy thanked him and said he would sort it out with Andy the following week, Mickey left.

Jimmy poured himself a drink before settling down to watch a bit of telly. Maria hadn't stirred all evening; she was still asleep when he turned in around one. Unsuccessfully he tried not to wake her as he got in the bed. Apologising for waking her, he asked if she was ok. Without speaking she just nodded. Putting his arm around her; he kissed her face, but out of character she didn't respond. Normally she would cuddle him, but she just laid there. Running his hand up her arm, he began kissing her neck, he hadn't intended to initiate sex; but he was becoming aroused. Still unresponsive, she just laid there as he slowly began fondling her breasts. Moving over, he rolled his tongue over her nipple before taking it into his mouth. Maria could feel his erection against her body, but still she didn't respond. Realising that she was trembling and her body was becoming more rigid, he stopped.

Propping himself up on his elbow; he gently stroked her head as he looked down on her. Tears were rolling down her face onto the pillow. Kissing her head, he assured her it didn't matter; it was his fault for wanting her. It was simply the effect she had on him. When he suggested them getting some sleep, she rolled over, while he just laid there looking at the ceiling. Finally his erection subsided. It was the first time she hadn't responded to his sexual advances.

Laying there he couldn't help but wonder if she'd told him everything. His feeling was that something more must have happened with the Jamaicans, he knew his Maria was tougher than this, he remembered how she had suffered with Nick, yet still she stayed strong. In his mind he was convinced there was more to it, he lay awake for hours thinking about it before finally dropping off.

When he woke the next morning, she was not in the bed. Getting up he headed for the lounge where he found her sitting looking out of the window. Calling her gorgeous, he said good morning. Slowly she turned to look at him; her eyes were red and swollen. It was obvious she'd been crying. Walking to her and putting his arms around, her asked what was wrong. Instantly she fell into him and sobbed.

"I'm so sorry Jimmy; if I'd listened to you in the first place none of this would have happened. If only I had taken things more seriously, I would never have gone into work. Or at the very least, I would have accepted Leon's offer to wait with me."

Jimmy tried to assure her that Samuels was to blame and she had nothing to be sorry for. Then in an effort to lighten the mood, he said all she needed to make her feel better was some of his scrambled eggs.

Having stopped crying, she giggled and suggested they settled for a bowl of cornflakes.

Throughout breakfast she kept looking at him while she ate. Unable to let it go, he asked her why and was shocked when she replied that she didn't understand why he loved her so much or how he put up with her. With sincerity he said she was very easy to love and it should be him asking how she put up with him. Before she could reply she yawned. He asked if she was tired, she nodded, but stated she shouldn't be because all she'd done was sleep.

Caringly, he said she'd been through a tough time and rest was good for her, so he suggested they went back to bed for a couple of hours as it was only quarter past eight. With a grin he promised he'd behave.

Jimmy was in bed first and asked if he could have a cuddle when she got in beside him. Laying her head on his chest she assured him he didn't have to ask.

Finding his hand that was wrapped across her, she gripped it when he said he wanted to ask her something and he didn't want her getting upset. After she nodded, he gently stroked her hair and asked what else had happened with the Jamaicans, because he knew something had.

Sitting up she looked down on him as the tears began rolling down her cheeks when she tried to tell him they had said horrible things to her and put their hands all over her. She'd tried to fight them off, but if Shaun hadn't turned up when he did they would have raped her. Her thoughts at the time were they would kill her, she was so scared. It was horrible, she sobbed, they'd told her that their boss wanted to fuck her and once Jimmy was out of the way there would be no one to stop him. They terrified her when they'd stated that after they'd all fucked her they would put her to work in one of their brothels in Jamaica.

As she tried to continue, she was becoming hysterical so he hugged her until she calmed down enough to continue.

They taunted her by saying that every day she would be getting, she stopped talking and just sobbed, momentarily unable to continue and just held him until she blurted out, "Big black cocks!"

Reassuringly, he said they were just trying to frighten her and even if he couldn't protect her, there would be other people that would. Shaun and Mickey to name but two, and anyway she didn't even have to think about it because it would never happen.

Although he remained calm, inside his anger was raging and even more so when she apologised for not telling him what had happened and not wanting sex the previous night, but she'd felt dirty where the Jamaicans had touched her. Eventually she calmed down.

In an effort to cheer her up, he told her it didn't matter, but he was glad she had told him because he wondered if he was losing his sexual prowess.

Snuggling her head to him, she said he knew she'd always loved it when he touch her. It was just that she couldn't get the Jamaicans out of her head. Their conversation was interrupted by his phone. It was Justin. Not wanting her to hear, Jimmy got out of bed and went into the lounge, using the excuse that the reception was poor. Once out of ear shot, Justin wanted him to know that everything was finished and he'd drop the keys off to Mickey. Explaining that he didn't have a motor at that time, Jimmy said he'd pay him as soon as he was mobile. Justin was happy to wait; he knew Jimmy was good for the money.

Whilst talking on the phone, he hadn't heard Maria get up; she was standing in the doorway. As the call ended she asked him what had happened to their car. Explaining he'd had it crushed as there was evidence linking him to the Jamaicans, she asked what evidence.

About three pints of their blood, he replied with a laugh before telling her they would be getting a Mercedes in a couple of days and if she felt up to it, he'd take her for a drive. As she nodded in acceptance she asked who Justin was. When he replied he was just a friend, the look on her face told him she was suspicious, so he quickly added he'd bought her a surprise gift which Justin had been sorting out for him.

"A gift?" she said curiously.

"Yeah a present which I was going to give you on our wedding day, but under the circumstances I think I should give it to you sooner. So I might just consider giving it to you early, but we'll have to wait until we get the new motor."

Only a few moments had passed when her curiosity got the better of her; she was unable to stay silent a moment longer. Excitedly she asked if her present was something big or small, something to wear and was it very expensive. With a grin, he teased her stating she'd have to wait and see as it was a surprise and if he hadn't mentioned it, she wouldn't have known about it.

"Oh Jimmy, that's so unfair because I do know and it's going to drive me crazy!"

Still he refused to tell her anything, she'd have to wait. Slapping him playfully, she said he was horrible and she couldn't wait, to which he replied "Patience is a virtue babe, or so I've heard."

"Argh, you're so infuriating!"

Jimmy just laughed.

Throughout the entire day she kept trying to find out what the surprise was, but he was giving nothing away.

Since their talk that morning, he could sense that she was feeling better. When she suggested he could go to the club that night with Mickey, he said it was a nice try to get round him, but he still wouldn't tell her.

Trying to look and sound sincere, she insisted that she hadn't suggested it so he would tell her.

"You little liar," laughed Jimmy "anyway I'm quite happy to stay home with you."

"Now who's a little liar," she said jokingly.

"No honest babe, although if Shaun could come over and keep you company, I wouldn't mind popping out for a couple of hours."

Giggling, she walked over and kissed him passionately. Jimmy knew with that kiss his Maria was back, whatever trauma she'd felt from her attack by the Jamaicans was over.

A short time later, he called Mickey to ask him to pick him up later as his good lady had said he could go to the club.

Mickey was actually on his way round to their place.

Ten minutes later he arrived at their apartment. Maria was the first to greet him.

The three friends sat down and talked over coffee about Monica and how quickly she was recovering and how she was looking forward to seeing Maria. They noticed Mickey had a funny grin on his face. Jimmy was curious and asked why. He could hardly believe it when Mickey said the reason he'd come round early was to tell them that Samuels had been round to the club and their plan had worked like a dream.

After stating that was quick, Jimmy asked him for the details.

"Samuels called into the club on his own. Tony and Shane were there with me. Samuels asked if any of us had heard anything concerning the Jamaicans. Apparently he'd heard a rumour that a local restaurant had some bother with them, and he just wondered if it may have been one of our restaurants. I could tell he was pissed off when I said all our places were fine. He did ask where you two were though, the cheeky bastard. I decided against the flu theory, just in case he said he called round. I told him Maria had roped you into going shopping for the wedding and chances where you would turn up at the club any minute. There was one thing I thought was strange though, he asked after Maria several times."

With a frown Jimmy asked him to be more specific. He looked angry to hear that Samuels had asked questions like was Maria looking forward to marrying Jimmy, only he didn't think for one minute he'd be her type.

Looking angry, Jimmy said Samuels needed to tread carefully or he'd punch his fucking lights out! Mickey's advice was to ignore him. Fortunately Jimmy agreed, but if Samuels stepped over the mark, he'd sort him out.

"Samuels asked if he could use the office phone because he had to make a private call. I asked Tony to take him to the office and told Samuels he wouldn't be disturbed there. He'd only been gone about ten minutes when he came out, thanked us and promptly left. Soon as he'd gone we watched the tape. I've brought it round, just wait 'til you see the slimy bastard in action."

Jimmy played the tape. They watched as Samuels took a large bag of cocaine and a roll of tape from his pocket; then he pulled out the metal filing cabinet and stuck the package to the back of it. As they watched, Jimmy said Samuels was a mother fucker who was definitely going to get what he deserved. Mickey believed the tapes alone would now be enough to send Samuels away for at least ten years and with him out of the way their only problem would be the remaining Jamaicans. Jimmy's answer to that was they could take care of the Jamaicans. When he asked what was happening about the drugs, he wasn't surprised to hear Mickey had passed them to Tony. They believed they could be worth about a hundred and twenty five grand to one of their buyers who Tony was setting up a meeting with that night.

"It won't be long before the Old Bill is tipped off by Samuels," said Jimmy "then they'll be round to search the club. It would be best if we could stop it before it happens. Another thing, we'll need to cover our tracks if the tape can be used against us. The first thing the drug squad will want to know is where the drugs are now."

"Already thought about that Jim, I've come up with a plan but we need to get Samuels back to the club. Once he's there we'll get one of the lads to call the office phone on his mobile. Whoever answers it can tell Samuels the call is for him; that way we get him on tape entering the office again. Then, unfortunately for Samuels, the tape will malfunction so nobody will actually be able to see him presumably take the drugs back, or leave the office. Monica thinks we'll probably get a visit from the drug squad within the next twenty four hours. Samuels won't leave it too long in case someone else finds the drugs, shame we already have! She also thinks that calling his bluff would be a good way of stalling him. I think she may be right. If he thought we were interested in selling the club, it will bring the Jamaicans to us. We have to assume Samuels doesn't know that we know he's the man behind them; so if we put the word out via him he will have no choice but to send the Jamaicans round to talk business."

Jimmy could see the logic, but he wondered how they could tell Samuels that they wanted to sell the club. He grinned when Mickey said Monica could get him to the hospital on the pretext that she'd remembered something. After Jimmy said it may just work, Mickey arranged to call Monica and get her to set it up.

Twenty minutes later, she had rung back to tell him that Samuels was going to visit her around seven that evening.

When Maria asked Mickey if he would like to stay for dinner, he said he would love to but only on the condition he could buy it. Maria should rest and not have to worry about cooking, so he would send out for something.

Mickey left to see Monica and meet with Samuels. He would come back to their place afterwards.

"Good luck with the dodgy detective," said Jimmy with a laugh as Mickey left.

It was turned eight o'clock when Mickey returned from the hospital. They were keen to hear what had happened.

"Monica fed Samuels a line about some threatening anonymous calls she'd had prior to the shooting," said Mickey "Samuels asked her why she hadn't said anything sooner. She acted very blasé and said at the time she had simply put it down to some hoaxer. It was after she'd talked to him about that, I chatted to him about us. I told him it was your idea about selling the club, reason being you wanted to spend more time with Maria after you were married. I dropped the fact that you want to try for a family straight away as one of the principal reasons. I led him to believe we knew a couple of people who might be interested in buying Sweet Cheeks. I even added that Tony, at the very least, would deserve first refusal. Samuels seemed more than interested; he even asked me what sort of figure we would be looking at. He didn't flinch when I said five hundred grand or there about. Cheeky bastard even mentioned the Jamaicans, said something like, 'rumour has it some Jamaicans are interested in your club.' When I questioned him about it and stated that we hadn't spoken to any Jamaicans, the cheeky bastard sneered and said, 'come now Mickey, do you really think I don't know what's been going on? I know you've had trouble with them; there's not much that happens that I don't hear about, despite the fact that you and your friend Jimmy keep trying to cover it up, I know all about it.' I simply bluffed my way out of it by saying we didn't want an issue made of it because it could be bad for business, plus the fact we didn't think the Jamaicans would be back. Funnily enough he disagreed with me, in his opinion they would be back. I have a strange feeling about Slimy fucking Samuels; it won't be long before we hear from him via our Jamaican friends, especially as I let him know that there were other potential buyers interested. So now we just sit tight and wait."

It was almost nine when the takeaway arrived. The two men were hungry, but Maria just picked at hers. Offering to make the coffee while the two men finished off the meal, she disappeared into the kitchen.

They were discussing Samuels when the intercom buzzed; Jimmy anticipated it would be Shaun as he had arranged for him to come round about ten to stay with Maria.

Answering the intercom, he immediately recognised the Irishman's voice.

Before they left for the club, they filled Shaun in on Samuels and Jimmy told Maria he would only be gone a few hours, but she could contact him anytime if she needed to.

Thanking Mickey for dinner, she kissed him on the cheek before kissing Jimmy and telling them to be careful as she said goodbye.

During the drive, Mickey asked how they should handle the Jamaicans if they turned up. Instantly Jimmy stated they should get rid of the fuckers because they'd caused them enough fucking grief.

Although Mickey agreed, he brought to Jimmy's attention that the Jamaicans didn't know the truth about Maurice's death; they'd only had Samuels version of what happened. Maybe if they explained it to them they could avoid any unnecessary bloodshed. Jimmy nodded, but was quick to say if they didn't believe them, they would run straight back to Samuels and tell him. There was also what they did to Monica and Maria. His thoughts on the matter were simple; he wanted them dead, they didn't need them.

They had the tape and Max, who he reckoned would turn on Samuels given the opportunity. Mickey agreed, but his main concern was how to deal with them. They didn't want anything coming back to them. Jimmy suggested offering to take the Jamaicans to a strip club; then get Reggie and Terry to meet them secretly en route. They could arrange a diversion so they could ambush their car and then take the bastards down the docks and off them.

"Fuck me Jimmy; it's so simple it might just work! It's quite worrying really; my best friend has the mind of a serial killer!"

They both laughed.

Pulling up at Sweet Cheeks they could see Kevin and Jacky Boy working the doors. Walking over to them and after talking for a few minutes about the club, Mickey explained to them about the Jamaicans.

Inside Billy was keeping an eye on the dancers. Shane was standing at the bar talking to Sue. They filled both men in on their plan, before asking Shane about Max. Shane hadn't heard from her, but he was going to phone her the following day.

They had only been at the club for about an hour when the three Jamaicans walked in. Two of them sat at a table; while Damon went to the bar. Mickey approached him and asked if his boss was still interested in buying the club.

"Dat dapends man," replied Damon.

"Depends on what?" asked Mickey sarcastically.

"It depends if ya tell me what happen ta ma friends."

"I've no fucking idea what you're talking about. If you're not interested in the club fine, we'll take our business elsewhere." Mickey turned to walk away.

"I dan't say I wasn't interested, but ya make a big mistake if ya fuck with me. Ya see I knows ya did something ta ma friends and I wanta know what."

Mickey continued walking away, only turning briefly to reply "Fuck you! I haven't got time for all your bullshit; there are others who are interested!"

Walking back along the bar towards Jimmy, he turned when Damon called out and told him to wait. He hadn't said he wasn't interested, he knew his boss still wanted the club.

When Mickey suggested going to the office, Damon nodded at the two Jamaicans sitting at the table. Immediately they got up and stood behind him. They all followed Mickey and Jimmy into the office and sat down. When Mickey started talking about their boss wanting to buy the club, Damon really pissed him off when he arrogantly stated he would only do business with Jimmy.

Mickey was put out by his attitude and quickly told him so, but Damon obviously wasn't intimidated.

"I dan't like ya Mickey and I dan't trust ya, if I find out yah hurt my friends I cut ya heart out!"

Jimmy intervened before things got out of hand and with a menacing look, told Damon if he didn't respect Mickey there wouldn't be any business and they weren't the only people interested so they'd take their business elsewhere.

"If ya have others interested, why would ya come ta us?"

"We didn't come to you; we never invited you here tonight, but now you're here we're prepared to give you the benefit of the doubt because we're good business men Damon, that's why. Truth is you're right, we know there is no mutual respect and to tell you the truth that pisses me off, but the fact is if we try to sell the club to someone else and you fucking lot give us grief, everyone will want to know why we're allowing you to live. You could make us look bad, so you see it would be in everyone's best interests to get on with business and stop fucking around!"

"I like ya Jimmy man, dares no messing with ya so we talk business."

Mickey poured them all a drink before going over the figures concerning the price and stating clearly it wasn't negotiable. That was the deal so they could either take it or leave it, but they wanted an answer within twenty four hours.

When Damon said he'd have to speak to his boss. Mickey told him to call him. Damon instantly stated he couldn't as he was busy, he would ask him the following morning.

The men agreed they would wait till the morning.

They talked business for another hour. The atmosphere was less tense by the time they'd had a few drinks. Jimmy was trying to think of a way to get the Jamaicans to leave with them.

Patronisingly, he smiled at Damon and said he was glad the meeting had taken place because he'd felt they'd got off on the wrong foot, which was a shame. They were all businessmen, he smugly added how he knew Mickey could be difficult, but in view of the fact that his girlfriend had been shot, surely they could understand why.

Damon and the others nodded.

Jimmy's advice to them was if they were going to set up businesses in London, it would be in their best interests to try and treat Mickey with a little more respect. Mickey had many contacts that could prove very useful to them in the future.

Damon looked over at Mickey and almost sincerely said maybe Jimmy was right and he did deserve a little more respect.

Mickey simply nodded.

"Right then," said Jimmy "now that's settled, might I suggest we either stay here to watch the dancers, or go on to a strip joint. I can recommend a good one."

Damon thought about it for a moment then said a strip club sounded good.

Continuing to lull them into a false sense of security, Mickey suggested they had a couple more drinks there first.

It was as they sat talking, Damon introduced the other Jamaicans. They were cousins of Maurice's, Jonah and Ric which was short for Ricardo.

Considering they were talking amiably, Jimmy saw the time as a good opportunity to let them know that they got on with Maurice; despite the fact he was going to kill them the first chance he got. When he spoke about Maurice, he could sense that they did not believe him, which in a strange way made him realise that killing them was, in his opinion, the right and only thing to do.

Mickey went up to the bar and ordered another round of drinks. Damon watched him as he chatted to Sue.

While they waited, Damon talked to Jimmy, asking him the name of the barmaid Mickey was talking to because he'd like to fuck her.

Jimmy really wanted to punch him over his lack of respect for Sue, but instead he laughed and told him all the blokes there wanted her and some had tried, but they'd wasted their time.

Shane walked over to the bar to speak to Mickey. They stood with their backs to the Jamaicans as Mickey told him to let Reggie and Terry know they were taking the Jamaicans to the club called G SPOT. Reg and Terry could wait until they left there then jump them. When Shane asked if he could come along for the ride, Mickey knew it was because he wanted to take a pop at Damon over how he'd treated Max so he grinned and nodded.

Damon kept looking over at them, trying to see what they were saying. Mickey was aware of this so as he walked back over with their drinks, he called back to Shane and told him they'd be going to another club, but any problems he could just bell them. Damon seemed content with the fact that Shane wouldn't be going with them.

As Mickey sat down, Damon said he didn't like Shane and rudely referred to him as a sperm donor with psychotic tendencies.

"Shane's actually a decent bloke," said Jimmy, now disliking Damon intensely "he's only downfall is pussy. One thing's for certain though, we'd rather have him as a friend than an enemy. Actually he's a lot like I was in my younger day."

Jonah said something a bit sarcastic about Jimmy soon being an old married man. Holding his temper Jimmy grinned and said he couldn't wait.

Mickey could see the aggression on Jimmy's face when Damon said they'd heard Maria was quite a looker, so he quickly interrupted and said they'd heard right, she was a real beauty. Sarcastically Damon laughed and asked what she saw in Jimmy.

"Yeah, I can't work that one out either," said Jimmy holding his need to hurt the Jamaican "not only does she bring out the best in me, but also the worst. She's more important than anything, she's everything to me."

Damon looked a bit baffled as to what he was really trying to say. Shaking his head he said no woman was worth everything.

"I thought that Damon until I met Maria, but like I said she brings out the worse in me. Rest assured I wouldn't hesitate to kill any man that touched her."

At that moment, Damon knew he was referring to the attack and rape he planned with his friends; he also knew they had killed his friends, but he couldn't say or do anything about it. Changing the topic, Mickey suggested going to the strip club. Damon nodded and said they would follow in their car.

G SPOT was about ten miles away and a far cry from Sweet Cheeks. It was a seedy little club, where for the right price the girls would do just about anything. Really it was nothing more than a cheap whore house, with a couple of dingy rooms upstairs if the dancers wanted to make a bit of extra cash. Ken Moor the owner was himself a seedy character. Now approaching seventy, he had never married. Always looked as though his clothes needed ironing and a wash and shave wouldn't go a miss. In his young days he had run a couple of very high class brothels, rumour has it he's a millionaire. When he reached sixty five he did try to retire, but he missed it. That's why he bought G Spot, just to give him something to do. Mickey had helped him out a couple of times when he had been raided by the Vice Squad, usually getting him off with a fine. Ken liked both Mickey and Jimmy and it was obvious he was pleased to see them when they walked in. Mickey introduced the Jamaicans to him and then ordered a round of drinks, which Ken said were on the house. They talked to him for a while and then found a table.

It wasn't long before a couple of the dancers picked them out, probably because they looked like money with the way they were dressed and the jewellery they wore. A petite pretty brunette aged about twenty made a bee line for Damon. Sitting down on his lap, she pushed her breasts into his face before rubbing her hand on his crotch. The Jamaican was lapping it up. Then she whispered something in his ear as she stood up. Taking him by the hand she led him up the stairs, nodding at Ken as she passed the bar to let him know she had a client.

She took the Jamaican to a small dingy room upstairs at the back of the club. It was sparsely furnished with just a bed, dressing table and chair. A pair of dirty curtains hung at the window. As she began to undress him, she told him fifty quid would get him a blow job.

Expressionless, he just looked at her; she felt a little intimidated by him as she asked what he wanted.

"I'm gonna fuck ya," he said in a cold arrogant tone. Compared to her tiny body, he was huge by comparison. Slowly she began taking her clothes off, but he grabbed her and threw her face down over the dressing table, knocking an ashtray that was on it onto the floor. Pinning her down, she asked him to take it easy. Ignoring her, he tore off her panties, then he began fucking her. Her cries fell on deaf ears when she shouted for him to stop because he was hurting her.

With him holding her by the neck to keep her in that position, she began struggling and calling out. Instantly he gripped her throat in his hands and shouted aggressively for her to shut up or he would shut her up. With every thrust he tightened his grip around her throat, she could barely breathe. Desperately wanting it to be over, she kept telling herself that he would come soon, and then he would leave her alone. Despite the fact that she had approached him for sex, this was not what she had intended. This was rape. When he finally finished she was crying as she stood up and put her panties back on. With a sickening smirk on his face, he told her she'd been a good fuck. Calling him a bastard, she stated it was rape. Laughing he threw a roll of money at her and said she could call it whatever the fuck she liked, it was what he'd wanted and she was a whore! Then he walked out and went back down stairs to join the others.

Picking up the money she counted it, there was a hundred pounds. After straightening her clothes and wiping her eyes, she left the room. Returning downstairs she went straight to the bar. Ken asked if everything was ok as she approached him. Looking at her, he knew something wasn't right, especially when she simply nodded. The only reason he didn't push the issue was because she hadn't asked him to. Without hesitation he would have had Damon thrown out had she asked or told him what had happened.

Back at the table, Damon sat down. When Jimmy asked if he'd had fun, he hadn't expected his reply.

"English women are weak," said Damon arrogantly "they dan't fight back enough; I like it when they fight back. Some women put up a real fight, they make ma real horny."

Jimmy just smiled and thought about what they'd done to Maria, at that moment he wanted to slit Damon's throat. Looking over at the bar he could see the young brunette, her neck and arms visibly showing red marks from where Damon had been rough with her. Jimmy went to order another round of drinks making a point of deliberately standing next to her and striking up a conversation. She recognised him as one of Damon's party from earlier. With a smile he asked if she was ok.

"Your friend is a fucking animal," she replied "he should be thankful that you're a friend of Kens; otherwise I would have him thrown out!"

Jimmy apologised for him hurting her, but stated they weren't friends just business associates.

While he waited for his drinks, he placed two fifty pound notes under her glass. Thanking him she asked if he wanted to go upstairs as she was available.

With a wink, he said "Maybe some other time babe."

When he returned to the table with the tray of drinks, Damon said he'd seen him talking to the whore and asked if she'd told Jimmy what a great fuck he'd been. Sarcastically, Jimmy made a point of shaking his head and stating that Damon obviously hadn't been that good, because she'd just asked him to go upstairs with her. Damon looked put out by his answer.

The time was four o'clock when Mickey said if no one objected he was going to call it a night. Everyone agreed that it was late and time to retire. They spoke to Ken on the way out, thanking him for his hospitality. The pretty brunette smiled at Jimmy and calling him sexy told him to come back soon. He simply winked and grinned at her.

Outside they shook hands with the Jamaicans. As Mickey shook Damon's hand, he said as soon as their boss agrees to the price, he would sort out all the paper work. Then they could call round to the club for it in a couple of days.

"Perhaps in time," said Damon "we could be friends Mickey."

Mickey just nodded.

They all walked towards their cars, the Jamaicans' BMW was parked about ten cars away from Mickey's.

Mickey honked his horn as he pulled away, Damon and the others waved out to them.

Just as the Jamaicans approached their car, they were jumped. Shane grabbed hold of Damon and head butted him in the face. The big Jamaican fell back against the car. The fact that he had been drinking heavily hindered his reaction.

Reggie hit Ric with such power that he was out cold. Terry had Jonah pushed up against the boot of the car with his arm twisted behind his back as they bundled them into the back of a transit van. Terry drove their BMW back to the docks.

Once inside the van, Reggie held a gun on them and laughing said he was shaking in his fucking boots when Damon said they would all die when his boss found out what they'd done. Realising Reggie couldn't care less about their boss, Damon changed tactics and told Reggie he would make sure he was rewarded well if he let them go, because he knew it wasn't down to him, Mickey had put him up to it.

"It'll be reward enough seeing you bastards dead after all the fucking trouble you've caused!" snarled Reggie "and Mickey didn't put us up to anything you dumb fucker!"

Shane couldn't resist interrupting and stated it was their own fault for getting involved with a slime ball like Samuels.

Damon looked surprised they knew who his boss was, especially when Shane added they were just doing Samuels dirty work and they should have listened to Hudson. The Jamaicans didn't reply. It was several minutes later when Damon asked where they were taking them. With a real smirk on his face Reggie said he was taking them to meet their friends.

Mickey flashed his head lights to let them know he was right behind them as they pulled into the docks. The moment the van stopped, Reggie's dogs ran over to greet him. Shane shook his head in disbelief as he heard Reggie say, "Sorry I had to leave you here boys, but I couldn't take you with me."

Mickey pulled in behind them. Terry forced the Jamaicans to walk in front of them. They were probably more afraid of Reggie's dogs than the gun he was aiming at them.

Inside the warehouse they tied them to the girder. In a very aggressive manner Mickey called them dumb bastards and asked if they'd really thought they could come over here and take their business. In his opinion trusting Samuels said everything about their fucking IQ! If they had simply been doing Samuels bidding, Mickey may have been able to let them live, but there was the near fatal shooting of Monica, plus the attack on Maria and not forgetting Reggie's dog so under those circumstances he wanted them dead.

Damon protested it was all Samuel's idea and they were simply working for him. They promised Mickey they would give him money and return to the Caribbean if he let them go.

The atmosphere changed to one of complete hostility when Mickey smugly told them they didn't need their money because Maurice had left them plenty. Instantly Damon called him a thieving pig and stated the money should have been his.

Mickey ignored him and asked Reggie to untie Ric who was still dazed from the blow at the car park. When Mickey ordered him to kneel down in front of him, it was obvious that he was going to execute him. Ric began screaming and begging for his life. Coldly, Mickey aimed the gun at his head and said "This one is for Monica you fucking pig!" Then he calmly pulled the trigger.

The other Jamaican, Jonah begged and pleaded with him not to kill him, but his executioner was oblivious to his cries. When Reggie untied him, he tried to run. Reggie hit him, knocking him to the ground then dragging him by his dreadlocks threw him down in front of Mickey.

Begging for his life, he was screaming and begging, until Mickey arrogantly ordered him to shut the fuck up as this would be his last chance to make peace with God and die with some honour.

He was still begging for his life as Mickey said, "This one's for Maria," then without flinching, took aim and shot him.

Damon was unlike the others. He belligerently told him he would not beg and he didn't believe in God.

Jimmy quipped that was probably just as well because where he was going it would be the other fella waiting to see him. Damon knew he was referring to Satan as he knelt silently in front of Mickey and waited for him to pull the trigger. Almost impatiently, he told Mickey to hurry up and get it over with.

"Are you that eager to die Damon?" said Jimmy "don't you want to know what happened to your friends? Well I'll tell you. I cut the cock off one of them; he squealed and bled like a pig! We sent his cock to Samuels, a little gift to let him know who he's dealing with, but I expect you already know that? Oh and something else you might be interested in knowing, Reggie's dogs finished off the other one they ripped his throat out."

It was obvious from the Jamaican's expression that he didn't know about the cock Samuels had been sent. Everyone knew it was typical of Samuels, he hadn't told them in case they changed their minds about working for him. It had also explained why none of Monica's colleagues had mentioned it when they visited her. Samuels had obviously kept his little delivery quiet.

Very aggressively, Damon assured them they wouldn't get away with this and they were all dead men.

He didn't reply when Mickey said smugly, "I take it you're referring to the drugs Samuels planted at the club? Well for the record Damon, the money we got for the drugs is going to be a wedding gift for Jimmy from you and Samuels."

The Jamaican had heard enough and snarled at him to get on with it. Mickey didn't need coaxing and aimed the gun at his head.

"This one is for me, because I don't fucking like you!" Without any hesitation, he pulled the trigger.

Reggie and Terry told them that they would get rid of the bodies. Shane offered to help them as he'd travelled in the van so would need a ride home.

Mickey nodded and said he'd drop Jimmy off then come back for him.

The two friends left. As they drove home they discussed Samuels and what he might do when he realised the Jamaicans were dead. Jimmy said he was too tired to even think about it so could they discuss it the following day. Mickey nodded. A few minutes later he dropped him off and headed back to the docks to collect Shane.

Jimmy entered the apartment. Shaun was sitting watching the door. After apologising to him for being late and telling him things with the Jamaicans couldn't have gone any smoother, Jimmy grinned and said that the Jamaicans won't be giving them any more trouble. Then he asked how things had gone with Maria.

Shaun nodded and explained how he'd talked her into going to bed. She had been worried because Jimmy was so late, she'd expected him back hours ago and she'd only agreed to rest because he'd reassured her that Jimmy would be fine.

Jimmy thanked him and said once they got rid of Samuels, he wouldn't need to watch over her. Without hesitation Shaun said he would always watch over her as it was a pleasure.

Jimmy knew he meant it and he felt quite honoured that he felt that way.

After Shaun left, Jimmy went straight to bed as the time was almost seven that morning. Maria stirred as he got in beside her and sleepily asked if he was ok.

"I am now I'm with you babe," he replied as she placed her hand on his shoulder and gently ran it down his arm onto his thigh. She kissed him tenderly on the lips as she put her leg over his body. It was clear by her actions that she wanted him. Despite his tiredness, he could feel himself becoming aroused. When he told her he was knackered but he wanted her, she told him to Sshh as she gently moved down his body.

Despite his tiredness, he laid there anticipating what she was about to do. Moments later he groaned with pleasure as she took him in her mouth, running her tongue over him to increase his pleasure. He knew he wouldn't be able to contain himself for many minutes, she knew exactly how he liked it. Within thirty minutes of him joining her in the bed, they were both fast asleep.

Neither one of them stirred until after ten that morning, he only woke then because he needed to use the toilet. Maria was still fast asleep. When he returned to the bed a few minutes later, she was lying on her back with her breasts exposed from where he had moved the duvet.

Gently he began fondling her, slowly moving over her to enable him to suck her nipple. Rousing from her slumber, she slowly put her arms around him and they began kissing. He knew from her responses she wanted him. Within minutes he was making love to her. Whatever she had thought since the attack at the restaurant, he was certain it had now passed.

Taking a shower together; they decided to have a light breakfast as it was almost lunch time. Whilst they ate, he told her what had happened with the Jamaicans. She asked what he intended to do about Samuels.

"I'll be discussing that very issue later with Mickey; we think we have enough evidence to put him away, but we're leaving nothing to chance. We'll need to speak to Max; if it does go to court we need to know she'll be prepared to give evidence. Obviously there would be her safety to consider. Samuels is a tricky bastard, he could have her arrested on some jumped up charge if he wanted to and especially if he thought she could incriminate him. Nothing is beyond him and kidnapping her son would guarantee her silence, so she'll need protection."

Before Maria could reply his phone rang. It was Andy Baxter calling to let Jimmy know that one of his boys could deliver the Mercedes to him that morning. Money wasn't an issue they could sort that out at a later date. Jimmy was only too happy to get a motor that day; he'd missed having his own transport.

When the call from Andy finished, he told Maria they would be getting a car later that day, but if she didn't like it he would simply trade it back in.

Maria giggled as she told him not to be daft; it was if he liked it as she didn't even drive. Instantly he offered to teach her. The look on her face told him yes long before she said it.

There was a knock on the door, then the lock turned and Mickey called out.

Jimmy questioned why he hadn't just come straight in. They all laughed when he said he'd heard voices and didn't want to walk in on them if they were up to anything. Maria was quick to explain they were talking about her learning to drive.

"Although she has been known to demand sex from me when I'm in the lounge," laughed Jimmy "so it was probably wise that you knocked Mick!"

"Ignore him Mickey," she said slapping Jimmy playfully.

Mickey had only been there ten minutes when the intercom buzzed; it was one of the men from Baxter's Autos. Jimmy told him they'd be right down.

A few minutes later, the driver asked if Jimmy wanted to test drive it. Jimmy nodded as the driver handed him the keys. Taking Maria with him, they left Mickey talking to the driver. Jimmy was impressed with the way it drove. It was a smart looking car and he could tell she liked it. Ten minutes later as they pulled up back at the apartment, Mickey opened the car door for her. Jimmy smiled at the driver and said the car was fine and he would square up with Andy the following day.

Handing him the spare keys the driver said it was a lovely car. One he wished he could afford. When he explained he had to call someone from the garage to come and pick him up, Jimmy threw the keys at Mickey and with a grin said he knew he'd be dying to drive it so he could run the driver back.

Mickey grinned and nodded.

Twenty minutes later, he returned telling them he thought the car was great. Maria made them all a drink as the two friends chatted. Jimmy asked him what the plan was regarding Samuels. Mickey said the first thing he needed to do was to ask Monica who the best person was to pass a copy of the tape to. Obviously she would have been his first choice, were she not incapacitated. He would sort it out when he visited her later that day. When Maria asked if they could go with him, Mickey was happy to say yes and he knew Monica would love it too. They continued talking about Samuels until they left for the hospital.

At the hospital, Mickey explained to Monica that they needed a reliable person to pass the information to about Samuels.

"My friend George Davage would be my first choice," said Monica "he's a good detective and another bonus is he hates Samuels. Many times he's told me he thinks Samuels is dirty, but thinking it and proving it are two different things."

When Mickey asked if she could set up a meeting with George at the hospital, she grinned and stated he'd already sent word with her friend Kathy that he would visit her the following afternoon around three.

Mickey would ensure he was there at that time.

The two ladies talked about the wedding dress while the men went for coffee. Maria explained to her that the dress she had liked was on order. Both of them were so excited at the prospect of getting married.

The three friends left the hospital at eight. They discussed whether Jimmy could go to the club that evening and they both thought it would be safe for Maria to join them. When Mickey suggested they should eat at Satins restaurant before going on to the club, Maria asked if she could go home and change first.

Jimmy nodded and said they'd eat then return to the apartment for her to change. When Maria asked if they thought she looked ok to eat out, Mickey was quick to reply she would look stunning if she was wearing a bin liner.

"Perhaps I should keep an eye on you Mickey," joked Jimmy "when Maria's out with us."

"As beautiful as she is I'd never go there, I'd like to keep my wedding tackle if it's all the same to you, and I've seen what you can do with a sharp knife Jimmy!"

They all laughed.

After they had eaten they went back to the apartment so she could change into something more appropriate for the club. The two friends talked while she dressed.

Mickey was happy to say it looked as though Maria was over the incident with the Jamaicans. He smiled when Jimmy said she definitely was because she told him she wouldn't want to live without him. Mickey said he never doubted it as she was nuts about him. Then Jimmy made a statement that worried him.

"Just as well she's nuts about me Mick, because I would rather see her dead than with another man. I gave her the chance to walk away, she didn't and I told her then I'll never give her another one."

"You need to control your temper Jimmy then hopefully she'll never want to leave. Threatening her isn't the way to go about it."

"I wasn't threatening her, I meant it," he replied with a serious look on his face.

Mickey was worried with what his friend had said but before he could say any more, Jimmy called out to her to hurry up as they needed to go. No sooner had he spoken when she emerged from the bedroom.

Both men stared at her; she looked stunning. Wearing a tight fitting, low cut red dress which showed her figure off perfectly, especially with the red stiletto shoes.

"You look lovely babe," said Mickey "good job we're not going to Sweet Cheeks, the dancers couldn't compete with you tonight!"

Blushing she smiled as she thanked him. Standing there she waited for Jimmy to say something, but he didn't. When she asked him what he thought, he said he hadn't seen her in that outfit before. Realising he was nit picking; she explained that she'd bought it weeks before when she was shopping with Monica. She asked him again what he thought.

"Yeah it's ok, you look good," he replied sounding less than convincing and from his tone she could tell all was not well and the last thing she wanted was to go out with him in strange mood. Instantly she offered to go and change into something different if he wanted her to.

"You can wear it this time," he said arrogantly "but I've got other preferences!"

Mickey looked at her and shook his head, which was his way of telling her not to push the issue. Even though she knew why he did it, she felt hurt.

"Jimmy," she said "do you want me to change it?"

"No leave it!" he snapped "I said you look fine!"

Mickey thought he was being unjust, but said nothing; he didn't want to make it bad for her.

Looking close to tears, she didn't reply. They left for the club. Despite his jealousy, both Mickey and she were surprised at his sudden mood change. Normally he would tell her how beautiful she looked.

As they walked from the car park to the club they could see Shane chatting to a couple of girls at the door. As they approached him, Shane wolf whistled at Maria. Knowing he hadn't meant anything by it she smiled, although she did blush. Jimmy looked angry. Mickey could tell he wasn't impressed, so he quickly said something to distract him as he was convinced his friend was about to say something nasty to Shane.

Inside the club, Jimmy scanned the area for a table after asking Mickey to get the drinks. Having secured a table, Maria gently touched his hand and asked him if everything was alright. She was shocked with his reply when he snapped at her and said, "I don't want you to wear that fucking dress again!"

"I offered to change and if it looks that terrible you should have told me. Why are you being so nasty Jimmy, if you don't want me here just call me a cab and I'll go home."

Realising how he was making her feel when he saw tears welling in her eyes, he took her hand and apologised saying she looked fantastic, but he knew the reaction she would get from other men by wearing it.

"Don't be so silly, you know I'm only interested in your reaction. I won't wear it out again."

Not about to let it drop, he reminded her that Shane had wolf whistled her, but she knew as well as him that Shane hadn't meant anything by it. Everyone knew he would wolf whistle anyone with a pulse.

Despite the fact she was right, in his mind nothing had changed, he didn't want her getting attention from other men. Maria looked sad at what he'd said especially as she had only ever wanted to please him. Looking at her he realised how dreadfully he'd acted, like a jealous school boy. He remembered back to when she had told him about Nick telling her what to wear and at the time he had called him a fucking control freak, which was exactly what he was now turning into. Holding her hand he apologised before stating Mickey had been right, she looked absolutely stunning and he was just a jealous idiot.

"I wouldn't change you for anyone Jimmy; anyway I quite liked the idea of someone thinking I'm beautiful, even though I'm not."

"You'd be the only person to think that babe, because you are a very beautiful woman who I know I'm so lucky to have."

Thankfully there was no further mention of the dress and everything ran smoothly at the club, there were no incidents; so they left just before closing.

Back at their apartment Jimmy told her he'd acted like a jackass over the dress and he was really sorry, but sometimes he has no control over his temper, especially when it involved her. With a smile she told him to forget about it and it was ok to be jealous as long as no one got hurt.

An hour later they retired to bed where they continued the conversation until the early hours of the morning. It was turned five o'clock by the time they fell asleep.

Over a late breakfast, Maria asked if he would visit Father Thomas with her after lunch. Despite trying to get out of it and using Mickey as the excuse, she was quick to say Mickey was going to meet George Davage and there had been no mention of Jimmy going with him. Knowing he couldn't get out of it, he begrudgingly agreed to go.

Ten minutes later, Mickey phoned to say he would call in after he had spoken to George; he thought it would be around five. Confident that they would hear from him, she had already asked Jimmy to invite him for dinner and as usual he didn't hesitate to accept the invitation.

When they arrived at the church that afternoon, she could tell that Father Thomas was pleased to see that

Jimmy had made the effort. While she chatted to the priest, Jimmy thought about the meeting his friend was having at the hospital. His thoughts being by now Samuels must be aware that something had happened to the Jamaicans.

At the hospital Monica was introducing George to Mickey. Although the two men had run in to each other on occasion they had never really talked. Immediately they took a liking to each other and it was clear that they would get along fine. Monica decided to tell George the truth as to their meeting. From that moment on, he was very interested in what Mickey had to say. They talked about the Jamaicans, including their involvement with Samuels. Mickey explained to him that they had only gone along with them so that they could get to Samuels. So as far as the Jamaicans were concerned, he was sorting out the paper work ready for them which they could call into the club for in a couple of days.

"Could you hold fire with the tape George," said Mickey "just until we've spoken to the Jamaicans again? Only we may be able to get some more information about Samuels."

Even though he knew the Jamaicans were well and truly dead, he had to go along with things because he couldn't tell George they had murdered them. Obviously the real reason for stalling for time was to get Samuels back round the club for the drugs, although he couldn't tell him that either. When Mickey handed him the tape, George said he would hold on to it for a couple of days. Mickey really appreciated it.

They continued to talk about Samuels. It was apparent that all three of them had a dislike for the man. George stated that for a long time he'd suspected Samuels of being dirty but until now had nothing on him.

They arranged to meet again at the hospital in two days and George would say that was the day he was given the tape. When George left, Mickey kissed Monica on the cheek and said he thought George was going to be an asset to them. Monica agreed. She really liked him, he was a really decent bloke.

Monica talked about her recovery, telling him how pleased the doctor was with her and if she continued to improve at such a good rate there was a chance she could go home within a week. Mickey was thrilled and quickly added Maria would also be pleased as she was looking forward to her staying with them. They both agreed how lucky they were, they really couldn't wish for better friends. She wasn't surprised that Maria had invited him for dinner again that evening.

"Don't get too used to it darling," she giggled "once we're married you won't be getting the same culinary delights as Maria cooks!"

"Well having three restaurants I'm sure I can get a decent meal!"

"Cheeky bastard," she said pinching him "I'll remember that!"

Mickey left the hospital fifteen minutes later after telling her he loved her and he'd see her later.

Arriving outside Jimmy's apartment twenty minutes later, he knocked on the door. Whatever Maria was cooking smelled delicious, he could smell it outside the door. When she opened the door, he instantly said hello and that Monica may be home within a week. Clearly delighted she hugged him, it was wonderful news.

When he asked where Jimmy was, he noticed she moved closer and in a quieter voice said he was in the bathroom and while he was out of earshot did Mickey know what the surprise was he had for her. Trying not to grin, he just shook his head and said he didn't have a clue.

They hadn't heard Jimmy enter the room until he asked Mickey what they were talking about. Without hesitation and laughing, he told him what she'd asked. Grinning Jimmy said she was worse than a kid.

Swiping Jimmy across the bum with a tea towel, she poked her tongue out at him. Playfully he grabbed her and said she'd have to wait, she'd find out soon enough, although he might consider giving it to her early, but it would depend on how nice she was to him.

"Oh I can be very nice," she giggled "although I don't think I should show you in front of Mickey!"

"It would take an awful lot to embarrass him babe."

"Oh I think we could!"

"If you two love birds want me to leave for half an hour," joked Mickey "I wouldn't mind."

"Half an hour," laughed Jimmy "with her you'd need to be gone at least three!"

"Well you never complain," said Maria blushing.

"I wouldn't imagine any man would say no to having three hours with you babe," said Mickey.

Despite it having been said in fun, Jimmy went quiet; his friend had obviously hit a nerve where his jealousy was concerned. Mickey was just about to redeem himself, when his phone rang. It was Shane calling from the club to tell him that something had just happened with Samuels and he wanted to know if they were coming down to the club. Feeling intrigued Mickey asked if everything was ok. Shane sounded well chuffed, everything was better than fine because Samuels been back for the drugs and they had him bang to rights on tape.

Sounding happy, Mickey said they'd see him at the club about nine. Just as he put the phone down, Maria served dinner. Sitting at the table, he repeated what Shane had said about Samuels. Knowing that going to the club was important, he phoned Monica and asked if he could leave visiting her. She was fine about it and said she'd see him tomorrow. Maria asked if she had to go to the club with them. After discussing it, both men thought it was probably safe for her to stay home now, providing she was careful. Just because the Jamaicans were no longer a threat, Samuels could be. She promised not to answer the intercom and if she changed her mind about the club, she would call Shaun to take her.

Mickey complimented her on the meal again as they were leaving.

Arriving at the club just before nine they could see Shane standing at the door. As they approached he grinned and said he couldn't wait for them to see the tape. They headed straight for the office.

Before watching the tape, Shane said Samuels had called at Max's for his money; while he was there she'd asked where his Jamaican friends were. Mickey asked what the dodgy detective had said.

"Apparently Samuels declined from answering," said Shane "although the dirty bastard did refer to Max having sex with him again to reduce the debt."

They asked if Max was ok and happy to hear she was fine. Both men thought Shane would have given up on her, despite knowing he liked a challenge. They were both surprised when he admitted he really liked Max and if he was thinking about having a regular girl, she would probably be the one.

"You're turning soft Shane!" laughed Mickey "still at your age maybe you should think about settling down?"

"Fuck off," laughed Shane "I'm not thinking of settling down, maybe in the future, but not now!"

"Here Mick," said Jimmy "I reckon Max had got to him, just goes to prove even the London stud isn't immune to the love bug! It gets us all in the end."

Shane laughed and stated they should watch the tape.

The tape showed Samuels entering the office after he'd asked Shane if he could use the phone in private. The moment Samuels closed the office door, he went straight over to the filing cabinet. The look on his face was priceless when he pulled it out and realised the drugs were gone.

Mickey asked what Samuels had said when he came out.

"Well he did look a bit pale and he asked if any Jamaicans had been in. I told him that you'd gone over buying the club with them. Then he asked if they'd been left alone in the office at any point. I said I didn't know then he asked if you two would be in today. I said probably; but not likely before ten."

"Well done Shane, Samuels probably thinks the Jamaicans took his drugs, because they knew that once the club was for sale, Samuels would call off the raid. Might be an idea to get Lenny round to doctor the tape so from the time Samuels pulled out the filing cabinet the tape lost visual contact. Then when I give the tape to George, there won't be any way to prove that the drugs had gone before Samuels went back into the office."

"I fucking love it when a plan comes together," said Jimmy "this calls for a celebration!"

They had only been back inside the club for ten minutes, when who should walk in, Samuels. Accepting Mickey's offer of a drink, he sat down. Unexpectedly, he asked if they'd seen anything of the Jamaicans. Mickey nodded and said they'd been in to discuss buying the club. They thought the deal would happen so they were just waiting for them to get back to them.

Looking concerned, Samuels asked if anyone had found something that belonged to him, only he seemed to have misplaced his note book. He thought he may have left it in the office when he used the phone before. Shane shook his head and said he wasn't aware that anyone had found it. Samuels asked how many people use the office. Jimmy said apart from them, hardly anyone. It was then Samuels asked if the Jamaicans discussed their business from the office. Trying not to grin, Jimmy said of course. They couldn't do business out in the club. Samuels asked if the Jamaicans had been left alone in the office. They watched him squirm when Jimmy said "No".

"Hang on Jim," said Mickey playing along "there were those few minutes when we went to see what the disturbance was outside; we left them in the office while we checked it out remember, but surely detective, you don't think for one minute that they would have taken your notebook, assuming that was where you left it?"

Now looking very agitated, Samuels asked what the disturbance had been and how long the Jamaicans had been left. Mickey made light of it stating it had just been a couple of yobs shouting their mouths off over some old tart and they had only been gone five minutes, but he didn't remember seeing any note book and doubted the Jamaicans would have been interested in it. Then he questioned Samuels that if he had thought he'd left his book there why had he left it so long to inquire about it. Samuels reply was he hadn't realised until that day. Jimmy offered him another drink, but he declined stating he had work to do. Once he'd left the club, they all joked about the crap story of the missing book; they could not contain their laughter, especially Shane.

"Fuck me," said Mickey "that couldn't have worked out better if we'd planned it."

It was obvious to everyone that the detective thought the Jamaicans had taken the drugs.

It was almost three o'clock that morning by the time Jimmy got home. Maria was fast asleep. Pouring himself a drink he went back over in his mind the events of the day. If everything ran smoothly, he really believed that Mickey could put Samuels away with the evidence they had, although they would still have to be careful. There were still some loose ends to tie up. Then he reflected on his jealousy regarding Maria, but try as he might, he couldn't bear the thought of other men getting close to her. Maybe it was because she was not the innocent young girl of two years ago. During her time there she had grown into an independent young woman, although in truth she never made him feel that she would ever want anyone else. Sitting there, he admitted to himself he had deep rooted insecurities about their relationship. When she first arrived he liked it that she relied on him for everything, even down to the fact that she did whatever he asked. He never gave her orders like Nick had and despite wanting to take her out and show her off, he now felt quite resentful that she had friends, be it only one or two. The more independent she became, the more insecure he felt. Truth was he preferred it when she just stayed home looking after his every need; but knowing she had never given him cause for not trusting her, he tried to convince himself that once they were married he would feel differently.

Throughout his life he had never felt jealousy toward anyone, even as a young boy when he had nothing and Mickey seemed to have so much, he had never resented him. It was different with Maria; she had cast a spell on him, to live without her would be impossible. She was not like anyone he had ever met before; she had the assets that drive men crazy. Yet she never flirted, rarely went out, except for the odd lunch with Monica and Simone. Without ever complaining, she willingly did everything for him, cooking, cleaning and sexually she was everything he could ever wish for and more, so why did he feel this way. Then he remembered something his mother used to say, 'when something seems too good to be true Jimmy; it usually is.' In his heart he knew this was not true of Maria, yet it somehow made his negative feelings easier to accept. Finally he went to bed.

Standing in the half light of the bedroom, he watched her as she stirred and wondered how someone so beautiful and loving could love him the way she did. Carefully he climbed into the bed next to her. Not wishing to wake her; he placed his arm around her and gently kissed her shoulder. Thinking she was still asleep, he whispered he loved her.

In a quiet sleepy voice she said she loved him too. They snuggled down under the duvet and fell asleep.

It was almost eleven the next morning when he finally got up, appearing in the kitchen as she cooked his breakfast. Mickey had phoned while he was asleep to say he would see him at Dixie's around two, he'd mentioned something to her about a meeting with the lads.

Jimmy asked her to go with him, it was just for the lads to go over their accounts of events concerning Samuels and the Jamaicans; just to make sure everyone said the same. Maria had heard all she wanted to about the dodgy detective so she'd decline if he didn't mind, although she would be grateful if he could drop her at the hospital on his way as she'd like to spend a couple of hours with Monica. She could call a cab to bring her home as Shaun would be at the club. Jimmy nodded.

Time flew by, with her doing the housework while he made some calls. Later that day he dropped her at the hospital. Five minutes later, she entered Monica's room. Her friend was pleased to see her, especially as it was rare that they got to see each other without their men. Maria expressed to her that she couldn't wait for her to leave the hospital. Once she was home they could discuss the wedding in more detail. Maria even suggested them having a couple of dress rehearsals while Jimmy was out. Monica liked that idea, but she'd been wondering if Maria would mind giving her some cookery lessons while she stayed with them, she wanted to surprise Mickey. With a grin Maria said she'd be only too happy to teach her.

They both giggled.

They were really enjoying their time together until Samuels turned up. Looking less than thrilled to see him, Monica asked why he was there. Sarcastically he replied he didn't think he needed a reason to visit a friend. Monica didn't reply she simply smirked. Several times during his visit, he leered at Maria making her feel uncomfortable. She didn't like the way he looked at her, like a dirty old man making her feel uneasy in his company. Eyeing her up and down he asked where Jimmy was. Keeping the conversation short she said out with Mickey somewhere. It was nice for her to have time alone with Monica so they could discuss the wedding arrangements.

"Ah yes the wedding, I can't help but say I'm surprised with your choice of men, especially you Maria. I wouldn't have expected a girl like you to be involved with a man like Jimmy Dixon."

"Jimmy's the best thing that ever happened to me detective; I can't wait to marry him."

"I hear he won you at a poker game," he said rudely "a royal flush wasn't it?"

Maria was dumbstruck and looked as though she would burst into tears any second.

Monica quickly jumped to her friend's defence.

"Yes wasn't that a wonderful way to get the one he loved. Did you know Jimmy had been prepared to lose his club for her, because he loved her so much? I only wish it had been the same for Mickey and me. I had to get shot and almost die before he proposed and for what it's worth I think your conduct was shameful Detective Samuels even mentioning it!"

Samuels knew from experience she would have an answer for anything he said, but being the arsehole he was he just couldn't resist another knock at Maria.

"I'm just amazed as to what type of business associates Jimmy deals with Maria, you know, the type who would bet their ladies on a hand of cards. I must ask you, aren't you afraid that when he's had enough of you he'll simply gamble you off in a poker game? Incidentally the man he won you from was Nick Orphanides wasn't it, quite a criminal if memory serves me right?"

Too upset to answer, Maria just shrugged her shoulders

"That's it," shouted Monica "I've heard enough, you're well out of order speaking to her that way! Her private life has got nothing to do with you, it sounds like you're jealous of Jimmy. I can understand that, Maria's beautiful and it's obvious to everyone except you just how much in love they are which considering you're a detective is rather ironic, wouldn't you agree?"

Without replying Samuels said he had to leave due to work commitments.

Maria simply nodded as he said goodbye. Monica didn't actually say anything; she just lifted her hand as a gesture to acknowledge his departure.

After he'd left, Maria tearfully said she hated him. Monica felt the same, but referred to him as a prick and said Maria shouldn't pay any attention to him, he was just a bitter twisted man and rumour had it the only way he could get sex was by paying for it.

Maria tried to laugh, but what he'd said had upset her.

"Maybe he was right Monica," said Maria close to tears "Jimmy did win me and perhaps one day he will do the same when he's tired of me?"

Reassuringly she said that Mickey told her years ago that Jimmy wanted her. In fact, Mickey was convinced that was why he'd never settled down, he was waiting for her. Maria hoped she was right because she loved him so much.

"You know I'm right, now put it out of your mind, everyone knows that Samuels is a wanker, so why are you allowing him to bother you?"

Maria knew in her heart she was right, no one could pretend to love someone the way Jimmy loved her. They were like two people who shared the same heart; she believed their love was real and forever.

"You're right Monica, Samuels is a wanker, a big one!"

They laughed together.

Maria said she had to go as she needed to prepare something for dinner, especially as they'd invited Mickey. She wanted to make sure everything was ready for when they got back. She would take a cab; there were usually a couple in the hospital car park. Monica thanked her and said she'd watch her from the window.

Maria kissed her on the cheek and left.

Monica watched from her room as she crossed the hospital car park to where the taxis parked, she could see there wasn't a taxi available; but fortunately there was a bench for people to wait on. Maria looked up at the huge building to try and find her friend's window; had it not have been for Monica waving she would never have found the right one.

A nurse entered Monica's room with her afternoon drugs, after giving them to her they chatted briefly before she left. Monica resumed her gaze out of the window to watch her friend. Spotting her, she was horrified to see Samuels sitting next to her on the bench and although they were quite a distance away, she could tell from their body language that Samuels was harassing her friend. She immediately called Mickey.

The moment he answered the call she told him Samuels was giving Maria a hard time in the hospital car park. Mickey said they'd be there within fifteen minutes.

Monica kept watching from the window, Samuels was obviously bothering Maria. Monica watched as he tried to put his arm around her, firstly as if to comfort her and then tugging at her in an effort to get her to go with him. Helplessly she watched as he tried to lead her friend away by the arm. Maria was shaking her head and saying something; it was obvious she was refusing whatever his offer was.

Ten minutes had passed; it looked to Monica as though they were rowing, because Maria kept shaking her head and backing away from him. Then Samuels stood up and said something to her as he began to walk away. Monica watched as her friend stayed sitting down. Maria was wiping her eyes as though she was crying. Desperate to help her friend, she had started to call Mickey's number again when a taxi pulled in. Maria was just about to get in to it when a car horn sounded behind her. It was Jimmy, who called out to her from the driver's window as Mickey got out of the car and walked towards her. He could see she had been crying and looked visibly shaken. Looking relieved, Maria asked what they were doing there. Mickey explained that Monica had called them and said Samuels was giving her a hard time. The moment he asked if she was ok, she tried to answer him but burst into tears. Putting his arm around her they started to walk back towards the car.

Leaving the engine running, Jimmy got out of the car and walked over to her. Throwing her arms around him she sobbed. Mickey said he'd drive so they could sit together in the back.

Sitting with his arm around her Jimmy tried asking her what Samuels had said, but she was so upset she couldn't answer.

Fifteen minutes later, Mickey parked the car at the apartment. Then he called Shane to tell him that they wouldn't be back at the club but he would probably call in later.

Once in the apartment, he put the kettle on while Jimmy sat on the sofa with her. Slowly she calmed down. Mickey brought her in a cup of tea.

"Thanks Mickey," said Maria "I'm sorry for acting so pathetic, but when Samuels started pressuring me I tried to keep it together, but as soon as I saw Jimmy I went to pieces."

"Yeah," laughed Mickey "Jimmy often has that effect on women!"

They all laughed.

They asked her what Slimy Samuels said to her.

Firstly she went over how sarcastic he'd been at the hospital; quickly adding that Monica was more than a match for him.

"That's my girl," said Mickey with a grin.

She explained how she was waiting for a taxi; she thought he'd gone because he'd left long before her. He'd obviously stayed in the car park and spotting her, he asked if she wanted a lift. Tearfully she said she wished now she'd simply accepted his offer but he gave her the creeps, especially the way he looked at her.

Jimmy said she'd done the right thing not taking a lift, and asked her to continue. It was when she refused a lift he turned nasty. It was Mickey who instantly took on an aggressive look and asked if Samuels had physically hurt her.

"No, but he insinuated I thought I was too good to travel with him and that it would be different if he was a low life criminal. I told him he was wrong to say that and if he was referring to Jimmy he was the most decent man I had ever met. Samuels laughed and said I had a funny idea of what decent meant. When I asked him to leave me alone he got angry and said if I ever needed another pimp I could phone him because I was nothing but a jumped up little whore, who thought I was too good for him."

"Well he got the fucking last bit right," snapped Jimmy aggressively as he thumped the arm of the sofa. "You most definitely are too fucking good for that slimy lump of dog shit!"

Mickey asked her to go on in the hope of defusing Jimmy's temper.

Waiting until Jimmy calmed down, it was several seconds before she continued. "Samuels said he knew you two were dirty and that it would only be a matter of time before he could prove it. He said that Mickey made him sick using the law to cover his tracks and how he thought he was so clever because he had a girlfriend in the force."

"That's fucking rich coming from him," said Mickey, "go on babe."

"It got worse after that. He said if I was nice to him he would look after me when you two were locked up, which in his opinion would only be a matter of time because he knew you two had done something to the Jamaicans. I had acted dumb and made out I didn't know what he was talking about. It was after that he became aggressive and started shouting at me, saying I knew exactly what he meant. Then he tried pulling me off the seat and said I was taking a ride with him whether I wanted to or not! He ranted and said he would find out what had happened to his friends, then he would have you both and that a good looking woman like me would not wait for someone like Jimmy. I told him I would never want another man and I'd wait forever if necessary. What I'd said about waiting for Jimmy seemed to enrage him even more; he just got nastier and nastier after that! When I told him I would report him, he laughed and said go ahead, see how far you get."

"I'll make Samuels pay for what he did!"

"Please don't do anything Jimmy, let Mickey deal with it so Samuels gets exactly what he deserves. Please Jimmy don't do or say anything to him that might jeopardise our plan."

"She's right," said Mickey "Samuels is a tricky bastard and we're only one day away from George Davage having enough evidence to arrest him."

Jimmy nodded and asked if she would rather he sent out for dinner, but she shook her head and said she wanted to cook, she was going to try out a new recipe on them. With a grin Mickey said that was a good enough reason to stay in.

While she worked in the kitchen the two men talked about Samuels until Mickey's phone rang. It was Lenny letting them know he'd done the tape and he'd drop it round to the club in the morning.

Jimmy was happy hearing the tape was ready, he just hoped Samuels kept out of his way because he couldn't guarantee he'd be able to hold his temper.

Maria called from the kitchen to say dinner was ready.

By the time they finished, Mickey felt like he would burst as he held his stomach and said compliments to the chef.

Later that evening when Mickey said he'd have to leave, Jimmy offered to drive him as he'd left his car at the club when they went to the hospital.

"I don't think so," said Maria "you two have drunk two bottles of wine!"

Mickey agreed and after thanking him said he'd call a cab.

Both men were thinking their ladies would have a blue fit if they knew how much they drank when they went to the club and then drove home.

Maria cleared the dishes while the men talked. Since Jimmy had bought the new dish washer, it only took minutes to clear the dishes.

Mickey had only just finished drinking his coffee when the cab driver rang the intercom. Standing up he kissed her on the cheek and thanked her again for another wonderful meal.

Two minutes later he left.

Sitting with Jimmy, she said she was sorry about the incident with Samuels. She hoped Jimmy was right when he said if everything went to plan she wouldn't have to worry about him. Then to his amazement, she asked if he'd ever thought she was a whore. Instantly he snapped at her stating he hadn't and he didn't appreciate her asking him. When she went quiet and just stared at him, he realised how abrupt he must have sounded and there must have been a reason why she had asked. Looking humble he apologised, but wanted to know why she'd asked.

Tears began rolling down her cheeks as she said everyone seemed to think that because he won her in a poker game, she must be a whore. Jimmy put his arm around her and said she was by far the most decent girl he'd ever met and it was just small minded idiots who would think otherwise.

She would never want their children to know about the poker game, but knowing there was nothing he could do or say that could change the past she quickly added he always made her feel special. To him she was special and he didn't give a shit what other people thought, he loved her more than anything in the world.

They kissed passionately before she suggested turning in for the night.

With her lying in his arms he said this was how he wanted it to be forever. No matter what happened she was never to doubt his love for her and to prove it he'd decided to give her the surprise the following day. Excitedly she asked what it was, but to her annoyance, he said she'd find out soon enough.

KAREN CLOW

CHAPTER 29

Maria was up at the crack of dawn cooking breakfast when Jimmy dragged himself out of the bed after the aroma of bacon cooking had woken him. Saying good morning, he asked why she was up so early and laughed when she said she was waiting for her surprise so could she have it then. Her curiosity was in overdrive when he explained they'd have to drive to get it, but first he needed to call Mickey to find out what time they were picking the tape up for George. It was obvious he had woken Mickey from the length of time his phone rang until finally he answered. After Jimmy explained he was taking Maria to see the surprise, Mickey said there was no need for Jimmy to pick the tape up, he would do it. Jimmy thanked him, but before he could end the call, Mickey asked if he could take them both out for dinner that evening. It was his way of saying thanks for the wonderful meals Maria cooked him. It would also give him a chance to talk about what George said about Samuels. Accepting his offer Jimmy ended the call.

Less than an hour later they were leaving the apartment. Throughout the drive, she kept asking him where they were going, but typically of him, he wouldn't tell her. They had driven for about fifteen minutes when he pulled into the driveway of a detached Tudor style house. Instantly she asked who lived there, but he didn't reply. He just grinned as he asked her to go with him; the people who owned the house were really nice so they wouldn't mind.

Surprised that he had a key to the door, she walked in behind him. As they entered the hallway she stated what a beautiful house it was. Shock was her reaction when he took her hand and said "I'm glad you think so, because it's ours. It's my wedding gift to you."

Standing there with her mouth open; tears began to roll down her cheeks.

"Stop crying babe and tell me what you think," said Jimmy "do you really like it?"

Wiping her eyes she exclaimed she loved it.

"Suppose we should look round then, after all we'll be living here soon. So if you don't like anything now would be the time to say so. My friend Justin completely refurbished it for us, he even hired an interior designer to select the furniture, but if you don't like it we can change it. There are wood floors throughout the ground floor, but if you want carpet I'll sort it out."

Still in shock, she was trembling with excitement as she squeezed his hand. First room she wanted to see was the kitchen. It was a cook's dream, everything you could ever want was there; right down to the last detail, there was even a stand with a cookery book on it. Maria was speechless; she simply flung her arms around him and said it was wonderful!

Next room was the dining room, furnished to a very high standard with matching oak furniture. The lounge, equally as stunning as the previous two rooms. Jimmy watched her; he could see by the look on her face that she loved everything.

"I thought the apartment was fabulous," said Maria "but this is beyond all my expectations! I would be happy to live here for the rest of my life."

"Maybe we will babe."

Continuing the tour of the ground floor, there was the cloakroom and a study. Unable to contain her excitement, on leaving the study she ran up the stairs, calling to him to hurry up because she couldn't wait to see it. Following her, he walked quickly up the stairs.

Looking down on him from the top of the stairs, she commented on how bright and airy the whole house was. A window half way up the stairs was letting in the sunlight. The house was huge compared to the apartment.

Showing her the master bedroom first, he asked what she thought of the fitted mirrored wardrobes. She knew why he asked, it was in reference to him being able to watch them having sex. With a sexy grin she said they were great. Her feet seemed to melt into the plush cream carpet. Looking round the room she pointed at a door and asked where it led. Walking to it, Jimmy opened it and she admired the en-suite. He showed her two further bedrooms followed by a stunning family bathroom complete with Jacuzzi.

When she said they'd only seen three bedrooms, he grinned that was because he'd saved the best till last.

As he opened the door, she was momentarily overwhelmed; it was a large bedroom that had been furnished as a nursery.

"Oh it's just lovely Jimmy. I've only seen rooms like this in magazines."

It was furnished with white fitted wardrobes and matching chests of drawers, a gorgeous cot with a lace canopy and musical mobile was placed next to a rocking horse along with several other large cuddly toys, including a four feet tall Winnie the Pooh.

"It's fabulous," she said throwing her arms around him "but we haven't got any kids yet!"

"That's why I deliberately left the nursery 'til last, in the hope you might want to get some practise in for making a baby to go in it!"

"I'd love to, not that you need any practice!"

They made their way back to the master bedroom; it was only a matter of minutes before they were making love.

Lying together afterwards, he said they only had ten more rooms to christen. Giggling she replied "Not all of them today though, hey babe!"

Still giggling, she told him to dream on when he said they could probably manage three or four!

When they finally got up it was around three that afternoon, Jimmy suggested stopping at a café on the way home for a coffee. Maria nodded and asked what he intended to do with the apartment. He wasn't sure whether they'd sell it or rent it out. As much as she loved it, she couldn't wait to move into the house. He suggested moving a few things into the house over the next couple of weeks and maybe even sleep over a couple of nights. Providing Mickey was available to stay with Monica, she loved the idea.

They spent the rest of the afternoon just talking about the house and the wedding. Having seen the house she couldn't wait to get married and start a family. Until then he had no idea she had already picked the babies name. For a boy it would be James Michael Shaun Dixon, or Jimmy junior for short! If they had a girl it would be Melanie Joanne after her friend from the orphanage and his mum Joan. With a grin he asked if he had a say in it. In a very matter of fact tone she said no, he would have done his bit nine months earlier, which reminded her that her contraceptive injection was due in two weeks' time.

Jimmy had a tiny smirk on his face as he told her not to bother, especially if they were going to have lots of babies.

"You'll make a wonderful dad Jimmy."

In that instant he felt an over whelming sense of pride; he had often thought about fatherhood, now it would be a reality.

When Mickey arrived at the apartment later that day, she couldn't resist telling him all about it, but not once did he let on that he already knew about the house. He listened intently, even acting surprised when she said about certain features.

Finally she went to dress for dinner and he was able to tell Jimmy that he'd passed the tape on to George Davage. Jimmy asked how it had gone with George.

"Everything went well; George implied he hoped to be able to arrest Samuels once the tape has been verified. Shame my friend Jeff Black is away on holiday in America, or he would have dealt with Samuels. Despite all the evidence it will take several weeks, if not months, before it goes to court and no doubt Samuels will try everything he can to have the case thrown out; he'll probably hire the best barrister London has to offer. Under normal circumstance, I could imagine him getting away with some of it, maybe even getting a paltry sentence, which in theory could mean he won't serve any actual prison time. As a solicitor I know only too well that the laws in Britain are as corrupt as some of the criminals. Basically if you can afford the best, you can save yourself prison time. You only have to look at child sex offenders to realise that. In a nut shell, you only have to be someone important with money to get away with it. However, that's where our old friend Quinton will prove useful, especially if he wants to keep himself out of prison, which I'm certain he will. There's another added bonus; internal affairs will be taking a good look into Samuels. One thing is pretty much a certainty; he'll be kicked out of the Force. The last thing the government want is a dirty cop slapped all over the papers. I'll look at the court rota to see when Quinton's available. I can probably talk to him at the courts; I just need to tell him to make certain he gets the case."

Jimmy was just about to call Maria when she appeared. Both men said she looked great.

Throughout dinner she talked about the house and the family they were going to have, although she did express to Mickey how bad she felt about Monica not being able to have children. Typically of him, he said there will always be babies that need a good home. In fact he knew several people who had even travelled to places like Romania to adopt babies and if Monica really wanted to do that he'd be happy to look into it.

With genuine happiness, she said wouldn't it be lovely if their children grew up together. With a laugh he suggested they get the wedding over with first.

They all laughed.

CHAPTER 30

With the wedding drawing closer the days seemed to fly by. Maria was thrilled to hear that Monica was being discharged from hospital that day, which meant they would have almost three weeks to go over all the final wedding arrangements. She had picked up Monica's wedding dress, so once she was home she would be able to try it on just in case it needed any last minute adjustments.

"They're here," called Maria as she watched Mickey and Monica get out of their car.

Jimmy had helped her to decorate the apartment with balloons and banners that read welcome home. There was a bottle of champagne and some tasty nibbles placed on the table, with a huge bouquet of flowers taking pride of place on the coffee table.

Maria embraced her friend as she entered the apartment. Monica's first words were it was great to finally be out of hospital and she felt fine, just a little weak.

"With Maria cooking for you," said Jimmy "you'll have your strength back in no time. Actually girls, as you've got lots of things to discuss perhaps me and Mickey could pop down to the club for a couple of hours later? Leave you girls to talk about the wedding and stuff."

Maria said it would be fine as she'd love nothing better than to sit and chat to Monica, but Mickey looked a little humble when he asked Monica if she was sure she didn't mind, after all she had only just come home.

With a smile she nodded, he'd earned a few hours out. They didn't need telling twice; as soon as they had finished dinner they kissed their ladies goodbye and left for Dixie's.

Billy was on the door, it was quiet as they had only been open an hour. Jacky Boy and Kevin were inside.

After stopping briefly to talk to Billy they entered the club. Inside, Jacky Boy said it was quiet, but it was always quiet for the first couple of hours.

They were talking as a pretty young girl came over and spoke to Jacky Boy, Jimmy recognised her as his girlfriend Lisa.

Saying hello he asked how she was and if Jacky Boy was taking care of her.

"Yes he's lovely," she replied "we're really looking forward to the wedding. We're looking for a place to live so we can move in together and then hopefully get married"

Mickey joked that she was finally going to make an honest man of him. Then he asked where they intended living. Lisa told him they weren't fussy as long as it was near to work, but property was like gold dust, especially in their price range. So they were going to rent in order to save for a bigger deposit.

Jimmy liked her; she was a decent sort, hardworking, honest and reliable.

"If you want some extra cash babe," said Jimmy "Jacky Boy could always get you a couple of night's pole dancing at Sweet Cheeks."

Jacky playfully grabbed her arse and said "Cheers Jimmy, but I'm the only one who'll be grabbing this bootie!"

Lisa blushed and told him to behave.

They had only been there two hours when to their surprise George Davage walked in; he was accompanied by a very pretty young woman, she was blonde in her early twenties. After he introduced her as his sister Rubie, he asked if he could talk to them in private. They asked Kevin to look after Rubie; adding her drinks were on the house. Kevin was only too happy to oblige because he liked the look of her and he quite fancied getting to know her.

The three men went into the office, George was off duty so he readily accepted the offer of a drink before telling them the reason why he was there. That very afternoon Samuels had been arrested and internal affairs were now looking at him. Samuels had protested his innocence until George told him about the tape he had in his possession, but even then he tried to convince George he'd been set up. Mickey asked if the police could make the charges stick. Both men were happy when George stated all the evidence pointed to Samuels being corrupt. There was also the fact the Jamaicans appeared to have returned to the Caribbean; so there was no one to collaborate his story.

In a blasé manner Mickey suggested it might have been the Jamaicans who took the drugs from the office. He couldn't help but grin when George replied, "No doubt about it!"

They'd both noticed that the off duty detective had a sort of a smug grin on his face when he'd said that. They were both thinking was he indicating to them he thought there was something dodgy about it, but letting them know he didn't give a shit?

"Things will move quickly once internal affairs have collected all the evidence;" said George "the powers that be will want the case dealt with as soon as possible. Nobody likes to hear about dirty cops, especially high ranking officers like Samuels. It makes everyone look bad. In my opinion with the evidence we have against him; they can't find him anything but guilty. As for the sentence that will depend on the judge. Oh there's one more thing, thought you might like to know Samuels has engaged the legal services of Alistair Fulton Monroe. I'm surprised he can afford him on a detective's salary."

Mickey agreed stating it would cost a small fortune to have him as he was probably one of the best barristers in London. His theory was it was Samuels's ill-gotten gains from drug dealing that would pay his bill. Out of curiosity he asked who was representing the people.

The moment George said the name Virginia Hollingsworth, Mickey grinned; she was very high profile, taking on some of the most difficult cases.

When the conversation moved to how some judges let people like Samuels off lightly, Mickey grinned at Jimmy because they knew it would be Quinton and it would be more than he dared do to let Samuels off.

Thanking George they expressed their gratitude that he'd taken the time to come over and tell them. As a gesture they invited him and his sister to enjoy the rest of the night as their guests. George nodded and after asking if they would be joining him and Rubie in the club, looked happy when they said of course they would.

George talked about Rubie; she was his half-sister from his dad's second marriage. There was a large age gap between them because his dad's second wife was considerably younger than him.

Back inside the club they chatted about Monica and the wedding, they knew she had invited George. Jimmy asked if he would be bringing Rubie along to the wedding. Unfortunately he was on duty that day, but he would try and drop in at the reception later in the evening. No one was surprised when Kevin suggested to George that if Rubie wanted to go to the wedding, he'd be happy to take her as his guest. Before he could reply Rubie thanked Kevin and said she'd love to.

It was obvious to her brother they liked each other. George had no objections to her going; after all she was old enough to decide for herself.

Jimmy suggested to Mickey about leaving and getting back to the girls. They invited George to stay, stating that Kev and the lads would look after him. Thanking them he declined as he had work in the morning. Rubie however didn't, and she was quick to say she'd like to stay if Kevin didn't mind.

Happy to spend time with her, Kevin nodded and said he'd take her home later. Aware that Kevin was a bit of a womaniser, George grinned and said "Thanks Kev, I'd appreciate that and I'm sure I don't have to remind you that I'm a copper, so I'll expect you to drive her straight home when the club shuts."

"Listen to him," giggled Rubie "anyone would think he's my dad to hear him talk!"

They all laughed as Kevin gave George his word.

Five minutes later the three men left. Mickey and Jimmy shook hands with George before they parted company outside.

Arriving back at the apartment they entered quietly. Maria was half asleep on the sofa as he asked where Monica was. Sleepily she explained Monica had felt really tired so she'd gone to bed around eleven, but she'd left a message for Mickey to say if she was asleep when they got back she would see him tomorrow.

Mickey thanked her and said he would push off home. Maria suggested he came early the following morning to eat breakfast with them.

After Mickey had left, Maria asked how things were at the club. Just after he began telling her about George, she interrupted and said maybe they should wait 'til the morning, so Monica could hear all about it. Jimmy agreed and with a sexy grin asked if she was going to take him to bed now.

"Oh I think I could be tempted," she replied running her hand up his leg.

CHAPTER 31

The days since Monica's discharge from hospital seemed to pass quickly, she had been at Maria's a week. All the girls had done was go over the wedding arrangements; the two would-be grooms had gone out at every opportunity. That day being no exception, Jimmy had taken Mickey to look at a pub that was up for sale. They had thought about buying a pub in the past, but just never seemed to get round to it. This one was different, within walking distance of Mickey's apartment; it did a good regular trade with not too much trouble. They had decided to find out for themselves what the lunch time trade was like. They knew it did a good regular evening trade, but lunch times could be the making or breaking of whether or not they bought it. They decided to drink there every day for the next week, which didn't exactly please the girls but they knew it was business.

Monica was getting about quite easily now, although it would be a couple of weeks before she could drive, so every trip into town meant a cab.

That lunch time the men left for the pub, Maria suggested arranging a dress rehearsal for the bridesmaids, just to make sure everything fitted.

They were just about to phone Ann to arrange it when the intercom buzzed, it was Father Thomas. Maria opened the front door to greet him, kissing his cheek as he entered. Apologising for just turning up, Thomas said he was in the area and thought he'd take pot luck on her being in because he wanted to tell them he'd arranged a rehearsal for all of them that coming Thursday. Monica explained that her parents wouldn't be arriving until two days before the wedding. Thomas didn't see it as a problem as someone could stand in for her dad. He asked who the best men were as originally Mickey was to be Jimmy's, but now he was a groom himself that had changed.

Maria explained Tony had stepped in to be Jimmy's and Mickey's brother-in-law Richard would be his, although he wouldn't be arriving from America until just before the wedding. Confident the wedding was well organised, Thomas left, but not before saying he would see them at three o'clock on Thursday.

They decided to leave the dress rehearsal as it was getting late and they needed to think about preparing the evening meal. Monica was excited because while staying there she had been taking cookery lessons. Maria was actually very impressed with how quickly she had picked things up; in fact that evening was to be her debut. They hadn't told the men, it was to be a surprise.

Under the watchful eye of Maria, Monica had cooked duck with orange sauce, served with a selection of fresh vegetables. Dessert was to be profiteroles with fresh cream and chocolate sauce. The two women had devised a plan to keep the men out until seven. Maria had phoned them and said that they were having a dress rehearsal of the wedding dresses, which was taking longer than anticipated, so they would have to stay out later. They knew that neither man would complain about having to stay in the pub.

Just before seven, Maria set the table while Monica added the finishing touches to the meal.

Maria, with a grin, congratulated the men for being on time as they entered the apartment and Jimmy stated that dinner smelled great.

A few minutes after telling them to go and sit down as dinner was ready the two girls brought the dishes through.

"Ah duck," said Mickey, "one of my favourites and as always it looks delicious babe."

Mickey ate the last mouthful and placing his knife and fork on the plate looked at Maria and complimented her on yet another glorious meal. The look on his face was priceless when Maria enlightened him that she hadn't cooked it, Monica had.

"Really," he asked looking shocked "only it was amazing are you sure she cooked it babe?"

"Yes she's sure you cheeky git!" said Monica "Maria's been teaching me while I've been here."

Everyone congratulated her on her success and Mickey redeemed himself by saying it had been fantastic.

With both men obviously in a good mood; Maria mentioned to them about the rehearsal at the church on Thursday. Jimmy looked less than thrilled, but said he felt they should go.

As they chatted Maria asked what they'd thought about buying the pub.

"Yeah we think it could be a good investment," said Jimmy "especially if we can get a license to have live music, which in our case wouldn't be too difficult, we've got a few council officials on our books and Mickey's not shy when it comes to bribery."

"I'll pretend I didn't hear that!" giggled Monica.

The pub was called the 'Jolly Roger' which really appealed to their sense of humour, as it was connected to pirates.

With the night drawing to a close, Monica asked if they would have any objections to Mickey staying overnight, only it was late and he'd drunk quite a lot.

Of course it was alright. Like her, Maria didn't like the idea of him driving and he could stay whenever he liked.

"Stay Mick," said Jimmy "but just because the guest room has a double bed, I don't want you getting up to any hanky panky!"

"No chance," giggled Monica "I'm saving myself for our wedding night, doctor's orders!"

"In that case I might as well fuck off home!" joked Mickey.

"Although the doctor was only referring to actual intercourse," she added with a grin.

"Maybe I should stay. Monica's right, I have been drinking!"

They all laughed.

Mickey and Monica were up first the following morning. As their friends appeared, Monica offered to cook the breakfast. Considering the gourmet meal she had cooked the previous evening; they all thought it was a great idea.

They had just finished eating when Mickey's mobile rang. It was his secretary Jan, who'd rung to tell him Virginia Hollingsworth's office had been trying to contact him in connection with the Samuels case. Thanking her, he would contact them. Mickey was just telling the others when Jimmy's home phone rang.

Maria answered it and a few seconds later handed him the phone, stating it was Virginia Hollingsworth's secretary wanting to make him an appointment to discuss the Samuels case.

The secretary spoke to Jimmy telling him she had tried to contact Mickey. He was quick to say Mickey was there with him, so she could make the appointment for both of them. The others listened as he made the arrangements before ending the call. They had an appointment at half eleven the following morning. Maria suggested taking their friends to see the house if they didn't have other plans. She was happy when Jimmy said all they'd planned to do was call into The Jolly Roger sometime during the afternoon. He suggested the girls going with them and combining the house with the pub visit. Everyone agreed.

They all got ready to see the house, within the hour they were parking in the house drive.

"Oh Maria," said Monica "it's absolutely gorgeous. If we do ever adopt, this is exactly the type of house I'd like."

"If I'd have known you'd say that I would have declined the offer to see the house," grimaced Mickey "actually there's some lovely little two up two down cottages just being built down near the railway station."

They all laughed when Monica replied, "Cheapskate!"

Excitedly Maria showed them around the house. It was clear to the others that she loved it and couldn't wait to move in.

Driving back toward the pub all the girls talked about was the house, even at the pub it was their main topic of conversation. Spotting a fruit machine at the far end of the bar Jimmy grinned at Mickey and asked if he felt lucky.

"Too right," laughed Mickey "anything to get away from weddings, houses and babies!"

Even the ladies laughed.

Once at the machine they talked about the pub. They didn't notice a group of blokes come in, two black and two white. Monica had noticed them, also that the landlord looked a bit intimidated as they went up to the bar. Watching them she saw the landlord give one of them an envelope, also a round of drinks, but no money changed hands. Curiously, Maria asked who she was looking at.

"I think something dodgy is going on between the landlord and the blokes who just came in," she replied in true detective style.

Before she could say anything else, she noticed one of them looking at her. Immediately she looked away and made it look as though she was chatting with Maria. One of the black guys looked over at them; then nudged the big white guy standing next to him. Within seconds the four of them were walking towards them. Monica discreetly told her not to look round, but the blokes from the bar were heading their way.

Without asking, the four men sat down at the girls' table.

"Can we buy you lovely ladies a drink?" said one of the white guys.

Politely Monica said no thanks because they were with someone.

"I don't see anyone," he replied cockily "are you sure you just don't think you're too good to have a drink with us?"

Maria felt uneasy, especially when one of the black guys put his arm around the back of her chair and calling her sexy asked if she was with anyone. Nervously she nodded her head.

"If I had such a lovely lady, I certainly wouldn't leave her alone in a pub. Now can I buy you a drink gorgeous?"

"No thank you, my fiancé will be back any minute."

Despite what she said he just wouldn't take no for an answer. Then things changed for the worse when he ran his finger seductively up her arm. Monica could see Maria was intimidated, so in a more forceful but polite manner, she stated they were with their partners, so could they please leave them alone.

"Leave sexy, we're only just getting to know you."

Then he placed his hand on her knee and squeezed it under the table. Instantly Monica snapped at him and ordered him to take his hands off her.

"You heard the lady;" said Mickey's voice from behind her "now take your fucking hand off her!"

Mickey looked very aggressive. Jimmy had been less polite with the black guy and aggressively shouted at him to get the fuck away from his girlfriend.

Within seconds a fight had broken out. Monica put a call straight through to her department, where her friend Jenny who answered the call said someone would be there within minutes.

Maria was petrified, she watched as Jimmy punched the guy several times in the face before one of the others held Jimmy so the guy could hit him back. Maria was screaming for them to let him go, but she was aware that Jimmy didn't seem to take much notice of the blows he was taking; it was as much as the other guy could do to hold him.

The landlord rushed over to try and stop it. By then Jimmy was free and hailing blows down on both men; much the same could be said for Mickey.

Suddenly three police officers entered the pub. Monica recognised them and complemented them on their quick arrival. They quickly dealt with the situation then afterwards one of the officers talked to Monica. She already knew procedure, but he had to say they would have to call in at the station sometime during the day to make statements. The officer couldn't help but grin when he added, judging by the state of the blokes faces, they'd picked on the wrong guys.

After they left, Mickey spoke to the landlord and apologising offered to pay for any damages. Telling Mickey it wasn't down to him, the landlord said the damage appeared to be minimal and he would take care of it. He offered them a fresh round of drinks, after getting the four trouble makers arrested, it was the least he could do. Mickey accepted, but only on the condition he joined them.

Without hesitation the landlord called over to the barman to bring them over a round of drinks.

"Larry Watson," said the landlord holding out his hand.

Jimmy shook hands with him then introduced the others before they all sat at a table.

"I'm sorry those blokes upset your ladies," said Larry.

"No harm done," said Mickey "are they regulars?"

"They're nothing but trouble, that's what they are. They started coming in round six months ago, bully boys who made it clear if I didn't want any trouble I'd have to pay them. Twenty years ago I would have sent them packing with a thick ear, but now I'm in my late sixties and to tell you the truth, I didn't want any trouble, so every week I give them fifty quid. Its peace of mind really, I know fifty isn't really a lot of money, but the word is they're doing the same to lots of pubs in the area." Monica instantly asked why he hadn't reported them to the police.

"The police," laughed Larry "I couldn't believe it earlier when they actually turned up! If every landlord in London placed a call about bully boys extorting money, they'd need a second police force just to deal with it!"

Jimmy asked him what he intended doing about it.

"Nothing, I'm retiring from the pub trade. I've been a landlord for forty years, now it's time for the quiet life. My wife Rose wants to move out of London and go down to Wales, our daughter and son-in-law have a guest house there. The pub game has been good to me, so we can buy a bungalow or cottage and still have enough to last us till I pop my clogs."

"Good for you Larry."

They chatted to him about the pub and how good the trade was; unbeknown to him they were fishing about what might become their future investment. Larry appeared to be completely honest with them when he said he'd only bought the Jolly Roger five years ago, before that he'd had a pub in the heart of London, but every week there was trouble and as he'd already said, he was getting too old for all that.

Jimmy looked at him, heavily tattooed, a well-built man, who looked younger than his years. Just like Jimmy, he had a look about him, the type of look that said don't mess with him. Jimmy certainly had the impression he could have handled himself, especially in his younger days, probably a lot like him. One thing was certain, he liked Larry.

The two friends decided to come clean as to why they had been drinking there for the past few days.

"Just my fucking luck," laughed Larry "the day you come in we have trouble with those fucking idiots! Sorry about the bad language ladies."

"It's not a problem," giggled Maria "we're used to it living with these two!"

They all laughed.

Larry didn't look surprised when Mickey told him not to worry about the bully boys because they wouldn't put them off buying the pub. As club owners they knew bullying and extortion were common place.

Seeing they were serious, Larry asked if they'd like to take a look at the accommodation while they were there. They thought it was a great idea, especially after Jimmy asked if his wife would mind and Larry stated she was at the hair salon and wouldn't be back for a couple of hours. Anyway she knew people will want to look round as they'd had quite a lot of interest from prospective buyers. They didn't think he was saying it just to hurry them into making a decision.

A couple of minutes later they were looking round the three bedroom flat upstairs, they all noticed how clean and tidy it was, especially the kitchen.

"We replaced all the units in here two years ago," said Larry "same with the bathroom, it had a new suite."

It was a good size flat, with newly fitted kitchen and bathroom and it was obvious to Larry they liked what they saw.

They eventually went back down into the bar and talked about buying it. Mickey was keen to let Larry know they would want their own people running it, so they wouldn't be keeping his staff.

He was happy when Larry said his barman was leaving at the end of the month to run his own pub. Leaving them to talk, Larry began clearing some glasses from the other tables.

When Mickey asked the girls what they thought, it was unanimous; they liked Larry and the pub.

Jimmy thought they should move quickly or they could lose it. Mickey agreed and called Larry back over to let him know they wanted to buy it. Larry looked chuffed; he'd give them the details for his solicitor so he could contact her. When Larry said his solicitor was Denise Wright, Mickey grinned. He knew her well and as Mickey would be handling all their legalities it wouldn't take long to get the ball rolling. He would call Denise that afternoon.

Larry shook their hands and joked with Mickey stating that for a brief he could handle himself.

"Ah well Harry that's because Jimmy taught me, he's a hooligan!"

They all laughed.

Larry had seen them in action; he didn't think they would take any shit from the bully boys. Before leaving, Mickey said they'd call back in a few days.

Monica reminded them they needed to call in at the station and make a statement regarding the trouble. It was best done sooner rather than later. They agreed.

Fortunately because of Monica's connections they weren't kept very long at the station. Most of her colleagues were more interested in her health and her forthcoming marriage than the earlier trouble, although the desk sergeant said he wasn't surprised they had trouble with the four blokes. They were well known for causing trouble. They were due to appear before a magistrate within a couple of days.

"Oh wonderful," said Monica sarcastically "so basically they'll get away with it! If we're lucky they'll get a fine and if we're really lucky they might even get a few hours community service!"

They all signed their statements before leaving.

Once they were outside, Jimmy asked if they fancied eating at Shades. It was a unanimous yes.

Forty minutes later they were sitting in their restaurant. They had a wonderful evening. It was almost midnight when they left.

The following morning the two men got ready to meet with Virginia Hollingsworth. Although Mickey wasn't a friend of hers, her reputation as a no nonsense prosecutor was known throughout the legal world. He often saw her at the courts, but thankfully had never come up against her. Driving to her offices, they went over their version of accounts.

"Fuck me Mick," said Jimmy as they entered the building, "this is a bit posh ain't it?"

"So it should be, the amount of money these people earn, they can afford posh."

Entering the lift their destination would be the third floor. They were greeted by a very attractive lady as they entered Virginia's reception area; she was about thirty five, with short blonde hair cut in a very modern style. Although she was slim, Mickey commented discreetly to Jimmy on the size of her tits. After asking if they had an appointment, she asked them to take a seat in the adjoining room and told them Miss Hollingsworth will be along shortly.

No sooner had they sat down when Virginia appeared.

"Hello Michael," she said offering her hand "and you must be Mr Dixon?"

Shaking her hand, he said she could call him Jimmy.

Taking them through to her office, she sat opposite them at her desk.

"This is quite a case we have here Michael. I'd like to go over a couple of questions with you both, if that's ok?"

They both nodded.

"Good, now I would imagine the first question the defence will ask you is why didn't you report the drugs as soon as Samuels planted them?"

"Simple," replied Mickey "because we wanted his devious act to show him for what he is, there was also the fact he may have decided to try something else. By leaving the drugs there, when the drug squad became aware through us, they would have Samuels's finger print which was why we didn't touch them, and of course we had the tape which showed him putting them there in the first place. We felt relaxed in the time which we had to disclose it."

Virginia looked at him and grinned.

"Good answer Michael. Now tell me, what do you think happened to the Jamaicans? Let me put that another way, Samuels believes they met with something nasty at the order of you and Jimmy."

"I personally believe the Jamaicans have either gone back to the Caribbean," said Mickey "or they have simply relocated somewhere else. As for Samuels's theory about us having done something to them; in my opinion it is little more than a weak attempt to throw doubt in. What does Samuels think we did with them, killed them and hid them under the floorboards?"

Even Virginia broke into a smile.

Virginia stated that Samuels was a desperate man and it seemed the further they delved into his private life the more desperate he was becoming. Jimmy asked if she had enough evidence to prove Samuels guilt.

"There's enough evidence to put him away for a long time," she stated "if I don't get a guilty verdict on this case I'll stop practising law. The tapes alone are very damaging, but a distressed witness is always a bonus."

They knew she was referring to Max; she would be a very valuable asset to the prosecution, especially as she taped Samuels harassing her, which although Lenny had done it for her she could simply say she did it.

"In theory," said Mickey "how long do you think he'll get Virginia?"

"That's the problem. Realistically he could get up to fifteen years, but you know as well as I do Michael, it will just depend what judge we get. Trouble is Samuels will be known to some of them, which might make it easier or harder for him; there's no way of telling. Unfortunately we won't necessarily know until nearer the day, if not on the day, what judge it will be. One thing is certain though; the powers that be will want this dealt with as soon as possible. I understand it's proving quite an embarrassment for certain departments. I'm hoping to be ready for court within six weeks. Hopefully the trial won't last long. As I've said, this entire case is one big embarrassment, they will want it wrapped up quickly. I don't think there's anything else I need to ask either of you today, my office will be in touch if anything crops up."

Shaking hands; the two friends thanked her then left.

CHAPTER 32

The days passed quickly. The nearer the wedding came, the quicker the time seemed to go. They had been called back to Virginia's office a couple of times, just to verify a few minor details. The sale on the Jolly Roger was going through nicely; even the rehearsal with Father Thomas had gone better than expected. The wedding was now just over a week away. Mickey's sister Fay and her family were due to arrive from America the following morning. Mickey had arranged to meet them at the airport; Monica was going along with him.

That evening Monica cooked the meal again, it was another triumph. While they ate they talked about Fay and her husband Richard, also their two teenage children. Mickey was so excited about seeing them all. Jimmy couldn't wait for them to meet Maria. Mickey hired a seven seater M.P.V after Charlie had expressed a wish to go to the airport with them. Monica smiled and said they wouldn't believe how pretty and grown up she is.

"It's heredity," laughed Mickey "she gets her good looks from me."

"Oh," joked Jimmy "nothing like blowing your own trumpet Mick!"

"Bollocks its true Jim!"

Monica told Jimmy they were staying over at Mickey's for the next two nights. They were also going to arrange a family meal while Fay and Richard were in London. She would let them know the exact details of when and where after they'd spoken to Mickey's parents. After Jimmy said they'd look forward to that, the topic changed to the Jolly Roger. They discussed who they would put in as a manager to run the Jolly. Their first choice would be Shaun, but only if he wanted to, with Shane being their second choice, although they knew how he liked working the clubs and a pub might cramp his style with the ladies although he and Max seem to be an item. Since Samuels' arrest they'd gone out several times together and Shane had stayed over a couple of nights. He even got on well with her son Harry. Their third and final choice was Jacky Boy and Lisa, simply because they were looking for somewhere to live and the pub could be the answer. They decided they would ask Shaun then take it from there. Monica could see Shaun as a landlord, as could Maria.

They talked more about Shaun and Ann running the pub. Mickey noticed Monica smiling and nodding her head at him, when Jimmy asked if he was staying over. He was well aware she wanted him to stay. Maria suggested to Jimmy that as Monica would be out the following day, they could take some more things over to the house. Nodding in approval, he suggested asking Shaun and Ann to join them so they could see the house. Everyone soon realised why he was so keen on the idea when he added they could stop at the Jolly for a drink on the way back. Nevertheless, she thought it was a great idea, so she would ring them first thing in the morning to invite them.

They talked into the early hours of the morning until Monica said she was retiring for the night as she was tired.

Everyone agreed that it was time for bed.

Lying in bed Maria snuggled her head into Jimmy's chest as he said it wasn't long now until the wedding and was she nervous about it. Confessing to him she was, but also really looking forward to becoming Mrs Dixon. Unexpectedly he asked if she remembered when she thought their life style would be unsuitable for children. Of course she remembered, but she thought they sorted all that out so, curiously, she asked why he'd mentioned it.

"I just want you to know I meant everything I said at the time, especially the bit about never letting you leave me once we're married."

"Tell me the truth Jimmy, if you've got cold feet and you don't want to marry me then just say so."

"I want to marry you more than anything, but I need to be sure you understand that no matter what, it will be forever."

"If I didn't think it was going to be forever, I wouldn't be marrying you in the first place!"

They kissed passionately for several minutes and then he pulled her onto him. Moments later they were making love. Knowing that Mickey and Monica could probably hear them, she asked him not to make so much noise. In true Jimmy fashion he began shouting in a loud voice, "Oh no more babe, you're killing me, please take the hand cuffs off! I'll be your slave! I'll worship your body!"

She tried to shut him up by going down hard on him and kissing him until finally he stopped. He grinned when she said how embarrassed she'd be with Mickey over breakfast.

"Don't worry about it babe, I've already told him you're a sex maniac!"

Pinning him down with her body she began tickling him, she knew he hated it, so it was a clever form of pay back. Desperately he tried to get up without hurting her, only managing to stop her by pushing her over onto her back and pinning her arms down before making love to her again. Finally they snuggled down together and within minutes they were both fast asleep.

The next morning she cooked the breakfast. Jimmy was reading the newspaper when Monica appeared and said

Mickey would be along any minute, he was just using the bathroom.

Thirty minutes later after they had eaten Mickey and Monica left to pick up the hire car. Jimmy reminded Maria to phone Ann. As Maria dialled the number, he told her to tell Shaun if he was expected at the club that day it wouldn't be a problem, someone would cover for him. Maria nodded just as Ann answered the phone. When she asked if they'd like to join them for the day, Ann jumped at the chance. It was arranged Jimmy would pick them up later that morning around eleven.

Looking at the clock and yawning, Jimmy stated it was only half eight so they could go back to bed for a couple of hours. She knew he was referring to sex. Since Mickey and Monica had been there they had been confined to the bedroom; she was also conscious of any noise they made in case they heard them.

Sitting down on his lap she kissed him and suggested that once she'd done everything she needed to maybe they could have an hour in bed. Pushing his hand up her top and squeezing her breast he offered to help if it would speed things up. Pulling his hand away, she giggled and stated she could manage. Unbeknown to him she had no intention of doing anything, she had only said that so she could surprise him. A moment later she disappeared into the bedroom on the pretext of making the bed and tidying it up.

Minutes later she returned dressed as a sexy French maid.

"Fucking hell babe!" exclaimed Jimmy, "are you trying to give me a heart attack?"

"Pardon me sir is there anything I can do for you," she asked as she knelt down in front of him and slowly undid his fly.

Unable to take his eyes off her, he wanted to take her right there right then. She was so sexy with the tiny black outfit barely covering anything and the white silk French knickers showing below it.

Taking him into her mouth, he called out her name as he grabbed her hair and pushed her head down onto him. She knew exactly how to please him; teasing him with her tongue she knew he wouldn't last long.

"Babe stop I want to fuck you," he said breathlessly.

Their love making was hot and passionate as she tore at his clothes when he entered her.

The time was almost ten when they finally stopped. Lying exhausted on the floor she glanced at the clock and exclaimed they needed to shower and dress if they were going to pick Shaun and Ann up on time. Jimmy nodded.

Once they were ready there was just time for a coffee before they left. As he drank his coffee, he asked where she had got the maid's outfit from. The moment she said Monica and Simone had bought it for her to wear on their hen night, his expression changed.

"Let me assure you Maria," he said arrogantly "you definitely won't be wearing it! In fact no one but me will ever see you in it!"

She felt angry at the way he'd spoken to her.

"I had no intentions of wearing it, but I resent your attitude towards me!"

"Let me put it another way Maria, if you did have any ideas about wearing anything remotely like that on your hen night, you definitely won't be fucking going! Do I make myself clear," he shouted as he aggressively grabbed her by the arm "my future wife will never been seen in public looking like a fucking whore!"

The moment he'd said it, he knew he shouldn't have. His words were cutting and she felt hurt. When she snapped back saying he hadn't minded her acting like a whore an hour ago, she could see the anger on his face. This was the side of him she feared.

"I don't appreciate you talking like that Maria! You know perfectly well how much I like you dressing up for me!"

"You're acting like a jealous idiot Jimmy, you of all people should know I would never dress like that in public, but as you've been so rude I might consider wearing it now!"

"You'd better be fucking joking Maria;" he snarled as he grabbed her arm again "actually you can cancel the fucking hen night!"

Tears rolled down her face, she was so angry and upset as she shouted at him to let her go as he was hurting her. Ignoring her request, he held her tighter and aggressively shouted, "I fucking mean it Maria! I'm not asking you I'm fucking telling you, cancel your hen night!"

"You're nothing but a jealous bully," she shouted trying to free her arm "I wish I'd never worn the stupid outfit! What's got into you Jimmy?"

She sobbed as they continued to argue and she said she didn't want to go out with Shaun and Ann now; he could take them on his own. Realising he had gone too far and she was right, he was a jealous bully; he released her.

When she began to walk away, he tried to pull her back, but she struggled against him. In the two years since they met he had never seen her in such a temper. For the first time he felt concerned, because he knew he'd gone too far and maybe on this occasion she wouldn't back down. After every row or misunderstanding, he had always been able to talk her round, but this morning was different. He had been wrong and he knew it. Finally when he released his grip, she hurriedly walked away and went into the bathroom locking the door behind her.

Standing outside the door, he apologised over and over again, but she didn't answer him.

Inside the bathroom, she was trying hard to hold back her tears, she loved him more than anything, but his jealous outbursts were escalating and taking their toll on her.

"Go and pick Ann and Shaun up Jimmy," she shouted "show them the house."

After he shouted he wouldn't go without her, she came out of the bathroom. Moving towards her, he tried to put his arms around her but she was having none of it. Reaching out he called her babe and expressed how sorry he was.

"Yes I expect you are Jimmy, so you should be! Go and pick Ann and Shaun up they'll be waiting."

"Fuck them! I'm only interested in us, and yes I know I'm a fucking jealous idiot, but I can't help it. Just the thought of another man seeing you dressed like that drives me fucking crazy!"

"You make me feel cheap Jimmy with the things you say, why do you do it? I only do things to please you, but you always end up rowing and making me feel dirty. I never asked to be sold to Nick, any more than I asked you to win me!" she said tearfully "I never intended to fall in love with you, but I did. Now I wish you'd just sold me on! Just lately you seem to have changed Jimmy."

"Babe I fell in love with you too remember?" he said hugging her as she burst into tears "I don't know why I do it. I'm so sorry I make you feel that way. I don't ever want to make you feel cheap or dirty, because you're not and I want to marry you more than anything babe, I'm sorry."

When he tried to kiss her his hands were all over her.

"Stop it, that won't work Jimmy, I'm not that easy a push over anymore. I believed we were a partnership, but it's always on your terms. As long as everything is how you want it everything's fine. I'm a person too, I have feelings!"

Sensing that he was losing the argument because everything she had said was true and he didn't have a valid reason as to why he behaved the way he did, he just stood there. Unable to justify his jealousy, except that the fear of losing her haunted him and it was always in the back of his mind. He loved showing her off when they went out, although if he was honest he would be happier if she stayed in when he wasn't with her; even he knew it was wrong feeling that way but that was how he felt about her.

"Please babe," said Jimmy humbly "what are you going to do about Shaun and Ann?"

Unable to look at him, she looked down at the floor and said she just wanted to be left alone, but she wanted him to take their friends to see the house.

Trying to kiss her again, he said how sorry he was, but he wasn't going without her. Pushing him away she told him to leave her alone, but he simply repeated his action to kiss her.

Feeling angry with the responses he was getting; he wasn't going to leave it. Forcing her against the wall he shouted at her that he loved her and he wasn't about to let anything go.

Determined not to back down, she fought against him, but he was getting angrier and she noticed that he seemed to be finding the argument arousing. Even though she knew he loved her, he had been wrong to say those things to her, so she was going to try and stand up to him. The more she continued to push him away, the more aggressive he became.

Grabbing at her and kissing her, he tried to justify his behaviour by shouting at her, "It's your fault I'm the way I am, because you do something to me! You bring out my bad side, the thought of you ever letting another man touch you makes me want to fucking kill you!"

They were screaming and shouting at each other and then totally out of character she slapped his face. Immediately he threw her down on to the floor and standing over her drew a fist. Automatically she put her hands up to her face to protect herself.

"God what is happening Maria! I would never hurt you, I fucking love you! Get up babe."

Ignoring him she rolled onto her side sobbing. Kneeling down next to her, he stroked her hair.

"Babe I'm so sorry. I don't know what happened, please forgive me. I need you babe."

Still sobbing she ignored him as she held her face in her hands. Getting down onto the floor he laid down next to her. Placing his arm round her, he kissed the back of her neck. He could feel and hear her crying as he caressed her and gently squeezed her breasts, but she didn't respond. Touching her he kept saying how sorry he was, begging her to forgive him. Still she didn't turn round, but she did speak to him and asked why he was so jealous, stating she'd never given him any reason to doubt her and she hated it when they rowed.

He was sorry too and knew he shouldn't doubt her, but he just couldn't control his jealousy. Admitting he had a problem, but he couldn't change, he tried to explain exactly how he felt, but it was difficult for him. Truth was she was always on his mind, especially on a sexual level. There was never a day that went by he didn't think about having her.

Slowly she turned round to face him; her eyes were all red and swollen as she said, "Jimmy you can't keep doing this, you need to think before you say anything, and your habit of thinking that after every argument sex will solve everything and win me round, has got to stop."

"You mean like this babe?"

Slipping his hand into her panties, he began touching her. At that moment she hated herself and him, but as always her body was responding. No matter how bad things were; the sex between them was always electric.

"That's exactly what I mean Jimmy and you're doing it again!"

Lifting her skirt, he pulled her panties down and moved slowly down her body with his tongue. She knew it was his way of proving he was in control again, she wanted to tell him to stop but it was too late, his head was between her legs. Feeling his hands on her as his tongue touched her intimately, her body now responding, she wanted him and was powerless to stop him. He knew it would only be a matter of minutes before she climaxed, then he would be inside her. To him that would be the end to their conflict, to her it was simply a compromise to the situation. In her heart she knew he would never change, this was the dark side of him. When he'd finished they just laid there, only stirring when the phone rang, but neither of them getting up to answering it. They listened as the answer phone cut in.

"It's only me love," said Ann's voice "is everything ok, only we're worried because you're an hour late."

Maria urged him to call her back and told him to do whatever he thought was best. She was going to take another shower. Telling her to wait while he called Ann, then he would shower with her. She simply nodded.

Two minutes later, he phoned Ann and apologised, making up some lame excuse about business and telling her they would be there around one o'clock.

Five minutes later, he joined Maria in the shower. She was painfully quiet and he knew that this time he would really have to make it up to her. He tried to kiss her.

"Leave off Jimmy; I'm ready to get out."

Reaching over she grabbed a towel and wrapping it round her walked off. By the time he went into the bedroom, she was dry and beginning to dress. Looking at her body, he noticed the scars on her buttocks from where Nick had branded her. Strange thing was, he had all but forgotten them, rarely noticing them anymore; yet today he noticed them with perfect clarity. He knew in his heart she hadn't deserved any of the bad things that had happened to her, his own dreadful behaviour being no different. No matter how he tried to tell himself that his behaviour was warranted, he couldn't justify it. Deep down he knew he was wrong with the things he said and did to her; but he just couldn't control his jealous outbursts. Then he remembered what his mother had told him about respecting women. When he thought about the way his father had treated her, he felt sick to the pit of his stomach. Wondering if he had inherited some dreadful genetic disease from his father, because his mother had been beautiful like Maria. There were many occasions when his father would call her terrible names like whore and slut before he beat her. Jimmy had wanted to kill him, but now for the first time in his life he could relate to his father's behaviour. Knowing in his heart that he would never change and if he loved Maria as much as he knew he did, he would do the descent thing and let her find a better life, but he couldn't do that, he would die without her. More frightening was he would see her dead before he'd let another man have her. With these terrible thoughts running through his mind, he made a promise to himself that he would not turn into his father and he would never lay a hand on her again. No matter how bad things may get, his children would never have to witness the dreadful things he had. Determined that history wouldn't repeat itself, he remembered his mother had often told him that when she first met his father he was kind and loving. Then as their time together went on, he became jealous and violent. Jimmy was adamant it wouldn't happen to him.

Walking towards her; he threw his arms around her. Unresponsive she just stood there.

"Please babe, say you forgive me. I can't go out unless I know we're ok."

Her beautiful eyes were filling with tears, she looked so sad, not the way a bride-to-be should look a week before her wedding. Although she knew he really was sorry; she also knew he had a problem that was deep rooted. Knowing he would never seek any help, in her mind she questioned as to why men behaved like this around her. She knew Nick was a sadist, but Jimmy was a good man at heart. She even asked if it was something she did but was unaware of.

As he held her, she knew he was desperate for her to reciprocate his affections. In her mind she was convinced that he had little to no control over his outbursts, but she loved him. Slowly she put her arms around him and held him then they kissed passionately.

"I love you so much Maria, I don't think you realise how much. I'm so sorry, it won't happen again."

"It will happen again Jimmy and you know it."

Knowing in his heart she was right, he didn't reply even when she continued and told him she would never want another man, but she couldn't cope with some of his behaviour. Like earlier when he'd drawn a fist, she truly believed he was going to punch her. His reply was, but he hadn't.

"I know Jimmy, but how long will it be before you do?"

Although she wasn't convinced when he stated he'd never hit her, she wasn't prepared to talk about it then, simply because she knew they would only end up arguing again. However she did say, with conviction, if he ever hit her in front of their children that would be the end of them. Convincingly he promised her it would never come to that. Hoping he was right, she said they should leave to pick their friends up.

Thankful that she was going with him, he knew it was better to drop the subject but he had made up his mind that he would make it up to her.

During the drive she was very quiet, he kept asking her if she was alright as he squeezed her knee. Keeping quiet she just nodded.

Once their friends got in the car, he noticed she seemed to perk up a bit.

It was obvious she enjoyed showing Ann around the house, especially the kitchen and the nursery; which were by far her favourite rooms. The two men talked about the renovations that had been done and how Maria had loved it when he first brought her there. It was then Jimmy mentioned briefly to Shaun about the pub they were buying, although he didn't say about them wanting him to run it.

They stayed at the house chatting for a couple of hours, the whole time Jimmy kept putting his arm around her and saying things like, 'We can't wait to actually move in and put the nursery to use, can we babe?' Ann had no qualms that Maria would make a wonderful mother and that Jimmy was lucky to have her.

After agreeing with her, Jimmy suggested they all went to the pub.

"Aye sounds good to me," said Shaun.

Larry greeted them as they walked in and asked what they were drinking. Jimmy introduced him to the others.

Five minutes later they were sitting at a table in the window. Ann glanced around the place before saying what a lovely little pub it was and how she'd always liked the area. Jimmy asked Shaun what he thought and if he'd ever fancied being a landlord.

"Aye it's nice and I quite like the idea of having a pub, we've thought about it in the past. It was only because of the kids we decided against it. Ann didn't feel that a pub was the best environment to raise a family in."

"How would you feel about becoming the landlord and landlady here at the Jolly Roger. Me and Mickey are buying it, although we've got no intentions of running it. The clubs keep us busy enough, so if you two want to give it some thought, all I'll say is we'll give you a free hand with everyday decisions. Also Shaun, if you fancied a few nights working the clubs, it wouldn't be difficult to get a couple of the lads to fill in for you. You'd have control over hiring and firing of staff, but obviously you would have to discuss the financial side of things with Mickey and I think I should tell you, the landlord's been having a bit of trouble with four bully boys, but I can assure you that would be sorted out before you took over."

"Fuck me Jimmy it's a nice offer, but unexpected."

It was obvious they would need to discuss it at home. There was no real hurry; nothing was going to happen for a few weeks until the sale went through. Leaving the others talking, Jimmy went back to the bar to order another round of drinks. Talking to Larry, he asked if there was any possibility his friends could take a look at the accommodation. Larry thought it would be fine, but he would just check with Rose first.

Jimmy took the drinks over and joined the others. Sitting down he said they may be able to have a look round upstairs while they were there. Maria told them it was very nice.

"I'm sure it is," replied Ann "are you alright Maria, only since arriving here you've seemed a bit quiet."

Maria said she was fine, just a little tired which was probably due to all the wedding arrangements.

Larry came over and introduced his wife Rose to them, and to tell them they were welcome to look round upstairs.

Jimmy and Maria waited downstairs as they wanted Shaun and Ann to make up their own minds.

After the others walked away, Jimmy leaned over and, kissing her on the cheek, asked if she was ok.

Smiling a half smile, she nodded. After telling her to cheer up, he stated he'd meant what he'd said earlier that he'd never hurt her.

"You don't have to punch someone to hurt them Jimmy, sometimes what people say is worse."

Knowing she was right, he changed the topic and asked if she fancied a go on the fruit machine.

"No thanks, but you go ahead. Or are you afraid to leave me here just in case I see someone I fancy?"

"Just fucking drop it Maria, this is not the time or the place!"

Turning away from him, she sipped her drink. A moment passed before he spoke and asked if she would like to take Shaun and Ann to one of their restaurants for dinner.

Although she didn't really feel up to it, if he really wanted to she'd tag along.

"Actually babe, with no house guests, perhaps we should have a romantic night in."

She just looked back at him. He was just about to say something to her when the others returned. They both noticed Ann was smiling and seemed to be getting along well with Rose.

As they sat down, Jimmy asked what they thought. Ann smiled and said it was bigger than she'd imagined and she'd really liked it.

Shaun gave a typical male response "Aye, it was ok."

Thinking they sounded positive, Jimmy suggested having another drink then pushing off home.

Forty minutes later around seven that evening they pulled up at Shaun's house.

Ann thanked them for a lovely time and how much she loved their new house. Maria thanked her and said she would call her the following day. Jimmy pulled away.

On their way home he stopped for a takeaway. By eight they were back in the apartment eating their meal.

When he asked what she fancied doing that evening, she said she was tired so she'd like to simply watch the TV. Jimmy nodded and said he would see what films were on while she cleared the dishes.

Waiting for her to return from the kitchen, he sat on the sofa, fully expecting her to sit with him when she finished, but totally out of character she walked straight over to the arm chair.

Looking over at her, he patted the sofa, indicating he wanted her to sit with him. Standing up she walked toward him. As she sat down he put his arm around her back, normally she would rest her head on his chest; but not this time. Telling her he'd found a good film to watch, she simply said "Fine."

"How long do you intend to carry on like this Maria?"

"Carry on like what Jimmy?"

"Don't act dumb; you know exactly what I mean. I don't like childish games!"

When she didn't answer him, he asked her again.

"This is all a game to you isn't it Jimmy? Have you forgotten what happened earlier?"

"I thought that was over and done with, as far as I'm concerned it's forgotten!"

His temper was beginning to surface again when she stated she couldn't forget it.

"Where is this going Maria? Or are you thinking of calling the wedding off again?"

To his surprise she didn't mention the wedding, she simply said she had more important things to worry about but she didn't want to discuss it. She burst into tears when he shouted that she had fuck all to worry about and he demanded to know what was going on. Unable to reply, she just kept shaking her head and sobbing. Holding her firmly by the shoulders, he ordered her to tell him. It was then she blurted out that she thought she was pregnant. To her disbelief he shouted "Fantastic!"

Telling him that to her it was anything but fantastic, they weren't married and she was a Catholic! His answer to that was, so what! Desperately she tried to make him understand that to her it was a dreadful sin.

"Bollocks," said Jimmy "how can it be a sin when two people love one another like we do? God owes you big time babe, he knows what a wonderful mother you'll make. Anyway, what makes you think you're pregnant, are you sure?

"My tummy feels bloated, my breasts are tender and I'm piddling more often."

"You forgot irritable and snappy," he said jokingly, "don't worry about it babe, we can talk to Doc Daniels in the morning."

She certainly wasn't comfortable about it like he was, but she wanted to talk to him and she didn't want him getting angry. Promising her he wouldn't, she referenced what he'd said earlier about his future wife leaving the house dressed like a whore. Instantly he stated he hadn't meant it to sound the way it had. Looking tearful she said in the eyes of other Catholics, that was precisely what she'd be if she was pregnant.

"And you wonder why I have no faith in the religion babe! It's ok for someone like my old man to beat the shit out of my mum every day, he can say three Hail Mary's and he's pardoned by God. Yet two people who love each other like us, who create something as precious and wonderful as another life are condemned as sinners!"

When she asked him to stop saying terrible things, he realised just how upset she was. Taking her hand and telling her she looked tired, he suggested leaving the film and instead having an early night.

Knowing it wouldn't be wise for her to push the subject, she nodded.

So much for the early night, they laid awake for hours just talking. They discussed being parents and the argument they'd had earlier. Assuring her he would always love her, and that it didn't matter what anyone else might think, they had each other and that was the most important thing.

CHAPTER 33

Jimmy was up first making tea and scrambled eggs when Maria appeared in the kitchen. Smiling at her, he said he'd spoken to the Doc and asked him to call round to see her before his morning surgery.

Maria had only just finished eating when the intercom buzzed. The Doc was early. After listening to her symptoms, he examined her. Relieved was how she felt when he stated he didn't think she was pregnant. It was more likely she was getting her period. With a smile, he handed her a small bottle and asked her to go to the bathroom and do a urine sample for him. When she returned, he dabbed a piece of thin card in it. They waited for it to change colour, but nothing happened. It confirmed she wasn't pregnant. They both noticed Jimmy looked disappointed. Maria shook her head when Doc asked if she'd ever had a period before she lived with Nick. Looking shocked, he asked if she had ever used oral contraceptives before he started giving her the contraceptive injection. Again she shook her head. Doc was aware that her past was anything but normal, so tactfully he asked about her time at the convent and if she'd been given some tiny pills to take every day.

"Yes, Sister Marjorie gave all the older girls a pill every night. One night Melanie had asked her what it was for; Sister Marjorie told her it was for protection. We all believed it would protect us from evil."

"It sounds like the contraceptive pill. Now because your injection is overdue, your body is producing eggs. You'll probably have some light bleeding, it will probably only last a couple of days. If however your symptoms persist and nothing happens, I'll come and see you again.

Jimmy thanked him for coming as he walked him to the door.

When Jimmy walked back into the lounge towards her, he noticed she looked sad.

Hugging her, he reassured her it didn't matter and at least she didn't have to worry about being pregnant before they married.

"I can't believe how stupid I am. Doc Daniels must think I'm so thick! I knew about periods, I just always assumed the injection stopped them and regarding my time before Nick, I just thought I was a late developer."

Jimmy knew Doc wouldn't think anything of the sort, he knew Maria's life had been difficult. Jimmy asked her why Sister Marjorie would think it necessary to give the girls the pill if they weren't allowed boyfriends. Maria's reply was simple; she could only assume it was in case one of the girls ever did meet a boy, at least they wouldn't get pregnant. Although she couldn't imagine for one minute that they would because they were never allowed to meet boys; it was forbidden.

With a look of love and sincerity, he told her once they were married she wouldn't have to worry about contraceptives. His expression changed rapidly when she said she was glad because the church didn't like it. Instantly he asked her not to mention the church again because it made him angry. Changing the topic, he asked what she fancied doing.

Assuming Doc was right, she suggested going shopping to buy some sanitary products.

"Oh yeah, then we should go out somewhere babe, we could stop at a chemist on the way. How do you fancy driving down to Brighton? It's a lovely day; we could go on the pier or sit on the beach?"

Liking the idea, she went to freshen up. Twenty minutes later, she appeared wearing shorts, T shirt and sandals. Jimmy laughed and said she looked like a tourist.

Even dressed casually, she still carried a certain upper class look. Jimmy didn't change; he wore jeans and T shirt.

Three hours later, they were walking hand in hand along Brighton sea front. Jimmy won a huge cuddly toy on the pier which she would put it in the nursery.

They ate whelks, cockles and candy floss. Maria was having the most wonderful time. Sitting on the beach he kissed her. Lying down on the shingle she gazed up at the sky as he said they should do things like this more often. Nodding she said she was having a lovely time.

Leaning over her he kissed her; she could sense the warm sun and the relaxed atmosphere were having a rousing effect on him. With a giggle, she stated people could see them and he was getting a little over amorous.

"I couldn't give a shit and I bet there's not a single bloke on this beach who wouldn't give his right arm to be in my shoes right now."

Maria was well aware he wasn't going to stop when he slid his hand inside her T shirt. She felt embarrassed as he squeezed her breast, so she suggested they should think about making their way back to the car.

Aware he was making her feel uncomfortable and considering the row they'd had earlier, he agreed. They stood up to leave, brushing themselves down. Picking up her bag she noticed a middle aged couple staring at them, she also heard the man mutter something under his breath. Jimmy also noticed. It was as they passed them that Jimmy turned to the man and arrogantly asked if there was a problem. Instantly Maria felt panic and pleaded with him just to ignore them. She could see him becoming agitated. Silently she prayed that the man would just ignore Jimmy's question, unfortunately he didn't.

"Yes actually there is," said the man "my wife and I found your behaviour unnecessary, especially in a public place. No one wants to watch two people mauling all over each other."

"Fuck off!" said Jimmy aggressively.

The man retaliated by mumbling some derogatory remark about Maria's morals. That was all it took for Jimmy to flare into a temper. Suddenly he hurled abuse at the couple.

"Your wife's so fucking ugly; no one would want to fuck her! I expect if the truths known you were getting a hard on just looking at my girlfriend."

A terrible argument raged between the two men as they hurled abuse at one another. Maria could see people watching, but no one intervened. The two women were trying desperately to calm the situation before it erupted into a full scale war. They would have succeeded had the man not referred to Maria as a tart. That was it, Jimmy had heard enough. Grabbing the man by the shoulders he head butted him in the face. The man fell to the ground, his nose pouring with blood. Jimmy kicked him several times, despite his wife screaming and Maria begging him to stop. Finally he did, the man was lying on the shingle groaning; his face and shirt covered in blood. Maria was shaking and sobbing as she pulled Jimmy away. Everyone was watching them, but Jimmy didn't seem to notice; it was as though he was oblivious to what had just happened. As they walked away, he looked at the man's wife who was crying while she tended to her husband.

"Next time lady," snapped Jimmy "tell your fucking husband to keep his fucking mouth shut and his opinions to himself!"

Maria could hear people mumbling under their breath as they walked past them. She cried all the way back to London.

"Stop crying, everything's okay," said Jimmy "if that bloke had kept his mouth shut it wouldn't have happened!"

He was trying to justify his actions by implying that it was the man's fault. Maria was quick to state it shouldn't have happened at all, why hadn't he just ignored the bloke.

"What and let him call you a tart! I'll never let anyone speak about you like that!"

She didn't reply. For her, the journey seemed to take forever before they arrived back at their apartment. Once inside she told him to take a shower as his hands and T shirt were covered in blood.

"So it is," he replied almost smirking.

There was a cut on his forehead which Maria wanted to look at, but he told her it was nothing and the bloke's head had been harder than he'd thought.

After pouring them a drink, he sat down. She just looked at him. He could tell she wanted to say something, so after several seconds he asked what. Her question was simple, why had he beaten the man on the beach? Why couldn't he just have laughed it off?

"Yeah right Maria, there was no fucking way I'd do that, the bloke referred to you as a tart or have you forgotten that!"

Although she knew he had defended her honour, she couldn't come to terms with the way he'd lost his temper and how he'd hurt the man. Desperately she tried to explain to him what she meant, but all she seemed to do was make him angrier. Finally he told her to just forget about it and maybe the next time they went they'd invite Mickey and Monica. Simply going along with him rather than have a row, she smiled and nodded.

With a grin, he asked if she fancied taking him to bed. Not wanting to say no, she told him she'd got a tummy ache. Typically of him, he said he had something that would cure it for her. Again she appealed to his gentler side by telling him she really didn't feel up to it. Ignoring what she'd said he started kissing her passionately and told her how much he'd wanted her on the beach. Unable to bring herself to speak, she just smiled.

Once they were in bed, she noticed he was not as gentle as normal. It seemed to follow a pattern; every time he had a violent outburst, he was much more dominant regarding sex. Finally he was satisfied and after kissing her they fell asleep. The following morning she was woken by the house phone ringing. Trying not to wake him, she crept out of the bedroom to answer it.

It was Monica ringing to let them know they'd booked a table for half seven that evening at Shades. Everyone was looking forward to seeing her, especially Mickey's sister Fay and her family. With the frame of mind Jimmy had been in, Maria hoped they would pop in that day and Monica would come back to stay within a day or so, but to her despair, Monica stated they wouldn't, because they planned to visit family with Fay and Richard and she would probably be staying at Mickey for a few days. It would be Saturday when she returned as it was their hen night and Jimmy had arranged to stay with Mickey.

Just as the two friends finished talking, Jimmy emerged from the bedroom and asked who'd been on the phone. Maria told him about the evening arrangements at Shades. She smiled and nodded when he said she'd really like Fay and Richard.

Over breakfast she talked about the arrangements for the stag and hen night. Jimmy was quick to remind her he wouldn't be happy with her wearing anything skimpy. Reassuringly she told him not to worry, because she wouldn't. It was then she noticed his expression changed before he said he wouldn't have to worry because he'd know exactly where she'd be and who she'd be with. Instantly she questioned as to why he would say something like that and she hoped he wasn't going to spy on her. With a grin, he said he couldn't spy on her, he'd be on his stag night, although he had no idea where he would be going or what he'd be doing as the lads were organising it. Wanting to change the topic of the hen night, she asked what his plans were for that day. He had some calls to make and some money to collect from a few places. He wanted her to join him, although when he said she may have to wait in the car at a couple of places, she told him she had lots to do and some recipes to go over, so she would be happy to stay home. Not liking that idea, he insisted she joined him. She knew that if Mickey had been available he wouldn't have asked her, but instead of debating it, she simply nodded her head in agreement.

Later that day they made several money pickups from different places. Maria never asked him what the money was because she knew it was business.

"That's the last one babe," said Jimmy as he returned to the car, "now all I've got to do is drop the money off at Sweet Cheeks. It's nearer to here than Dixie's."

Ten minutes later they were entering the club. Twins Simon and Steve were watching a couple of dancers practising their routines; they were covering for Shane and Billy who were out collecting money from a couple of businesses that were behind with their payments.

Jimmy joined them at their table. Maria wasn't really comfortable because she had only met the twins briefly once or twice before. While the three men talked business, she just sat quietly sipping her orange juice.

Looking round the club in an effort to occupy herself, she noticed a young girl in her mid-twenties walking towards them. She was petite, peroxide blonde and pretty, wearing just a skimpy pair of panties and she was topless. Jimmy looked surprised as the girl approached. Then to Maria's horror the girl completely ignored her as she sat down on Jimmy lap and landed a full kiss on his lips.

Looking embarrassed, he pushed her off but now standing behind him, she placed her arms round his shoulders and referring to him as lover boy asked if he'd missed her.

"Hi Della," said Jimmy in a blasé manner "when did you get back? This is Maria, were getting married."

"Who's a lucky girl then," she said throwing Maria a dirty look.

Maria felt intimidated; she could sense the animosity from Della but before Jimmy could say anything she looked at Maria again and said rudely "Well if you can't satisfy him Maria, he knows I can!"

"You're out of order Della" said Jimmy angrily "and we were a long time ago, before I met Maria!"

"Looks like I shouldn't have gone away Jimmy, still I'm back now."

Simon could sense the tension mounting, so tactfully he told Della to go back to the dressing room as they were talking business. Della protested, stating she hadn't practised her pole routine. Not taking her crap, he said she'd have to practise later. She began walking away but turned and told Jimmy he knew where to find her and she'd be waiting for him.

Steve looked at Maria and told her not to take any notice; Della wasn't a bad sort, she just obviously hadn't heard that Jimmy was getting married as she'd been away a long time.

Maria couldn't answer him, she felt sick to the pit of her stomach. Forcing a smile, she simply nodded. If she had said a word she would have burst into tears. Jimmy knew she would never make a scene in public; by the same token, he knew Della had humiliated her. A few minutes passed when he asked if she was ready to leave, she nodded. Minutes later they were saying goodbye to the twins.

Driving back to the apartment she never said a word.

"Sorry about what happened back in the club babe; Della worked for us a couple of years ago but she left to do a bit of travelling."

He was trying to make it sound as though she meant nothing to him; but it had been obvious to Maria that she had. Several minutes passed and she still didn't reply.

"Say something babe, don't give me the fucking cold shoulder. I can tell you've got the hump with me, believe me I had no idea she was back."

Although she didn't answer him, she had believed him.

Once inside the apartment, she tried avoiding him by busying herself. He knew why she was doing it and it was bothering him, so angrily he shouted at her and told her to stop acting like a child and talk to him.

"Ok Jimmy, if you want to know what I'm thinking, I'll tell you. I thought your friend Della was absolutely horrible, little better than a common slut! And if she ever humiliates me again like that in front of people, I will simply walk out, there so now you know!"

Shocked by her sudden outburst, he was quite taken aback; he wasn't used to seeing her act like that.

"You're blowing it all out of proportion Maria. I told you Della meant nothing to me; she had only ever been a bit of fun. I hadn't even met you at the time!"

"Do you still want to sleep with her?"

"No I fucking don't!" he said with a laugh, "you're the only woman I want to sleep with!"

Maria wasn't as naïve as he would like her to be, she knew from the way all the men used to talk at Nick's poker games that very few, if any, were faithful to their wives. She had hoped it would be different with them. She hoped she would be enough for him, but she did believe what he'd said that Della was before he had met her. Truth was she didn't like her, in Maria's eyes she was nothing but a cheap lay. Deciding to put it out of her mind, she was determined that it wouldn't spoil her evening out with

Mickey and his family. Wanting to avoid any conflict over Della, she left to get ready to go out.

Jimmy looked at the clock and in an effort to cheer her up asked why women needed hours to get ready, yet men only took five minutes.

"Well for a start you haven't got hair and you don't have to wear makeup."

"Fair point babe," said Jimmy with a grin.

It was turned quarter past seven when she finally appeared. Standing in front of him, she twirled round and asked his opinion on how she looked. She could tell there was something about her dress he wasn't sure about, especially when he asked what she was wearing underneath. Asking him why he wanted to know, he was quick to say he couldn't see any bra straps. With a giggle she explained it was a strapless dress, so she had to wear a strapless basque underneath. Then she asked again for his opinion.

Noticing the anger on his face, she wasn't surprised when he said he thought it was too sexy for a dinner date.

"Oh I don't," she said looking disappointed "but you obviously do, so I'll change into something more appropriate, although I haven't got a clue what. I thought you'd like this."

"Don't worry about changing now. You look lovely; it's just me being paranoid."

He knew she would attract attention, which was why he'd said the things he had; truth was he knew she looked sexy in most things and that night was no exception.

Knowing how quickly his mood could change, she asked him again if he wanted her to change. Although he said no, he did ask what jacket she intended wearing with it. Explaining to him that the dress came with a silk wrap, she put it on to show him. Instantly she could tell by his face he preferred the dress with it, rather than without it, basically because it covered her shoulders and cleavage. Telling her it looked good, he told her to keep it on throughout the evening. Sensing he still wasn't happy, she asked again if he wanted her to change.

"I said its fine," he replied in an arrogant tone "just make sure you keep the jacket on."

She simply nodded.

Once at the restaurant, she soon fitted in with Fay and Richard, she could understand why Jimmy liked them so much. While he chatted to Fay and Mickey's parents, Richard seemed happy talking to her and Monica about his family, especially his children.

Maria made conversation asking him why the children hadn't joined them for dinner. She giggled when Richard said they had planned to until their cousin Charlie offered to take them to a friend's birthday party and boring oldies just couldn't compete. They all laughed.

It was well past midnight when the evening began winding down. Mickey knew when his mum said she was feeling tired, it was a cue for them to leave.

"It's been lovely to meet you," said Maria to Fay and Richard "I've had a wonderful evening. I hope to see you again before the wedding."

"It's been lovely to meet you too Maria," said Fay "you're as lovely as everyone said you were. I'm sorry, but I can't make the hen night due to other commitments. You know what it's like; everyone wants to see us."

Maria understood, so she would look forward to seeing them at the wedding.

Everyone kissed and shook hands as they made their departure from the restaurant.

On the drive home, she noticed Jimmy was quiet. Hoping to lighten the atmosphere, she said how much she'd enjoyed the evening and how lovely Mickey's family were. They'd made her feel like she'd known them for years. Without replying to what she'd said, he said arrogantly the meal was ok. Surprised, she giggled and stated he'd looked as though he was thoroughly enjoying himself talking to Fay and her parents.

"I could say the same about you. You looked like you were enjoying yourself a little too much with Richard!"

She refrained from answering him because she knew he was implying something and she didn't want another fight.

"What's the matter Maria, did I hit a nerve?"

"I don't know what you're talking about Jimmy, I was only talking to him and he was very nice."

"Yeah, he's probably saying the same about you."

"I'm not having this conversation, I know where it's leading and you're wrong!"

He never spoke again during the journey.

Once home, she decided she would try to ignore the situation, rather than cause a row. When she asked if he wanted a coffee, he nodded.

Moments later she returned with their drinks and sat down. To her horror, he looked menacingly at her and asked if she fancied Richard.

"Don't do this Jimmy. I told you I thought he was very pleasant and nice, but no, I didn't fancy him!"

She felt as though she was treading on egg shells when he was like this. Not wanting to talk about Richard, she said once she drank her coffee she was going to bed. He said he'd join her.

Within minutes of getting into bed, he tried to initiate sex. Maria apologised, but stated she couldn't have sex because her period was starting and she had stomach cramps. Only thinking of his needs, he instantly implied there were other things they could do. She knew he was referring to a blow job. In truth she would have done whatever he wanted, rather than bring the subject of Richard up again.

Thankfully after she'd satisfied his lust, he fell asleep. Unlike him, she laid awake for hours thinking about how he'd changed over the past few weeks. Something about him was different, but she couldn't work out exactly what.

CHAPTER 34

Saturday morning arrived and Jimmy still seemed quiet as they ate breakfast. Maria asked if he was looking forward to his stag night. After replying with a simple yeah, he asked if she was and if she'd decided what she was going to wear.

Shaking her head, she explained that Monica was coming over early to help pick something out.

"I'll help you, I'm happy to have a clothes show. Go and put some gear on and I'll give you my opinion."

She was reluctant, because she knew he would be critical of anything he deemed as sexy. However as usual he talked her into it.

She had tried on several things before showing him a short black halter neck dress. Immediately she knew from his expression he wasn't happy with it. He hadn't seen it before and asked where she got it from. Monica had given it to her. He asked her to walk up and down the lounge, so he could watch her.

It was when she began walking back towards him; he beckoned her to him with his finger and pulled her onto his lap as she approached him. Kissing her, he asked if she was still bleeding. When she shook her head he began kissing her passionately, at the same time he undid the neck ties and pulled the dress down exposing her breasts. Breathing heavily, he kissed and fondled her as he slipped his hand inside her panties and told her to take the dress off and stand in front of him.

Moments later she was standing there, wearing just her panties which he then told her to remove.

When she'd done as he'd asked, he stood up and lifted her onto him. Carrying her to the lounge wall with her legs wrapped around him, he pushed her against the wall and began thrusting into her, erratically grabbing at her buttocks as he bit her neck. She could feel the tension with every thrust; it was almost as though he was using sex as a release for his aggression. Despite the fact that she wasn't ready for him, she said nothing for fear he would get rougher, but she did ask him to slow down a couple of times.

A few minutes after they'd finished, she went into the bedroom to fetch their dressing gowns. Returning to the lounge she giggled and said she hadn't expected to have sex. His mood changed instantly as he snapped at her, "Neither did I, it was that fucking dress so you definitely won't be wearing it tonight! I want you to wear trousers!"

"Everyone else will probably be wearing a dress Jimmy. Maybe I'll wait and see what Monica and Simone think when they come round later," said Maria trying to skip round the issue of what he deemed appropriate.

"I'm not interested in what everyone else is wearing, I'm not marrying them! I don't give a fuck what they think; I've told you to wear trousers!"

Simply agreeing with him in an effort to avoid a row, she suggested making coffee. When she passed him a mug five minutes later, he asked who was going out with her that night.

"Just a couple of Simone's friends, me and Monica don't know them. Simone invited them; she said a hen night needs more than three of us."

"I'm not interested in what your fucking friends think, and while we're on the subject you'd better remember to behave yourself. If I find out you've flirted with anyone; I won't be happy about it!"

"Why are you being so nasty Jimmy? I wish I wasn't having a hen night, it's only because Monica insisted!"

For the rest of the day she tried to avoid the subject; simply because she knew he didn't want her to go. Trying to keep out of his way she busied herself with house work, while he lounged about making business calls before eventually settling down to watch the sport on the telly.

Finally Mickey and Monica turned up. Thankful for some light relief from the atmosphere between her and Jimmy, she welcomed their arrival. One of the lads had phoned Mickey to say they wanted them to meet at Dixie's by seven. Out of character, Maria asked Mickey if they'd be going to Sweet Cheeks. Shrugging his shoulders, he had no idea. Jimmy knew why she had asked, it was because of Della.

Jimmy told her to remember what he'd said as he hugged her before they left.

After the men had left Monica asked her if everything was alright, only she'd sensed a bit of an atmosphere between her and Jimmy. When Maria explained to her what he had said about what she could wear, Monica looked and sounded angry when stating he had a bloody cheek and that Mickey would never say anything like that to her. Maria asked if she trusted Mickey.

"As much as anyone can trust men in the club game," said Monica "the trouble is young girls see them as sort of play boys. It's because they own clubs, they offer them sex on a plate. I would like to think Mickey wouldn't be interested, but I wouldn't bet on it, after all he is a man!"

Maria spoke to her about Della.

"Now there's a fully paid up member of the slut society! A couple of years ago before Jimmy met you, he went out with Della. At the time she was young and fancied herself as the club owner's wife. Jimmy knew about her reputation from blokes like Shane. She had slept with just about everyone who worked at the club. I asked Mickey once what Jimmy saw in her, she had slag written all over her. Jimmy just saw her as someone to fuck, but unfortunately she didn't see it like that. When Jimmy tried to cool it down, she gave him grief. Apparently she kept turning up acting as though she was his girl, according to Mickey she became something of an embarrassment. I asked him why they didn't just fire her, turns out her father was a good friend of Den's; it came down to a loyalty issue. When she left to go travelling, I hoped that was the last we would see of her, obviously I was wrong. Don't worry about it. Jimmy would never do anything with the likes of Della, especially if it jeopardised his relationship with you."

Maria hoped she was right because lately she'd noticed Jimmy seemed different. Monica wondered what she meant by different. Maria explained how she knew he'd always been jealous and everyone knew what a temper he had, but lately he'd seemed more aggressive. Dictating what she could wear, that type of thing, he'd even accused her of flirting with Richard. Monica suggested it could be due to the stress. Maria agreed, although he didn't say much about it other than he couldn't wait. One thing was certain, he was changing. Seeing the concern on her friend's face, Monica reassuringly said he was probably worried she would change her mind.

No matter how hard she tried to take some comfort from Monica's words, in the back of her mind she had a bad feeling that there was something Jimmy was hiding from her, also that Della would come back to haunt her at a later date.

The intercom buzzed, it was Simone. They waited at the door for her to get out of the lift.

The lift doors opened and she stepped out. They both noticed instantly the black bin liner she was carrying. Monica was the first to ask what was in the bag.

Simone giggled when she told them it was their clothes for the hen night. Looking concerned, Maria instantly stated Jimmy wouldn't like her wearing anything sexy.

"Well it's a good job he's not coming with us then!"

Once inside the apartment, Simone pulled out two white basques which had white silk and lacy bits sewn on to them; along with an L plate on the back. Laughing, Monica asked which one was hers. Simone passed her one, before handing Maria the other. Eagerly Monica insisted they should all try them on.

The outfits left little to the imagination. Knowing the grief it could cause her should Jimmy find out, Maria apologised, but said she couldn't possibly wear it, Jimmy would have a fit.

"Well he won't know will he," said Simone with a grin "wear it Maria, I spent half the night sewing the lace on."

When she repeated she couldn't wear it, Simone could see how worried she was. Not wanting to upset her, she explained how she'd brought some spare material in the bag, so if she could make it a bit more decent, maybe Maria would reconsider and try it then. Monica told her to stop worrying about Jimmy as it was their hen night and if Simone made it so the basque wasn't showing anything, it shouldn't matter. Feeling embarrassed, she told them Jimmy had insisted she wore trousers.

Simone called him a cheeky bastard and said she could never imagine letting her boyfriend tell her what to wear.

Monica felt sorry for Maria because she knew what Jimmy was like, but on this occasion she too thought he had a cheek. It was their hen night and they were going to enjoy it. Finally, the two girls badgered her into wearing it, despite her not really wanting to. By the time Simone had finished adding material all that was showing were her arms and legs. Despite this, Maria still said she would prefer to wear trousers, but they wouldn't hear of it. Finally she agreed to wear it because she knew they wouldn't take no for an answer.

Monica attached the homemade veil and then offered to fix Maria's. She had just finished when they heard a car horn outside. It was their taxi.

Maria wished she felt as comfortable in her outfit as Monica did in hers, despite Monica's being far more revealing.

"You all look lovely girls," said the cab driver "it'll be a sad day for all the single blokes when you two get married next week."

The cab stopped at a pub where Simone said they were meeting her friends. Maria was nervous as several men at the bar wolf whistled them as they entered. Blushing profusely, she felt sick to the pit of her stomach but never said anything to her friends. Monica thought two men who came in just after them looked familiar.

Simone introduced her friends to the girls; there were three of them, Debbie, Dawn and Jayne all single and all out for a bit of fun. It was obvious they had been drinking heavily before the others arrived. Some blokes came over to them and bantered with them, the others girls lapped it up, but Maria felt uncomfortable, especially when Simone handed one of the guys a felt tip pen so he could sign his name on their outfits. Leaning over Maria, he wrote his name across the material on her chest, she was blushing profusely. Within minutes at least six others had joined in wanting to sign. Maria wasn't at ease with any of them; unlike Monica who was lapping it up.

Much to Maria's relief, they only stayed at that particular pub for about an hour, but even as they were leaving some men stopped them and asked for a kiss. Maria declined.

"Go on Maria," said Simone "that's what hen nights are all about, it's your final night of freedom!"

Monica kissed all that asked and some full on the mouth, where Maria tried to get away with a peck on the cheek, although some of the guys were insisting it was on the lips.

Within minutes of arriving at the next pub on Simone's list; it was an exact replay of the first pub. Despite Maria now being under the influence of alcohol having had two glasses of wine, she was still not really comfortable, although she was by then beginning to relax a little. Monica noticed the two men who she thought she'd recognised in the previous pub had followed them. Moving next to Maria, she pointed to them and asked if she recognised them. Maria shook her head stating she'd never seen them before. Monica's thoughts were they looked suspicious. With a giggle, Maria told her to stop being a detective and just enjoy herself.

When one of the men approached Maria, he was promptly offered a pen by Simone.

"Bend over gorgeous" he said smuttily "so I can write my name across your arse."

Nervously, Maria was quick to tell him she'd prefer him not to.

"Doesn't your boyfriend mind such a pretty bride to be dressing in such a skimpy outfit?"

Seeing that she looked embarrassed, Monica laughed and said, "He doesn't know, you can sign my arse if you want to!"

As he walked towards her, she bent over to accommodate his signature. That was Maria's chance to get away; she headed for the ladies telling her friends she would only be a minute.

The moment she stood up, the man with the pen moved towards her, grabbing her round the waist he aimed the pen at her stomach, then leaning forward he rested his head on her chest. Instantly she backed away. Pulling her back towards him he tried to kiss her. Not wanting him to make a scene she offered him a peck on the cheek, but he tried to kiss her on the mouth. Feeling sick and trembling she was relieved when another couple of guys interrupted and asked if they could sign.

When they moved on to the next pub, again the same two men followed them, although this time the one who had been friendly before didn't speak to them. Monica was suspicious when she saw him taking photos on his phone. Despite having drunk several shorts, she seemed to remember that one of them had been taking photos at the previous pub, but due to the fact that she was quite tipsy and couldn't really be sure, she never said anything.

The time was approaching midnight and Maria was only slightly tipsy, unlike the others who were well and truly merry. Maria didn't want to be a party pooper or upset anyone, especially Simone as she'd gone to a lot of trouble, but she was ready to go home. Deflated was how she felt when after asking when they would be leaving, Simone enlightened her to the fact they were going on to the Denbigh to see the male strippers she'd bought tickets.

Maria knew if she went and Jimmy found out there would be hell to pay. Apologising she told them she would probably call it a night after the pub. Simone wouldn't hear of it. Maria was hoping that Monica would back her up, unfortunately she didn't.

"Monica I really should go home," said Maria "Jimmy wouldn't like me going to see male strippers."

"Its women only," laughed Monica drunkenly "so how will he know? Anyway you're going, even if I have to drag you. We're not doing anything wrong, it's our hen night and we're going to have fun, regardless of whether your Jimmy likes it or not!"

Walking into the Denbigh thirty minutes later, Maria could feel butterflies in her stomach; she really didn't want to be there, especially as they stuck out like sore thumbs in their outfits. Thankfully the front tables were all taken so they had to sit at the back which suited her.

Five male strippers were gyrating on the stage. Maria watched with disbelief as a group of women tried to grab at the men's bits, especially when a couple of them even managed to get up on stage. Watching them she thought it was disgusting the way they rubbed themselves up against the strippers. Secretly wishing her friends would stop shouting things out, she felt relieved an hour later when the show finished and they made their way home.

Maria asked the cab driver to drop her and Monica off first. Although she wasn't falling over drunk, Monica had definitely had enough.

Once home, Maria suggested her going straight to bed. Fortunately Monica was too drunk to argue. A couple of minutes later, she was out cold on the bed, still wearing her outfit.

With her friend retired for the night, Maria made herself a coffee. Sitting drinking it she wondered what their future husbands were doing. If she'd have known, she wouldn't have felt so guilty about going to the Denbigh.

All the lads had taken them to a strip joint where all evening naked girls had been sitting on their laps and slobbering all over them. At one point, two girls had turned up dressed as police women. They had handcuffed the two grooms and told them the only way they would release them was if they could take the girls' garters off with their teeth. Neither man had any objections even though they knew Shane was taking photos, which he intended to hang at the club once they were developed. There had been one point during the evening when Mickey thought there might be some trouble. They had run into a couple of blokes they hadn't seen for a while, cousins John and Dave Marchant, they were well known within the London criminal world. They had done business with Nick on occasion, but since Nick's demise the others had been reluctant to continue doing business with them. It was while the stag party were drinking earlier on that they ran into the cousins. When John had asked why they hadn't been in touch, Mickey had tried tactfully to convince him that since taking over the business from Nick they were keeping things low key. Obviously feeling that he was being fobbed off, John had got a bit mouthy; had Jimmy not have opened his mouth the situation probably would have passed without any bother, but Mickey knew the moment John said he couldn't believe that Jimmy was marrying the whore that Nick kept, all hell would break lose. Ten seconds after saying it, John was picking himself up off the floor because Jimmy had head butted him. Had it not been for Shaun, the situation would have quickly spiralled out of control. Even though the cousins were outnumbered, it could still have turned nasty but with Shaun's intervention, five minutes later they were all shaking hands and drinking together.

Fortunately there were no more incidents; although Mickey had been annoyed over Jimmy's quick outburst, he could understand it. Maria was anything but a whore and had they said anything about Monica, he would have done the same.

It was gone four that morning by the time they got back to Mickey's place. Both men in a drunken stupor, they simply collapsed onto the sofas.

CHAPTER 35

It was two o'clock the following afternoon before either man stirred. It was only Jimmy's mobile ringing that woke them. Mickey noticed when Jimmy took the call he was very coy, answering just "yes" and "no" and then ending the call by saying he'd call in for them later.

Mickey had a look of curiosity when he asked who he'd been talking to on the phone. Noticing that his friend seemed secretive as though he didn't really want to tell him, he decided he would ask again later after Jimmy replied, "Just a mate."

Thirty minutes later, they were sat drinking coffee when Mickey broached the phone call again. Jimmy didn't like keeping things from him although he would have preferred not to have been asked.

"Tell you the truth Mick, it was one of the blokes I paid to follow the girls on their hen night, they took a few photos for me. I was worried. They're good looking girls Mick, I thought some blokes might try and take advantage of them."

Mickey wasn't convinced of his friend's reason for doing it and quickly told him so, asking how he'd feel if Maria did it to him. He trusted Monica and stated Jimmy should trust Maria, regardless of what they might have got up to as it was probably nothing compared to what they did at their stag do. Jimmy looked a bit sheepish when Mickey asked if it had been the photos he'd referred to when he'd said about picking something up later. Jimmy nodded. Feeling angry, Mickey told him he was lucky to have someone as lovely as Maria. He was going to phone Monica to check they were ok.

"Don't mention about the blokes Mick."

"Why would I, I can't believe you did it!"

Taking his phone out, he called Monica. A few moments later she answered. Sounding happy, she joked about him surviving the stag night.

When he asked how the hen night had gone, she said it was brilliant, but she didn't go into detail over where they'd been, just in case Jimmy was within ear shot. Happy they'd had a great time, before ending the call he arranged to pick her up within the hour.

As Mickey put his phone down, Jimmy asked if the ladies had a good time. Mickey nodded and said they had, but when Jimmy said he was glad they got home ok, Mickey couldn't bring himself to reply after what Jimmy had done, he simply said he was going to take a shower.

Forty five minutes later they were on their way back to the apartment.

Mickey pulled up outside the pub where Jimmy had arranged to meet the two men so he could pick up the photos.

As Jimmy began exiting the car, Mickey said he would be best leaving well alone and forgetting about the photos. Jimmy said he was just curious and then he tried to justify his actions by adding he had no intentions of telling Maria about them and asked Mickey to keep it secret. Mickey didn't have a problem with that; he would prefer not to have any part in it.

He waited in the car while Jimmy went in. When he returned a few minutes later, he was carrying an envelope which he put in his pocket before getting into the car. The photos weren't mentioned as they drove, Jimmy didn't even take them out to look at them.

Fifteen minutes later, the two friends entered the apartment. Spotting Monica in the lounge, Mickey walked over and kissed her. Jimmy acknowledged her then asked where Maria was. She was in the bathroom.

Maria could hear them talking, her stomach was churning for fear that Monica would let something slip, the strip club being foremost in her mind. Plucking up the courage to finally greet them, she walked out into the lounge with a smile on her face.

Instantly, Jimmy pulled her to him and calling her sexy asked if she'd had a good night. Nervously she smiled and nodded before asking if anyone wanted a drink. Jimmy said coffee, but their friends declined stating they were going back to Mickey's to crash out.

After their friends left, Maria offered him another coffee. Nodding he said his mouth felt like the bottom of a budgies cage because he had a hangover.

With Maria in the kitchen making his coffee, he took the envelope out and opening it glanced at the photos. Every one enraged him, especially when he saw what she had been wearing. Not wanting her to see them, he quickly put the envelope back before she returned.

Five minutes later they were drinking their coffee when he asked where she'd gone on her hen night. Despite feeling nervous, she tried to stay calm and said "Just a few pubs."

When he asked what she'd decided to wear, she instantly said "Trousers."

Fortunately, she had put the wedding outfit in a bin liner and thrown it in the bin. She felt quite unnerved as he continued to question her, especially when he asked if she was sure she wore trousers. Hoping to change the topic she nodded then quickly asked about his stag night. Coldly he stared at her but didn't answer. With that look she knew something was very wrong. Taking the envelope from his pocket he threw the photos at her and shouted aggressively "So who the fuck was this then Maria?"

Picking one up and looking at it, she felt panic stricken. It was of a man signing across her chest. Trembling she started to cry.

"Stop fucking crying Maria, did you listen to what I said last night, or are you that fucking stupid you didn't understand!"

She pleaded with him to let her explain, but he wasn't interested in her explaining. Standing up he pulled her to her feet and shouting demanded to know where she'd put the outfit she'd worn. Terrified she begged him not to get angry.

"Where is it Maria and don't fucking lie to me!"

Physically shaking, she nervously pointed to the bin.

"Fucking go and get it!"

"Please leave it Jimmy," she sobbed "let me explain."

Aggressively he walked over to the bin. Again she begged him to stop but he ignored her and tipped the contents of the bin onto the floor. Picking out the bin liner which had white material sticking out the top, he threw it at her and shouted "Fucking put it on!"

Too afraid to do as he'd asked, she tried to run to the bathroom, but he grabbed her by the hair causing her to lose her balance and fall backwards onto the floor. Ripping the bin liner open, he pulled the dress out and threw it down on her. Now in a terrible rage, he shouted again for her to fucking put it on. In that moment she was truly afraid of what he might do.

"You're a fucking liar Maria;" he shouted as she fumbled to dress, "you fucking knew all along what you intended to wear! What do you take me for, some sort of prick!"

"I swear Jimmy, I didn't even know about it until Simone turned up with it, she made them as a surprise for me and Monica. I told them over and over that I didn't want to wear it, but they insisted."

Coldly he stared at her before ordering her to fucking hurry up and put it on. Feeling sick as she stood in front of him, shaking with fear she began putting it on. Grabbing her, he began trying to read the signatures as he snapped "You look like a fucking whore!"

Suddenly she felt angry toward him and shouted she hadn't done anything wrong.

"If you don't fucking shut up I'm going to belt you!"

She remembered when he had promised he would never hit her, how quickly he had forgotten that. Raging with anger he shouted, "Did anyone fuck you!"

Without thinking she slapped his face and through her tears said how dare he ask her that. Immediately realising her mistake, she tried to run.

Grabbing her, he punched her in the face so hard it threw her against the wall. Hitting her back against the door frame she collapsed onto the floor. Sitting astride her he grabbed at her dress and the wedding basque she had on over it, almost tearing it in half. She was screaming, her arms and legs frantically hitting and kicking him as she desperately tried to fight him off but he was too strong.

Grabbing her hair, he banged her head on the floor. After ripping the dress off, he pinned her down, pushed her legs apart with his knees and raped her. When he finished he stood up, punched the wall and without even looking at her, walked to the front door. Opening it he stormed out, almost slamming it off the hinges.

With a searing pain in her head she just lay there stunned, asking herself why he treated her like this; she hadn't done anything to warrant it. Then she remembered all the good things about him, how for the first year he had barely raised his voice to her. What had happened to make him so angry, so jealous? Was it simply that he had a fear of marriage, or had someone broken his heart in the past? Maybe he wanted to stay single now that Della was back. Whatever the reason, she couldn't live like this. Her head was telling her to leave, but her heart was telling her to stay. Where would she go, she had no money of her own. Despite having the restaurant, everything including that ran around him. In her heart she knew something was very wrong and that she could help him, but again her head was telling her he didn't want any help.

Slowly and unsteadily, she got up and walked to the bathroom. Standing in the shower she wondered what she had ever done to deserve all the things that had happened to her. Not once in her life had she flirted or acted tarty, she could understand if she behaved like Della. She wondered if he ever treated Della the same way, somehow she doubted it. Wiping the bathroom mirror; she looked at her face, it was beginning to show a bruise from where he had hit her. Looking at her reflection, she tried to recall just how many black eyes and split lips she'd had during her life, there were just too many to remember. Her head was pounding as she stood there. It was then she asked herself if she would actually be better off dead. Had suicide not have been a sin in the eyes of God and go against her religious beliefs, she would have done it. Asking why she was allowing this to happen to her, she was stronger now than she had ever been in her life. Deep down she knew it would be in her best interests to leave and in some strange way she thought it would also help Jimmy. He wouldn't have to think about the threat from other men if she wasn't there.

Going into the bedroom, she dressed before pulling a suitcase down from on top of one of the wardrobes. With her head and face throbbing, she began to pack. Despite feeling devastated at the thought of leaving him, she began placing her clothes into the case. Finally she convinced herself that leaving would be best for everyone. When she had packed the essentials that she needed, she carried the case through to the lounge. Knowing he always kept about three hundred pounds in spare cash in the cabinet, she had no choice but to take it, but she would leave a note telling him she would send it back once she found a job.

The note read 'Dear Jimmy this is very hard for me, but I want you to know that I truly did love you and I hope one day we can be friends. Thank you for all the kind things you've done for me, especially rescuing me from Nick. Please wish Monica and Mickey all the best for their future together and to tell them I'll miss them. My dearest wish will be that one day we'll all meet up again. I hope you find true love and happiness. I'll never be able to repay you for all the wonderful things you've done for me. I'll remember you every night in my prayers and ask God to watch over you. I'm so sorry for not being able to stay with you. Love always Maria xxx'

Leaving the note on the table along with her engagement ring and her door keys, she phoned a cab. Her destination was to be St Augustus church.

Thirty minutes later she walked into the church, she felt relieved to see Father Thomas.

"Hello Maria this is a nice surprise," said the priest as she walked towards him, then noticing the bruises on her face he added, "is everything alright?"

"Hello Father, could you hear my confession please?"

The priest, looking concerned, nodded. They walked over to the confessional booth.

Once inside, she began telling him about what had happened between her and Jimmy and about the terrible man (Nick) that she had lived with before she met him. As Thomas listened to her plight, a tear ran down his cheek. Like her, he felt that Jimmy needed help because his troubles were deep rooted, probably from his childhood. When they left the confessional he asked if she would like to join him for a cup of tea. In a soft voice she thanked him and said that would be lovely.

They went into his private quarters where minutes later they sat drinking tea. When he asked if she had any idea where she would go, tearfully she shook her head.

Caringly, he touched her hand and reassuringly said she could go into any Catholic church and ask for help.

Looking sad she asked if he thought she would have made a good nun. Obviously surprised at her question, he hesitated before replying that in his opinion she would have made a wonderful nun and if she ever thought seriously about it, he would endeavour to help her.

Feeling it may be her calling, she expressed how much she would appreciate his help. Kissing his cheek she made ready to leave, stating she didn't fancy travelling alone through London at night. Feeling concerned he asked again where she was going and offered her to stay the night with him. Politely she declined, but did say she would probably head south, maybe to the coast. There were lots of hotels and restaurants in Brighton, so her hope was to get some casual work, maybe even live in.

Before she left, she embraced and thanked him before asking if he would watch over Jimmy for her. Thomas could see the sadness and apprehension on her face when he asked if she was sure about leaving. When she nodded, he passed her his bible, he wanted her to have it. Despite the fact she had already packed her own, she would treasure it always.

When she left the church, he watched her until she disappeared from sight.

At the train station, she bought a one way ticket to Brighton. Sitting quietly on a bench reading the bible Thomas had given her; she looked around at the people in the station. She couldn't help but notice that many of them looked sad and destitute. Trying not to stare at them; she reflected on her own life. Maybe she could have a place in this world as a nun, at least then she wouldn't have to worry about men because she would be married to God.

Finally the train arrived. She sat in a carriage with a young couple. They were kissing and cuddling. They reminded her of her time with Jimmy. Without a doubt she would miss the tenderness they so often shared, but she was confident she was doing the right thing.

It was just before nine when she arrived in Brighton so her first priority was to find a bed and breakfast.

The first two she called at were full, but luckily the third one had a single room available. She paid for three nights in advance. Once she had unpacked a few things, she laid on the bed. For the first time in her life she felt at peace. Lying there, she decided that after breakfast the following morning she would try and find a job. Eventually she fell asleep.

CHAPTER 36

Jimmy returned to the apartment around midnight fully expecting her to be waiting for him. Then he found the note. Reading it, his first emotion was anger; how dare she leave him but after reading it again his next emotion was one of total despair and sadness. After all he had put her through, she still wrote nice things, even thanking him for rescuing her from Nick. Feeling ashamed, he sat at the table and sobbed. Never in his life had he cried like that. The only decent thing in his life had been her, now he'd driven her away and he hated himself.

Clutching the note, he felt a panic race through his body, he had never experienced such an over whelming feeling of fear. A sudden need to vomit came over him, he rushed into the bathroom. In his mind he kept trying to tell himself he would never intentionally have hurt her, he loved her so much, his life was nothing without her. Then he thought about her being alone and wondered if she was alright. Was she afraid, where would she go? For the first time ever as an adult, he didn't know what to do, so as always he phoned Mickey.

Mickey had never heard his friend in such a panic, barely able to understand what he was saying because he was talking so fast and obviously crying. When Mickey finally got him to calm down, he said they would be there in fifteen minutes.

When Mickey ended the call he started to tell Monica what had happened. She dressed quickly and within minutes they were on their way to Jimmy's.

Walking into his apartment fifteen minutes later, they could see him pacing up and down, only stopping when Mickey spoke to him and asked what happened.

"Maria's left me Mick; I don't know where she's gone!"

Still clutching the note, he was almost hysterical as he repeated over and over it was his fault. Monica asked him to tell them exactly what had happened.

Obviously embarrassed, he tried to talk about the events which had led to Maria leaving. Intently she listened as he confessed about the two men he'd paid to follow them.

"You don't deserve Maria!" she snapped "how could you do that? Did you have any part in this Mickey?"

Fortunately, Jimmy backed him up when he swore to her he hadn't.

"Come on babe you're the detective," said Mickey "where has she gone?"

"Perhaps she doesn't want to be found after the way you have treated her," she replied looking at Jimmy "now I know why she was so nervous about our hen night. I hope you're pleased with yourself Jimmy! If it's any consolation to you she didn't enjoy herself; she was terrified every time a bloke spoke to her. How could you treat her like that, it's beyond me. She never did anything but tell everyone how much she loved you!"

"I know what I did was wrong," said Jimmy "don't you think I feel bad enough without you giving me a lecture? When we find her, I'll make it up to her. I'll never hurt her again."

"I should think you would make it up to her! Just for the record Jimmy, she is one of the sweetest, kindest, most decent people I have ever met. My only regret is that I didn't see what was going on; if I had, maybe I could have helped her!"

Jimmy got up to use the bathroom, they could hear him vomiting.

Once alone, Mickey asked her to go easy on him, he'd never seen him like this and he was concerned. He knew Jimmy had issues from his past.

"Issues!" stated Monica, "I should think if anyone's got issues it's Maria! I can't even begin to imagine what a dreadful life that poor girl's had. If she's got any sense she'll stay gone!"

"Keep your voice down babe. Jimmy was treated badly as a child, terrible things have happened to him too. He's never told anyone except me, but his past still haunts him. It's not only Maria who deserves our sympathy. One day I might tell you his story, then you'll change your opinion, but until that day I'm asking you never to mention it. We need to find Maria before something bad happens to either one of them."

With his words, he noticed she seemed a little less hostile towards Jimmy when he came out of the bathroom and she politely asked to see the note. Taking it out of his pocket he handed it to her.

Reading it, she started to cry, unable to hold back her tears. When she finished she handed the note to Mickey. While he read it, she talked to Jimmy.

"It's unlikely we'll find her tonight, it's already past one o'clock. Try not to worry Jimmy, I'm sure Maria would have gone somewhere safe; she certainly wouldn't be walking the streets. My advice to you is stay by the phone tonight just in case she rings. First thing tomorrow morning I think we should contact Father Thomas, I'm confident Maria wouldn't leave London without saying good bye to him. Can either of you think of any where she might have gone?"

They both shook their heads.

Jimmy looked totally exhausted when he stated Maria had no one but him. Wanting to keep the house phone free in case she called, Monica rang the local hospitals and the police station from her mobile. Jimmy looked worried at the prospect of Maria being injured or worse. Thankfully Monica's inquiries drew a blank. When she suggested making them a coffee and left the room, Jimmy asked Mickey if he thought Maria could ever forgive him. In an effort to comfort him, Mickey thought they could work it out but Jimmy would need to trust her, especially as she'd never given him reason not to.

Jimmy swore if she gave him another chance, he'd make everything right.

They waited up all night in the hope she would call. By six o'clock that morning Jimmy was beside himself and unable to wait any longer, he phoned Father Thomas.

The phone rang and rang before Thomas finally answered, his voice sounded as though he had just woken up.

Apologising for calling so early, Jimmy needed to know if he'd spoken to Maria. Relief was how he felt when Thomas said he had the previous day when she went to see him. Jimmy asked if they could come over to the church to talk to him.

The priest was waiting when they pulled up ten minutes later.

Jimmy pleaded with him to tell him where she'd gone, but he believed Thomas when he said he didn't know. Monica asked if there was anything he could remember that may help them.

"I will not be able to discuss anything that was said in confession, only what she said outside to me as her friend. She was very upset, she talked about becoming a nun and I think she was serious. I'm sorry, but there isn't much to tell you, except she was hoping to catch a train when she left. She didn't want to be in London on her own at night.

She was going down to the south coast in the hope she could find work there."

They all thanked him for his help. Then just as they began to walk away, Thomas called to them and said she had mentioned Brighton.

Suddenly their fortunes changed; at least now they had somewhere to look. Although it would be like looking for a needle in a hay stack, it was a place to start.

From the back seat of the car, Monica worked out from the times Thomas gave them that Maria would have arrived in Brighton quite late the previous night. Her first priority would have been to find somewhere to stay. Most likely somewhere near to the station. Chances were she was staying at a guest house near there.

Jimmy grabbed her head through the seats, kissed her and stated she was a fucking genius!

"Not only a genius," said Mickey "but a great detective!"

They drove to Brighton station. Parking the car they continued on foot, trying guest house after guest house, but to no avail. Jimmy was beginning to lose heart.

"We may have a result," said Monica as she returned from a particular house "one of the owners from a B and B said a young woman checked in last night, her description was sketchy, but she did remember the girl only had one suitcase and that she was carrying a bible. She paid for three nights in advance; but she left this morning straight after breakfast. I'm confident it was Maria."

The men agreed.

For the next three hours they walked up and down the sea front looking in every restaurant and café to see if she was asking for work. Finally Monica said she must rest and eat something.

It was as they sat down at a cafe on the pier, something happened by chance. Mickey looked along the beach. The weather was overcast, so there were just a handful of people on the beach, but to his amazement he spotted

Maria sitting on her own reading the bible Father Thomas had given her.

Jimmy felt overwhelmed as he looked to where Mickey was pointing and Monica said it was definitely Maria.

Jimmy was on the verge of tears when he asked them to wait while he went and spoke to her.

"Just don't push her Jimmy," said Mickey as his friend stood up to leave.

Maria was totally unaware they were nearby; she hadn't even noticed Jimmy walking along the beach until he startled her when he sat down beside her. Unable to suppress his emotions, he cried as he looked at her. He couldn't help but notice how calm she appeared. Jimmy knelt down beside her on the shingle and through his tears, repeatedly told her how sorry he was and how much he loved her. Maria smiled as he tried to tell her how he felt, but through his crying she found him difficult to understand. Feeling empathy for him, she asked what he was doing there. She wasn't surprised when he said he'd come to take her home. Looking lovingly at him, she squeezed his hand and stated she wasn't going back.

At that moment she expected him to lose his temper. Surprisingly he didn't, instead he cried and begged her to go home.

With her heart breaking for him, she was fighting back her own tears as she asked him not to cry and it would be better for everyone if they'd stayed apart.

"Not for me it won't, I love you so much; I'll die without you Maria. Please come home babe, I'll do anything you ask. Please, just say you'll forgive me."

Gently she touched his face and said she'd already forgiven him. Jimmy said if that were true why wouldn't she give him another chance, he would never give up on her; she was the only woman he wanted.

"I love you too Jimmy, but I'm staying here. You wouldn't understand even if I tried to explain and I don't want a scene on the beach. Just go home Jimmy."

"Babe I promise I won't do anything to upset you, just tell me why Maria. I don't understand. We love each other, so why won't you come home?"

In the hope of stopping his constant pleading, she changed the topic and asked how he'd found her. Jimmy pointed to the café and explained how it was Monica who'd seen her. She could see their friends waving at them as he asked why she'd chosen Brighton. Her answer was simple. With the exception of the holiday Mickey gave them for her birthday, it was the only place she'd ever been.

Feeling his chance was slipping away, he begged her to give him another chance or at least tell him why she couldn't.

"Last night Jimmy was the first time I can ever remember being able to lie down and not have anyone make any demands on me. I don't expect you to understand, but for me it was wonderful."

Looking at her for the first time since they had met, he truly realised how hard her life had been. All he wanted to do was put his arms around her and tell her that everything would be alright. How could he have said and done such terrible things to this beautiful, loving young woman. Unable to hold back his tears he broke down again. Trying to comfort him, she gently placed her hand on his shoulder and in a gentle voice told him, if the church would accept her, she was going to join a convent. Seeing the look of total despair on his face, she tried to lighten the mood by saying it was her calling and at least he would never have to worry about her meeting another man. Her words made him feel sick to the pit of his stomach; he knew he had driven her to such despair that she was going to hide herself away from society. Unable to accept what she'd said, he squeezed her hand.

"Please babe, I'm begging you, please come home, don't end what we have Maria, surely its worth fighting for?"

No longer able to hold back her own tears, she began to cry as she told him go back to London and just leave her alone.

He could tell she was beginning to weaken when he said he would never leave her and he would die if that's what it took for her to believe how much he loved her. He swore that he wanted to marry her more than anything in the world and have lots of babies with her.

Watching the tears begin to trickle down her face, he started crying as he said she was the only person who really knew him and he couldn't live without her, he would rather be dead.

Just like him, tears were flowing down her cheeks; she knew how desperate he felt. Summoning all her courage, she told him to stop; she couldn't listen to him anymore. There were things she had to do, so she suggested he went back and joined the others. Refusing, he stated he wanted to stay with her and questioned as to what she could possibly have to do. Knowing he didn't believe her, she explained she was meeting a restaurant manager about a job and didn't want to be late. Instantly he snapped at her, stating she didn't need to work in a restaurant, she had her own.

"It's not mine Jimmy, it was never really mine, it's yours just like everything else. It doesn't matter anyway, you can sell Maria's restaurant if you want to. I certainly won't need it when I become a nun."

He knew what she had just said was true. Lowering his head into his hands he cried and told her she was wrong, the restaurant was hers. Desperately, he pleaded with her to tell him what he could do to make her go home with him. Placing her arm around him and looking sad, she said he didn't really need her, there were lots of young girls who would want him. Totally distressed he didn't want anyone else, only her.

"Please stop it Jimmy it's over. I'll always have love in my heart for you and I'll always be grateful to you, but I can't live that life anymore."

"Please babe, I promise you if you give me just one last chance I'll prove to you just how wonderful your life can be."

Waiting for her to reply, he just watched as she sat there with tears streaming down her face. Wiping her face with his hand, he asked why she was crying.

When she didn't answer him, but simply shook her head, he asked her again. Still she sat silently.

"Considering you've been so adamant about not coming back Maria, I'm surprised you're so upset."

A few moments passed then with her beautiful eyes all red and puffy, she looked lovingly at him.

"You wouldn't understand Jimmy and I find it hard to talk about it, but for most of my life I have been abused in one way or another. I've been beaten, starved, at times denied all my human rights, raped and treated like an animal and I just can't take anymore. I don't expect you to understand, but I just want peace now, that's why I want to become a nun."

"I know exactly what you mean babe. I've been there; my father did all those things to me."

Raising her head, she looked at him with disbelief. Jimmy knew he'd hit a nerve because for the first time since meeting her on the beach she really appeared to be listening to him.

"If you don't believe me ask Mickey, that's why Den ordered the hit on my father. They're the only people who know, but now you do."

Patiently he waited for her to say something, hoping against all hope that she would give him another chance. His heart was racing as they sat there looking at one another. Barely a few seconds had passed when she put her arms around him. Resting his head on her chest as she held him tight in her arms, he sobbed like a baby. It was as though years of pent up anger were flooding out of him. Several minutes went by; he could barely catch his breath when she lovingly said everything would be fine and for him to cry and just let it go. Barely coherent, he said nothing would ever be right if they were not together.

A feeling of total relief surged through him, he was trembling, but he couldn't stop hugging and kissing her when she said she couldn't make him any promises, but she would go back to London with him. Maria was well aware he would see it as everything going back to how it was. She needed to convince him it wouldn't, so again she repeated about not making promises and how they would need to talk a lot more before she committed to anything. When he asked if she was referring to the wedding, she nodded.

Not wanting to push the subject, he knew the time wasn't right, he just wanted her home.

Taking a tissue from her bag, she passed it to him to wipe his face. Looking at her, he noticed the bruises as she swept her hair back. Gently he touched her face.

"I promise as God is my witness, I'll never lay a hand on you again babe."

"Come on Jimmy let's go home."

Despite what he'd said, she knew their problems were far from over.

Mickey drove back to London. Jimmy slept most of the journey with his head resting on her shoulder as they travelled in the back. They were all very quiet. It wasn't until they pulled up outside the apartment he woke up.

Monica kissed her friend on the cheek and said she would call her.

"Thank God we found you babe," said Mickey as he kissed her "I couldn't have taken another night like last night."

Tearfully, Maria apologised for all the trouble she had caused them. Mickey was the first to tell her not to be daft; they were all worried about her. Looking at her, Mickey asked himself how anyone, especially his best friend, could treat her so badly. Monica had been right when she'd said she was a lovely person.

Even on the drive back to his place with Monica after dropping the others off, he thought about Maria. She never deserved any of the terrible things she had endured, she was everything that was good and kind and loving. Then for a brief moment, he wished they hadn't found her simply because she would have found peace by becoming a nun, and if anyone deserved it, she did.

Inside the apartment, Maria offered to make him something to eat. Jimmy wasn't hungry, but he was tired. Promising her he wouldn't want sex, he asked if she would lie down on the bed with him so he could hold her.

Smiling she held out her hand. They walked toward the bedroom.

Lying on the bed with her in his arms, Maria rested her head on his chest. In the relaxed atmosphere, he asked if she'd been serious about becoming a nun. He felt her nod as she said yes because she felt it was her calling; she wanted to help save people.

"You're already doing that, you've saved me. I know I have no right to ask, but do you think you might still marry me on Saturday?"

When she didn't answer, he asked again. Knowing his temper was still just under the surface, she didn't want to say anything that might anger him.

"Up until yesterday Jimmy, I wanted to marry you more than anything, but now it feels different. I had often questioned why God had allowed all those terrible things to happen to me, I would pray and pray for an answer. Then when I left yesterday, I watched the people at the train station, the down and outs here and in Brighton. It was then I realised, had I not have suffered myself how could I possibly connect with those people. Perhaps God had intended all along for me to be a nun, that's why everything's happened the way it has."

When he suggested that God may only have intended for her to save him, she couldn't give him an answer so she suggested he asked Father Thomas.

Pulling her closer to him, he snuggled his head onto her breasts, "Please don't leave me babe. I'm a better person when you're here. Hopefully you love me enough to think I'm worth saving. I know I don't deserve another chance, especially after all the terrible things I've done but I love you babe."

"I love you too and I know you're a good person Jimmy, I only doubt myself."

Confused by what she'd just said, he lifted his head and stared at her before questioning what she meant because she was an angel. Lovingly, she stroked the side of his face and stated it wasn't important. It was important to him and he asked her to tell him.

"Ok, but I expect you'll laugh. For the first time in my life I experienced jealousy. It was when Della kissed you. I felt terrible, but for that instant I loathed her."

"Believe me babe; you've got nothing to be jealous of. If it makes you feel any better, if it had been a bloke who had done that to you I would have ripped his fucking head off!"

Despite his joke, she looked at him and said as this was a day for home truths; she wanted him to know how she resented his mistrust of her. He of all people should know she would never be interested in anyone else. Just as she'd anticipated he instantly stated he did trust her. If that were true she wanted to know why he'd become so much worse in the last couple of months. From the moment he answered, she knew he was keeping something back because he couldn't look at her.

"More than anything in my life, I want to marry you Maria. Stupidly I thought by making you fear me, you would be too afraid to even look at another man. Truth is babe; I'm terrified of losing you, I see every man as a threat. I promise I'll try not to think like that anymore.

Even if you call off the wedding, I'll wait for as long as you need to, just as long as we're together."

Accepting what he'd said, she asked where he'd gone when he'd left the apartment the previous night. Her first reaction to his reply was shock when he said he'd been to the cemetery to talk to his mum. There in the darkness he'd asked her to ask God to help him make things right with Maria, although he didn't know she'd left him then.

"Obviously God listened Jimmy."

Rolling over onto his side, before propping himself up on his elbow, he looked down upon her, and with sincerity told her she'd never know or understand how much he loved her.

Then he kissed her tenderly. When she responded, he so wanted to make love to her, but he remembered what he said about just needing her to lay with him. Fighting his desire to touch her, he refrained from being intimate. Maria knew he was struggling to keep his promise which was why she asked him to make love to her.

For the rest of the night they kissed and touched each other, making love until the early hours of the morning.

Maria was up first the next day. As she prepared their breakfast she reflected on the previous day. In some strange way, she felt as though she'd achieved something, quite what she didn't know, but there had been a break through with Jimmy. The fact he'd told her about the abuse he'd endured at the hands of his father was a positive thing. For the first time she had a feeling of complete calm, never before had she been so in control of her life. In her heart she wanted everything to work out with him; she loved him with every fibre of her being, but for the first time ever she felt she had options, not an experience she was used to.

Gently she woke him up, taking him in a cup of tea and telling him breakfast would be ready in five minutes. Looking at her, she was the best person he had ever known. Watching her leave the bedroom, he asked why he'd allowed himself to come so close to losing the one thing in his life that was truly wonderful.

Joining her a few minutes later, he sat at the table as she attentively poured him another tea and served his breakfast.

When he asked if he could have a kiss, without replying she leaned over and kissed him. When she moved away, he took her hand preventing her from leaving and told her how truly sorry he was for what he'd done.

Seeing he was calm, she wondered whether or not to broach the subject of his father's abuse, her thoughts being, she would have to at some point so it might as well be then. Just as she was about to speak, he asked if she'd thought any more about the wedding. He knew he shouldn't pressure her, but he wanted to marry her more than anything in the world.

Reaching over, she took his hand and squeezing it gently said she wasn't sure, things had changed. Knowing she was referring to the events of the previous night, he gave his word he would never treat her badly again. All he wanted was another chance.

"It's not about giving you another chance Jimmy, I came back didn't I? It's just there are things we need to discuss before I'll even consider making such a huge commitment. Like your temper and the way you've become so sexually aggressive, it frightens me. I think all your problems stem from your father."

When he quickly looked away from her, she knew he was embarrassed so she told him to finish his breakfast but added he didn't have to talk to her, but she felt he should talk to someone.

Without saying anything, he just looked at her and shook his head. Now she wasn't about to let the issue go, especially if she was going to spend the rest of her life with him. When she asked if he'd ever thought about seeing a counsellor, he shook his head but said nothing. In the hope of reassuring him, she squeezed his hand and smiled as she waited for him to say something, but it wasn't the answer she'd hoped for when he stated firmly, he could never talk to anyone about it.

With his words and the look on his face, she imagined the terrified young boy he must have been, knowing as she did what it felt like to be terrified and powerless. Wanting so much to help him conquer the demons from his past, without hesitation she assured him he could always talk to her in absolute confidence and she felt the same about Father Thomas, she knew he would always help him.

His reply wasn't what she'd hoped for when he stated that once they were married he'd be fine.

Although she disagreed, she decided to leave debating it; simply because it was obvious he wasn't going to talk to her, especially as he'd changed the subject. What she'd already said would have to be enough for that day. After asking if he had anything planned and his reply being as long as he was with her they could do whatever she liked, she suggested spending the day together. They didn't have to do anything in particular. Liking that idea, he suggested taking a picnic over to the house and eating in the garden. Maria thought it was a lovely idea.

After breakfast they showered together. He was very tender with her as they sponged each other down. Sex in the shower was something they both enjoyed, so it was inevitable that morning would be no exception. Gently sponging her back, he asked again about the wedding. Although she knew he was desperate for her to say yes, she needed to be sure, knowing this would not be an easy marriage simply because she knew his new found trust in her would be short lived. There would hopefully be children somewhere in their future; so she would need to be absolutely certain. For those reasons, she asked him to give her time. Apologising, he said she was there and that was all that mattered.

Just before they left, he called Mickey to let him know they were going over to the house and he would be turning his phone off, so if there was an emergency he'd have to call at the house. Mickey was happy to hear they were working things out. They just wanted time on their own, preferably without any interruptions. Mickey understood and said he'd see them the following day.

On the drive to the house, he kept squeezing her knee and telling her he loved her. Throughout the journey, he kept reassuring her that everything would be ok, making several references to the wedding.

When they arrived at the house he still dropped hints, like hopefully the next time they came to the house, he'd be carrying her over the threshold as Mrs Dixon and wouldn't it be wonderful if their children grew up here.

Trying to get away from the topic of the wedding, she asked if they should eat at the table in the garden, or have a proper picnic with a blanket on the ground.

"Definitely the blanket babe," he said with a grin.

An hour later, they were sitting on the blanket in the warm sunshine when she told him it was her first picnic.

It was Jimmy's too, but he couldn't help but add he was looking forward to taking their kids on picnics.

Maria knew, although he meant it, there was an undercurrent as to why he said it; he needed her to reassure him the wedding was still on. Leaning over he touched her face, then placing his hand behind her neck gently pulled her head towards him and kissed her passionately. Maria giggled when saying she hoped their neighbours couldn't see them.

Jimmy didn't care and said they didn't really have any neighbours. Raising her eyebrows, she pointed to a couple of houses whose bedroom windows overlooked their garden.

"Oh well," he said "looks like we'll have to go indoors to make love."

"I thought we were here to spend quality time together?" she giggled as she tickled him.

"Don't I always give you good quality, and let's not forget quantity!"

"Jimmy Dixon you've got a one track mind!"

Tickling him again, she could feel him becoming aroused, so with a grin she suggested going back inside the house.

Maria knew that to him every problem they had could be resolved with sex; it wasn't the same for her.

Back in the house, he led her by the hand up the stairs, stopping on the landing to kiss her before pulling her T shirt off over her head and removing her bra. He was breathing heavily as he hurried to undo her jeans. Lovingly she told him to slow down. There was no hurry they had all day.

Picking her up, with her arms secured around his neck, he carried her to the bedroom. With a giggle she said they could have made love on the landing.

"But we haven't got mirrors on the landing babe!"

Laying her on the bed with her feet facing the headboard, he kissed her. Then taking the pillows, he placed them at the bottom off the bed under her head. That way he could watch as they made love in three different wardrobe mirrors. Jimmy had introduced her to the real world of love making; she had no one other than Nick to compare him to which was a totally different thing. Nick had only ever wanted to please himself; he got sexual pleasure from hurting her. The actual time between him penetrating her and coming was barely minutes; it was the terrible things he did before that he liked. Jimmy was different; apart from his temper he was loving and passionate, always keen to satisfy her. They enjoyed using sex toys, but only for pleasure. This day would be no exception as he was desperate to please her. After tying her hands loosely to the headboard he slowly kissed her body all over before pushing her legs apart and giving her oral sex. Maria fully expected him to enter her after she came, but instead he surprised her when he took a vibrator from the bedside cabinet and seductively rolled it over her mouth. He watched as she licked it before he took it away and rolled it down over her nipple before finally pleasuring her with it. With her hands still tied, he finally fucked her. Lying together exhausted, he untied her so they could cuddle.

He confessed to her that he'd wanted Justin to put a mirror on the ceiling above the bed but he wasn't sure if she'd like it.

The moment she said it would have been ok, she wouldn't have minded, he said maybe they could try to have it done before the wedding then.

Despite his happy banter, she realised it was yet another reference to them getting married. Feeling she had to say something, she said she knew he needed an answer about whether they'd get married or not, but she needed be sure. To her, marriage would be a lifelong commitment.

"And me babe" said Jimmy "I love you more than anything, but I can understand how you feel. Believe me babe if I could take back the things I've done to you I would in a heartbeat. I wouldn't blame you if you didn't want to marry me, but one thing I can promise you if you do; I will love you 'til the day I die and I promise I'll never hurt you again."

"Jimmy, don't make promises you know you can't keep. We both know your jealousy isn't going to go away."

"You're probably right babe, but I'm sure I can control it."

Gently stroking his face, she looked at him and knew at that moment in time, he truly meant what he was saying. Realistically, she also knew it probably wouldn't be long before something would make him jealous again and his dark side would surface. Feeling relaxed with him, she tried to tell him about her fears; but he was in denial over his outbursts.

"This is what I mean Jimmy, you're trying to justify your temper, you're in total denial, you need help and I don't think I'm qualified to give it. You told me before you would never let me leave you once we were married. You said you would see me dead first, surely you must realise that is not a normal thing to say?"

"I know I shouldn't have said it and I even feel angry towards myself for thinking the way I do. I don't know why I do and say those dreadful things, especially to you babe."

For the first time, she thought that maybe they could talk about it without him become aggressive. Rallying all her courage, she asked if the horrible things he'd said and done to her were things his father used to do and say to his mother.

She knew she'd hit a nerve when in a raised voice, he ordered her to stop asking because it was about him and not his mother. Maria wasn't about to leave it and said she believed he'd seen and heard his father abusing his mother and that was why he did them.

He didn't answer straight away, but she could see his breathing beginning to labour when he aggressively shouted he fucking hated his father and he wasn't like him.

"I know Jimmy, but you were afraid of him. You knew what he was capable of; you must have felt so helpless."

Waiting for his reply, she felt him clench his fist under the duvet, but she was not deterred as she placed her arm across his chest to hold him.

"This is what I mean Jimmy. Just look at you, I can feel the anger coming from you. I only want to help you, but I can't if you won't talk to me."

Sitting up quickly, he began to get out of bed but she pulled his arm and asked him to stay.

"I can't do this Maria! You've got no fucking idea what you're asking of me!"

Since living with him, she knew he had issues he'd never told her about, but this was it, if their marriage was to have any chance, she couldn't back down now. For both their sakes, all she was asking for was the truth.

Jumping out of the bed with his fist clenched, he arrogantly snapped at her.

"You're asking me to talk about things I've kept buried for years, things that are too painful to remember!"

Quickly getting out of the bed, she grabbed hold of him and tearfully said she loved him and wanted them to have a future together, he'd carried this alone for long enough.

"What is it you want to hear Maria! That my mother knew what my father was like, that she heard me begging him to stop? The nights when he would come home drunk and beat us, or the nights when my mother would lock herself in the bathroom, knowing my father would take it out on me! Have you any idea what it feels like for a ten year old boy to be held down by his father and raped!"

In his anger he turned and punched the wall, tears streaming down his face as he struggled to breathe.

"Let it go Jimmy, stop blaming yourself, you were a little boy. What could you do?"

"I could have stabbed him if only I'd had the courage. I could have put an end to it, but I was afraid!"

Now he was really struggling to breath. She felt concerned for him and told him to calm down, take some deep breaths.

Unable to reply, he just burst into tears and sobbed. In his mind he was reliving the whole terrible nightmare of his father abusing him. The terrible pain he felt after every attack, the night tremors when he was too afraid to go to sleep in case his father come into his room threatening to kill him, unless he did what he wanted.

Suddenly he pulled away from her and rushed into the bathroom, instantly she followed him. Standing behind him as he leaned over the toilet and vomited, gently rubbing his back she reassured him everything would be alright, he just needed to let it go.

Several minutes passed before he stopped being sick. Still shaking, he washed his face and cleaned his teeth before walking back into the bedroom with her.

Jimmy sat down on the bed while she stood naked in front of him. Putting his arms around her waist, he held her tight as he pressed his head against her tummy. For the first time in years, he felt a sense of relief. Unable to control his sobbing, softly she held his head against her.

"That's it baby, let it all out," she said tearfully "I'll always be here for you Jimmy. I love you, we can work this out. You're a good man; you're not like your father."

For the first time, she felt his aggression subside without the need for him to act violently or force himself on her. Lovingly she asked him to get back into bed and lie down. Moments later, she climbed in next to him; this would be the test to see if he didn't need sex. Still sobbing, he held her tight and begged her not to leave him, he had nothing without her, he loved her totally.

A wave of relief flowed over him when she said she wanted to be with him for the rest of her life and she would help him deal with the past.

"Now you know my terrible secret Maria, do you still feel the same about me? Knowing what my father did to me can you bear to be with me?"

"Do you really think that would make any difference to me? With everything you know about me, I think that makes us soul mates, don't you?"

As he looked at her, he had a strange feeling of calm. Seizing the moment, he asked if she would please marry him on Saturday.

"I will" she giggled "but only if Justin can fit the mirror by then!"

Gently he pushed her over and rolled on top of her, kissing her through his tears, he promised she wouldn't regret it.

When he finally stopped crying, she could see the pain of almost thirty years of silence etched on his face. Finally facing his demons had taken its toll on him, yet in some strange way he looked at peace. At last someone had told him none of what had happened was his fault; he had carried the guilt for long enough.

Gazing up at him, she lovingly touched his face and asked him to make love to her.

Moments later he was inside her. Finally she felt she had her Jimmy back.

They spent the rest of the day in bed talking about their future together. After all those years of silence, he was finally able to talk about his family. To his mother, he had been a relief from the rapes and the beatings she endured. In some strange way, he could even understand why she had tried to pretend that it wasn't happening. Even her suicide wasn't all down to what his father had done; it was also because of her guilt over Jimmy. Knowing how important her faith was to her, he knew how desperate she must have been to have taken her own life. Despite her unwavering belief in God, she was prepared to commit the ultimate sin of suicide. Regardless, he had still loved his mother, but he also felt hatred towards her because she'd been aware what was happening. Although they had never spoken about it, he still questioned as to why she hadn't protected him, especially now, because he knew if Maria ever found herself in that type of situation, she would do anything to protect her children, as would he.

Eventually he fell asleep with her cuddled up to him. In her mind she felt today had been a turning point in their lives, but she wasn't so naïve as to think from then on everything would be a bed of roses, more on the lines of a fresh start. She would be his counsellor if that's what it would take for him to let go of his past. Watching him sleep, she noticed how peaceful he looked. Convinced she had found her soul mate, she believed that through all the painful events of their pasts, God had brought them together. This was her calling, to love him.

They didn't leave the house until nine that evening. Maria suggested getting fish and chips on the way home. She noticed that he seemed a bit quiet as he drove, but that was only to be expected considering the last couple of days.

Back at their apartment as they ate she asked if he was alright. Before answering her, he hesitated; it was as though he wasn't sure whether to say what he obviously wanted to. Reaching over and taking her hand, he looked at her and said he wanted to tell her he would never hurt their children.

Instantly she asked why he'd said that as the thought had never even entered her head.

"I've heard people say that children of abuse can often go on to abuse. I would never want any child to experience the terrible things I had. I want our children to have the type of life Mickey and Fay had, with loving parents. One final thing on the topic, I think I should warn you, if anyone ever so much as looked at my kids in a sexual way; I wouldn't hesitate to beat them to death!"

"I know that" said Maria with a big grin on her face. "Our children will be loved Jimmy, that's one thing I'd never doubt."

Having said all he needed to, he changed the subject completely and asked if she fancied a jacuzzi.

Two hours later, he was lying in the bubbling water watching her as she undressed. By the time she was actually getting into the bath, he was almost at fever pitch. From the moment she sat down his hands were all over her. Slowly she lowered herself onto him as he took her nipple into his mouth. Deliberately she moved up and down him slowly and seductively, although she could sense he wanted her to be quicker and more forceful. Caressing his head to her breast with one hand, she placed her other hand into the water and gently began touching herself. Jimmy was quick to move his hand down to help her. Feeling her body nearing to orgasm, she moved quicker.

Leaving him stimulating her, she put both her arms around his neck as she moved on him. Her body now jerking, he squeezed her buttocks to increase their pleasure. Gradually they stopped. Totally satisfied she moved off of him and sat between his legs. Her breasts were just under the water line; gently he caressed them as he kissed her neck and told her she was wonderful and he couldn't wait to marry her.

CHAPTER 37

They were woken by the house phone ringing. The time was a little after nine that morning. Jimmy listened to whoever was on the line for a few seconds.

"That would be fine," said Jimmy "thanks for calling."

Because of the way he'd spoken, she knew it wasn't Mickey or one of the lads. It was Virginia Hollingsworth's secretary; she wanted to see him and Mickey again. She'd scheduled an appointment for three o'clock the following day. It was only to go over their statements, as she was hoping to take it to court within the next four weeks.

Everything sounded as though it was moving along nicely and four weeks was very quick, although seeing Samuels banged up couldn't come quick enough for Jimmy. Maria felt the same way, referring to Samuels as a horrid, creepy little man.

Jimmy picked his phone up and switching it on, noticed there were four missed calls. Putting it onto speaker phone so she could listen, the first call was from Shaun, a brief message to say that they were going to take the pub. Then there were three from Mickey, 'hope you two had a good day at the house yesterday? If you've got any energy left, I've got four complementary tickets for the Lion King tonight; thought Maria would enjoy it.' The second said

'Let us know about the show by five, and the final message said 'Virginia's office called.'

Jimmy asked her if she wanted to see the Lion King. When she excitedly nodded her head, he called Mickey to say they would love to accept his offer, he also confirmed the meeting with Virginia.

After Mickey told him the appointment was fine, he went on to say the Lion King also included a meal in the West End, compliments of him. When he asked how things were going and if the wedding was back on, he laughed when Jimmy said of course it was Maria couldn't get enough of him. Jimmy arranged to pick them up about half five.

Once the call ended, Mickey told Monica the good news. She was happy to hear the celebrations were back on but said she'd need to spend time with Maria as they needed to go over a few last details concerning the wedding. That wouldn't be a problem as he and Jimmy could check in on the clubs if she wanted to spend the following evening with her.

He was curious when Monica said that would be great, but could he do her a favour and not go to Sweet Cheeks in case Della was there. If Maria thought Jimmy was seeing her it could throw a spanner in the works.

"You're right babe I never gave it a thought. Della's nothing but an old tart, but I wouldn't put anything past her, especially where Jimmy's concerned. If she thought she could cause trouble between him and Maria, she would. Della always saw herself as the next Mrs Dixon, but Jimmy only saw her as a Friday night fuck."

"Eloquently put darling!

Back at their apartment, Jimmy and Maria were talking about having the evening out with their friends. Joking with him, she asked if she could wear a dress or would he prefer a suit of armour.

"Very funny, tonight gorgeous you can wear whatever you like. As long as you're with me whatever you choose will be fine babe. The West End won't know what's hit it. No doubt you'll outshine the cast."

They spent the rest of the day packing items they wanted to take to the house. It seemed to her that he was calmer; she hoped it was due to their talking about his past but only time would tell.

It was almost four o'clock when he reminded her they had to leave about five to pick up the others. Maria left the room to get ready.

It was approaching five when she finally reappeared. As always she looked beautiful; wearing a figure hugging midnight blue strapless dress, black jacket and black high heeled shoes. Her hair was pulled up at the sides with two matching gold slides. Standing in front of him, she waited for his reaction.

"Fuck me babe, you look great! Maybe we should have a cosy night in?"

"Never mind that, do you like it and more importantly is it appropriate for the theatre?"

Waiting for his answer, she thought to herself that the last thing she wanted was him thinking she was drawing attention to herself. Relieved, she smiled when he said she looked fucking beautiful, but she did ask if he was sure because she didn't want him changing his mind once they were there.

"Truthfully babe, you look fucking good enough to eat. I'll be honest with you, if I wasn't going with you tonight, I wouldn't want you wearing it. Honest babe the dress looks lovely, but just out of curiosity when did you buy it?"

It had been a gift from Monica as a thank you for letting her stay after she was discharged for the hospital. He thought it had been a nice gesture and all the more reason for her to wear it that night.

They picked the others up just before half five.

Monica said the dress looks fabulous. Maria repaid the compliment, telling her she looked stunning.

"I agree," said Mickey "you both look breath taking tonight. We should be so lucky hey Jimmy, with these two beauties."

Jimmy agreed.

During the show, Jimmy was aware that several men eyed Maria up, but he never said anything, although throughout the performance he'd sat with his arm round her and kissed her cheek every now and then. Maria knew it was just his way of letting other men know she was his property.

After the show, Mickey took them to a classy restaurant. Having been there before with Monica, he boasted that the food was superb. Jimmy looked at the menu and commented with the prices they were charging it ought to be.

Whilst enjoying their meal, the waiter came over to them with a bottle of champagne.

"Compliments of Mr Sheridan," he said placing it on their table.

They all looked over to where the waiter had indicated the champagne had come from. A large built, well-dressed man looking to be in his sixties raised his glass to them. He was sitting with two heavies and a very pretty young girl who looked young enough to be his granddaughter. Mickey and Jimmy nodded their heads in appreciation.

When Maria asked who he was, Monica was quick to say she really didn't want to know.

"His name is Dave Sheridan," said Jimmy "he runs the West End, he's nothing but a loud mouth prick that makes Reggie and Terry look like choir boys."

It was as they finished their meal, Dave Sheridan walked over to their table. Standing in front of them, he eyed Maria up and down before speaking.

"Alright boys," he said "what brings you to my neck of the woods then?"

Mickey mentioned they'd been to the theatre to give their ladies a night out. Dave looked leeringly at Maria; she felt uncomfortable and nervously held Jimmy's hand.

"I see your taste in women has drastically improved Jimmy."

Trying hard to keep his cool, Jimmy introduced Maria to him. Dave held out his hand to her, out of politeness she offered hers and calling him Mr Sheridan said she was pleased to meet him.

Lifting her hand up, he kissed it and said the same to her.

There was something about the way he looked and spoke to her that made her uneasy. Mickey tried to make conversation, because he could see that Jimmy wasn't impressed, but it was obvious that Dave was more interested in Maria than talking to either of them.

Dave bantered with Mickey for a few moments before he looked at Jimmy and asked if Maria was the girl he'd won on a royal flush. Instantly, Maria felt intimidated along with nervous. Despite her earlier breakthrough regarding Jimmy's temper; she knew he wouldn't stand too many snide remarks like that from anyone. So without hesitation she looked at Dave.

"Yes that's right Mr Sheridan," she said "romantic isn't it? In fact it was the best day of my life."

Her friends knew why she was doing it, simply because she knew Jimmy would retaliate and she wanted to avoid that.

"If I'd have known how right they were for each other Dave," joked Mickey "I would have fixed the game years ago."

"When you've had enough of Jimmy here and you want a real man," quipped Dave "just give me a call Maria, unless of course you'd prefer to play poker for her Jimmy?"

Immediately Jimmy sprang to his feet. Everyone in the restaurant stopped eating and watched them.

"Please Jimmy leave it," said Maria grabbing him by the arm "you're better than that, please babe sit down."

Looking evil, Jimmy stood with his fist clenched.

"Maria's right," said Mickey "just leave it Jim. You're treading on dangerous ground Dave, why don't you just go back to your table?"

"Yeah," snapped Jimmy "why don't you fuck off back to your table, your granddaughter looks lonely!"

"Still got that short fuse then Jimmy," laughed Dave "that temper of yours will get you in trouble one day!"

"If you ever talk about Maria like that again, you'll see just how bad my fucking temper is granddad!"

"No need to be like that," said Dave smugly "I didn't realise you thought that much of her, let's face it Jimmy she is up market for you. What happened to that little blonde slapper you used to knock about with, what was her name, Della wasn't it? Have you still got her on the side then; she was a bit of a goer by all accounts, definitely more your type."

Maria was trembling and trying hard not to cry.

Stating Dave was out of order, Monica told Maria to ignore him in an effort to comfort her. It was obvious that Jimmy was seething. Just as it was about to kick off, Dave casually begun to walk away, calling over to them as he reached his table.

"Nice to see you boys again, you should come to the West End more often; maybe we can have a few drinks and a game of cards one evening."

Then he sat back down. Within seconds the young girl sitting with him was all over him like a rash, but he took no notice of her, he just stared at Maria.

Tearfully, Maria asked if they could leave. Agreeing it was a good idea; Mickey hailed the waiter and asked for their bill. Jimmy just sat there with his fist clenched. Maria was terrified that something would happen while they waited for the bill. Gripping his hand, she asked him to stop staring at Dave and not to start anything. Reassuring her he wouldn't unless Dave said anything about her, he told her to stop panicking as he was fine.

Five minutes later as they were leaving, Dave called out goodnight to Maria and added for her not to be a stranger.

That was all Jimmy could take, he spun round and looking aggressive, started heading towards Dave's table. Mickey grabbed him and bundled him out through the restaurant door. Jimmy was hurling abuse at Dave who just sat there laughing.

Outside, Mickey told him to calm down; he didn't want him starting a war.

Arrogantly Jimmy snapped that he couldn't stand Dave the fat bastard and he'd take the fucker out!

Punching a parked car he triggered off the alarm, momentarily it seemed to bring him to his senses.

Noticing how scared Maria looked; he put his arm round her and began walking in the direction of their car. Minutes later they were pulling away. Jimmy's driving was erratic.

By the time he dropped their friends off, he was slightly calmer. Mickey apologised about what happened, he'd intended for them to have a great night.

Declining his offer of a night cap, they assured him they had a great night and Jimmy would see him the following day. Monica waved at Maria as they pulled away.

Back at their apartment, Maria asked if he wanted a drink. In an arrogant manner he said a large one.

Because of what had happened, she was anticipating his temper flaring up. Passing him a drink she sat on the arm of his chair and placed her arm around him. To his surprise she apologised for wearing the dress, stating that if she hadn't maybe Dave Sheridan wouldn't have said anything to her.

Pulling her onto his lap, he slid his hand up her dress, rubbing it up and down her thigh as he kissed her passionately.

"Dave Sheridan is a fat bastard," snapped Jimmy "I fucking hate him! Believe me babe, if he hadn't said something about you it would have been something else. There's no love lost between me and Sheridan, he hates me as much as I do him. It's a long story, one which I'll keep for another time, because right now I want to shag the arse off you!"

Sliding his hand inside her panties, he kissed her passionately. She knew he needed sex, only this time was different, he was loving and gentle. Unzipping her dress, she slipped it off revealing the strapless bra she was wearing. Kissing her breasts, he undid the clasps while Maria undid his trousers and pulled at them. Within seconds they were rolling about on the lounge floor making love.

Over breakfast, Maria said she needed to check with the caterers that everything was running smoothly as the wedding was now only two days away. Jimmy had to drive into town to pick their rings up from Martin, so they could stop off at the hotel. Continuing to chat, Maria said she felt really bad about what happened at the restaurant. It had been nice of Mickey to take them out and she was sorry it had ended so horribly. Reassuringly, he convinced her Mickey would understand, especially regarding Dave Sheridan. She asked why they hated him so much.

"Well that's one reason," he said lifting his T shirt and pointing to a scar on his stomach. "About five years ago, Dave Sheridan came to Sweet Cheeks with a couple of his boys; we were hospitable towards him out of respect. Everything was going ok, until he got a bit rough with one of the dancers. He just wouldn't leave her alone. She was only a kid working to pay her way through university. Anyway, when she went back to the dressing room after her stint, unbeknown to us he followed her. By the time me and Mickey got there he had beaten her to a pulp and was raping her. I gave him a fucking good hiding and warned him never to set foot in any of our clubs again. We thought that would be the last we'd hear from him. I should have known he couldn't take the beating I gave him like a man. After we closed that night, Dave and two heavies waited for us, they jumped us in the car park."

"Oh my God Jimmy, he could have killed you!"

"If it hadn't been for Reggie and Terry working there that night, he probably would have."

"What happened to the girl?"

"Poor cow was a nervous wreck after that; she didn't come back to work, dropped out of university. We compensated her with money, but basically, Dave fucking Sheridan ruined her life. So you see babe that's why I hate the fat bastard. Don't worry about the fucking likes of Dave Sheridan, I'd take the fucker out before I'd let him touch you! Did you mean what you said to Sheridan about when I won the poker game?"

"I'm glad we left the restaurant," she said lovingly touching his hand "I didn't like him. He gave me the creeps and yes, I meant every word; it was the happiest day of my life when you won me, but it doesn't take anything away from the way he made me feel when he mentioned it. I feel cheap and dirty when people use the fact that you won me. If I could change it I would."

"You'll never be cheap," he said as he pulled her to him "you're a lady in every sense of the word. Sheridan was only jealous; he can only get pretty young girls because he pays for it."

Their conversation was cut short when the phone rang; it was Monica. Apologising for calling so early she wanted to ask Maria if she would go into town with her that day as she had a couple of last minute things she needed to pick up. Mickey was going to take her originally, but his office has just phoned and said there was a client who needed to speak with him.

Telling her they were also going into town they arranged to pick her up on the way.

Less than an hour later they were pulling up at Mickey's. Monica was waiting.

"Alright babe," said Jimmy as Monica got in the car "what time do you reckon Mickey will be finished at the office? Only I was thinking maybe we could all have lunch together down at the Swan."

"Yep," giggled Monica "no doubt about it you two are psychically linked! When Mickey left this morning he told me to tell you he'd meet us for lunch in the Swan."

They all laughed.

As Jimmy parked the car, he turned to the girls and said he'd meet them in the Swan at one o'clock. Until then, he would go to the jewellers and have a chat with Martin while they shopped for whatever it was they wanted.

Maria kissed him as they separated.

He was relieved when just over an hour later; Mickey phoned to say he was on his way. Since leaving the jewellers Jimmy had bumped into the girls who had talked him into going shopping with them, so he'd spent the last hour being dragged in and out of shops. With a look of relief on his face, he told the girls Mickey was early and waiting for him at the pub, so he'd see them there at one o'clock.

"Now he's gone," said Monica "how about we buy the two grooms something? I was thinking along the lines of maybe a day out at a race track. There's a booth in the precinct that does those red letter days, there are loads to choose from. They do hot air balloon rides, flying a plane, that sort of thing. I reckon they'd both enjoy driving a racing car."

"Yeah so do I, the way Jimmy drives I often think I'm at Brands Hatch!"

They made their way to the booth where a nice young man talked them through the brochure. Both ladies decided on the racing cars and paid for the full package.

After sorting the trip out, they started making their way to the pub. On the walk there, Monica joked about the salesman at the booth being gay. Maria asked how she could tell. Monica was just about to answer when they heard a voice call out from behind them.

"Doing some shopping for your big day Marsha?"

They looked round; it was Della with two very unsavoury looking friends.

"Her name's Maria," said Monica aggressively.

"Marsha, Maria who gives a shit!" said Della sarcastically.

Monica could feel the nastiness oozing from the group. Not about to let them get the better of her, she looked at one of the girls with Della and said she hoped she wasn't shop lifting that day.

The girl pulled a smug face but ignored her.

Monica spoke again, this time even more sarcastically when she said "Well nice talking to you delightful young ladies, but we really must be going, we're meeting our soon to be husbands, you know what it's like. Oh no, of course you don't, you're all single, I can't understand why, can you Maria?"

"See you on Saturday," called Della as the girls walked away "oh and by the way Marsha, don't think for one minute he'll be faithful to you, I know what makes him tick, because I don't suppose you take it up the arse do you lady muck!"

In a moment of rare bravado Maria turned round.

"Funny," said Maria "if you're so hot Della why didn't he marry you when he had the chance?"

Monica threw her arm round her shoulder.

"Well done Maria you're catching on. We'll make a scrapper of you yet!"

They laughed as they walked away. Della just stood there, momentarily lost for words before hurling abuse at them. They just laughed and continued walking.

The Swan was busy as they looked for their men then Maria spotted Jimmy walking towards her. With a grin he asked if he was bankrupt. With a giggle she said "Not quite!"

They ordered lunch.

While they waited, Mickey asked if they'd enjoyed their shopping trip. Monica didn't mince her words when she announced they had, until they ran into Della and her slags. Jimmy looked straight at Maria who looked embarrassed that Monica had mentioned it. When he asked if she was ok, Maria simply nodded.

Maria cringed when Monica stated she wasn't alright because Della, the old slag was nasty to her. However, Maria had done herself proud which had impressed Monica. Jimmy asked Maria to tell him what happened. No one was surprise when looking tearful, she said she didn't want to talk about it and hoping to avoid his questions said she was popping to the ladies. Everyone could see she was close to tears.

The moment she was out of earshot, he asked Monica what had happened. He looked angry when she told him what Della had said.

"I'll be having a fucking chat with Della," he said aggressively "if need be I'll sack the bitch! After all her father's dead now, so there's no loyalty issue."

"Leave it Jimmy," said Mickey discreetly "Maria's on her way back to the table."

Maria felt a bit uncomfortable as she sat down, she could sense that they had been discussing her. A waiter arrived with their meals. Everyone tucked in except her, she barely touched hers. When Jimmy asked if the food was ok, she nodded and said she just wasn't hungry.

When they ordered dessert she declined; she just sipped her wine and making conversation, asked Monica if she was coming back to their apartment that afternoon. Monica declined as she would be spending the evening with her.

Two hours later, they parted company in the car park. Inside the car, Jimmy could sense she was still hurt over what Della had said to her. Squeezing her knee as he drove, he told her not to let Della get to her. She didn't reply, she just nodded and forced a smile.

Back at the apartment, he tried to lighten the mood by putting some music on and asking her what she'd bought.

Despite her saying she only bought some cosmetics, by the look on her face, he could tell she was still thinking about Della, he knew whatever had been said was playing on her mind. Trying to reassure her, he said Della was nothing but an old dog and she should ignore her.

"That's easy for you to say, you weren't there Jimmy," she replied with a sad expression on her face "just tell me the truth; have you invited her to our wedding?"

"Fucking hell no, she's the last fucking person I'd ask. I can't even believe you've asked me that!"

"Ok," she said tearfully "so you tell me what she meant then, because she said she would see me on Saturday? I'll tell you this Jimmy, if she's going I won't be!"

He assured her that Della had not been invited, but if by chance she turned up, she'd be told in no fucking uncertain terms to leave!

He watched the tears well up in her eyes as she asked why Della was being so nasty to her, she didn't even know her and she certainly hadn't done anything to warrant it.

His answer was simply that the relationship he had with Della meant nothing to him. There was never any possibility of them being a real couple.

Believing him, she asked why he would even want to go out with someone like her.

Wanting to be honest, he said there had been times when he was lonely. Della simply filled a void at those times and unfortunately she misread his intentions.

"She said you like anal sex Jimmy, yet you've never mentioned that to me."

Knowing that Maria would consider anything he wanted to do with her, he needed to explain why he hadn't.

"Making love with you could never be bettered babe; it wasn't like that with Della; she was the one who liked it. With you the issue has never come up because our sex life is so fantastic and so varied. You are the sexiest, most beautiful woman I've ever dated and the only one I've fell in love with."

"Thank you," she replied in a quiet voice.

Hoping she was now less concerned about Della, he listened to music while she packed a few more things for the house.

Knowing that she just needed to keep busy to take her mind off Della, he let her carry on. As the time passed she seemed to be a little more relaxed. So much so she said she wouldn't mind cooking, if he wanted to invite Mickey and Monica over early to have dinner with them. Thinking it was a great idea and knowing it would keep her occupied was an added bonus. Two minutes later he called them with the dinner invitation which they were only too happy to except. Jimmy arranged for them to be there by seven.

Their friends arrived a little early, bringing wine and flowers with them. Monica helped in the kitchen while the two men talked in the lounge.

"I want to go to Sweet Cheeks later Mick to have a word with Della."

Remembering what Monica had said, Mickey suggested leaving it until after the wedding.

"No I can't," snapped Jimmy aggressively, "because the bitch implied to Maria that she was going to the wedding, and I'm going to tell her in no uncertain terms she's not!"

Maria called out to them that dinner was on the table before Mickey could reply.

They chatted for a while after the meal, then Jimmy suggested them going. They kissed the girls and told them they would be back by one.

They called in briefly at Lazer, just to confirm that everything was sorted before the wedding. Simon assured them everything would be fine and asked where they were going on honeymoon.

"Actually we're not going until Monday," said Mickey "it's a surprise, the girls don't know about it, so keep it quiet Simon. We're going to St Lucia in the Caribbean. I've lied to the girls about a big case that will tie me up for at least another three weeks."

"How unusual," laughed Simon "a solicitor that tells porkies!"

They all laughed.

Jimmy took the opportunity to thank Simon for trying to calm the situation with Della at Sweet Cheeks.

"No problem, but you need to watch her Jimmy, she's bad news, a nasty little tart. Your Maria seems a really good sort, well above Della's league. Just be careful Jimmy, jealousy is a fucking dangerous animal and your Maria is worth a thousand Della's. Just a shame she decided to marry you before she gave me a chance."

"She wouldn't look twice at a pretty boy like you and regarding Della you're right, she's not in the same league. If she thinks for one minute she's going to give me grief, she's fucking kidding herself!"

From Lazer they went on to Sweet Cheeks where they were greeted by Shane who said he hadn't expected to see them that night. When Jimmy said they were just checking everything was sorted before the wedding, Shane laughed and told them to stop worrying about the clubs as they would be fine! They both grinned when he said he was taking Max and her son Harry to the wedding.

It was obvious to both of them that he was growing very fond of Max. When Jimmy asked if Della was dancing that night, Shane nodded and said he'd heard about the incident with Maria.

"Fuck me talk about bush fucking telegraph!" laughed Mickey.

"Simon only told me ten minutes ago when I rang him about work; he mentioned you'd been in and that you were on your way here. Then he said about Della. He's right Jimmy, she's bad news."

Jimmy didn't reply, he simply nodded and turned to go into the club. Inside, one of the dancers told him Della was in the dressing room.

Mickey asked if he wanted him to go with him. Shaking his head Jimmy said he'd deal with her.

Jimmy acknowledged the other bouncers with a nod, as he made his way to find Della. On entering the dressing room he saw two other dancers talking to her. Without asking why, they both left when Jimmy asked them to give him a minute with Della.

Della was only wearing a pair of lacy knickers as she stood smiling at him.

"What's up lover?" she said "got cold feet about marrying her already, need some arse?"

"No I don't," he snapped as he grabbed her around the throat "and if you ever speak to Maria again I will fucking kill you! As far as I'm concerned you were never anything other than a quick fuck! So if you want to carry on working here you'd better keep your fucking mouth shut!"

With him still holding her by the throat, she squeezed him between the legs, she could feel he had a hard on.

On releasing her, she kissed him on the lips and for a split second, he began to respond, then he pushed her against the wall and aggressively told her to fuck off.

"What's the matter Jimmy," she said smugly "scared because you know you want it? Doesn't lady muck take it up the arse, or aren't you rough with her? We both know what gets your rocks off, you'll be back and I'll be waiting!"

"I'm fucking warning you, never to speak to Maria again! Unlike you slag, she is a lady and don't flatter yourself, I won't be back! As for what I like Della, she's everything I like and if you think for one minute I'm going to fuck it up for an old dog like you; you've got another thing coming! Oh, one last thing slag, if I so much as glimpse you at my wedding you'll be fucking sorry!"

Walking out he slammed the door behind him.

Returning to the bar, Mickey asked him if he was ok. The look on his face was enough to tell his friend that he'd been aggressive and that he'd warned her to keep away from Maria and the wedding.

They kept out of Della's way. Even when she danced Jimmy turned his back to her. They were just about to leave when she walked over to them and asked Jimmy if she could speak to him. Having finished dancing for the night, she had clothes on.

With a look of anger on his face, he stated they had nothing to say and told her to fuck off. Almost pleading with him, she asked for just two minutes of his time, just to listen to her.

Knowing Jimmy would either ignore or snap at her, Mickey asked what she wanted.

"I just want to tell Jimmy how sorry I am about Maria; I was jealous. Please Jimmy can we still be friends? I really am sorry. Truth is I need this job; I owe some bad people money. Please just give me another chance, I promise I won't let you down."

"You can keep your job, but just keep out of my way. Another thing, never speak to or about Maria again, do I make myself clear?"

Thanking him, she walked away.

Driving to Dixie's they talked about her. Both men had reservations about her sincerity, but with the wedding so close they saw it as a good compromise. Della knew if she stepped out of line she would be gone.

Jacky Boy and Kevin were on the door at Dixie's, they spoke to them as they went in. The atmosphere was always good at Dixie's, both Mickey and Jimmy felt very comfortable there. Standing at the bar they talked to the bar staff.

Tony arrived just after them; they went into the office to talk about business while they would be away. Tony would be their first in command should there be any problems that couldn't wait until they came home.

The time was approaching half twelve when Mickey suggested them going home to the girls. Jimmy agreed, but said he needed to use the toilets first.

It was almost ten minutes later when he returned and apologising stated he'd been talking.

"Goodnight lads," said Tony "I'll see you both on Saturday if not before."

Back at the apartment while the men were out, the brides to be had gone over all the arrangements at least twice. They also talked about when Maria ran away to Brighton. Having complete trust in her friend, she even mentioned to Monica how often Jimmy wanted sex.

"That does sound a bit excessive" said Monica "but I know some people have a very high sex drive; maybe Jimmy's just one of those people?"

"Yes, I suppose he could be."

Monica was shocked when she spoke about her time at Nick's. She knew things that Mickey had told her, although he had never really gone into detail.

"When Jimmy won me it was the best night of my life Monica, even though Nick almost beat me to death, I knew I'd been saved. I never imagined a man truly loving me the way Jimmy does, or that I'd have such nice things and a beautiful house. One of the best things for me is having such wonderful friends like you and Mickey, Shaun and Father Thomas."

"For what it's worth Maria, we feel the same about your friendship. Although I must say, I think you deserve a medal for putting up with Jimmy and his temper, not to mention his jealousy!"

"I love him unconditionally Monica, he's the love of my life."

Suddenly a familiar voice echoed behind them.

"I hope your referring to me babe?"

They hadn't heard the men come in until Jimmy had spoken.

"No Jimmy," giggled Monica "Maria was actually referring to the man who drives the ice cream van."

Leaning over the back of the chair that Maria was sitting on, he put his arms around her chest. She tilted her head to kiss him. It was a long lingering kiss.

Monica giggled and referring to them as love birds, asked if they'd like to be left alone.

They carried on kissing, oblivious to her question.

Mickey sat down next to Monica and pulled her to him then he kissed her passionately. When Mickey finished his kiss, he glanced over at the others, they were still kissing. It was then he noticed that Maria was trying to pull away, but Jimmy had a firm grip on her head.

"Let the poor girl up for some air Jimmy."

Mickey's words had the desired effect. When Jimmy let go of her, they both noticed she looked very embarrassed.

"Fuck me Jimmy," said Mick trying to lessen Maria's obvious embarrassment "for a minute there I thought I saw Maria turning blue!"

Jimmy laughed and said she couldn't get enough of him. A few minutes later Mickey said they were leaving. Maria felt embarrassed that she hadn't even offered them a drink or something to eat.

"Well you were a little preoccupied with that future husband of yours," laughed Mickey "anyway we're fine babe; I only came in to pick Monica up."

Monica pulled Mickey by the hand and calling him sexy said they had to go.

"Sexy?" grinned Mickey "that sounds like you're hoping to take advantage of me whilst I'm under the influence of alcohol!"

They all laughed as they made their way to the door to see their friends out.

When they'd gone Jimmy grabbed hold of Maria and began kissing her again. As the kiss ended, she told him how embarrassed she'd felt in front of their friends. Jimmy laughed it off, stating he just needed a long kiss and Mickey and Monica were also kissing. It was then she noticed he had a strange look about him; his pupils looked larger, a sort of wide eyed look, so she asked if something had happened at the club. When he asked what she meant, she hesitated momentarily, simply because she'd thought he'd looked aggressive when he came in and she didn't want to sound as though she was provoking him.

"I'm waiting Maria," he said impatiently "what exactly did you mean?"

Quickly she said she hadn't meant anything it was just that he'd seemed a bit tense when he'd kissed her and he was usually like that after something had happened.

Everything was fine, nothing had happened. He never mentioned Della, although the scene with her from the dressing room was now racing through his mind. Going over in his head what Della had said, he could feel the anger knotting up in his stomach, a surge of sexual ego was starting to overwhelm him.

Pulling Maria to him, he kissed her passionately; she could feel his strength holding her. Instantly she asked what was wrong.

"Nothing's wrong babe;" he replied acting agitated "I just want you so bad it hurts!"

Then he began undressing her erratically as he pushed her against the back of the sofa. Sensing that something wasn't right and despite what he'd said, she knew giving him sex would calm him down. Trying to slow him down, she tried to undo his shirt buttons, but he was desperately pulling at her clothes. Within seconds she was naked.

Standing there in front of him, she expected him to push her down onto the sofa or the floor.

"God Maria," he gasped "I could fucking eat you."

When she asked if he wanted her to lie down, he said no and told her to stay standing as he started kissing her breasts.

Maria held his head in her hands as he continued kissing her breasts and neck. Despite his rush, he was still passionate, her body wanted him.

Working his way down her body, he knelt on the floor in front of her. She was anticipating his next move, as he pushed his head down onto her. A second later his tongue was touching her intimately, her legs were shaking from the impact of what he was doing. Suddenly she cried out his name, unable to control herself a moment longer she climaxed. Trembling, her legs felt weak. Standing up he kissed her passionately.

Knowing he enjoyed taking her from behind, she willingly did as he'd asked when he told her to turn round and bend over the sofa.

Leaning over she felt him touching her intimately, within seconds he was inside her. Anticipating his thrust, she was surprised when there wasn't one and then she felt him withdraw from her. He didn't reply when she asked him what was wrong, he simply told her to Sshh. Seconds later she felt him moving her buttocks with his hands and realised what he was about to do.

"Jimmy, please don't do that."

Before she could move away or say another word, he was taking her from the back. She groaned as he pushed himself into her. Desperately she wanted him to stop, but she remembered what Della had said to her and Maria wanted to please him regardless. Over the years she had endured anal sex many times with Nick and she hated it, she knew it was something she would never enjoy. When Jimmy thrust himself harder and harder into her, she winced with the pain. Several times she tried to move position to lessen the severity of his thrust, but he was having none of it, holding her down firmly.

"Please Jimmy you're hurting me!"

"Sshh babe, I've got to take you. God babe I love you, please babe I can't stop now!"

Giving a powerful thrust, she groaned as he held her down and told her he was coming.

"Jimmy! Please stop, you're hurting me!"

He ignored her until seconds later when he had finished. Motionless she just laid there over the sofa with tears in her eyes, she knew in her heart that the sex they had just had was in some way connected to Della. Cupping her face in his hands, he looked at her tear filled eyes before he kissed her.

"Babe I'm sorry, I just couldn't help myself did I hurt you? I'm sorry. I just wanted you so much I couldn't stop myself."

Too upset to answer him, she just shook her head as she bent down to pick her clothes up. He told her to leave them and speak to him.

With tears rolling down her face, she looked at him and asked "What do you want me to say Jimmy, that it was great, why didn't you just ask me? You were hurting me, why didn't you stop when I asked you to?"

His excuse was he'd been drinking and it felt so good he couldn't stop. Fighting back her tears, Maria said she needed to take a shower before going to bed.

When she had finished in the bathroom and went to bed, he was already fast asleep. For several hours she laid awake thinking about what had triggered off his need for anal sex, her mind kept coming back to Della. Her thoughts were simple, if he really needed that kind of sex she would go along with it. Even though she didn't really like it; she wasn't going to give him a reason to want Della.

By the time he got up and showered the following morning, she had been up for over an hour and was already cooking breakfast. Walking up behind her in the kitchen, putting his arms around her waist he kissed the back of her neck. Turning she kissed him and told him breakfast was nearly ready.

Moments later they were eating.

"Babe last night was wonderful. I'm sorry if I got a bit carried away, it's your fault for making me so fucking horny! God I'm a lucky bastard, tomorrow I'll be marrying the girl of my dreams, she's beautiful, kind, loving, a great cook and sexually there's no one in the world to better her!"

When Maria just looked at him and smiled, he asked if everything was ok. He knew something wasn't right when she simply nodded, so he asked her to tell him what was on her mind. Shock and anger was how he felt when she asked if he'd had sex with Della the previous night. Looking angry he stated he hadn't had sex with anyone but her.

"Then why did you need to have sex like that last night? You've never needed it before. Be fair Jimmy; look at it from my point of view; it does seem like a bloody big coincidence that it should happen after what Della said to me. Oh, and let's not forget last night you went to Sweet Cheeks! I just want the truth Jimmy, I don't want an argument."

"Ok Maria, I'll tell you the fucking truth! I did see Della last night, I told her if she ever said another word to you, I'd fucking kill her. I also told her that you're the only woman I want, that you're everything I desire and that I love you! Oh and I called her a slag and warned her to keep away from the wedding! Do you really think I would arse fuck her two days before our wedding, or any other fucking time for that matter! With all that we've been through in the last few days I can't fucking believe you don't trust me!"

Feeling very humbled, she just sat there looking at him as he pushed his plate away, leaving half of his meal. Saying she was sorry for mistrusting him she told him to finish his breakfast.

"I've lost my fucking appetite!"

Tearfully she apologised adding they were supposed to be getting married the following day, so they shouldn't be arguing.

Patting his knee, he asked her to sit with him. Sitting on his lap with her arms round his neck he kissed her.

"Don't you know how much I love you Maria? I wouldn't do anything to jeopardise what we've got. I nearly lost you once; it's never going to happen again. I'm sorry about last night; we don't have to do that again if you don't want to."

"No it's ok, I just imagined terrible things that's all, I'm sorry."

"Forget about it babe, tomorrow is our big day, then you'll be Mrs Dixon."

Sitting on his lap she was aware that he would have sex again right then, but she wasn't up for it. Despite all that he'd said, she still wasn't totally convinced about his account of the previous evening. Changing the topic, she asked if he could run her into town that day, she needed to check with the florist that everything was running smoothly.

"If I say yes, is there any chance of us going back to bed for an hour first?"

"Not if you want us to get married tomorrow!"

Later that morning he ran her into town. At the florist she chatted to the manager about the wedding flowers, while Jimmy talked to the young girl who was serving. Confident that Maria was out of earshot, he asked the girl to deliver two dozen red roses to his address that afternoon, he wrote his address down on the back of a florist's card.

He had only just finished writing it when Maria came over to him to say she was ready to go. When they turned to leave the shop, Jimmy winked at the young sales assistant as she picked up the card.

They stopped at a small café for a sandwich and a cuppa. Jimmy asked if she needed to go anywhere else. He wasn't surprised when she told him they should call into the church to see Father Thomas. Begrudgingly he agreed, providing they were quick.

Maria knew it was always a struggle for him to go to church, especially as, on this occasion she knew he was only doing it to please her.

Father Thomas was as always pleased to see her. Although they had spoken on the phone when she returned from Brighton, it was nicer for them to actually speak in person. After kissing Maria on the cheek, Thomas shook hands with Jimmy and asked how things were going between them. He was happy to hear things were good. When he asked if Jimmy was ready to marry, Jimmy stated he'd been ready for the last two years!

The priest gave them a lecture on the sanctity of marriage, before Jimmy said they had to be going because he was expecting a delivery later that afternoon.

Maria thought it was simply a ruse so they could leave. Once in the car, she humorously said it wasn't wise to lie to a priest.

"So you think I was lying? For your information mother superior, I am expecting a delivery."

The fact he hadn't mentioned it earlier, she asked what it was. Calling her nosy, she pinched his leg. Despite asking him again he remained secretive.

Having arrived back at their apartment block they were just getting out of the lift on their floor as a young man was waiting to go down, he was carrying a huge bouquet of red roses.

"Who's the lucky girl then?" said Jimmy admiring the flowers.

The delivery lad explained he tried to deliver them but the lady was out and he couldn't leave them with a neighbour as none were in. When Maria asked which apartment they were for in the hope of helping, she said there must be a mistake when he gave their address. After asking her surname, the delivery boy handed her the flowers when she told him it was Davis.

Automatically she thanked Jimmy and said they were beautiful. Her face took on a different look when he said he hadn't sent them, especially when he added that perhaps she'd made an impression on someone during her hen night.

Shaking her head, she was beginning to feel a bit nervous. Seeing by her face she was worried, he suggested she simply read the card as he opened the apartment door. Nervously she opened the tiny envelope and began to read.

A tear ran down her cheek when she read 'to my darling Maria can't wait to marry you, don't ever doubt my love, forever yours J.xxx'

Jimmy laughed as he explained there wasn't room on the card to write Jimmy.

"Oh thank you Jimmy," she said as she hugged him "they're absolutely beautiful. Will you still buy me flowers when I'm old and wrinkly?"

"I'll buy you flowers every week for ever if it makes you happy."

Looking lovingly at him, she said he made her happy before she kissed him. When he asked what time Mickey and Monica were coming round, she reminded him they were going out first with Mickey's parents so they could meet Monica's parents before the wedding. Her guess was they wouldn't be back before ten at the earliest.

"Great, so this could be your last chance to have me while I'm single. By this time tomorrow I'll be a married man and as it's not even four o'clock yet, we'd have ample time."

She kissed him before leading him by the hand into the bedroom. After sex they laid and talked, they were both a little nervous about their big day. He confessed to her that his only fear was she wouldn't turn up. Giggling she gave her word that she would. It was when he asked her if she feared anything; he could see she did by the look on her face. After a lot of coaxing she finally told him that when she used to watch weddings from the children's home, she'd noticed lots of people kissing the bride. Sister Marjorie had told the girls it was tradition, although being old and set in her ways, she personally didn't agree with it. Maria was worried he would get angry with her if other men wanted to kiss her.

"From what you told me about good old Margie," interrupted Jimmy "I'd imagine she'd find anything that meant showing affection to someone else very distasteful. Sounds to me babe like she needed a fucking good porking, most nuns are frigid old hags!"

Although she thought what he'd said was disrespectful, she did giggle.

"Regarding you being kissed babe, I'll be surprised if there's a man there tomorrow that doesn't want to kiss you," he said squeezing her hand "it'll be fine babe; surely you don't think I'm that bad? I know everyone one will kiss you and I promise I won't be jealous. When you first moved in with me I hated the way you seemed frightened of me all the time. I told myself then I'd never want you to feel like that, now I know that's exactly how I make you feel. A bride shouldn't be worrying about kissing people on her wedding day."

"I'm always on edge, even when another man speaks to me Jimmy, especially if I don't know them and even more so when you're with me. I will never want another man; I just wished you believed that."

Lifting her head gently with his hand, he looked lovingly at her and promised that in future he'd try not to be so jealous, although he couldn't guarantee anything, but he'd given his word he'd try. Feeling she could talk openly she asked about his previous girlfriends and if he'd been jealous with them. And did he always want sex like he did with her.

When he didn't answer, she apologised and said she shouldn't have asked. With a grin he explained he hadn't answered because he was trying to remember and the answer to both questions was no. Feeling a bit braver she asked if that included Della.

"Especially Della, why would I be jealous of anyone with her, she'd already had everyone at the club."

Questioning his term everyone, she asked if that included Mickey.

"Yeah even Mickey, although I was there at the time. We were here in the apartment; I was fucking her when Mickey turned up. When he realised what was happening he apologised and turned to leave. Della told him he didn't have to go and that the bed was big enough for three."

"Oh my God," said Maria feeling sick to the pit of her stomach "promise me Jimmy that will never happen with me!"

"Are you fucking kidding me, best friend or not I'd rip his fucking balls off if he ever so much as touched you!"

"I wasn't actually referring to Mickey, I was referring to threesomes."

"You need never worry about that babe, it was a one off and if you think for one minute I could lay here while someone else fucked you then you don't know me very well!"

When she suggested changing the subject, he grabbed her and kissed her passionately. Moments later he suggested they practice making babies. It was a suggestion she liked.

With a sexy grin he asked if she fancied messing around with the handcuffs and stuff.

"As long as you're gentle with me," she said as she playfully pinched him, "I don't want to walk up the aisle bow legged!"

Jimmy took the handcuffs from the bedside drawer and humorously calling her wench, ordered her to lie on her back.

"Yes Master" she laughingly replied.

For almost two hours they made love, both enjoying it. Cuddled up together afterwards, Jimmy dozed off, but Maria just laid there thinking about the conversation they'd had earlier. Despite being upset by his revelation about the threesome with Della, she could see why it happened, although she had always believed that Mickey would feel differently about such things. Maybe Monica was right about men in the club game; they simply couldn't let an opportunity for sex pass them by. Snuggling her head onto Jimmy's chest, he stirred and tightened his grip around her before dropping back off to sleep.

It was almost half nine when they finally got up and took a shower, only dressing minutes before their friends arrived.

They chatted about the wedding most of the evening. Several times the grooms had tried to change the topic, but the girls were relentless.

It was approaching midnight when Monica told the men to leave, stating the brides needed their beauty sleep.

"Neither of you need worry about that;" said Mickey "you're already beautiful."

"See Maria, this is why I can't wait to marry him!"

Maria double checked with Jimmy that he'd taken everything from the apartment he would need, because she wouldn't let him back in on their wedding day as it was considered bad luck to see the bride.

"I've got everything I need," he replied as he hugged her "just promise me you'll turn up!"

Reassuringly she promised she'd see him at the church at two. They kissed each other and then the men left.

"Thank God they've gone," said Monica "pour us a drink."

Maria looked surprised; she thought they were going to bed. Monica grinned, she was far too nervous to sleep. Maria felt the same, but suggested trying to sleep as they would be up early the following day.

Back at Mickey's the two men were drinking. Jimmy talked about his fear of her changing her mind; he couldn't bear the thought of being jilted.

"No chance," laughed Mickey.

"When I thought I'd lost her Mickey I wanted to die, even now I can't believe the effect she has on me and I can't get enough of her where sex is concerned."

Mickey said it was good he felt that way and everyone could see there was a strong sexual chemistry between them. The only thing that bothered him was Jimmy's temper and jealousy. He grinned when Jimmy said he was working on that.

It was turned three that morning when they finally turned in for the night. As Mickey walked towards his bedroom, Jimmy called over to him and thanked him for everything.

Telling him he was welcome, Mickey disappeared through the door.

Jimmy couldn't get to sleep, everything was going through his mind, like the terrible way he had treated her, the argument he'd had with Della and knowing in his mind that if she ever tried to come between Maria and him, he would kill her. His mind took him back to Maria's hen night when he attacked and raped her barely a week before. His stomach ached, if he was with her now he would need to have sex and tell her how much he loved and needed her.

That night without her, he would have to masturbate to relieve his tension.

CHAPTER 38

Both girls were up by half six the next morning. Their wedding dresses were hanging on the wardrobes.

They both settled for a slice of toast for breakfast, eating it as they went over the time schedule for the day. Everything planned to the last detail; hopefully the day would run like clockwork.

Both men were still asleep as nine o'clock approached. Mickey was the first to surface followed ten minutes later by Jimmy, who had laid awake until the early hours of the morning.

Mickey commented on the state of his friend as he entered the lounge.

"Fuck me," he laughed looking at Jimmy "England's last hope!"

In true Jimmy fashion, he just smiled and stuck his middle finger in the air at his fellow groom. When Mickey asked if he wanted some toast, Jimmy said he was used to full English, including toast and fried bread.

"Oh are you now, well today your majesty it will be toast or digestive fucking biscuits, which would sire prefer?"

Laughing Jimmy said toast would be fine.

After breakfast, Mickey noticed Jimmy seemed edgy; he kept pacing up and down the apartment. Telling him to stop because he was making him nervous, Mickey reassured him everything would be fine.

Looking stressed, Jimmy said it was the longest fucking morning ever and did Mickey think it would be ok if he called Maria. When Mickey nodded, he looked relieved.

Nervously Jimmy phoned the apartment, Maria answered. After asking if she was ok, he told her how much he'd missed her the previous night, but since hearing her voice he felt fine. Telling him she missed him too, she said she had a lot to do, so she'd have to go. Repeating three times that he loved her, he'd see her later at the church. She knew he needed reassurance, so she said the same and that wild horses wouldn't keep her away.

Mickey could see the relief on Jimmy face as he talked to her. Jimmy passed him the phone before hanging up so he could speak to Monica. Just after he'd said hello, she had to go as the hairdresser was on her way up.

They blew each other a kiss into the phone as they ended the call.

Ellie the hairdresser asked to do Maria's hair first because it was so long. They'd decided between them to put a slight curl in it before sweeping it up on to the top of her head leaving a couple of curly bits hanging down the sides and the back.

The florist had brought miniature rosebuds for their hair that matched their bouquets. Ellie was still doing her hair as the bridesmaids arrived.

"Shall I put the kettle on?" said Ann seeing that the two brides were looking a bit stressed.

Thankfully, unlike her friend, Monica's hair was short by comparison. Ellie was simply going to style it with the sides pulled up and entwined with the flowers. The three bridesmaids were each having a French plait with flowers. Ellie was confident that they had plenty of time, she was right. Monica had her nails done whilst the bridesmaids' hair was finished off. Fortunately, Ann was very organised. By half one the bridesmaids were ready, they looked absolutely gorgeous. Both brides noticed how proud Ann looked as she checked her grandchildren. Charlie looked beautiful, her dress being different because of her age, but it complemented her figure perfectly. She was a pretty girl anyway, but today it could be said that she would definitely turn heads.

With the time fast approaching two o'clock, Ann helped Monica dress first. Her gown was white with lace, low cut, figure hugging and stylish. A traditional lace veil which gently cascaded from her head down onto her shoulders was secured with a delicate row of pink rose buds to her crown. Feeling like a princess she walked into the lounge, everyone stared. Charlie looked in awe at her soon-to-be step mother and stated Monica looked absolutely beautiful!

Maria agreed and said Mickey was a lucky man, Monica looked absolutely stunning.

They all waited in the lounge as Ann helped Maria dress. Time was slipping by; it was quarter to two when they finally came out of the bedroom.

The ladies noticed Maria was visibly trembling.

"God Maria," said Monica "you look like a super model! Jimmy won't be able to take his eyes off you."

Her dress was fabulous; white silk, strapless with a dropped back that went into a swag with a criss cross detail in the back space; tight fitting to show off her figure with a fish tail trail which cascaded around her feet. The letter J was beautifully detailed in tiny diamond sequins on the bottom, only visible when the trail was fully extended.

Maria stated she was so nervous she felt sick. Monica assured her she'd be fine and that she was the most beautiful bride she'd ever seen. Maria thanked her and said the same about her.

Ann had a tear in her eye as she positioned them all for a photo.

"You all look absolutely wonderful," she said as she took the photos "both grooms should be grateful you agreed to marry them."

Charlie called out that the cars had just pulled up and she'd also spotted Shaun and Monica's dad entering the building.

Telling them she would leave with the bridesmaids once Shaun came in, Ann made her way to the door.

Megan was shaking, she was as white as a ghost; it was a big day for her as she had never been a bridesmaid before. Ann put her arm round her as they waited for the lift. Shaun and William stepped out. Ann snapped at them stating they were cutting it a bit fine!

Always ready with a reply, Shaun said it was traditional for the bride to be late. Then both men complemented her and the bridesmaids on how lovely they looked.

"I just hope my hat stays on," said Ann.

"You look grand me darling!" said Shaun.

Just before the lift door closed, Ann called out she'd see them at the church.

Shaun and William entered the apartment. Walking into the lounge both men stopped and just stared at the two brides.

"Aye," said Shaun "now there's a vision of loveliness if ever I've seen one!"

"You look absolutely beautiful darling," said William as he walked over to Monica "this is a very proud day for me and your mum."

Thanking him she kissed his cheek and said he looked very smart.

"Your Jimmy's a lucky fella," said Shaun as he kissed Maria affectionately on the cheek "you look wonderful. Well this is it, are you sure this is what you want?"

Looking nervous she smiled and nodded her head.

Shaun looked at William and suggested they take the two beauties to the church. Instantly William agreed and stated the time was running short. With a grin Shaun told him not to worry about the time as both ladies would be worth the wait.

He was like a proud father. Maria was so grateful to have him there; she loved him like a father.

By the time they arrived at the church even Monica was showing a few more nerves. Father Thomas was standing outside with the bridesmaids.

"You both look absolutely lovely," said the priest as the brides approached him, "I'm so glad you're here. The grooms are getting nervous, especially Jimmy. So are you both ready?"

They both nodded.

Leading them into the church, he signalled to the organ player. Maria didn't think her legs would carry her up the aisle. Shaun could feel her shaking. Placing his hand on her hand that was through his arm, he winked at her. Maria always felt safe with him and today was no exception. Walking up the aisle she could hear people whispering at how beautiful they looked.

It was only after Father Thomas took his position at the front that the two grooms had a full view of their brides. Mickey smiled and winked at Monica, but Jimmy just stared at Maria. She felt unsettled that he didn't smile at her.

Thomas asked the grooms to join them at the front before he began the service.

"You look beautiful," whispered Mickey as he stood next to Monica.

Smiling she squeezed his hand. Thomas asked Shaun to step forward and then repeated the process. Shaun passed Maria's hand to Jimmy, but still he just stared at her. She was shaking from head to toe, as was Jimmy.

The best men looked on as the wedding service began. Maria could barely talk by the time she had to say her vows, yet Monica, in true detective fashion sailed through hers.

Maria was wondering why Jimmy hadn't smiled or tried to say anything, her fear being he didn't approve of the dress, her hair or makeup.

Thomas asked the best men for the rings. Richard and Tony passed them to the two couples.

Thomas then went through the normal service requirements. Maria was nervous as he asked if anyone knew of any reason why they couldn't marry. A deathly silence followed, she had an overbearing fear that Della would be there and say something, but the moment passed without incident and moments later they exchanged rings. Thomas spoke to the congregation.

"As many of you know," said Thomas "normally at this time the happy couples would be pronounced man and wife. However, today will be slightly different because Jimmy has asked if he can say a few words."

Maria was terrified; this was not something she would have ever expected from Jimmy.

"Babe," said Jimmy "I just want you to know while we're here and God is my witness, I love you with all my heart. I will love you for eternity; you are the love of my life. Lastly, I want to say thank you for marrying me."

A tear ran down her cheek, it was the same for some of the guests. Gladys and Ann were both clutching their hankies.

Feeling totally overwhelmed, she held his hands tightly and in a shaky nervous voice said he was the love of her life and she would die without him.

The entire congregation clapped.

"I now pronounce you, men and wives," said Thomas with a chuckle.

The newlyweds kissed and then a cello player sitting at the front of the church next to the organist played Amazing Grace while the couples entered the vestry to sign the marriage certificates.

Outside people threw confetti as the couples appeared and Shaun was the first to kiss Maria. After the photographs they made their way to the hotel where their guests were waiting in another room. A master of ceremonies announced their arrival, before leading them into the banqueting hall. It was breath-taking. Each table had place names and a seating plan was displayed on entering.

Every guest had a gift on the table. The women had a small pink and white satin bag filled with sugared almonds, also a small box containing a silver brooch to commemorate the occasion. The men also had a small gift wrapped box containing a pair of silver cuff links.

With the guests seated, the waiters and waitresses served champagne before a toast was given to the brides and grooms. A prepared speech was read by the master of ceremonies, followed by speeches by Tony and Richard.

Everyone clapped and cheered. Mickey was the first to stand to give his speech as the master of ceremonies called order.

"I think everyone here is probably aware that I've always felt as though Jimmy was more like my brother than my best friend. I can't even begin to tell you about the laughs we've had together over the years, and of course a few hair rising moments, but I promise I won't rabbit on. Jimmy knows how I feel about him, so let's talk about someone else who's found a special place in all our hearts, Maria. Little did I know when they met two years ago, she would be the one and only woman who could tame him. I for one never imagined him being this happy. Now we all know Jimmy has a bit of a jealous side, not to mention a temper, but I think today is probably the only day I can say I love her, kiss her and keep my teeth!"

The room erupted into laughter.

"Everyone who knows her well will know Maria has a unique quality; she brings out the best in everyone. On a final note I'd just like to say I hope we will always remain best friends. It's a good feeling knowing I've always got Jimmy watching my back."

When the speech finished they shook hands and he kissed Maria.

Jimmy stood for his speech.

"Thanks Mickey, you know I feel the same way about you. It's no secret I think of your family as my own, so I'd like to take this opportunity to thank Mary and Den for treating me like a son, and if I didn't think of you as my sister Fay, I'd probably have married you!"

"Believe me sis" said Mickey "you dodged a bullet there, no offence Maria!"

Everyone laughed.

"Mickey is the best friend anyone could wish for and I feel honoured that he's mine. Let's not forget Monica. I'm sure everyone here will agree today she looks absolutely beautiful. You're a lucky bloke Mick. Now on a more serious note as everyone here knows, I'm not the most romantic man in the world, but I'd like to say a few words about my lovely wife. I never imagined I would be standing here making a wedding speech, simply because I never thought I'd love anyone enough to want to marry them, but being with Maria has changed all that. She is without a doubt the best thing that's ever happened to me. I was worried she'd come to her senses and stay at home today, I'm so glad she didn't! You've changed my life babe; I hope I'll be the type of husband you deserve. I love you with all my heart, so thanks for turning up!"

Everyone clapped and laughed. Before he sat back down he leaned over and kissed her. Maria had tears in her eyes.

Last on the agenda was the giving of gifts to certain people, both wedding couples stood up. Shaun and William were each given a gold watch. Monica's mum was given a beautiful ladies watch, along with a bouquet of white roses as were Ann and Ellie. Father Thomas was surprised to be called. After kissing him affectionately on the cheek, Maria handed him a gift wrapped box, it was larger than the other men's. Inside was a beautiful bible with Father Thomas's name and church etched on the front in gold italic scribe. Inside the cover it read, 'To dear Father Thomas, thank you for always being there for us,' it was signed 'with love always Maria and Jimmy.'

Everything ran perfectly, the food was superb, even up to Maria's standards. Everyone had the most wonderful time. The newlyweds took the first dance, Unchained Melody by the Righteous Brothers.

They danced into the early hours of the morning. As Jimmy danced with his wife they chatted.

"I want to tell you something babe," said Jimmy "when you walked in the church I thought I was going to pass out. I couldn't say anything because I couldn't come to terms with the reality that this absolutely stunning woman would soon be my wife."

"I thought you didn't like the way I looked. I know you were nervous Jimmy, but when you didn't say anything I was worried."

"What's not to like, to say you looked fucking stunning would be an understatement. Perhaps later when we get back to the house, you could leave the dress on? I've never made love to anyone in a wedding dress before!"

"By the time we get home," she giggled "I doubt you'll be in any fit state to do anything!"

"Do you want to bet on it?"

Finally the celebrations came to an end with the last guests leaving around half two that morning. The four friends kissed each other and shook hands as they left for their destinations.

Mickey and Monica were booked in to the bridal suite for the night, but Jimmy and Maria had decided they were going to their house.

The limo driver opened the car door for them as he congratulated them. The groom was quite tipsy, especially once the night air hit him.

Pulling up outside the house fifteen minutes later, the driver asked Maria if she needed any help. Thanking him she said she could manage. As they entered the house she looked at Jimmy and said she should try and get him to bed. Shaking his head, he asked her to wait and make him some black coffee.

Maria couldn't help but notice him staring at her as he drank the coffee. Finally her curiosity got the better of her and she asked what he was staring at. The love he had for her was obvious when he said he couldn't believe she was his wife, Mrs Dixon.

Standing up he held out his hand, Maria took it. He led her back through the house to the front door. Opening it she was surprised when he walked her back through it. Then scooping her up into his arms, he carried her over the threshold, closing the door with his foot.

"Put me down Jimmy," she said when he started to carry her up the stairs, "you've been drinking and I don't want to end up in casualty on our wedding night. Put me down, I'm frightened I'll fall!"

"No babe, I'm determined to get you to our bed and I'll always be here to catch you."

After several stops to steady and kiss him, they eventually made it to the bedroom.

Laying her gently on the bed, he kissed her. When she suggested they could wait till the morning if he wanted to, he grinned and said he didn't think so because they'd be doing it all again in the morning! Maria giggled.

Jimmy pulled the zip slightly down on her dress so that he could feel her breasts, before hurriedly taking his clothes off. The silk next to his bare skin felt good as he ran his hand up her leg. Scooping the dress up, as his hand reached the top of her thigh he felt the edge of her panties under her basque. Pushing his hand inside them, he could feel that she wanted him when he gently pushed his fingers inside her. Her body's responses were telling him that she was enjoying him touching her. Pulling her dress right up, he moved between her legs and then tenderly and slowly he kissed her as he gently entered her. They continued to kiss as he slowly moved inside her, their breathing getting heavier with every movement. Squeezing his buttocks she pushed him deeper into her. Moving faster, holding her shoulders before moving his hands up to meet hers. Now her arms out stretched past her head; their fingers entwined, their bodies arching in symmetry. Finally they were coming, slowly collapsing onto her before he rolled over. Maria gazed up at the ceiling, totally fulfilled with their love making.

"Jimmy, open your eyes and look up."

There above them on the ceiling was a huge mirror. He watched as he touched her breast and played with her nipple.

"Tomorrow we'll be able to watch ourselves making love babe."

Finally the day had caught up with them, within minutes they had both drifted off to sleep.

It was ten the following morning before either of them stirred. No sooner had he woken when he rolled over and kissed her tenderly and said "Good morning Mrs Dixon."

"Good morning husband. Oh God I need to get out of my wedding dress, I slept in it last night."

Lustfully he watched her as she took it off, unable to take his eyes off her as she stood next to the bed, still wearing the white basque, panties, stockings and suspenders, although two of the suspenders had come open leaving a baggy top to the stocking. Despite having slept in it; she carefully hung her dress over the back of a chair. When she'd undressed, Jimmy called her to him; she said she needed to take a shower first. He sounded dominant when he ordered her to come to him. Walking towards the en suite, again she asked for time to take a shower.

"Fucking get your arse over here now Maria!"

Instantly she turned, he could see that she was frightened. Realising how he was must have sounded; he smiled and told her not to be too long because he didn't want his breakfast getting cold!

As she stood in the shower, he came in to use the toilet. Then he pulled open the shower door. Moving towards her they embraced.

"Fuck me I fancy you," he said "but I'm saving it for the bedroom so I can watch us in the mirror."

Her hair was still up having tried not to get it wet. Jimmy kissed her passionately as she dried herself. Heading towards the bed a few minutes later, she noticed a gift wrapped box on her pillow. Sitting down on the bed she opened it while he sat down beside her and kissed her shoulder. As she opened the gift, he gently began taking the hair pins out of her hair. It fell loosely down, still wavy from the day before as he pushed it back off her shoulders. Excitedly she opened the box, inside was a beautiful eternity ring that matched her engagement and wedding ring.

"Oh thank you Jimmy," she said tearful "it's beautiful."

Taking it from her, he slipped it onto her finger and stated it meant she was his forever, no matter what.

"I expect we'll have our ups and downs like most couples Jimmy, truth is I never thought I would want us to be apart and then I found myself in Brighton."

"I mean forever, no matter what. I told you before babe I will never let you leave me."

Gently he pushed her down onto the bed and said he wanted to experiment with the mirror.

Several hours later they finally left the bedroom. Had it not been through hunger, they would have stayed there all day.

CHAPTER 39

Monday morning they were eating breakfast when Maria asked if they were doing anything specific that day. She looked curious when he said they were packing because they had to be at the airport by ten. They were going on honeymoon to St Lucia for ten days with Monica and Mickey.

"Come on" she excitedly said throwing her arms around him "we've got a lot to do!"

First she wanted to phone Monica, who like her had just found out about the trip. They were both so excited.

Maria wasn't keen on the flight, she felt air sick; but once they landed she was fine. They all had a glorious honeymoon although Jimmy did have a couple of jealous outbursts, but nothing serious.

By the time they returned home, Maria had the most fantastic tan, she looked almost foreign and although she'd had the most amazing time, she was happy when she walked back through her own front door. There was a stack of mail on the table from where Ann had been popping round to check on the house. There was also fresh bread and milk which she had left for their return. Maria kicked her shoes off and flopped into a chair. When

Jimmy asked if she was ok, she shook her head and said she felt a bit queasy and really tired. He suggested she rest for a while as it was probably down to all the travelling they'd done that day.

She dozed off while he opened the mail. There was a letter from the courts stating he would be required to give evidence on Tuesday the 24th of July at two thirty, which just happened to be the next day. The letter had arrived nine days earlier. Jimmy immediately called Mickey.

"Yeah I had the same letter waiting for me" said Mickey "I'll pick you up at quarter to two tomorrow, I'll drop Monica off so she can spend the afternoon with Maria, if that's ok? Oh and we'll pick the wedding photos up en route."

Jimmy knew Maria would love that.

When she woke up, Jimmy noticed she looked pale and wondered if she was going down with something. He suggested seeing the doctor. Convinced it was down to the travelling she thought she'd be fine in a couple of days.

As they chatted, he told her Mickey was picking him up the following day because they had to give evidence in court and that Monica was picking up the photos and would stay with her..

Maria spent most of the day sleeping on and off, as soon as she did anything she felt exhausted. Jimmy didn't think she looked well at all and suggested an early night.

The following morning she felt sick and was still feeling tired and unwell when their friends arrived with the wedding photos. The men left the girls looking through them as they left for the court.

Jimmy could understand what Mickey had meant about Virginia Hollingsworth; in court she was like a pit bull, although Samuels looked smug and over confident as usual. That was until he was questioned by Virginia.

When they were called they were ready for anything his barrister, Alistair Munroe, threw at them. They had talked it through a dozen times.

Virginia had managed to have the tapes brought into evidence and it came as no surprise to Mickey and Jimmy that the RT Honourable Quinton Randal-Scott was the judge presiding over the case. Mickey had spoken to him when Samuels was first arrested and convinced him that it would be in the judge's best interests to ensure he got the case.

"I definitely think it's looking a bit dodgy for Samuels," said Mickey driving back from the court that afternoon, "especially as the star witness, Max, is due to be called tomorrow. I reckon her evidence will just about put the lid on things."

Maria seemed to have perked up when they returned. Jimmy sent out for take away to save her having to cook.

The four friends chatted until the late night hours before Mickey and Monica readied themselves to leave. Maria said they were welcome to stay over. Mickey declined because they were running Fay and the family to the airport first thing in the morning.

"Fuck me that time's passed quickly," said Jimmy "don't seem like yesterday you was picking them up. Send them our love and tell them to have a safe journey back."

Once their friends had left, Jimmy talked about the case and how he felt it was looking bad for Samuels.

Despite being glad over Samuels, Maria asked if they could talk about it later, she felt so tired she just wanted to go to bed. Feeling knackered too, Jimmy nodded.

Maria slept through till half nine the next morning and throughout the day she felt nauseas and lethargic. Mickey had arranged for them all to go to the clubs that evening, but Maria asked if they would mind if she stayed home. Mickey was confident that Monica would stay with her rather than go to the club.

As usual he was right; Monica was only too happy to stay in with her when they arrived later that evening.

Telling the girls they'd be back by one o'clock, the two men left.

Checking in at Lazer first, it was heaving with punters; the club was packed. Both men were happy not to stay too long after being told that everything had run smoothly during their absence.

At Sweet Cheeks, Sue was working behind the bar; she greeted them both before asking about the honeymoon. They hadn't noticed Della going to the bar.

"I thought the words you said to Maria during the wedding were beautiful Jimmy," said Sue "they brought a tear to my eye. If Maria ever doubts how much you love her, she will only have to remember your wedding day. I never realised just how romantic you were!"

"You would have thought they'd have calmed down after all this time," said Mickey "but oh no, you should have seen them on the honeymoon. It was sickening Sue, he couldn't get enough of her!"

"I don't doubt it if the wedding was anything to go by."

"Never thought I'd hear myself saying this Sue" said Jimmy "but Maria has changed my life, she's the best thing that's ever happened to me."

Their conversation was cut short when they heard a noise like glass breaking. Looking round they noticed a broken glass on the bar. Della was walking away; she had obviously heard what had been said.

"Don't worry about clearing it up Della;" called Sue sarcastically "I'll do it! Sorry Jimmy, but I can't stand her the dirty cow; she gets right up my nose!"

They knew Sue was not one to mince her words, she had never liked Della and by the sound of it never would.

They checked with Shane that Max had done ok at the courts that day and were pleased to hear that Virginia had told her she had sealed Samuels' fate. They all agreed that was great news.

After leaving Sweet Cheeks; they made their way to Dixie's. Tony was there. Shaking hands with them he said business had been good while they were away. He'd deposited several grand into the club account and the rest he'd put in the club safe. Money collections from the lads had also been good.

"Thanks for holding the fort Tony" said Mickey "we're calling a meeting Friday lunch time, can you tell all the lads to be here at midday?"

They talked with Tony and the other staff until after midnight and then they left.

CHAPTER 40

The rest of the week passed without any great developments. Maria was convinced she had picked up a virus on honeymoon after feeling fine one day and poorly the next. Repeatedly Jimmy had told her to see the doctor.

Friday morning, Mickey picked Jimmy up for the meeting at the club, everyone was there. It was no surprise to them as they walked in that everyone looked curious as to why the meeting had been called.

"You can all stop looking so worried," said Mickey pulling out a chair "nothing's wrong."

They all laughed.

"So I expect you're wondering why we called this today. Well the reason is, as you all probably know the court case against Samuels is going well, better than any of us expected and as a result of that, we no longer see Samuels as a threat. Therefore, it's going to be a good day all round, thanks to Tony and the drugs that Samuels planted at the club, everyone is getting a nice bonus. Getting married has obviously made me and Jimmy a bit soft, because on this occasion we've decided to share all of it out between all of you. It's not just because of Samuels though; you have all probably noticed that since the demise of Nick everything has run smoothly, the crew are doing a good job. Our appreciation of which will be shown in the envelopes. Well that's about it, unless Jimmy wants to add anything?"

"Yeah I do Mick. You all know Mickey and me got married recently, not to each other I might hasten to add!"

Everyone laughed.

"Anyway, as I was saying it was a great feeling to be able to leave the country knowing that everything would be taken care of and like Mickey said we do appreciate it."

Mickey handed everyone an envelope, but nobody opened theirs, they just put them in their pockets as they thanked them.

"If we get a good result on Samuels," said Mickey "I think everyone will agree this will have been one of the best years the firm has ever had."

They all agreed.

None of them realised just how good until they went home and opened their envelopes. Each one contained ten thousand pounds in cash.

CHAPTER 41

The time passed and the case drew to a close, but no one could foresee the outcome. They attended court on the final day and were ecstatic when the jury returned a guilty verdict on several serious charges against Samuels. Virginia Hollingsworth had certainly earned her money. When the court was called to order, she quickly turned to Mickey.

"Now let's hope old Quinton does the right thing," she said "and Samuels is looking at ten to fifteen years."

A deadly silence hung over the court as Judge Quinton Randal Scott spoke.

"Detective Samuels, you held a high position of trust within our great police force. Not only have you let yourself down but the very people who strive to keep this country safe, often putting their own lives at risk to infiltrate criminal activities such as drug rings. Based on that I feel you should be made an example of, therefore you shall receive the maximum sentence of twenty years and to serve no less than fifteen."

Samuels looked pig sick. His barrister was obviously in shock, but immediately said they would appeal against the judge's decision. Mickey leaned over the chairs and kissed Virginia.

They couldn't wait to get home to tell the girls. Twenty minutes later, Mickey dropped Jimmy off before heading home to Monica.

Entering the house, Jimmy called out to Maria but the house was empty. She had left a note on the table, which read, 'gone to the doctor's back soon love M.'

He had just poured himself a drink when she returned. Happy that she'd gone to the doctor's because he'd been worried about her health since the honeymoon. The moment she sat down he asked what the doctor had said.

"Not much really, but he did think a shopping trip would help me!"

"What fucking doctor did you see, a fucking witch doctor! Why on earth would he tell you to go shopping?"

"Because soon none of my clothes are going to fit me," she giggled "you see I'll be putting on a bit of weight over the next few months!"

His heart started pounding as he grabbed hold of her.

"Babe, are you saying what I think you're saying?"

"You're going to be a dad Jimmy!"

Unable to contain his emotions he burst into tears and punching the air shouted, "Babe that's fucking wonderful!"

ABOUT THE AUTHOR

All my life I've been passionate about writing, even as a child. Little did I know then I would have to wait until I was 50 to fulfil my dream and actually publish my novels.

My family have always been of paramount importance to me, so it seemed natural to put my life, as a would-be writer, on hold until my children were settled and happy. There never seemed to be enough hours in the day, especially when my girls were growing up. Time was the only thing I could never control and between fostering teenagers, raising money for worthy causes and rescuing guinea pigs, I never seemed to have any left for me! Often I would write during the night hours so as not to upset my family's routine. I still do, old habits die hard.

I felt confident enough to try and secure an agent, but I quickly realised I probably stood more chance of becoming the next Prime Minister than actually getting signed up! Everyone loved my books and constantly said I should publish. So, with the help of my lovely 'little' Ian (a young man who we all consider family), we looked at eBooks and print publishing.

Despite having to fit my writing around my working life, I always run two books together. Fortunately, I never get bored with writing or writers block, but there are, on occasion, times when I feel the need for change so I write a few chapters in one book then switch to the other and repeat the process. I also love writing poetry about real topics. Some are funny some are sad. I was thrilled when, after entering a competition, two of my poems were selected for publication.

I have written several novels in different genres which I'm told is quite unusual. Truth is all of my writing comes from the heart and from some of life's experiences. One question I'm always asked is where my story lines come from. My answer is simple. Like most of my friends I attended the school of hard knocks, but I feel truly blessed to have a large extended family and to have met so many people from so many walks of life, some good, some bad and some decidedly dodgy, but never dull. Without any doubt they have helped to inspire some of my characters, but for the story lines my colourful imagination has come into play.

Earlier this year, I was asked to ghost write the autobiography of a bona fide, old school, London bad boy and I must admit, I'm loving every minute of it. I felt honoured to have been entrusted to write this amazing story, along with flattered as an author to do the book justice. No sugar coating no fancy words, just writing it as it is. Ironically it's like writing a non-fictitious book for my Ruthless series!

AVAILABLE TITLES IN THE SERIES

Ruthless Series 1
- **Book 1: Jimmy's Game**

Addictive, obsessive, sexually driven and all consuming; Jimmy's Game is a book that will dominate your darkest desires of control and power.

- **Book 2: Maria's Journey**

Compelling, brutal and stretching every boundary of love and loyalty to its limits; Maria's Journey will leave you wondering how she ever survived and remained the lady she is.

- **Book 3: Mickey's Way**

Touching, loving, merciless and unforgiving, only a father knows how far he will go to protect the one's he loves.

- **Book 4: Billy's Move**

Sexy, passionate, body pulsing, when you find true love and someone has wronged them, there has to be revenge and it's always served best when it's unexpected.

- **Book 5: Tony's Business**

Totally absorbing, a boss driven by power, control and greed. Now he has to make the toughest decision of his life, but can this king relinquish his crown?

Ruthless Series 2 - The Next Generation
- **Book 1: Carlo's Law**

When you double cross the king of London, be prepared to pay the ultimate price.

- **Book 2: George's Ascent**

Can a man kill to prove himself?'

- **Book 3: Vito's War**

His greatest fight will be for his life.

- **Book 4: Shaun's Call**

Some fights you just can't win.

- **Book 5:** Coming Soon…

Ruthless Series 3 Coming Soon…

Other Genres and Standalone Titles by Karen Clow:
- **The Angels Are Dying**
- **The Diary Of Angel Moon**
- **Brassick**

SNEAKY PEEK AT MARIA'S JOURNEY RUTHLESS SERIES BOOK 2

Dave Sheridan was sat at a table facing towards the bar in his favourite club. It was one of four that he owned in the West End. Despite his age he still liked to be seen as a player, he was always in the company of young girls. Money talks volumes and he flashes it about like confetti. A group of girls caught his eye as they came through the doors. Instantly he recognised the tarty blonde amongst them. It was Della.

Thinking as he watched her, nothing changes, still the same old Della, anybody's for a drink and a packet of crisps. He eyed her up and down as she ordered some drinks. She was wearing a tiny mini skirt, which barely covered her arse; a low cut black top and white boots. He thought she looked like a prostitute. With her drink in her hand, she turned and faced the dance floor; it was then he caught her eye. As she spotted him, she thought she recognised him but couldn't place where from.

One of her friends spotted an empty table behind his. It was as they passed him, he spoke to her.

"Della isn't it?"

"Yeah that's right, I thought I recognised you, but I can't remember where from?"

Dave offered his hand as he said it was nice to see her and it had been a long time.

"Dave, yeah, I remember you now. You used to come to Sweet Cheeks when I danced there before."

"That's right darling; it was never the same after you left, although I could never understand a young lady of your obvious talents dancing in a dive like that."

Della was quick to tell him she used to date one of the owners, Jimmy Dixon. He never said he knew Jimmy. When he asked if she and her friends would like to join him, they nodded.

Della sat down next to him before looking at the young girl sitting the other side of him and saying, "Alright."

The girl begrudgingly smiled a half smile while Dave Sheridan's two heavies just sat there with faces like setting concrete. Dave nodded at one of them and told him to get the ladies another round of drinks before turning to Della and asking where she was working nowadays. When she said she was back at Sweet Cheeks, he tried to look surprised, but he knew everything that went on with the other clubs, especially when they belonged to Jimmy Dixon.

In an effort to flatter her, he stated Jimmy must have been mad to let her go, but he expected they were still good friends.

When Della's friends burst out laughing, he asked if he's said something funny. One girl stated that Della still had the hots for Jimmy, but they'd had a falling out. Dave said he'd heard Jimmy got married a while back.

Della nodded, his new wife spoilt everything, if she wasn't on the scene her and Jimmy may have got back together.

Telling her that was a shame, he asked what Jimmy's new wife was like. Despite his question, he remembered only too well what she was like. Since the moment he had laid eyes on Maria in the restaurant, he'd thought how he would really like to fuck her, she was a beauty. Della arrogantly stated that in her opinion, she was a right toffee nosed cow, who went to church, didn't swear, a real miss prim and proper. Quite frankly she didn't know what Jimmy saw in her. Dave knew very well what he saw, unlike Della, Maria was a lady.

Acting sympathetically, he touched Della's hand and said it must be difficult for her working at the club knowing Jimmy might be there…

You can download or purchase this book and any of Karen's other titles on Amazon.

Printed in Great Britain
by Amazon